MW00460007

the HERBWITCH PRINCESS

the Herbwitch Princess

IREEN CHAU

ILLUSTRATED

This book is a work of fiction. Names, characters, places, and incidents are the product of the author's imagination or are used fictitiously. Any resemblance to actual events, locales, or persons, living or dead, is coincidental.

Cover Design and Illustrations: Ireen Chau
Formatting: Enchanted Ink Publishing

ISBN: 979-8-3556962-4-5 (Paperback)
ISBN: 979-8-3753124-1-5 (Hardcover)

Illustrated edition March 2023

Printed in the United States of America

For Jenni

Antonio watched as the sun dipped below the water's edge, its fiery rays setting the sky ablaze in shades of passionate crimson. The waves rippled, distorting the reflection of the woman behind him—the woman he spent three long years waiting for.

"Carla," he whispered.

She approached the dock, wind tousling her glossy black curls.

Heavens, she was beautiful. He could stare at her forever. Her shoulders shone like gold in the sunset, her brown eyes glossy with yearning. She was clad in a fine silk gown, so unlike the rough cotton Antonio was used to.

"My love," Carla said, her voice tender and sweet like the kisses they used to share.

Antonio turned away, jaw clenched. He mustn't fall under her spell again. Not when she was the duke's bride-to-be.

"Antonio, I didn't mean for this to happen." Carla ducked her head, inky tendrils falling over her face. "You were going to lose your boat and—"

"I never asked for your help!" Antonio's voice broke.

He shouldn't be shouting at Carla. If not for the money she sent monthly, Antonio would have lost everything. His boats. His fishing business. Even the roof over his head. Not only that, Carla was the woman he wanted to raise a family with. The woman he intended to hold and cherish forever.

Now, she belonged to someone else. And that shattered Antonio's heart.

—from *A Sailor's Seduction: Tales of Romance at Sea* by Erasmus Lenard

1

THE TRAITOR'S DAUGHTER

1

A loud meow stopped me from turning the page.

What in the blazing fires are you reading? Misty demanded.

I closed the anthology and set it beside me on the stone bench. The embossed letters gleamed by the light of the overcast sky: *A Sailor's Seduction: Tales of Romance at Sea.*

"What is it?" I said as my cat brushed against my skirts. "Are you cold again?"

Yes. I told you five minutes ago but you were too absorbed in your humiliating romance novel.

Misty shook off the frost on her paws. A few droplets flew onto the lawn, threadbare from the cold. Even the gardeners Father hired couldn't keep the grass in prime condition during mild Olderean winters.

"Forgive me for entertaining myself," I said, raising a brow as I scooped her from the ground. "Would you rather us return to our room?"

Not a chance, darling, Misty said drily. She nestled into my arms. Despite her complaints, she was warmer than I was. *You forget I can go where I please, unlike you.*

"Right."

I stared blankly at the three-tiered fountain before us. What little water the basins held had since frosted over. At the marble base, bare patches of dirt replaced the daffodils that used to flourish there. In contrast, the white heather bushes around us bloomed without restraint, obstructing everything within view with snowy blossoms.

This corner of Greenwood Abbey was the only place I frequented during the past six months. Its isolation was part of its charm, though it was beginning to grow tiresome.

"Why not visit the kitchen, then?" I said, scratching Misty underneath her chin and around her ears. "There's a nice big fireplace and probably a chicken roasting for supper."

Misty purred as I continued to pet her. *I'm warm enough. Besides, there's wild poultry out here.* She eyed the maple tree behind the fountain, green eyes glinting.

"Chickadees are not poultry."

Could have fooled me, she said.

An angry chirp sounded within the tree. A small round bird fluttered out and landed on the barren branch above, her inky feathers popping against our dreary surroundings.

Not you again, she said disdainfully.

Misty stilled, flexing her jaw. I held her down lest she got any ideas. "Good evening," I said to the chickadee.

She gave a chirrup. *I wish you would stop bringing that cat here. I plan to live long enough to nest.*

"Misty won't be any trouble. Isn't that right, Misty?"

Misty made a disgruntled noise. *That's right. No need to weigh me down like a prisoner.*

I let her go and resumed petting her in her favorite spots.

The chickadee chirped a laugh. *You domestics,* she said haughtily. *I'm glad I'm not forced to repress my natural instincts.*

Misty hissed.

I frowned. "Don't push your luck," I said to the bird, "or I might accidentally set her loose."

I was bluffing, of course. If Misty ate the chickadee I would be down to one companion instead of two. I was nearly finished with *A Sailor's Seduction.* There was only so much I could fill my day with.

Oh, very well. The chickadee fluttered to a higher branch and rearranged her feathers. *You know, you should come here more often. Those pesky gardeners want to remove my nest.*

I raised my brows. "And how does my presence solve anything?"

You scare them away. They treat this place like the plague whenever you're around. I see them turn and leave all the time.

My cheeks flushed, though not from the cold. After all my time living at Father's abbey, I had only caught brief glimpses of the gardeners. Certain spots of the garden had seen drastic improvement, but not this corner.

Of course they were avoiding me. Who wouldn't after hearing the rumors?

Nearly every servant in the household knew that Lady Narcissa was a snobbish, ill-tempered girl who had assisted her mother in her scheme to assassinate Queen Cordelia. Such a shame she hadn't been locked up too, instead of becoming a burden to Captain Greenwood.

Misty pawed my hand. *Don't listen to her. Birds are ridiculously stupid creatures.*

Why I never! The chickadee chirruped in indignation and fluttered back into the maple tree, muttering profanities.

"It's getting dark." I set Misty aside and stood, leaving the book. "Let's go back."

She twitched her tail and walked the length of the bench, making a point to leave a dirty paw print on the cover of the anthology.

This is because your brother bad-mouthed you all over the abbey, she said.

My mood dampened at the mention of my half-brother, Maddox. I would have to see his sour face again this evening. But even without his bad-mouthing, I was sure nothing would change. I was, after all, Mother's daughter. My reputation preceded me.

Misty landed noiselessly on a patch of grass. *Well. It's nearing dinner time. Save me a morsel, will you, darling?*

I sighed.

Meals were always tense. Tonight would be no different.

I WAS SUMMONED for dinner shortly after I returned. I didn't bother to dress for the evening and instead headed straight for the dining room where Father, Lady Vanessa, and Maddox were already seated. A late entrance was better than an early one. At least I would not have to engage in small talk.

A serving maid placed a slice of chicken breast on my plate as I settled. A steaming bowl of cheddar pear soup sat on the side.

"Thank you," I said.

She darted her eyes away and proceeded down the table to serve Lady Vanessa.

I sipped the wine from my goblet, focusing on the taste of watery raisins instead of the humiliation blooming over my cheeks. Social interaction was easier when I hid behind sharp words and a condescending air. No one questioned me when I acted superior. Now, everything I did felt fraudulent.

"The weather is getting warmer," Father said from the head of the table, jovially ignorant to the tension. He shoveled a spoonful of soup into his mouth. "I daresay winter is coming to a close."

"Nonsense, Maverick. The winter solstice has not yet passed," Lady Vanessa said, her voice barely audible over the clinking silverware.

Proper ladies never raise their voice, Mother once said. *Others must quiet to hear her.*

Lady Vanessa was the epitome of a proper lady, from her neat, straw-colored hair down to her oval fingernails. She was everything I imagined Father's wife should be:

soft-spoken, gentle, and refined. Nothing like Mother. Perhaps that was why I found her so unapproachable.

"I swear it. Last night I fancied the fireplace a little too hot. Wasn't it, Cissa?" Father turned to me with an earnest look.

"I wasn't near the fireplace," I mumbled. As much as I hated speaking, I couldn't bear to upset him by keeping silent—not when he called me by my pet name. It reminded me of happier times.

"Because you were in the dungeons visiting that woman last night."

I turned to the contemptuous face of my half-brother. Misty said the kitchen maids found him handsome—something about his blond hair and "storm cloud eyes"—but I couldn't fathom what they saw in him. He had grown from the stocky, loud-mouthed boy I saw glimpses of as a child to a stocky, loud-mouthed man.

"Maddox," Father and Lady Vanessa said in unison. They exchanged a glance before Lady Vanessa touched her son's arm.

"There is no reason why Narcissa cannot visit her own mother," she said.

Maddox's eyes flashed. "The former duchess is a traitor. If the woman who bore me were a traitor, I would have turned her in the moment I knew it."

Lady Vanessa jerked her hand away.

"Maddox! Apologize at once!" Father said, dropping his fork with a clatter.

"But Mother could never be like that traitor or her daughter—"

Father glowered. "That is enough. Show your sister some respect."

Lady Vanessa turned to me. "Please don't take offense dear. Maddox is still…adjusting." She offered a gentle smile.

I dropped my gaze to the gilded rim of my plate.

Maddox slammed his goblet down. Wine sloshed onto the tablecloth, staining the linen a deep red.

"She is *not* my sister," he hissed. With a venomous glare, he stormed out, his blond ponytail disappearing behind the tapestried corner.

I chewed a piece of my chicken. It was dry and bland, somewhat a reflection of my feelings. I had heard worse insults from him both spoken to my face and behind my back.

The chickadee in the garden was a big gossiper. I could have gone without the knowledge that my half-brother thought me a cold-blooded snake demoness, but I had little choice in my companions, much less what they chose to talk about.

"I apologize on Maddox's behalf," Lady Vanessa said after a beat, as if the same thing hadn't happened two nights ago. "He always had a temper."

"We've spoiled him, that's what," Father grumbled. "He has no ambition and no interest in joining the Royal Guard even at his age. Shameful."

The edge of the tapestry moved almost imperceptibly.

I took another bite of chicken, which had already gone cold. The little appetite I had since disappeared. Perhaps Misty would appreciate the tasteless poultry more than I did.

I stood from my seat. "Excuse me. I will have the rest of my dinner in my room."

"Are you sure, Cissa? There's pumpkin pie for dessert. Your favorite." Father put both hands on the edge of the table, as if ready to spring up and fetch the pie himself.

"I'm sure."

"If you need anything at all, just ask, dear," Lady Vanessa said, brows furrowed.

I nodded, avoiding her searching eyes.

"I'll take your meal to your room, milady," the serving maid said, moving toward me. I grabbed the dish before she approached.

"No need," I said. "Good night, Father, Lady Vanessa."

I swept away before anyone could wish me a good night back. When I made it out of the dining room and into the hall, I heaved a sigh and leaned against the stone wall, watching the firelight flicker over the faded tapestries.

Greenwood Abbey was old-fashioned in every way, from the crumbling ceiling down to the ash-colored bricks that tiled the floor. The walls were thick and the windows minuscule, blocking out what little winter sunlight there was.

The structure would have served well during a siege, but the darkness and sterile decor seemed to lay siege against me. If it weren't for Misty and the chickadee, I would have been alone for the entire six months I'd been here. Father tried to organize a celebration for my nineteenth birthday this coming spring, but I refused. Mother always said I would be queen at twenty. She promised to organize the grandest of parties and invite everyone of consequence to celebrate.

Now, even if there were a celebration, I didn't know who would dare come.

"Congratulating yourself?"

Maddox stood a few paces down the hall, arms crossed. I merely stared. I had no interest in picking fights with anyone, especially not with someone who believed I was wicked to the core.

"Hey. I'm talking to you," Maddox said, marching toward me. I turned on my heel, though it was the opposite way to my room. Before I could make much distance, he blocked my path.

“Speak when you’re spoken to, witch,” Maddox spat.

Irritation spiked in my chest. I wouldn’t have tolerated such treatment in the past. Despite everything that had changed, I was not going to tolerate it now.

“What do you want me to say?” I demanded.

Maddox scowled. “Admit it. Admit you’re taking advantage of Father and Mother’s kindness and turning them against me. Admit you’re poisoning their minds with your magic.”

I barked a laugh, the mirthless sound achingly loud in the empty hallway. “You know nothing of magic. And yet you are half-witch yourself.”

Maddox clenched his jaw.

Father revealed to the court last summer that he was indeed a witch, but that he had removed his and Maddox's magic decades ago with a potion. Both Maddox and Lady Vanessa were in shock, though the latter had taken the news more gracefully than her son.

"You're turning them against me," Maddox repeated.

"That is your own doing. You heard them. You're spoiled and immature."

"That's rich, coming from Father's *favorite*," Maddox spat. "I never had a second of his day when you were born. But you don't even bother holding a conversation with him. So why are you here, if not to leech off of us as you scheme with your mother?"

A flood of frustration washed over me. He was impossible. Everything about this was impossible.

"Just..." My eyes stung, and I channeled all the venom I had left. "Just leave me alone!"

I fled to my room, hardly caring that the gravy from my plate had dripped onto my skirts. A sob threatened to burst from my throat as I shut the door and sank to the cold floor.

What was dinner? Misty slunk over from the bed and sniffed the gravy stain on my gown. I swallowed my tears. She meowed in delight, tail curling when she spotted the plate of half-eaten chicken on the floor.

Despite my efforts to appear composed, I trembled.

Misty looked up. *That brute of a brother bothering you again?*

I wiped my eyes dry. Mother said there was nothing more humiliating than crying in earnest. Tears were a waste if not used to manipulate.

"I don't know why I bother speaking to him," I said. "Or to anyone."

Misty gnawed at the meat. *Then don't. Take your meals in here again.*

"Father will worry."

She lapped a puddle of gravy off the plate. *Your father seems harder to please than your mother. I don't recall you being in such a state before this.*

I hugged my knees to my chest. Misty was right. I knew exactly what Mother expected of me. I knew how to win her approval. Father was a different matter. A part of me craved to have that certainty again.

If you decide to run off and free her, I certainly have no objections. Whatever will make you happy.

I jumped, forgetting that Misty could read my thoughts as well as I could read hers if she pleased. Our bond was strong enough to go both ways, though I had gotten used to speaking with her out loud—something I wouldn't have dared to do before.

I shook my head. "You know I've made my decision."

Misty blinked slowly. *You humans and your morals. If all that mattered was good food, life would be a great deal easier.*

I sighed. Misty was the most human-like animal I've connected with, but even then her feline instincts prevailed.

She yawned. *It's getting late. I think I'll take another stroll around the gardens before I sleep.*

"Leave the chickadee alone," I said as Misty sauntered over to our open window.

She bristled. *I know.* She leaped over the windowsill and disappeared into the bushes below.

I sank into my four-poster bed and buried my face into the pillows. I didn't bother to ring for my maid. The girl was terrified of me, anyway.

2

"I am *not* going, Father!"

"Yes you are and that is final! Honestly, you're acting like it's a public beheading instead of a…"

I jerked up, squinting at the watery beam of sunlight slicing through my curtains. Misty was curled up next to me, unbothered by the shouting in the hall.

"Oh! Good morning, milady," came a tremulous voice.

"Tizzy," I said to my maid.

She stood at the far corner, furiously wiping down the top of my vanity and avoiding eye contact. A stray curl popped out of her bonnet as she worked.

I was too exhausted to dwell on the awkwardness of our relationship. Still, she was a great improvement from my previous maid, Karen, who was as unkind and selfish as could be. Perhaps that was why Mother chose her for me—to have near an example of what she wanted me to be at all times.

"What is going on?" I asked.

"Oh, milady," Tizzy said, rubbing at a spot on the mirror, "there came a letter from the palace. Invitations to the winter solstice ball, milady. Master Greenwood insists that Young Master Greenwood go and acquaint himself with the Royal Guard, but Young Master Greenwood is unhappy, milady."

I rubbed my eyes. Father had made several attempts to get Maddox to join the Royal Guard since I moved in. None had been successful, but none had resulted in this much shouting.

"I see." I eased myself out of bed, wincing at the ache in my neck.

Tizzy gasped when my blankets fell away. "Did you sleep in your day dress, milady?"

I looked down at my gravy-stained skirt. "It appears so."

"Oh, this won't do," she said, setting the rag down. She rushed toward me, but at the last second, took a step back. "M-may I help you out of your dress, milady? And draw you a bath, milady?"

I wondered how "milady" hadn't already become meaningless to her. "You cannot do both at once," I said. "Go draw a bath. I'll be fine."

Tizzy bobbed a curtsy and scampered off to the washroom. I sighed.

Strange one, that is, Misty meowed.

THE SHOUTING DID not cease even after my bath. As Tizzy combed my damp hair, Lady Vanessa's pleading voice joined the masculine bellows.

"You know how he feels about joining the Royal Guard, Maverick. It isn't for him."

"Honestly, Vanessa. I cannot believe the way you are coddling that boy! He doesn't want to join the Guard? Fine. What else does he want to do?"

"I...my love. Maddox just needs *time*."

"He doesn't need time, he needs a purpose! Listen here, boy. If you are not spending your time more sensibly next month, you'll have no place in my will!"

Maddox barked an incredulous laugh. "Good heavens, Father. Last time I checked we are *nobility*. How could you disown your only heir for not slaving away like a commoner? What about Narcissa? Doesn't *she* need a purpose?"

Tizzy lifted my hair away from the nape of my neck. I stiffened. My witch traits—the mark of a possessor of magic—marred the spot in a smattering of golden birthmarks. It was the reason I never wore my hair up and always made sure to conceal that area with powder. I stopped after Father took me in, but it still garnered whispers from the abbey's staff.

At least Tizzy had stopped fainting at the sight of it.

"I just want Narcissa to be happy," Father said.

My half-brother laughed again. "And you don't want *me* to be happy? Ever since that witch came you've been treating me like dirt."

"Maddox, please," Lady Vanessa pleaded.

"Can nobody see that?" he demanded. "Mother, I do not know why *you* are supporting this. That witch must be using her magic!"

"You will not speak ill of witchkind, Maddox," Father growled, his voice dangerously quiet. "*You* are half-witch. Do you condemn yourself? Do you condemn me?"

"I don't have an *ounce* of magic. You made sure of that when you rid us both of those cursed powers!" Maddox shouted. "That seems to be the only decent decision you made in your entire life!"

The thud of a boot striking the stone floor reverberated in the hall. "We are all going to the ball. Maddox, you will meet with the other members of the Royal Guard and be happy to do so. That. Is. Final." Father's heavy footsteps faded away, leaving shocked silence in their wake.

"Gah! I can't believe him!"

"Your father needs time to cool," Lady Vanessa said. "And so do you. Join me for tea?"

"I'm going for a ride."

Another set of footsteps stormed off, followed by a quiet sigh.

I sat still as Lady Vanessa left the hall. Father's last words swirled in my head. *We are all going to the ball.*

Did he mean me as well?

I turned, taking the ivory comb from Tizzy's hands. "That is enough, Tizzy. You're dismissed."

"Yes, milady." The maid bobbed several curtsies and scampered off, no doubt to tell the rest of the staff what she overheard.

Misty sauntered over from the bed and leaped into my lap. I stroked her midnight fur on impulse, trying to calm my heartbeat.

Your first appearance in society after switching allegiance? Misty said. *That's going to be interesting.*

"Second," I corrected. My first was the engagement party Amarante invited me to all those months ago.

The faces of the other guests were enough to convince me never to emerge from my room again. There was nothing quite so humiliating as being the jewel of high society, then having everyone witness my downfall. How was I supposed to act in the presence of those same people half a year later?

And even worse—how would the royals treat me? The palace had been my second home growing up. The last I saw of them was the masquerade ball that changed everything. King Maximus hadn't even summoned me when he decreed me as Father's ward. He wanted nothing to do with me, I was sure.

Calm yourself, darling. You know I like being pet slowly, Misty meowed.

"Father can't possibly expect me to go to this ball," I said, setting down my comb with a clack.

Talk to him. You know he'll do anything for you.

Misty jumped to the carpeted floor as I stood. Tizzy had left, so I was stuck dressing myself. After throwing on a simple gray gown and a wool spencer, I opened my window.

The garden was just below. I knew Father frequented the fountain when I wasn't there. It was where he and I used to play when I was a child.

I threw my legs over the windowsill and eased myself out. My damp hair grew icy against my neck as I traversed the lawn, ducking behind a rose bush when I passed the gazebo where Lady Vanessa took her tea.

On the other side of the garden, Father sat on the stone bench before the tiered fountain, his head buried in his hands. His figure was nearly drowned by the white blooms around him.

I hesitated. I hadn't spoken to him much since I arrived, and now I was only doing so because I wanted something. Guilt warmed my cheeks. It was bad enough I was the smear on his reputation as a loyal, upright guard. What right did I have demanding things from him on top of that?

"Do you remember when your favorite kite got caught in that tree, Cissa?"

Father had removed his hands from his face, his gaze fixated on the maple tree behind me. The branches were bare now, but I could easily recall a time when they were thick with fiery orange leaves. The same shade as my hair, as Father used to point out.

"You called for the pigeons to get it for you," he said, a ghost of a smile on his lips. "You named them too. Periwinkle and Gossamer, was it?"

His words resurfaced the memory of a pink silken kite and a pair of sassy pigeons.

I gave a weak laugh. "That was the day I learned not to do that."

Wild creatures found it highly offensive when people named them, whether humans or witches. The two were one and the same, for all they cared. A name labeled them as domestic—something undesirable in their world. Needless to say, the pigeons never returned to the garden.

Father chuckled and shook his head. "You were only eight. And with such control over your magic! You didn't even need an enchanted object to help you along."

Being isolated from witchkind since I was born, I hardly knew that witches my age needed enchanted objects to keep their magic under control. I doubted that Father could have acquired one for me, anyway.

I meandered over and sat next to him on the stone bench, ignoring the cold seeping through my dress.

"I reckon you heard everything this morning?" he said.

I nodded.

Father heaved a sigh. "Sometimes I wonder what would have happened if I kept my magic...and your brother's. What if I told Vanessa I was a witch instead of Wilhelmina?"

"Father..."

"I was a charmwitch, did you know? Cleaning spells and protection charms were my specialties. Fellow guards were jealous how my sword gleamed brighter than theirs and how I never got a scratch during training," he said, gray eyes alight with amusement. They faded as he looked down. "The day you were taken from me was the day I decided magic was too dangerous to have outside Witch Village. That woman...I know she made you do terrible things."

I did not recall the exact day Mother took me under her care. I just knew I never visited Father again, and I was not allowed to call him Father even when I saw him at the palace. The time I spent playing was replaced by Mother's experiments. She wanted to see what I could do. And more importantly, how she could use it to her advantage.

Most days took place in a small room with caged animals. The first time, I forced a snail to crawl into a bed of salt. The second, I made a fish jump out of a bowl of water. I left that session with the fish stuffed under my dress, scales and all. I had promised to return him to the pond.

Unfortunately, he did not survive the trip.

Coercion was not my true magic, but I let Mother believe it was. She would not have cared for my ability to converse with animals.

I shut my mind to the memories as Father plucked a white bloom from the bush next to him. He spun it between his fingers. "I would have removed your magic too. There was enough sickleweed potion left for you after I gave Maddox his dose, but I couldn't bring myself to take something that gave you so much joy."

"Sickleweed potion?"

"The herb itself looks quite similar to this," he said, pushing the bloom around on his palm. The petals were crinkled and white, like pieces of organdy. "In small doses, it's good for removing jinxes or spells. In a concentrated form it strips a witch of their magic entirely. Painless and quiet, said the herbwitch who sold it to me. She didn't tell me the silence would hurt."

"I'm sorry," I said.

"Don't be, Cissa. It was my decision." Father smiled mirthlessly and flicked the flower away. "My only *decent* decision, as Maddox said. Maybe he is right. Vanessa would have divorced me on the spot if her son started shooting sparks out of the blue."

"I don't think so."

Father wallowing in misery unsettled me. He had done nothing but smile in my presence the moment I moved in.

"Thank heavens the boy was a late bloomer." He studied his hands, brown and weathered from training. "I wonder what his magic would have been."

We sat in silence for a minute, listening to the rustling of the heather bushes and the chirping of the chickadee.

"Well, Cissa, now you know a little more about this old man's life," he said in a lighter tone, patting my shoulder. "All we can do is move on, eh? The Winter Solstice Ball will be a fresh start for both you and Maddox. We'll show that our family is bigger and stronger than ever, despite everything."

I parted my lips but closed them when I saw how his eyes shone. It would break his heart if he knew I cared less about this family than he did.

"When is the ball?" I asked at last. Misty said Father would do anything for me, but I was not so selfish as to let him.

He smiled. "Five days. There isn't time to get you fitted for a new gown, but I am sure Vanessa has something suitable for you to wear," he said. "After all these dreary months you can finally mingle and have fun. It will be a nice change, yes?"

Every fiber of my being protested. "Quite."

Father sighed. "I was worried you wouldn't want to go," he said, giving me a sidelong glance. "It's worse enough with Maddox. I need at least one of my children to make a good impression."

If he knew the truth, he would be sorely disappointed. But Father didn't need a hermit daughter *and* a sluggard son. The least I could do was appease him and endure a three-hour ball.

I returned to my room afterward, numb as the tips of my ears. Misty looked up inquiringly and I let my thoughts—a jumble of words and images—flow into her mind.

Do you think you made the right decision then? Misty asked. I couldn't discern whether she was impassive or disapproving.

"Perhaps," I said, sinking onto the floor, "this is one of my only decent ones."

3

A few days later I found myself on a low platform in Lady Vanessa's chambers. Father had informed her of my need for a ball gown, so I had no choice but to accept her invitation and try some of hers. I had disposed of my extravagant dresses before I came to Greenwood Abbey. They were all in Mother's favorite styles—none of them were truly to my taste.

I surveyed the heavy velvet covering my arms. It seemed that Lady Vanessa's gowns weren't faring any better.

"It's a little old-fashioned," Lady Vanessa said, "but quite flattering nonetheless."

"Oh yes, I believe so too, milady," Tizzy piped up from behind me.

The two of them were clearly lying through their teeth.

The dress was forest green with a low waistline embroidered with pale gold thread. Mother never allowed me to wear green. She claimed it made me look like a carrot with my coloring. It didn't help that the fit was all wrong. If Tizzy hadn't pinned back the excess fabric, I reckoned it would've slouched right off.

"It'll do," I said.

It was the fifth dress I tried, the past four being too bright, too dark, too drab, and too outrageous respectively. I was tired of standing and listening to Lady Vanessa and Tizzy make conversation.

"Are you sure, dear?" Lady Vanessa asked, joining Tizzy in the back. Her fair brows raised as she took in the mess of pins in the back. "I can find something that fits better. There was a time I slimmed down quite a bit—"

"It's fine," I interrupted.

Lady Vanessa and Tizzy exchanged glances in the mirror.

"It's fine," I repeated in a softer voice. "I...actually have somewhere to be."

The two exchanged another glance. For all they knew, there was only one place I went—the palace dungeons to visit Mother. They weren't wrong.

"Very well, I won't keep you if you have plans," Lady Vanessa said, her face breaking into a warm smile. I wondered how she could muster such an expression despite what she must be thinking. "Tizzy, help Narcissa dress. And take the gown to a dressmaker. I heard there's a new shop downtown doing quite well."

Tizzy began removing the pins on the ballgown. "Yes, milady. It's called Jeraldine's Dress Emporium. Witch-owned and run, I heard."

"How lovely!" Lady Vanessa said, clapping her hands together. "I'm sure they have spectacular service. I'll have to order from them sometime."

"Perhaps for future gatherings, milady," Tizzy said around a mouthful of pins. I stepped out of the gown and bent for my sage green day dress.

"Yes, of course. It's lovely having these magic businesses pop up," Lady Vanessa continued. "Just the other day I visited a quaint little bakery. They had my order whipped up in seconds and enchanted the coffee to stay hot even in these temperatures."

Tizzy helped me into the dress. "I'll take a look in my free time," she said. "Oh, but have you seen the one uptown, milady?"

My gut sank as they chatted enthusiastically about witch-owned businesses. It only confirmed my assumptions—that the people of Greenwood Abbey feared me. Not my magic.

SOON AFTER, I took the carriage to the palace. A guard rode in front, his posture stiff and disapproving. Father had insisted I go with some sort of protection during my visits. The cramped carriage and the narrow-eyed glances of the guard, however, made me feel more like a prisoner than a lady protected.

When the gleaming towers of the palace grew close, we rounded to the back entrance where the dungeons were situated. The guard followed as I took my route down the dark hallway of wailing prisoners. I had come so often that their cries no longer startled me and the acrid smell didn't burn my nostrils. The numbers on the cells grew with every step until we reached cell one hundred and fifty-six.

The burly prison guard before the door gave me a nod.

"Visitor," he said gruffly into the slot. He unfastened the lock and chains, leaving the door ajar.

I wished I had Misty with me, but she didn't like the

dungeons. I suspected she didn't like Mother either, though she would never admit it for my sake.

I clenched my fists and stepped in.

Mother sat in the middle of the cell, her knees tucked under her chin. Not a speck of dirt marred her chemise despite being surrounded by old hay and grime encrusted bricks. No doubt she had bullied her guard into allowing her various vain luxuries.

"Come to pay your dear mama another visit, have you, Narcissa?" Mother said, her words drenched in sarcasm. Her eyes flicked up my gown. "I told you you look awful in green."

I kept my hands folded in front of me. "Mother," I said. "How are you?"

She snorted, the sound echoing in the dank cell. "Why keep up this charade, Narcissa? If you cared I wouldn't be here. Aren't you busy enough frolicking about with your father and those other *creatures*?"

Witches, she meant. I pressed my lips together. The only witch I had ever come in contact with was Amarante, and after the way I treated her, I didn't expect any of the others to accept me. She was practically their savior.

My throat tightened when I recalled the events of last summer. Six months alone cleared Mother's influence like spring fog dissolving in the afternoon sun. Without her praise and affirmations, her pretty gifts and rare shows of affection, the things she made me do became all the more horrifying.

Forcing Amarante into servitude was perhaps the worst. I had drawn her blood and bullied her into silence. The bullying was nothing new, but the physical assault was a line I didn't think I would ever cross. The knowledge that I had done it without so much as a blink—that my desperate need to please Mother pushed me to do something so cruel—was the most sickening of all.

My silence was enough.

"So. You've been wasting away in your room like a prisoner. It shows." Mother sneered. Her once full, deep voice had become tinny. I suppose being shrill was more advantageous in the dungeons, so as to better annoy her guard. "You always were a sulky girl. Pathetic and friendless. If I raised you right you would be queen by now. But alas. With that gaunt face of yours you won't stand a chance with any prince."

"If you don't want anything I will be on my way," I said flatly, turning on my heel. I touched my cheek for a brief moment.

I had hoped to find Mother in disarray, like a proper prisoner. But once again I was disappointed. Satin smooth hair. Clean face. Straight spine. And that glint in her eye.

What I would do to get rid of that glint.

"Tell me, Narcissa. Why do you come unless some part of you wishes to free me?"

I wanted badly to take calming breaths. The rancid air did little to settle my nerves.

"I hear the Winter Solstice Ball is around the corner," she said.

I should have walked away. But I never left as long as Mother had something to say. If I closed my eyes I could imagine us in her suite again, days before an event, her mahogany comb running through my hair as she drilled me on etiquette and noble lineage.

I could defy her with no consequence now, but old habits held me back. She knew that.

I looked over my shoulder. "Where did you hear that?"

Mother tipped her head back and gave an airy laugh. "I'm not so foolish as to tell you," she said. "Well? Are you going?"

I stiffened. "That is no longer your concern."

"You must go," she said gleefully. "When you were my daughter you were admired by all. Did you think betraying me would grant you their good graces? They will not accept you, Narcissa. You are nothing without me, only the bastard daughter of Greenwood. And a *witch* at that."

She was playing one of her mind games again. To confuse me in the midst of my own confusion. Did she loathe my existence and want nothing to do with me? Or was she trying to draw me back under her influence? Or perhaps she had lost her sanity completely. The last, I knew, was wishful thinking.

Whatever it was, I couldn't stand another minute of it.

"Goodbye, Mother."

I exited the cell. The prison guard slammed the door, the sound of chains being fastened reverberating through the corridor.

My guard showed no sign of having heard anything as I brushed past him, but I knew he was going to recount the conversation to every other staff member in Greenwood Abbey. Roaches scurried across the floor, a cacophony of little voices echoing in my head.

Food, food, food, food, food...

They were hungry, off to find a crust of bread a prisoner had hidden for himself. I shook their thoughts away, too overwhelmed with my own. I pressed my fingers to my eyes, but they came back dry.

What a fool I was. Was I not satisfied with the knowledge that she was locked away in the most secure corner of the palace dungeons?

No.

I would not rest until I saw her broken.

"ENJOY PLOTTING WITH your mother?" Maddox said when I returned to the abbey. He was in the stables, his horse beside him.

"Enjoy behaving like a brat?" I retorted, eying his muddied trousers. He had taken another one of his rides, evidently.

I had been around long enough to know he only rode when he was upset and took great pleasure in tearing up the fields. When the groundskeepers weren't whispering about me, they were muttering about Maddox.

He scoffed and turned his attention back to his horse, a steed with a glossy black coat, and attempted to lead it into his stall. The horse did not budge.

"Come, Midnight," Maddox said, tugging on the reins.

Leave it up to him to give his horse the most unoriginal name. Midnight whinnied in protest, his thoughts floating over to me. *There's a rock lodged in my hoof!*

"There's a rock lodged in his hoof," I said as Maddox continued to struggle.

He stopped. "What?"

"Your horse," I said, jutting my chin at Midnight. "Check his hooves."

He glared. "This is some sort of joke, isn't it?" He tugged on the reins again but Midnight held his ground. "What are you doing to my horse?"

There's a rock in my hoof, you idiot!

"There's a rock in his hoof, you idiot," I said coolly.

"*What* did you just call me?"

Are all humans like this or is it just him? Midnight huffed.

I sighed, wondering why I was bothering with this. *Show him*, I thought to the horse.

Midnight whinnied and raised one of his front hooves.

"What are you—" Maddox's words cut off when he caught sight of the offending rock.

"You're welcome," I said, turning on my heel. I pretended not to hear him cursing me under his breath.

4

It was funny how in a place I used to thrive, all I wanted to do now was hide.

The royal ballroom was as grand as ever, but it was always something special during the winter solstice. Dangling crystals threw iridescent shards of light against the marble walls. Tapestries depicting snow-capped mountains hung between pillars. The dance floor was aglow with thousands of flickering candles speckling the ballroom. Some sat in blown glass orbs, meant to be carried by the dancers as they performed the candle waltz—a dance that only came around during the solstice.

A courtier's daughter once whispered to me that the candle symbolized hope and new beginnings, a fiery promise that spring will come bearing all things good. The last person you dance with is said to be your true love. I thought it rather romantic as a child, but romance was one of the many things Mother spurned.

I glanced over at Father, whose eyes were nearly as bright as the chandeliers.

"Would you look at that. I haven't attended a ball in years," he said as the four of us emerged from a crowd of guests. I wedged myself behind him as more people entered through the archway. King Maximus and the princes still had to be announced, meaning the night had yet to commence.

"It was kind of General Turner to take your place tonight," Lady Vanessa said, her diamond earrings glittering. "I thought I would have to attend without you."

"Killian is a generous man. He knew I needed a break from the Royal Guard," Father said with a chuckle. "And what better time than now? Maddox, stand straight, my boy. You have an impression to make tonight."

Maddox grunted at my left. At first glance, he looked the part of a perfect gentleman. At my proximity, however, his pout was about as obvious as his bright blue necktie.

He shot me a venomous glare when he caught me looking at him. I rolled my eyes in response.

"Listen to your father, Maddox," Lady Vanessa said. She reached over to straighten his lapel, but Maddox jerked away.

"I am not a child," he muttered.

She withdrew her hand, brows furrowing. "Very well then."

I closed my eyes, hoping there wouldn't be another family outburst just because my idiotic brother couldn't keep his temper in check. People were already looking at us, some greeting Father and others blatantly staring at me.

Last summer when Father pronounced me as his daughter and not the late Earl Whittington's, he received some disapproval for having me out of wedlock. But it seemed that his noble services to the kingdom outweighed his sins. I, however, had nothing to redeem myself.

Many among the guests were Mother's friends, or rather, noblewomen who befriended her out of fear and desire to advance their own positions. The same women who sang my high praises now looked at me in contempt. My hair was on full display, half piled up with pearl pins and half cascading down my back. Tizzy chose the style for me as I had no preference, but now I wished she had covered my head with a scarf. Anything to hide the glaring fact that I was my mother's daughter.

"Do my eyes deceive me? Greenwood!" a hearty voice exclaimed.

"Hello, old friend," Father said warmly to the gray-haired gentleman who approached us. The dark mustache on his upper lip made him instantly recognizable.

Lord Frederick Huntington was one of His Majesty's most trusted former advisors. He had stepped down to join the Royal Guard as a commander next to Father instead, claiming that regulating royal affairs was far more strenuous than maintaining palace security.

If I recalled correctly, he lorded over some parts of Coriva.

Mother didn't like him. She didn't like any of Father's friends.

"When was the last time you attended a ball?" Lord Frederick asked.

"Why, just last month. I was outside armed to the teeth. Didn't you see me?" Father said, eyes twinkling.

Lord Frederick laughed a deep, bellowing laugh. "I see the cold hasn't damaged your humor." He turned his bright gaze to Lady Vanessa, Maddox, and me. If he was surprised by my presence he didn't show it. "Ah, greetings! A rare family gathering, I see."

Lady Vanessa inclined her head. "It is the winter solstice, after all."

"So it is! Unfortunately, that wasn't reason enough for my wife and daughter to join me," he said with a rueful smile. "They insisted on going to the opera to see some new singer or whatnot."

"Celeste Carr from the Grand Alevine Opera?" Lady Vanessa asked. "She has been making quite a name for herself lately."

Lord Frederick shrugged. "Ah yes, that's the one. My Izzy has been talking nonstop about her, though just a month before she was begging me to take her to the palace to see the crown prince. But I suppose young girls enjoy a good show more than anything else!"

"Shame." Father clapped him on the shoulder, clearly wanting to change the subject. "Say, Frederick, how is the security at Huntington Abbey?"

"Horsefeathers, Greenwood. You're concerned enough about palace security. Why must you involve yourself with mine?"

"My son has recently taken interest in becoming a guard," Father said, motioning for Maddox to step forward. Maddox looked ready to deny the blatant lie, but to my surprise, he forced a smile and joined Father and Lord Frederick in conversation.

No doubt the rest of the night would go that way for him. I took some pleasure in the fact that Maddox would have to suffer as much as I would.

Lady Vanessa touched my arm. "You look beautiful tonight," she said, retracting her hand when I met her eye. "Green suits you."

The gown she lent me hung much better after it had been tailored to my measurements. Still, I didn't feel beautiful. Not after Mother claimed I had grown gaunt.

"Thank you," I said quietly.

"I suppose we should leave the men to their own devices." A smile pulled at the edge of her pink lips. "Perhaps you can introduce me to your friends if any are in attendance?"

I glanced at the table behind her, filled with flickering candles in small glass orbs.

Friends. What a novel concept.

"Or perhaps we can take a trip to the refreshments table? A spiced cider will warm us up nicely," Lady Vanessa said.

I racked my brain for a polite refusal. The truth was, I didn't want to spend the night with her. Not with the pity and guilt in her eyes.

Before I could think of something to say, Lady Vanessa shook her head. "How silly of me. A young thing like you shouldn't be chained to her stepmother all night," she said with a forced laugh. It was the first time she referred to herself as my stepmother. She wasn't looking at me anymore, which was a relief.

Instead, she stepped back and retrieved a candlelit orb, pushing it into my hands. This one had a blend of snowy blue and periwinkle glass, textured like a honeycomb. The surface felt like ice despite the large flame flickering within.

"Why don't you find a nice gentleman to dance with? They'll all be head over heels for you, I'm sure," Lady Vanessa said with a smile. "I have a few acquaintances to catch up with. We'll be at the benches if you need me."

I nodded. With that, she slipped off, the silvery train of her gown disappearing into the rabble.

The ballroom was at full occupancy now, crowd and conversation concentrated at the archway. I made a beeline to a corner between the staircase and the refreshments table, well hidden from view.

A bench waited for me there. I took my seat and leaned against the wall. On the balcony above, the orchestra was tuning their instruments. I always attended public events without Misty, but this time, there was no one to occupy me. I felt her absence sorely.

A rustling sounded within the wall. I tilted my head closer.

I'm starving, Ma, a rodent squeaked.

Have a little patience. The humans will leave eventually.

But I want to eat now.

You just had some parchment.

I'm tired of parchment! I want real food.

We're mice, child. Everything is real food.

A disgruntled squeak came from the young mouse.

I managed a smile. Mice were far more friendly than the average kitchen maid would think. I spent hours of my childhood listening to them in the corridors of Mother's estate. They were my only companions before I found Misty.

A myriad of cakes and sandwiches were stacked on the refreshments table. None of the guests had approached yet, thankfully. I picked out a honey-glazed pastry and ran my hand down a hairline crack in the damask wallpaper.

There was a hole the size of a child's fist at the bottom. The staff had cleverly placed the table over the entrance, though part of it was still accessible.

I broke the pastry into pieces and swept it into the mouse hole. A squeak of delight came from the wall, followed by the pitter-patter of feet. A flash of snowy white paws appeared and disappeared.

"What are you doing?"

I jerked up, narrowly missing the edge of the table.

"Are there mice in there? I love mice." A girl in a shimmering violet gown hovered over my shoulder. The fabric was eye-catching, shifting to pale green at certain angles. Her hair was braided in neat rows against her scalp, piling into an elaborate chignon on top of her head. It tipped dangerously as she craned her neck to catch a glimpse of the mouse hole.

"There are." I hardly knew how to react. I had never done anything so undignified as shove dessert into a wall at a royal ball. And never had I been approached by strangers.

The girl popped back up. She had wide silver eyes and a crescent moon smile. Light from the chandeliers danced over the freckles on her cheeks, shining gold.

A witch.

I didn't let my surprise show. It seemed that much had changed during the six months I spent in my room.

"Were you going to dance?" she asked, nodding at the glass orb I had abandoned on the bench.

I reached for it, running a finger over the textured surface before blowing out the flame. A wisp of smoke rose from the wick and dissolved.

"No."

"Oh, shame," she said with a sigh. "I want to dance. But you're the only person who would talk to me tonight."

I blinked slowly. "One does not simply approach someone in a royal ballroom unless they are previously acquainted."

She huffed. "Then how is anyone supposed to meet new people?"

"Find a mutual acquaintance and have them introduce you. Those are the rules of society."

"Sounds inconvenient." She crossed her arms, the fabric of her bodice bunching. "No one I came with knows anyone. Not Rowena and certainly not Ma." The girl straightened. "I know Prince Ash. Maybe he can introduce me." She shook her head abruptly. "Ah. He's in Vandil on royal business. I forgot."

"I see," I said. How did a chatty, oblivious witch girl know the second prince?

"I have an idea! Can *you* introduce me? We're acquaintances, aren't we?"

I looked heavenward, hoping her mother would find her and lead her away. The last thing I wanted was to spend the next two hours entertaining a prattling teenager.

"You don't know me. And you wouldn't want me as an acquaintance," I said, standing up from my crouch. My right foot had fallen asleep, sending stinging needles up my leg.

"You're Lady Narcissa. Amarante told me all about you, and we met once. Well, actually, I was invisible then. I'm Elowyn, by the way."

My eye twitched.

"You helped Amarante and Prince Ash escape the duchess. Amarante said you were really brave during the masquerade ball."

Of course she did. How spineless of her to not say vicious things behind my back after all I had done to her.

"I wish I was there to see you summon those animals, but I wasn't allowed to attend," Elowyn said, kicking the floor with embroidered satin slippers. She shrugged. "Well, I'm making up for lost time now. This is my second ball, you know? I wish I could've attended all those fancy dinners with all the others, but Ma said I wasn't allowed to. Royal business or whatnot."

I tilted my head. "Royal business?"

"Oh, you didn't hear? The princes organized a witch, er, group. I forget the word."

"Committee?" I supplied.

"Right. Committee. We don't have many groups in the village. Anyway, you see, the committee is in charge of reporting the comings and goings of witches in Witch Village to the royals. And they help witches who want to move above ground get settled. Rowena told me their first meeting was about licenses needed to open magic shops in Delibera. But you probably already know this since you seem important and—"

"Only in Delibera?" I wanted to shut down the conversation earlier, but it turned out that isolation gave me a thirst for kingdom-wide news, which I was so used to getting before.

"For now. It is the biggest city, after all. But I heard they plan to organize more committees for Olderea's other regions. Coriva and Vandil and such." She leaned in and lowered her voice. "I don't think the older witches are too happy about the politics and groups. They're too used to living without authority in Witch Village. They don't like it."

"And you do?" I asked, raising a brow.

"Of course! It's much freer up here, especially in the palace," Elowyn said, as if she hadn't just complained about the rules of high society minutes before. "I hope to join the committee when I'm old enough. Traveling and exploring the kingdom—doesn't that sound great?"

"I don't like traveling," I said, once I realized she was going to prattle on about something else. I turned on my heel, hoping she would take the hint and go away.

No such luck.

"Why not?" Elowyn said, trotting to keep up with my strides. "I haven't traveled much, but it all sounds like great fun. Plus, afterward, you can just appear to all the places you've been—but oh, silly me, not everyone can do that, so I suppose I'm just lucky in that regar—"

Thankfully, a blast of regal fanfare interrupted her. The steward's high voice rang through the ballroom. "His Majesty King Maximus Median and His Highness Crown Prince Bennett Median of Olderea!"

I stopped several feet away from the grand staircase and nearly tripped over Elowyn's skirt in the process. My cheeks warmed as I righted myself. Elowyn giggled loudly, drawing glances from the group near us.

"What is *she* doing here?" a noblewoman in lime green whispered to another. Dame Alderidge, I recalled. One of the biggest gossips in Mother's circle who stuck her bulbous nose in places it had no business in. Her daughter was equally annoying.

I shot Dame Alderidge a glare. She immediately turned her attention back to the figures on the staircase. When the king and crown prince came to the last few steps, I lowered my head. I had yet to know what they thought of me. A part of me prayed I'd be ignorant to that forever.

Raise your head, Narcissa, the phantom voice of Mother echoed from many balls past. *Look them in the eye. Make it known you are their equal. Someday, you will surpass them.*

I winced, squeezing my eyes shut as my heart pounded wildly against my ribs.

She's not here, I reminded myself. *Nothing is going to happen.*

Then, all hell broke loose.

Shattered glass rained from the ceiling and screams pierced the air. Elowyn yelped beside me. With a bright violet flash, she disappeared. I hardly had time to wonder where she went when the window above the dais shattered. Crystalline shards rained onto the floor as a band of people in black garb streamed in. An arrow whizzed across the ballroom, embedding itself inches away from Crown Prince Bennett.

"Guards!" King Maximus bellowed. His voice was drowned in the chaos of the guests, who all at once surged away from the assailants.

My gaze jumped wildly to each assassin, trying to identify any of their covered faces. None looked like Mother's men, but she hired many. I could never be sure.

One of them was suspended eerily above the thrones, floating on thin air. They fired another arrow.

"Guards!" the king shouted again, swinging himself over

the staircase and ducking for cover paces away from me. The crown prince followed suit.

This time, his call was answered. Members of the Royal Guard flooded in—some from the staircase and others from directly behind the assassins. The ones at the entrance had no such luck as the crowd was pushing themselves through the singular archway near the row of benches.

The benches. Lady Vanessa.

I forced my legs to move but promptly tripped over an extinguished candle, crushing the glass beneath my knees. Pain shot up my legs like daggers. I cursed, clenching my fists to gather myself.

Before I could attempt to stand, strong hands hauled me up by my upper arms. I turned to thank whoever it was, only to find myself face to face with Crown Prince Bennett. Surprise flashed through his eyes. He released his hold, as if burned.

I didn't have time to dwell on his reaction—nor did I want to. I turned and ran, ignoring my spinning vision. Luckily, my thick velvet skirts took the brunt of the glass. A quick look down confirmed I wasn't trailing blood across the marble. I only hoped it would stay that way.

The shrieks of guests grew even louder as I fought through the crowd. Somehow I avoided getting shoved or knocked to the ground. At long last, the benches appeared beyond the throng. Many were flipped in the chaos.

Lady Vanessa sat pressed against the wall near the archway, small and pale. My nails dug into my palms. What was wrong with the woman? Didn't she have the sense to run like everyone else?

"Lady Vanessa!" I called out.

Relief flooded her face. "Narcissa!" She stood up. "Thank heavens you're alright. I didn't want to leave in case you came looking for me. What is happening?"

The crowd and commotion must've obstructed her view. "Assassins," I said, catching my breath.

Lady Vanessa paled. It was then I noticed she had a scratch on her forehead, dotted with minute spots of blood. I tore my eyes away from it.

"They're outnumbered by the Royal Guard," I said, attempting to keep my voice level. "It should be fine."

The singular levitating assassin came to mind. Could they possibly be a witch? My blood ran cold at the thought. Mother detested witches—but only those she could not control. Before my mind could wander again, Lady Vanessa grabbed my hand.

"Narcissa. Have you seen Maverick?" Worry lined her face. And with her hand grasping mine, trembling yet warm, something indescribable flooded my chest and threatened to burst.

It must have been my nerves.

By some miracle, Father emerged from the crowd, sword in hand. His shoulders sagged in relief when he locked eyes with us. Maddox materialized behind him, eyes wide with fear. It was the first time he looked anything other than angry.

"It's over," Father said, breathless. "One assassin killed. The rest...gone."

Despite the brevity of the attack, the chaos did not subside for another twenty minutes. By then, most guests had already fled. Those injured from the throng stayed to be treated.

Father remained behind, as did General Killian Turner and several others. We were instructed to wait at the benches for him, but I found myself listening in.

"Why," King Maximus said as he paced before his throne, "do these things always happen in the blasted ballroom?" Broken glass crunched beneath his boots.

Father knelt, his borrowed sword clattering to his side. "Forgive me, Your Majesty. If I had been more aware—"

General Turner stepped forward, his arm hanging in a sling. "No, Maverick. I was on duty. It is my fault, Your Majesty. If you deem it appropriate to strip me of my title—"

The king exhaled. "No, General. The attackers came from above and you were injured. But I expected you to appoint trustworthy guards in the back. It seems an excess of…winter solstice *cheer* caused them to neglect their duties," he said drily, brushing off his ermine coat. "Be sure this never happens again."

General Turner lowered his head. "They will be properly punished."

King Maximus nodded, then turned his eyes to the body laid out on a stretcher. It was clothed in black. The covering had been lifted, revealing the face of a long-chinned man with gold marks speckled across his cheeks.

"Someone explain this to me," he said, frowning heavily at the group of people—witches, I realized—behind Father. All of them had an ornate golden pin in the shape of an acorn on their clothing, which gleamed underneath the remaining candlelight. They were the witch committee Elowyn was speaking of.

Behind them was a cluster of old men dressed in emerald green robes. The king's council. One of them stepped up.

"These witches have outstayed their welcome," the councilman said with a sneer. "They have become bold enough as to attack the royal family."

A woman from the witch committee bristled. She looked a great deal like Elowyn. "We can assure you witches have no part in this," she said.

"What proof do you have, Rowena, when that man was levitating before our eyes?" Crown Prince Bennett asked from his seat on the dais. He sounded surprisingly calm for someone who was almost killed. "Surely you cannot speak for all witches."

Rowena walked over to the body and rubbed her finger over a spot of gold on the dead man's cheek. It flaked off. She examined the substance.

"Gold leaf," she said, "not witch traits. He was an impersonator."

King Maximus frowned. "The fact that he is not a witch himself does not mean he was not working with any. Perhaps a witch levitated him."

Rowena directed her gaze to the shattered window above them. She stared for so long I was convinced she had fallen asleep standing, until she lifted her hand and grabbed something I couldn't see.

"Suspension wires," she said. She let them fall to the marble, where the wires curled in on themselves with a twang. "Imperceptible during the night. They're common in theatrical productions, if I'm not mistaken."

Crown Prince Bennett stared at the wires. "Someone must've built a rigging system above the window frame for that to work."

"Actually…they have," Father spoke up, his brow furrowed. "Just last week, in fact, my men reported beams of wood and rope on the ballroom roof. It was the same time general repairs were going on in the palace—I assumed that was what it was."

"So the intruders had access to the grounds," the crown prince said.

King Maximus flushed red. "Has palace security gotten so incompetent as to let these things happen?" he demanded.

Father and General Turner bowed their heads.

The king muttered to himself, dragging a hand over his face. "Maverick. I need to know who those assassins are and what their motive is."

"Father," the crown prince said. "I believe I have an answer."

"What is it, Bennett?"

"The riots."

King Maximus paled. "Heavens, you're right."

The king's council murmured in agreement. The witches looked uncomfortable. I waited for someone to elaborate but no one did.

"It seems we have a lot to discuss," the king said. "Come, Bennett, to my study. Will you join us, Maverick?"

Father threw a concerned glance in our direction. I hoped he would tell us to return home without him, but I knew he didn't feel it was safe, especially with assassins on the loose.

King Maximus seemed to catch on to his dilemma. "Have Captain Greenwood's family escorted to my library," he said to a servant. He turned to everyone else. "The rest of you, dismissed."

6

Servants led us into the king's library where we were given blankets and warmed cider. I sat before the fireplace with Lady Vanessa and Maddox, clutching my mug as if my life depended on it.

Voices came from the door of His Majesty's study. The king's voice rose and fell. Father's was a low, steady rumble.

Of all the things I expected to happen tonight, an attempted assassination was not one of them. And even worse, it led me here: in close proximity to the royals. I took a sip of cider to calm myself, but the spiced beverage only burned my throat and made my stomach turn.

Maddox rose from the couch and crouched before the fireplace, scowling at the flames. "They're going to make him investigate this, aren't they?"

Lady Vanessa sighed. "It's only natural. He is Captain of the Royal Guard. His title comes with duties," she said, pulling her blanket tighter around her shoulders. The scratch on her forehead had scabbed over, but it was still disconcerting to see it on her calm, refined face.

"It's not fair!" Maddox exploded. He slammed his fist into the rug.

I turned around, slinging an arm across the back of the couch. "Don't tell me you're going to throw a tantrum in the king's private library." The words slipped out before I could stop them.

Maddox's face flushed. "You have no right to judge me! If I had to place my bets, those assassins were witches, through and through. Why don't you save Father the effort and go tell him it was your kind who caused all this?"

I opened my mouth to retort, but to my surprise, the angry voice that spoke next was not my own.

"Enough, Maddox! You are not the only one hurting."

I stared incredulously as Lady Vanessa stood from her seat, hands fisted at her sides. Her eyes blazed with the reflection of the fireplace. "Do you think I want my husband gone for months on end to protect a family that isn't his own? Do you think your sister asked to live in a home with more strangers than kin? I am trying, Maddox. I am trying my best to hold this household together," she said, her voice almost hysteric. She took a shaky breath. "I know how you are feeling right now and I am sorry. But for once, can you please be *quiet*?"

"Mother," Maddox began, but seemed to think better of it. He was too surprised to even throw me a scathing glare before sinking back into the rug.

I took another sip of cider just to occupy myself. The air simmered with raging silence as Lady Vanessa reclaimed her seat. The voices in the king's study had stopped some time ago. I winced, hoping the three of them hadn't heard our little outburst.

It wasn't long before the knob turned and Father emerged from behind the oak door, his face grave. Relief swept through my limbs. Was it finally time to go?

"Narcissa, come. His Majesty wants an audience with you."

My gut seized. I stared, wide-eyed at the gap between the library and the study.

The king wanted to see me? Did he think the assassins were hired by Mother? That I had something to do with it? I wanted to scream and run.

Instead, I nodded and followed Father inside. I caught a glimpse of Lady Vanessa's questioning look before the door clicked shut and I was standing before the very people I wanted to hide from.

"Your Majesty. Your Highness." I executed a smooth curtsy in their general direction, gluing my gaze on the dark walnut floorboards.

"Narcissa. I hope you are well," King Maximus said. I saw from my periphery that he was standing behind his desk with Crown Prince Bennett to his right.

"Perfectly well, Your Majesty. Thank you." I was dangerously close to vomiting. No doubt I had too many sips of cider.

"You must be wondering why I asked to see you," King Maximus said, clasping his hands behind his back. "Maverick. I believe it would be best for you to explain."

Father's warm hands weighed on my shoulders. "Cissa. As you know, we've figured the assassins were humans. But as for their intentions, we have strong suspicions they are witch-related." He heaved a sigh. "With the influx of witch magic in Olderea's biggest cities, lives of human civilians have seen many changes. Changes to riot over."

"Have...witches taken traffic away from human businesses?" I asked slowly, recalling Tizzy and Lady Vanessa's mention of witch-owned shops. I wouldn't have known otherwise, having spent all my time in my room.

"Precisely," he said. "Local farmers can't compete with herbwitches who specialize in growing crops, as one example. I'm afraid public opinion about reincorporating witches is skewing downward."

"I hardly knew it could skew even lower," King Maximus said. "The benefits of witch magic seemed to outweigh the disadvantages a few months ago."

Father sighed. "We fear that after the awe of magic has worn off, civilians will start seeing witches as an invasive people taking over their livelihoods."

I nodded. It all seemed grave, but expected. There were still people eager to push witches off the land—people like Maddox, no doubt. For it to escalate into an assassination attempt was dangerous indeed. The royal family was no longer as popular as they once were before ending the Non-Magic Age.

I had never studied witch history. Mother didn't find it necessary for me, so I was ignorant of human and witch relations before the late King Humphrey banned magic.

"How were they living with humans before?" I said. "Were there not witches working in the palace as royal inspectors?"

The crown prince spoke, his voice quiet but domineering. "That was a special case. History only shows us that most witches kept to their own circles despite living amongst humans. There was tension from the start."

I pressed my lips together. This all seemed like royal business, something I had no part in. "What does this have to do with me?" I asked Father.

"His Majesty feels that the first step toward harmony

is setting an example of unity," Father said. He took a deep breath. "Through...marriage."

"Marriage," I repeated, unable to comprehend what he was saying.

King Maximus gave the slightest nod. "Bennett?"

Before I knew what was happening, the crown prince strode out from his corner and knelt before me with a ring in hand—an onyx stone set in a gold band. It must've been one of his, for there was a pale band of skin wrapped around his index finger.

"Lady Narcissa, I humbly request your hand in marriage for the wellness of our kingdom," he said, his voice stiff and emotionless.

I took a step back, looking from King Maximus's calm face, the crown prince's blank one, and finally to Father, whose expression I could not read.

I pinched my arm hard, convinced this was a dream.

Not just any dream. *Mother's* dream.

But the crown prince's bowed head did not disappear, neither did the winking onyx. I was at a loss for words.

A beat of silence passed before King Maximus cleared his throat. "Perhaps this is too sudden for you, Narcissa," he said, taking a seat behind his desk. "It has been a long night. How about we schedule another meeting to go over the logistics?"

I nodded wordlessly as Crown Prince Bennett stood. His boots, which were spotless even after the chaos, retracted back to the corner of the room. Father and the king murmured about the time and location of the next meeting, but I barely heard them.

Somehow, even locked away in the dungeons, Mother got exactly what she wanted.

7

The ride back passed in a blur. Lady Vanessa and Maddox asked frantic questions which Father answered. I said nothing, and I said nothing even until the next morning as Tizzy tended to my toilette.

She, on the other hand, was more talkative than usual.

"Which gown would you like to wear on Monday, milady?" she asked as she braided my hair back.

Monday was the day Father and King Maximus settled on to meet again. It seemed that in a span of a night, news had spread all over the household about the crown prince's proposal.

I met Tizzy's gaze in the vanity mirror, deciding to throw the girl a bone. "Whatever you deem fit for a newly engaged."

"So you accepted?" she exclaimed. Her eyes widened with a million questions. Whether I was in love with the crown prince was surely one of them. Little did Tizzy know,

I was not a romantic. Mother had crushed the dreams and silliness right out of me at the age I started finding boys handsome.

"It is a royal arrangement. I hardly think my acceptance matters," I said drily.

Tizzy fastened my braids in place with pearl-tipped pins. "Oh." After a moment's hesitation, she said, "Does that mean milady does not want to marry the crown prince?"

I didn't speak. Tizzy finished attending me and left with a pout, clearly disappointed at my lack of response.

But I had answered her question. King Maximus, who rarely yielded on his decisions, seemed set on the arrangement. Meanwhile, Crown Prince Bennett's emotionless proposal made it clear he would avoid me like the plague once we were wed. Neither he nor the king could possibly trust me to take part in royal affairs after what happened last summer. I would be a figurehead to show off at public events, nothing more.

The situation must be dire indeed for the king to choose you, Misty said as she jumped off from her perch on the window seat.

"He wouldn't be able to find another gentrified witch with a competent bloodline," I murmured. I looked at my hands. "Do you think she did it?" Now that I was alone, I finally voiced my fears.

Who, darling, your mother? Misty curled herself around my chair. *You think she schemed all this up so you can become the crown princess?*

I gazed at my reflection. My cheeks looked paler and hollower than I remembered. "I wouldn't put it past her."

I suppose it all seems quite convenient, Misty reasoned. *Still. You must be paranoid. You're in shock.*

"I am not. I am being cautious."

Misty meowed. *Why don't you go ask her then?*

"Visiting right after the proposal?" I scoffed. "People will talk."

Really, you have a dizzying intellect.

The contents of my vanity rattled as I searched the drawers for rouge. "I won't let her win."

My. Even when she's in the dungeons your life still revolves around that woman. Misty turned up her tail and sauntered out the door, which Tizzy had left open. *I'll be in the kitchen when you decide to pay me some attention.*

THE REST OF the day passed uneventfully. I took my breakfast and lunch in my chambers, mainly to avoid Father. Whenever I did see him, I caught him throwing apologetic glances at me. I wondered if he was the one who proposed the idea of marriage. Protecting the royal family—and thereby the kingdom—was his duty. If that involved pulling me into an arranged marriage, I couldn't blame him.

But the possibility of all this being Mother's plan still gnawed at my consciousness. Scenarios of every shape and form ran through my head. It was possible she still had access to her network of thugs. Perhaps they were the ones inciting riots, if not the actual assassins. But how? I was no longer sending messages to them through rodents and pigeons. Could she still have people working for her, even without her wealth and position?

I pressed my forehead against the window in frustration, the icy glass burning my skin. Even after years of living with her—of assisting her with the most unscrupulous schemes—I could not fathom how her mind worked.

Maybe Misty was right. I was in shock. I was being paranoid. After all, six months of solitude being broken by an assassination attempt could not be good for my health. I made a discontented noise in the back of my throat and collapsed onto the window seat.

A light tap next to my ear nearly sent me to the floor.

Lady Vanessa, of all people, stood on the other side of the window, smiling sheepishly. She had a plate in hand and a furry shadow against her skirt, which, if I wasn't mistaken, was Misty.

I lifted the window with some effort.

"You missed dinner. I thought you'd like some dessert," Lady Vanessa said, placing the plate on the windowsill.

"Thank you." Pumpkin pie with a dollop of whipped cream on the side. Just how I liked it.

"And this little lady has been scratching at your door for some time," she said, lifting Misty from the grass.

"Oh," I said, grimacing. I had kept the door locked after lunch and somehow didn't hear a thing. Misty jumped through the window and hissed at my outstretched hand. She stalked away.

I would have to sleep on the floor tonight, it seemed.

"May I?" Lady Vanessa asked, gesturing to the window seat.

I fiddled with my sleeves. Avoiding her forever was impossible. And after her outburst at Maddox last night, I figured the best thing would be to appease her.

She hopped onto the windowsill with the nimbleness of a woman half her age and settled comfortably beside me.

"Help yourself," she said, gesturing to the pie.

I cut into the slice with a fork, though I had no intention of eating it in front of her. It felt a little too familiar.

Lady Vanessa leaned forward, clasping her hands before her knees. A few blond curls fell from her chignon. Even with disheveled hair she looked beautiful.

"If you don't mind me asking, how are you feeling, Narcissa?"

I blinked, shifting in my seat. "Perfectly fine, thank you."

She didn't look convinced. "I see."

A beat passed. I continued to push the pie around the plate, smashing the crust into crumbs.

"I was in an arranged marriage once," Lady Vanessa said. "I was seventeen—younger than you. My father said it was my duty to marry into a good family. Preferably one with... influence, as he liked to call it."

I glanced at her, wondering why she was telling me this.

"I was stubborn at first. Having the freedom of choice taken away from me was suffocating, especially at my age." She sighed and straightened her shoulders. "But even then I knew I had to do it. My family was depending on me. We were on the brink of financial ruin, but my father had a title that was respected enough to make the match. Can you guess what happened next?"

I shook my head.

She smiled and looked around the stone walls. "This happened. I'm the lady of Greenwood Abbey with a wonderful husband and son, and a stepdaughter, of course."

"You and Father...that was arranged?"

Lady Vanessa nodded. "I suppose you expected some great romantic adventure where I ran away and found true love, no?"

I gave a mirthless smile. I was the last person to expect anything of the sort. When I was thirteen, Mother had promised me to General Turner's son, Dominic. The experience was unremarkable at best and unpleasant at worst. It was some time before she broke it off, setting her sights on the crown prince instead when my face began to show promising signs of beauty. It was funny how things turned out in her favor.

"Going through with the marriage was my duty," Lady Vanessa said. "Luckily, I ended up with a gentle husband and a sweet son. When they're not at each other's throats, that is."

I managed a smile.

"That is my story. But yours..." She turned and placed her hand in the space between us. "You don't have any obligation to go through with the marriage if you don't want to."

"I don't?"

"No," Lady Vanessa said. "There are thousands of witch girls in Olderea who could make the perfect crown princess. You're the best choice, but you're not the only choice. You have the option to refuse if it makes you unhappy."

"What does that have to do with anything?"

Lady Vanessa stared, blue eyes wide. "My dear, it has to do with everything. Don't you know that your father would go to the ends of the earth for your happiness? He worries that you're angry with him for even suggesting you as a possible bride. On the other hand, he heard that you and the crown prince were...close."

I laughed, which seemed to startle her. "Merely rumors started by my mother," I said.

"In that case, you have every right to back out of the arrangement."

Did I really have the option to reject this proposal? Did I *want* to?

"I'll get out of your hair now," Lady Vanessa said after my prolonged silence. She brushed imaginary dust from her skirts as she stood, flustered, a stark contrast to her earlier serenity. She headed to the door instead of back out the window like I expected. "Good night, Narcissa."

"Good night."

The door clicked shut. I took a bite of the pumpkin pie, savoring the buttery crust and thick filling.

You have that look on your face, Misty said from the corner of the room. Her eyes popped out from the darkness, missing nothing.

"What look?"

You're realizing something.

She was right.

I recalled how Lady Vanessa's face shone when she spoke of duty. Her shoulders had straightened with pride. Father's duty was to serve the royals and lead the Royal Guard. Maddox...he had none. Perhaps that was why Father was so angry with him.

As for me?

I stared out the window. Night had fallen. I could see nothing but my reflection, which stared back with a surprising hunger.

I used to have a purpose. A certainty. A goal. They were never my choice, but the moment they were taken away from me I had been miserable. Now, a new opportunity presented itself in the form of this marriage. It was a road that led to a life with purpose again.

I could help this kingdom more than Mother had harmed it by being the very thing she wanted me to be—crown princess.

8

Monday morning, our carriage rattled down the road. Greenwood Abbey shrank behind us. The horses' hooves clomped outside. I caught snippets of their grumpy thoughts. They were hungry and didn't appreciate being put to use so soon after their breakfast.

"Cissa...you're not angry with me, are you?"

I turned my attention to Father across from me, his brows knit. It was the first time we had spoken alone since the night of the ball.

"Not at all," I said.

He exhaled and ran a hand over his beard. "I didn't expect for this to happen, truly. But His Majesty proposed the idea of marriage, and your name slipped out. You were the perfect choice."

"I know."

"If you don't want to go through with it, you don't have

to," Father said earnestly. "Perhaps Crown Prince Bennett convinced His Majesty to withdraw after all."

I raised a brow. "The crown prince was not pleased with the idea, then?"

Father shook his head. "He wanted to reevaluate the existing witch laws, but King Maximus claimed that was too time-consuming. Marriage is the quickest and most effective way of bringing peace."

"Do you think that's true?"

Father shrugged. "It's an old-fashioned solution, to be sure, but I suppose it's effective enough. Tension with Aquatia was why His Majesty married Queen Cordelia. As you can see, their two kingdoms have yet to destroy each other," he said with a rueful smile.

It was odd how a loveless union between two individuals could prevent wars. Politics rarely made sense. It was a wonder so many people went along with it.

"But even if you can't back away, Cissa, I don't think you'll be too miserable," Father said, patting my hand. "Think of it: Olderea's first witch princess! That is something to be proud of. Plus, the crown prince is a good man. Accomplished and dutiful." He waggled his brows. "And handsome too, don't you think?"

I couldn't help but smile. It didn't matter if the crown prince had warts all over his face and was three heads shorter—nothing would change.

The palace pulled into view, and soon enough we were escorted into the king's study. The room looked much larger in the daylight. Nonetheless, the dark, woodsy furniture and animal skin rugs felt stifling.

"Captain, Narcissa," King Maximus said as we entered. Crown Prince Bennett gave a stiff bow beside him.

We returned the greeting and took our seats before the king's desk.

King Maximus clapped his hands together. "No use dragging this on, now is there? I just heard over breakfast that Vandil's textile trade has gone up in flames. Foreign merchants want witch-woven fabrics instead of the usual from local weavers. There is only one witch-owned fabric shop in Vandil. Can you believe it? One!"

The fabric of Elowyn's gown was no doubt witch-made. I had never seen anything like it. It was no wonder the merchants wanted their share.

The king pressed his fingers to his temples. "Why did I let that Amarante girl convince me to allow these blazing witches back into the kingdom?"

Father coughed. "With all due respect, sire..."

"What my father means is that ending the Non-Magic Age has created far more changes than we expected," Crown Prince Bennett said. "Handling them has been difficult, and our laws—"

"Yes. You've complained endlessly about the laws, Bennett," King Maximus said irritably. "I told you they will take too long to reform. The more immediate solution is your marriage. You were set to marry last Season but it is better you waited. Perhaps this will be more effective than any witch committee you and Ash can pull together." His tone surprised me, but I schooled my features when he met my eye. "Lady Narcissa. I reckon the three days were enough to make your decision?"

I wrung my skirts beneath the table. "Yes, Your Majesty. I have decided to accept."

The king breathed a sigh. "Good. Very good. I am afraid the future of the kingdom depends on this union."

I bowed my head. "I am honored to serve Olderea."

"As am I," Crown Prince Bennett said shortly. "May I suggest something, Father?"

The king stiffened again. "What is it?"

"Perhaps we should have an engagement tour."

"A tour?" I said, unable to mask my surprise. The crown prince hardly seemed pleased with the arrangement. Why would he want to parade our marriage around the kingdom?

Crown Prince Bennett turned to me. "I hope you won't be opposed to it, Lady Narcissa. A crown princess has many duties."

I pressed my lips together. Was he belittling me? "Not at all, Your Highness."

King Maximus raised his brows. "That is the most reasonable thing you suggested all week, Bennett," he said, tapping his armrest. "It is a good idea. The people ought to see for themselves what a proper non-magic and magic union looks like."

Father looked similarly astonished. "And when will this take place?"

"As soon as possible, preferably. We will target the regions with the most unrest: Coriva, Vandil, and Alevine," Crown Prince Bennett said, pointing at the map splayed out on the king's desk. It seemed like he had prepared for this beforehand. "We will need a procession of guards."

Father sat straighter. "I will put together a group of my most trusted men."

King Maximus nodded. "Of course. But you must stay here with me, Captain. There are many things to be done here."

Father dipped his head, albeit reluctantly. "Yes, Your Majesty. May I suggest that Lord Frederick lead the men?"

"A capital idea. Frederick can house the procession in Coriva as well. I will have to write to my sister for lodging in Vandil…" The king's reply faded in the background as my mind raced.

A kingdom tour? I expected a grand wedding. But touring the kingdom and appearing before the people was entirely different. A tendril of panic raced up my throat. Seeing so many people after half a year of isolation…

You're doing this to defy Mother, to fix everything she destroyed, I reminded myself.

The king stood, straightening his ermine coat. "Bennett, I believe you have a few words to say to your fiancée. I will leave you to it. Captain, join me for a walk in the gardens?"

"Of course, Your Majesty. In fact, there is something else I wish to speak to you about." Father followed the king to the door. He threw me a concerned glance, but I shook my head ever so slightly, assuring him I'd be fine. Hopefully.

The door clicked shut, leaving me alone with the crown prince.

Though neither hulking nor grizzled, Crown Prince Bennett was an imposing figure—tall and elegant, and broad enough around the shoulders to fill out his mulberry coat. His cravat was crisp and white, setting off his tanned skin to perfection. Father was right that he was handsome. Though I wished he wasn't, so it would be easier to face him.

The crown prince pulled a velvet box from his waistcoat, flipped it open, and slid it across the table. Inside was a blood red ruby set in an embellished gold band.

"For you, Lady Narcissa."

I dipped my head, though I did not reach for it. "Thank you, Your Highness."

"The tour…" He glanced down at the spot between us, running a hand over his knuckles. "You seem reluctant."

"I assure you I am not." I cringed. The words sounded

more defensive than I meant them to. "It came as a surprise, that is all."

He flicked his gaze to me, dark eyes guarded and calculating. Of course. What did I expect? Soft words and sweet nothings?

"Understandable."

There was nothing understanding about his manner. In fact, everything about him said otherwise. Unlike the king who had mentioned nothing about my switch of allegiance, Crown Prince Bennett was suspicious.

So be it. I exhaled.

"You do not trust me, Your Highness," I said.

If he was surprised he didn't show it. "I don't," he agreed. "I advised my father to find someone else, but it seems you are the most suitable candidate at this moment. The kingdom cannot wait. It would be unwise to put more citizens at risk because of my baseless suspicions."

"I could hardly call them baseless," I said, folding my hands on my lap. I had my fair share of backhanded conversations. My feathers were not so easily ruffled. "I hope you will trust I have no ulterior motives other than to help Olderea. My mother is under the watch of your men. If you suspect us of cavorting you can ask them."

Crown Prince Bennett stared

unblinkingly, his shoulders tense. He reminded me of Misty before she targets her prey. The resemblance was uncanny.

I tore my eyes away and looked past his shoulder instead. "I apologize for my past actions, but I believe I've since made my allegiance clear. That is all."

I felt my cheeks heat despite my best efforts to appear unaffected. He was there at the masquerade where I attacked my own mother quite publicly. That was the moment I denounced her forever.

But why was my heart pounding like I had just lied?

Perhaps it was the mutual knowledge that I had flirted with him before per Mother's orders, and that the coy facade was the only side he had seen of me until now. No doubt my sudden switch of personality was not helping my case.

He was as unflinchingly stoic as he had always been.

"My duty is to my kingdom, Lady Narcissa," Crown Prince Bennett said at last. He stood and rounded the table. "Whether yours is remains to be seen."

He bowed low at the waist, then straightened. "Excuse me. I will return with Father and the captain shortly."

The door swung shut. I glared at the spot he had stood seconds before.

Insufferable! He was as bad as Maddox, though with cleverly twisted words and a mask of politeness. The ring glittered in its velvet bed, as if mocking me. I snapped the box shut and stuffed it into my pocket.

I acknowledged his suspicions and apologized. Wasn't that enough? What more did he want?

The box weighed heavily against my thigh. I closed my eyes, forcing myself to calm. Somehow the change in me I thought was so obvious was not so to everyone else. There was much I still had to do.

I just had to figure out what.

"I REFUSE TO go!" Maddox bellowed.

"You have no choice. I've settled it with His Majesty and Lord Frederick. You will join the guards accompanying Narcissa and Crown Prince Bennett on their engagement tour," Father said, the picture of serenity as he poured himself a glass of whiskey.

It was evening. Father had summoned us to his study after supper to share what he spoke to the king about. It seemed that Maddox now had a position in the Royal Guard.

"This isn't fair!" Maddox said, arms trembling as he gripped the sofa.

"It isn't," Father agreed. He took a sip of the amber liquid. "Others have to spend years upon years training to get a place in the Royal Guard. You're lucky enough to have the king himself grant you your position."

"I am not spending the next four months of my life trudging around in the cold and following *her* like some slave!"

"Any guard would be grateful to serve the future crown princess."

"Crown princess? Crown princess my a—"

"Maddox. You are a fine swordsman. With work, you will have the patience of a guard," Father said. "You have greatness in you, son. I'm merely pushing you to unlock it."

Maddox's jaw opened and closed. Apparently, praise was difficult to argue with. He swung to me instead. "You have ruined my life!"

With that, he stormed out of the room, no doubt off to throw a tantrum in the stables.

"You're not going after him?" I said.

Father took another swig of whiskey. "No. Defying me is one thing. Defying the king is treason."

I laughed. "Clever."

He looked at me and smiled. "I haven't heard you laugh in months. Is your new fiancé to your liking? What did he say to you?"

The mention of the crown prince wiped away all amusement. I smoothed a cushion to avoid Father's gaze. "He is perfectly respectable."

Luckily, the whiskey made him less observant than usual. "Good. There's little joy in matrimony if you do not like your partner."

I shifted. "So...Maddox will be my personal guard?"

"One of several," Father said. "I'm sorry I will not be there to accompany you, Cissa. My primary duty is to the king."

"I know, Father," I said.

"Nevertheless, I trust Frederick. He is an impeccable captain and his men are competent. I hope your brother can learn discipline under him. That boy is too lazy and careless for his own good."

He seemed to be talking more to himself than to me. I took the opportunity to slip away, knowing that his whiskey was companion enough.

Misty meowed loudly when I returned to my room.

Please don't tell me you're leaving me in this dingy place while you go frolicking with your new beloved, she said, pacing at my feet.

I blinked. It was rare to see her so worked up, much less over something that wasn't food. "Since when have I ever gone anywhere without you?"

Since recently. You didn't bring me to the ball. Or to the palace this morning.

"I didn't know you were upset about that. You hate traveling."

She sat down on the carpet. *I know why. You're trying to sway public opinion. Having a black cat follow you around doesn't exactly paint the picture of innocence, does it? Perhaps you'd prefer a white cat? A ginger tabby?*

I squatted to her level and rubbed the downy spot behind her ears. "Silly girl. We've been locked up in this room for far too long, haven't we?"

Misty mewed, batting my hand away half-heartedly. We both knew she liked it when I petted her there. *Are you bringing me or not?*

"Of course I am. Together forever, remember?"

She purred in satisfaction at our oath.

I couldn't help but smile. "Besides, who else am I going to talk to if you don't come?"

Misty surrendered to my petting. *I thought your fiancé. Not much of a conversationalist, is he?*

My smile faded. "He doesn't trust me."

Well, that makes things difficult.

I set my shoulders. Having complications to solve was better than moping around the abbey. It gave me something to work toward.

"Well, Misty," I said, lifting her into the air. "It looks like we have a long road ahead of us."

9

Crown Prince Bennett never liked me.

I knew this the spring I turned eight. Mother had taken me to the palace on one of her weekly visitations to the king. She claimed he was under the weather and none of the servants–or even Queen Cordelia herself–were competent enough to care for him. So, the duty naturally fell to her.

"Narcissa," Mother said as we rattled through the grand gates, "remember to invite the crown prince to your birthday celebration. The two of you must become good friends."

"But why, Mama?"

She was Mama to me then, before I learned that Mother was a more preferable title to her.

I tugged at the scarlet ribbon in my hair so my waves fell free. Father always said I looked prettiest that way. The cream envelope on my lap slipped to the floor, denting a gold-embossed corner.

Mama sucked her teeth, a harsh sound she made when she was displeased. "Because it must be so." She picked up my birthday invitation and put it back into my hands. "You don't want to be known as the friendless girl who pretends animals understand her, do you?"

She pulled my hair and tied it sharply back with the ribbon. I knew better than to argue with Mama, but animals *did* understand me. And I wasn't without friends. In fact, I made a new one last week—the kitten I found in the palace dumping grounds. She was a darling thing. I had fashioned a cot out of old shifts for her under my bed.

That morning I decided to name her Misty, after the springtide mist that hung over our gardens during sunrise. I promised her we would be together forever, and even though she couldn't talk yet, I knew she promised the same.

Mama had yet to know about Misty. I'd have to make sure she was well-trained before making the introduction.

Mama finished tying the bow. My hair felt too tight, but I didn't touch it lest it angered her. "Smile, Narcissa," she said as the coach stopped rolling.

I pulled on my winning smile. "Like this, Mama?"

She softened a little and kissed my cheek. "That's it, my darling."

My heart sang at these pieces of affection. They certainly never came about when she was upset.

Which is why, I told myself sternly, *you must always do as Mama says.*

Outside, the grand palace spires glistened in the sunlight. The two of us entered the south wing, servants bowing as we passed. That seemed to please Mama. As she clicked down the hall toward King Maximus's chambers, she stood a little straighter. I did too. It felt good when Mama felt good.

When we stopped before the oak doors, she knelt before me, tutting. "You look a mess, Narcissa." She straightened my sleeves and rubbed something off my cheek.

I touched the spot. It was the imprint of her rouge when she had kissed me earlier. I wished she hadn't smudged it away. Mama's kisses were hard to come by.

"Now, you know what to do," she said, pointing at the smaller entrance to the left. Crown Prince Bennett's study. "Give His Highness his invitation and stay there until I come get you."

"Yes, Mama." I smiled brighter, but my slippers scuffed against the marble floor. I was glad my skirts concealed the movement.

Mama wouldn't be pleased to know I didn't want to talk to the crown prince. He was two years my senior—much too old to become friends with. And he was always so serious.

"Good girl. Be off now."

Swallowing my displeasure, I waved goodbye to Mama and followed a footman who escorted me inside. The grand double doors closed behind us.

"His Highness is at his desk, milady," the footman said, gesturing to the far end of the study.

I took in the tall mahogany furniture and books with muted covers. It looked like a place for adults who had nothing better to do than pour over yellowed pages of text all day. The damask rug was lit with panes of sunlight from the window, against which a desk was placed. Sure enough, Crown Prince Bennett was bent over a dusty old book. He turned when we drew close.

The footman bowed. "Your Highness, Lady Narcissa." He departed shortly, though I knew he was behind the shelves as a chaperone. I didn't know what part of the meeting needed chaperoning. All the crown prince did was sit around and read, whether there were visitors or not.

I dipped into my best curtsy, making sure to rise gracefully as Mama instructed. "Good morning, Your Highness."

Crown Prince Bennett blinked, his face impassive as he looked at me. I wondered if my hairdo looked as tight as it felt. "Girls aren't allowed here," he said. His dark hair was neatly combed back, not an unruly strand in sight. The style made him look impossibly grown-up, especially paired with his neat ensemble.

It irritated me to no end. "Says who?" The words came out before I could stop them. Mama would have sucked her teeth at my behavior.

"Father," the crown prince said, turning back to his book. His feet dangled from his chair, the only indication that he *wasn't* a grownup.

But horsefeathers, he was as boring as one. I ran my fingers over the gold embossing on my birthday invitation, watching it reflect light onto the floor. Misty loved shiny things. I'd have to bring her toys or make some myself. Some pigeons feathers on a string, perhaps? I tugged my hair ribbon loose and held it up. It was the perfect length.

Throat clearing drew me out of my thoughts. Crown Prince Bennett was staring at me again, his cheeks pink, no doubt annoyed that I hadn't left.

I retied my ribbon and sighed. Too bad. I was stuck here for another hour, unless I managed to sneak off to the dumping grounds like last time. Maybe I could find another kitten.

But not before carrying out Mama's assignment. I walked over to his desk and stuck out the invitation. "Will you come to my birthday celebration this week?"

He didn't take it, only looked. I grew self-conscious, wondering if the invitation wasn't fancy enough for him or if my fingernails were still caked with dirt from the garden.

No. They were spotless. Mama had scrubbed them raw the other night.

"Birthday celebrations are frivolous," the crown prince finally said, turning away.

I stamped my foot. "They are not." I hadn't a clue what 'frivolous' meant, but I refused to give him the satisfaction of knowing that. "I'll have a chocolate fountain at mine. And ponies for riding."

Mama said I could have whatever I liked, as long as the crown prince came.

"I'm busy," he said. A few dark locks fell over his forehead as he studied the book. He had ruffled his hair when I wasn't looking. The messiness made him more approachable.

"You can't be busy all week," I said. "It's on the weekend. You're supposed to have fun on weekends."

"Fun is frivolous."

Again with that word.

"Please?" I dropped the invitation over his book, leaning my cheek against the hard desk to catch a glimpse of his face. "I'll show you my new kitten."

I hadn't shown Misty to anyone yet. I didn't plan to for at least a month, but I figured I'd make an exception for the crown prince.

Crown Prince Bennett frowned, leaning away. "No. I don't care."

Irritation spiked again, along with a twinge of hurt. I didn't offer to introduce my animal companions to just anybody. I stood upright. "You're not very nice for a prince."

"Princes aren't supposed to be nice. They're supposed to be wise," he said with an air of superiority.

It wasn't wise to be in the company of friendless girls who talked to animals. That was what he meant. My cheeks grew hot as Crown Prince Bennett swept my invitation off his book like a crushed insect.

"Go. You're distracting me."

I bit my lip hard, willing the tears away. This wasn't the first time he had evaded my company, but he had never explicitly told me to leave. He wouldn't even look at me, or the invitation I spent hours picking out.

"Fine," I said, grabbing the card. The crown prince had just sentenced me to a miserable birthday thanks to his stubbornness. I could kiss the chocolate fountain goodbye. And the ponies.

But Mama would understand, wouldn't she? The crown prince's will was out of my control. I tried my best.

The footman emerged from behind the shelves. "I'll escort you to the parlor, milady," he said.

I fumed silently, glaring at Crown Prince Bennett's straight back. He even sat like a boring person. I heard Mama's tongue clicking in the back of my mind.

Take your leave properly, Narcissa, she would've said.

I dipped into another perfect curtsy though he couldn't see it. "Goodbye, Your Highness."

The footman walked me back to the door. When I turned, I was surprised to see that the crown prince had followed. Maybe he changed his mind after all.

Before I could extend the invitation again, he reached for the knob and shut the door in my face.

Tears threatened to burst from my eyes. I huffed instead, lifting my chin so they wouldn't fall. Mama always said I looked disgusting when I cried.

I couldn't tell her what had passed on the carriage ride to our manor. Mama's visit to King Maximus had put her in a glowing mood. She was all smiles and cheerful comments. I basked in them as long as I could. But the dreaded question came when we arrived home.

"Did you give the crown prince his invitation?" Mama asked, peeling off her gloves.

His invitation was buried in a bed of pansies in the royal gardens. But I left that part out as I ducked my head and relayed what had happened.

When I looked up, Mama's face was creased into a harsh frown. No trace of her previous levity was in sight.

"You had one simple job, and even that you couldn't do correctly. You've ruined your chance, Narcissa!" My name was harsh on her tongue.

Nar-cis-sa. Each syllable had the lash of a whip.

My eyes welled with tears at these invisible injuries. “Mama I didn’t mean to!” My voice took on the whine I knew she hated.

She scoffed, rapped me three times on my wrists, and sent me to my room.

That night I sobbed with Misty in my arms, missing Father and his warm hugs. But my kitten’s soft fur and gentle nuzzles comforted me immensely. Even if nobody liked me, at least Misty did.

And that was all that mattered.

10

Greenwood Abbey had never felt more alive than it did in the next three weeks. Servants and palace staff bustled through the stone halls with luggage and letters, a stark contrast to the usual stillness and gloom. A sketch artist came to take my likeness for the city papers. I spotted a rendering of Crown Prince Bennett's regal profile in his portfolio.

The next morning, the portraits were featured at the front of the morning papers on an article detailing my royal engagement with the crown prince. I couldn't bring myself to read past the sensational headlines, so I busied myself with packing my gowns instead—which turned out to be unnecessary.

The king had hired many witches into the palace since the end of the Non-Magic Age, one of them a charmwitch who went by the name of Giselle Phula. The fashion publications lauded her as the luckiest royal seamstress yet, as she was to work on "the finest figures of Olderea". I was told she would be making most of my clothing during the tour. A small trunk arrived from her the week before, filled with new gowns of the most fashionable styles. Tizzy fawned over them for the entire evening, but I was too preoccupied to do the same.

The royal steward, Ulysses, had informed me of the first stop of the tour: the city of Coriva which lay beyond a few hills outside of Delibera. It was there we were to reside for the next month in Lord Frederick's Huntington Abbey. Our route crossed one of the busiest parts of the city—the Witch Market. There was a witch market in every region of Olderea now, Ulysses had said, but the biggest by far was on Deliberan soil.

I hardly knew how the witches would react. Rumors of last summer's ordeal had spread far and wide. Whether they were in my favor or not was a mystery. And the public's opinion, I was sure, would sway the crown prince's.

THE DAY OF the tour arrived. That morning, our procession filled the palace courtyard, most dressed in Royal Guard purple. Three carriages awaited—one large and ornate, the other comparatively modest, and the last for cargo. There were horses in front for Lord Frederick, the crown prince, and our personal guards.

Father and Lady Vanessa came to see me and Maddox off.

"Best of luck to you, Cissa," Father said, taking my gloved hands as Maddox and Lady Vanessa said their goodbyes.

"Thank you, Father."

"I always knew you were meant for greater things, though I wish you didn't have to leave. It felt like just yesterday you were returned to me," he said with a sad smile, eyes crinkling.

My chest ached. This time I couldn't attribute it to nerves.

I threw my arms around his neck like I used to as a little girl.

"I'll miss you," I whispered. It was unlike me to say such things out loud, but there was plenty of time to recover from any embarrassment I felt afterward.

Father tightened his hug, sharing none of my awkward hesitation. "I'll miss you too, Cissa." He pulled back, eyes glassy, and bent down to pick up the feline beside him. "Don't forget Misty."

I took her. Misty looked disgruntled, too used to sleeping in to appreciate being awake at this moment.

"Maddox, my boy," Father said in a louder voice, "you look dashing in uniform."

My half-brother merely grunted, more subdued than usual. Perhaps he accepted his fate. But the more likely reason was that he didn't want to act impertinently in front of his new colleagues.

Lady Vanessa went to stand next to Father. "Take care, Narcissa," she said earnestly.

"You as well," I said.

She looked as if she wanted to say something more, but thought better of it.

Ulysses the steward glided up at that moment. "Milady," he said as he adjusted his wire-framed spectacles, "His Highness has arrived. It is time to leave."

Maddox and I nodded, and with one last goodbye to Father and Lady Vanessa, we headed across the tiled courtyard toward the group. Crown Prince Bennett was instantly recognizable, dressed in a double-breasted lavender coat with crisp lapels. His crown glinted in the watery sunlight as he stood next to an impressive white mount, conversing with a woman with a dark braid.

My skirt jerked back abruptly. I stumbled as Maddox let out a string of curses. Misty hissed in displeasure as I turned to him.

"You're supposed to protect me from danger, not endanger me yourself," I said coolly, surveying the damage he had done to my hem. The sage green was now stamped with a muddy footprint. Misty jumped to the ground.

"Don't start with me you…you spoiled society *brat*!" he said fiercely.

I pursed my lips. "How strange. *You're* always the one to start with *me*."

Maddox flushed. "Listen! I'm stuck here because of you and the last thing I need is your—"

He choked when the crown prince approached.

"Your Highness." I dipped into a low curtsy, but Crown Prince Bennett held out a hand.

"No need for formalities, Lady Narcissa," he said.

"In that case, you should call me Cissa," I said, giving him my best smile—the one that accentuated the dimple on my left cheek. I knew he wasn't easily charmed, but it didn't hurt to try.

The crown prince merely blinked twice.

I bit back a sigh. It was frustrating, not knowing what he thought of me. Mother always made her approval and displeasure known. Father practically wore his heart on his sleeve. The crown prince, on the other hand, was a book I couldn't read.

Misty took the liberty of rubbing herself against his leg and purring loudly. I raised my eyebrows at her.

What? she said. *I thought we were trying to win his favor.*

Crown Prince Bennett moved aside. "You brought your cat," he stated. I couldn't tell if he was displeased.

"Her name is Misty," I said. "She's usually...not that friendly."

Misty meowed indignantly.

The crown prince wet his lips. "The carriage is ready. It's time to go." He looked a little past me. "You may rise."

I turned to see Maddox straighten from a deep bow.

"Thank you, Highness!" he said loudly.

Crown Prince Bennett nodded and headed back to his spot at the front. Maddox's face was already aflame, no doubt anticipating a snarky comment from me.

"In that case you should call me *Cissa*," he said in a high-pitched voice before I could get a word out. "If you won't let me keep my freedom, at least let me keep my breakfast."

I scoffed. "You are a child."

"Better than a two-faced fraud," he shot back. "His Highness will see through your façade in no time."

Maddox turned on his heel and marched to the other guards.

"Well. Smiling didn't work," I muttered to Misty as I approached the large carriage in the front. The coachman helped me inside. The interior was smaller than anticipated, having room for only four passengers. Nevertheless, the plump velvet seats looked more than welcoming. I relaxed into them as the coachman closed the door.

And he doesn't seem to have a liking for felines, Misty meowed. *Ridiculous.*

Shortly after, a soft knock came at the window. I moved the curtain aside to meet Lord Frederick's smiling face.

"Good morning, milady," he said. "Are you comfortably settled?"

"Quite. Thank you, Lord Frederick," I said.

"It will be a long ride to the outskirts of Delibera. Two hours or so, with the size of our company, and two more to reach my residence. You won't need to make an appearance until we reach the witch market. We have a mare prepared for you when it's time."

I nodded and thanked him again. "Will His Highness join me in the carriage?" I asked, peering past his shoulder.

"Er, His Highness informed me that he will be on horseback for the majority of the tour," Lord Frederick said. He looked askance before giving me a tight-lipped smile.

So! He refused to even share a carriage with me. No one in their right mind would want to be on horseback for four hours, much less for an entire four-month tour in the midst of winter.

Looks like our high and mighty crown prince would rather suffer a sore backside than endure our company, Misty said, licking her paw.

I kept my face neutral. "I see."

Lord Frederick cleared his throat. "Well, if you need anything, don't hesitate to come to me. I'd be happy to assist if you need to pass any messages to His Highness."

"Thank you, Lord Frederick," I said, "but that won't be necessary." If I wanted to win the crown prince's favor, I'd have to do it myself.

He nodded and glanced over his shoulder. "Looks about time to go. Enjoy the ride, milady."

I let the curtains drop.

Misty jumped to the opposite seat and stretched herself out on the cushion. *Looks like you have your work cut out for you.*

"I know. This is going to be—"

The carriage door burst open, letting in a flood of cold air. A young woman with a leather satchel stood outside, eyes flicking around the interior of the carriage until they settled on me. I recognized her as the dark-haired woman speaking to the crown prince earlier.

"Are you Lady Narcissa?" Her eyes glinted gold, as did the freckle on her left cheekbone.

Did all the witches in the palace have no manners?

"I am. And you are?" I said, pulling the collar of my spencer tighter around my neck.

"Giselle. Charmwitch, dressmaker extraordinaire, peacekeeper, and your carriage companion for the next hour."

She threw her braid over her shoulder and swung inside, shooing Misty back onto my side of the seats. Misty hissed, baring her fangs, but the charmwitch didn't seem to mind.

"I see you're wearing one of my ensembles," she said, looking me up and down. "Gorgeous, isn't it?"

I shifted. I had never witnessed someone admire their own work so shamelessly.

She raised her brows at the brown footprint on my hem and tutted. "And it's ruined already. Good thing I sew quickly." Giselle flipped open her satchel and dug into it so deeply that her shoulder disappeared inside. "A bottomless bag enchantment," she said when she caught me staring. "Quite simple. I can show you sometime."

"That is...fine," I said.

"Aha! Here we are." Giselle fished out a hefty wad of fern green fabric I couldn't make sense of. "Where's my thimble?"

She rummaged through her satchel again, this time sticking her head in as well.

Heavens, what an annoying woman, Misty said in displeasure.

I couldn't help but agree. I expected to spend the ride contemplating my next steps and perhaps take a nap. Now I was stuck with the seamstress of all people, who clearly wasn't the quiet type.

Giselle reemerged with her sewing supplies just as the carriage jerked into motion. The palace courtyard disappeared behind us, as well as all hope of getting rid of her.

"So," she mumbled as she slipped an end of thread into her mouth, "how was your morning?"

I frowned. The woman had barged inside, barely introduced herself, and now was inquiring about my morning like we were old friends.

I folded my gloved hands on my knee. "Excuse me, but I hardly know who you are."

Giselle threaded her needle, which was rather impressive as the carriage rattled over cobblestone. "Ah. You're the prim and proper sort," she said. "Well, milady, I am the newly appointed royal seamstress, here to dress you and the crown prince during the tour."

I glanced at the left side of her bodice, where an acorn pin glimmered against the teal fabric. "What else do you do?" I said.

Giselle looked down at the pin and smiled. "Observant, aren't you?"

"You're on the witch committee," I said. I tried to recall if I saw her in the ballroom the other night.

She shrugged a shoulder. "Yes. In addition to my many talents, I also have a knack for keeping everyone calm when things…escalate."

I raised a brow. So that was what she meant when she called herself a peacekeeper. "Using magic on angry masses who already hate magic? That can't be wise."

Giselle thinned her lips, ducking her head over her work. "It's only for emergencies, milady," she said. She flashed a smile, though it seemed false. "Thankfully I do have a naturally calming presence."

I exchanged a look with Misty. Would things *escalate*, as Giselle called it?

Of course, Misty meowed. *People are rioting over fabric. Think of what they'll do when they find out their future queen is a witch.*

Giselle looked at me suddenly. Her pale gold irises were unnerving. "Say, you and the crown prince aren't exactly the lovebirds you need to be, are you?"

"Pardon?" I said, affronted.

She shrugged and began stitching. "He made it public enough that he didn't want to be in this carriage."

I bristled.

"No need to get your knickers in a twist...not that you're wearing any, I presume." Giselle shifted closer so that our knees bumped. "Listen, I want to help."

"What are you saying?"

She darted her eyes around the carriage before pulling something out of her bodice. Two decorative charms made of knotted twine and colorful ceramic beads dangled from her hand.

"Love charms," Giselle whispered from the side of her mouth. "Keep one on you and the other on the crown prince. Anywhere will do, as long as it's on his person."

I am positive that is treason, Misty drawled.

"No," I said.

Giselle raised her eyebrows. "You're not even going to consider it? Think of how much more effective this tour will be if you two are actually in love. Besides, how long will it take for that to happen organically? After what you did last summer—"

"No," I repeated.

"Are you sure?"

I turned to the window. "I'm here to atone my wrongdoings, not commit more." My lip curled as I looked back at Giselle. "It seems that Crown Prince Bennett made a mistake bringing you onto the witch committee."

My sneers intimidated the haughtiest of courtiers, but Giselle didn't shrink back. Instead, she shrugged, unconcerned, and shoved the charms back into her bodice. "Alright. I'll hold on to these if you change your mind," she said, returning to her sewing.

"I won't," I said stiffly.

I sincerely hoped the rest of the witch committee weren't as lawless as her.

Giselle sighed loudly. "The crown prince is about as difficult to woo as a brick wall. Just you wait. After the wedding, you'll be spending the rest of your life alone."

I saw it fit to not respond. As insane as she was, Giselle made something very clear: making the crown prince fall in love with me was impossible. I had tried under Mother's orders but to no avail. And from our interaction this morning, it didn't seem like I would have any more luck on my own.

What mattered now was winning his trust.

I recalled what the crown prince said to me in the king's study.

My duty is to my kingdom, Lady Narcissa. Whether yours is remains to be seen.

Of course. I would have to show him that Olderea matters to me as much as it does to him.

And what does that entail? Misty asked from my side.

It means, I thought to her, *that I will be the best crown princess this kingdom has ever seen.*

"Antonio, look at me," Carla cried, taking his face in her hands. "I don't want the duke. I want you. It has been you all along, don't you understand?"

"But you accepted his hand."

Her brown eyes clouded. "His Grace...you do not know him."

"What did he do? Did he hurt you?" Antonio demanded, trapping her in his arms.

Carla gave into the embrace, pressing her cheek against his chest. "H-he forced me into the arrangement." Her voice trembled like a flower in wintry winds. "Oh, my love. Help me run away. I don't want to go through with it. I mustn't go through with it.

—from *A Sailor's Seduction:*
Tales of Romance at Sea by Erasmus Lenard

2

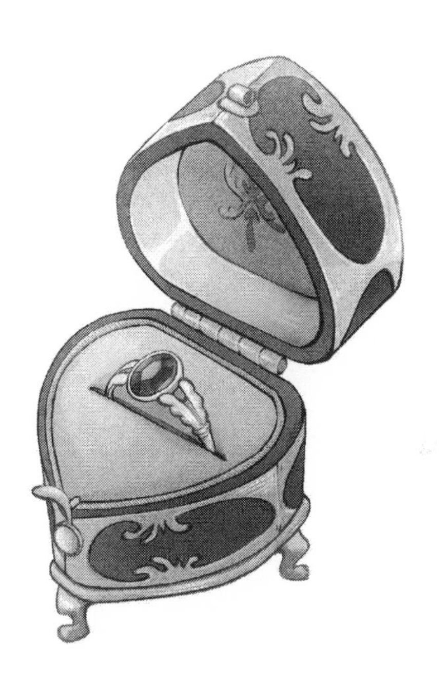

THE HERBWITCH PRINCESS

11

Two hours later, the carriage rolled to a stop. Lord Frederick opened the door.

"We're approaching the marketplace, milady," he said. "It's time to proceed on horseback."

I descended eagerly.

Misty pawed at my sleeve. *Please do not leave me with this woman.*

Giselle had stopped making small talk ages ago, opting instead for studying me with narrowed eyes. She made no attempt at concealing her scrutiny for the entire two hours. I found her shamelessness unnerving.

Giselle yawned and stretched before I could send Misty my condolences. "I'll walk with the others for the rest of the way," she said, hopping lightly to the ground. "I'm in dire need of some exercise." She saluted me and Lord Frederick and skipped off.

If Lord Frederick found her as strange as I did, he didn't

show it. He led me to the front, where Crown Prince Bennett sat atop his white gelding.

He held the reins of a speckled gray mare, which I presumed was mine. Her tail swished meekly and her ears drooped. Certainly not a lively mount.

"Have your travels been comfortable, Lady Narcissa?" the crown prince asked as Lord Frederick helped me onto the saddle.

"Very much," I said, my words stilted. I took the reins from him. He didn't call me Cissa like I requested.

Our procession stood in the center of the short field that divided Delibera's residential parts from the bustling witch market at the edge of the city. The ground was bare and brown, gray frost clinging to the patches of withering grass that remained. A cluster of teal-topped structures sat on the horizon of the bleak scene. It was odd seeing so many buildings in the once empty land.

"Is there anything I must do when we pass?" I asked.

Crown Prince Bennett hardly spared me a glance. "No. I will handle it."

I bit back a scoff. I highly doubted His Royal Stoicness could handle a proper procession. If being a duchess's daughter taught me anything, it was how to flaunt—just enough to impress an audience of commoners without appearing too gaudy. Processions were my specialty.

My mount, on the other hand, needed work.

We continued forward. I leaned over to stroke the speckled mare's mane. Her thoughts were quiet compared to the others, but I managed to pick it out of the rabble.

So hungry...so bored...

I prodded her thoughts with my own to make my presence known, gentle enough not to spook her.

Hello. I continued to stroke her mane. *My name is Narcissa. What's yours?*

Cozbi, she replied. She didn't seem too interested in talking to me, or surprised that I could.

That wasn't a promising start. I leaned back and looked around. Crown Prince Bennett rode to my right, and Lord Frederick to his. The three of us were flanked by two guards. Four rode behind us. Maddox, thankfully, was the furthest away from me. I didn't need any snarky remarks from him.

"Excuse me," I said to the young guard to my left. He looked not much older than me, with a crop of red hair and freckled cheeks.

He turned, as if surprised by my attention. "Did you need something, milady?"

I flashed him my best smile. "Yes. Do you happen to have any fruit on you? My mount is hungry."

The guard blushed a deep scarlet. I felt some relief that I hadn't lost my charm entirely.

"Ah. Y-yes milady." He fumbled in his pocket and pulled out a small pear. The yellow skin was dull and bruised. "Will this do?"

I thanked him sweetly, then leaned into Cozbi again, now holding the fruit in her line of sight. Her ears perked up.

May I have that? she asked with a small snort. She was a rather polite horse. My old mount would have snapped it right out of my hand.

"Do me a favor and it's all yours," I said.

"Pardon?"

I jumped at the sound of the crown prince's smooth voice. He looked down at me, puzzled.

"Apologies, I was...talking to myself."

He nodded and returned his attention ahead. I pinched my arm, hard.

It was all those months talking out loud to Misty. I seriously had to stop.

Is this your first time in a parade, Cozbi? I asked, this time through my thoughts.

First time with fancy folk like you, Cozbi said. *My last owner was a farmer. I pulled his cart...but he didn't have much use for me anymore when he had a witch enchant his wagons to be weightless.*

I pursed my lips. Witches again, this time putting horses out of work.

Alright, I thought to her. *I'm going to need you to show off a little.*

Show...off?

I smoothed the stray hairs in her dark mane. The stable-hands had done a decent job grooming her, though compared to the crown prince's snowy white gelding, Cozbi looked rather mediocre. Still, she had the potential to be stunning if she carried herself in the right way.

You're a lovely horse, I said. *It would be a shame if you let* that *one take the spotlight.*

Cozbi swiveled her head to Crown Prince Bennett's gelding and snorted.

We horses were never meant to be that perfect, she said loftily.

No, I agreed. *Better rustic than extravagant.*

Cozbi nickered. *Very well. Have that pear ready for me.*

I allowed myself a satisfied smile as the entrance to the market grew closer. Soon enough, we passed beneath the archway and into a wide cobblestoned street.

The witch market met us in a shock of jewel tones and spices. I expected outlandish aesthetics, but the buildings were recognizably Olderean and the wares on display appeared to be common objects—scented candles, glinting brass jewelry, and bottles of medicine and makeup. I couldn't pick apart which items had magical properties and which didn't.

I found myself straining for a closer look, but Ulysses blew his horn, the high timbre cutting through the bustling of the streets. "His Highness Crown Prince Bennett and his future princess, Lady Narcissa Greenwood!" he announced.

The vendors and hagglers quieted at once, parting for us to pass. A few children ran up to the sides, jewel-colored eyes wide and curious. The adults stayed back. Their expressions, though not hostile, were unreadable.

Crown Prince Bennett held up his hand, gracing the silent crowd with a stiff, close-lipped smile. Describing the situation as uncomfortable would be an understatement.

I will handle it indeed!

I straightened my shoulders and began to pull my lips into a proper smile until Cozbi reared her front legs.

Ulysses yelped. "Lady Narcissa!"

My backside nearly slipped from the saddle as the mare leaped forward. I grabbed the reins just in time. The children squealed, darting out of the way before they got trampled by her clattering hooves.

"Cozbi!" I exclaimed, clinging on for dear life. "What are you *doing*?"

Showing off! she replied with a loud nicker. She pranced in a circle, throwing back her glossy mane.

I gave an incredulous laugh as a few strands smacked my cheek. The witch children giggled as Cozbi continued her ridiculous dance. I could only imagine how we looked cavorting in the middle of the street like a circus act.

The pear bounced in my pocket. I grabbed it and held it over her head in hopes she would calm.

Cozbi snatched the fruit, her hairy lips encasing my fingers. *Yum! I love the yellow ones.*

"Where'd you get a creature like that, princess?" an elderly witch hollered from the crowd.

"She's so cute," a witch girl cooed.

I smiled sheepishly as I took Cozbi's reins and turned her around. A young boy with a head of inky curls stepped out into the street and pulled out another pear from his satchel.

"May I feed her too, milady?" he asked. A gaggle of children surrounded him, gushing at Cozbi's liveliness and silky mane.

"Of course," I said as graciously as I could. This was good. Princesses interacted with children all the time, didn't they?

Cozbi, delighted by the attention, ate the second offering with enthusiasm.

The boy bowed low and melted back into the crowd with a giggle.

I steered Cozbi forward and returned to my place beside Crown Prince Bennett, who gave me a brief glance before looking away.

Lord Frederick gave a low whistle. "You certainly have a way with animals, milady. I hardly realized what a beauty that mare is."

Cozbi practically preened at the praise.

"She only needed some encouragement," I said, smoothing her mane.

"The committee did say witches wouldn't respond well to our usual pomp and circumstance," Ulysses said with a sigh. "Good thinking, milady."

The prancing was far from my intention, but it seemed to have worked out in my favor. Crown Prince Bennett's expression, however, remained neutral. I colored, hoping he didn't think I was putting on an act for his sake. A part of me knew that was the case, but I couldn't dwell on it. Shame had no part in my duty.

That's enough for today, I thought to Cozbi. *You certainly showed that gelding who the better horse is.*

The mare behaved normally for the rest of the way—which was all I wanted in the first place—and the procession proceeded onward.

When the scenery reverted once again to dreary hills, Lord Frederick asked if I wanted to return to the carriage. I gladly agreed.

"It will be some time until we reach Coriva," he said as he helped me dismount. He threw a glance at the crown prince. "Perhaps you would like to rest in the carriage as well, Your Highness?"

"No need," Crown Prince Bennett said.

Lord Frederick sighed a sigh only I could hear. "As you wish, Your Highness."

THE SUN HAD set when we arrived at Lord Frederick's residence. Huntington Abbey was a silhouette against the dreary gray sky, speckled with elegant spires and golden window panes. We stopped before a spacious courtyard encased by a ring of second-floor balconies. In the middle, a large marble fountain in the shape of a bear reared on two powerful hind legs.

Lord Frederick descended his mount. "Welcome to my humble abode," he said cheerfully, "and yours for the next few weeks. Do make yourself at home, Your Highness, Lady Narcissa."

I held Misty closer as an icy gust of wind blew against my back. Ulysses said that part of the tour was to keep friendly relations with powerful families in Olderea—the Huntingtons included. If that was the case, I doubted I could make myself at home.

Inside, the halls were lively with bustling servants. White marble tiles shone like mirrors beneath my feet, and plenty of windows spanned floor to ceiling, so unlike Greenwood Abbey's somber interiors. I hoped Father would consider remodeling in the future.

The second floor was luxuriously carpeted and equally as grand. Lord Frederick looked over his shoulder as we followed him through a set of double doors. "I'm afraid Lady Huntington and Isabelle have already retired for the evening," he said apologetically. "Introductions will have to be made tomorrow. Meanwhile, here is where you will be staying."

We stood in a cozy, comfortably furnished common area swathed in rich blue velvet.

"Your quarters, Your Highness," Lord Frederick said, pointing to a door on the left. "And yours, milady." He pointed to one on the right.

Crown Prince Bennett twisted the ring on his finger. "Are there no separate suites?"

Lord Frederick shrugged. "I'm afraid not. Unless Your Highness wishes to switch with one of the guards?"

"If you're worried about propriety, Your Highness, we share a common room, not a bedchamber," I said, irritable from the journey and the cold. All I wanted was to pass out unconscious.

What a prude that prince is, Misty meowed.

Crown Prince Bennett frowned. "Very well. Good night, Lord Frederick. Lady Narcissa." With a stiff nod, he strode off to his side.

Lord Frederick shook his head. "I'll leave you to your rest, milady."

12

The night passed far too soon. I slept late as a result of the creaking doors and murmuring that came from the crown prince's chamber, though I was too tired to wonder who he was speaking to.

In the morning, a maid who introduced herself as Serena assisted in washing and dressing me.

"Lord and Lady Huntington and Miss Isabelle are downstairs breaking fast," Serena said, buttoning up my gown. "I'll show you down shortly, milady."

After I finished dressing, Serena led me out to the hall. She looked down at Misty when we reached the set of stairs. "Forgive milday, but M-Miss Isabelle doesn't like animals," she stuttered.

What am I supposed to do then, starve? Misty said grouchily.

"She's very well-behaved," I said.

"Oh…of course, milady. The dining room is right down

these stairs to the left. If you'll excuse me, I have much to attend to. Good day, milady!"

She bobbed a quick curtsy and practically dashed off, brown skirts flying.

I frowned, reminded very much of Tizzy. Was I that frightening to serve that every lady's maid dissolved into a puddle of stutters and "milady"s?

Who cares? Misty meowed, cutting through my thoughts. *Let's get something to eat.*

We barely made it down two steps.

"Lady Narcissa."

I turned. Crown Prince Bennett strode toward me, dressed in a soft blue waistcoat and a dusky purple coat, both tailored impeccably to his form. But it was evident he was ill-rested, the darkness under his eyes betraying him. What *had* he been doing last night?

"Good morning, Your Highness. Are you off to breakfast?" I inquired. I wasn't sure how to act. Civility, therefore, was best.

He nodded. "And you?"

"To breakfast."

He studied the railing, then his shoes, before looking back at me. If I didn't know better, I would think him shy. Odd, after his usual stoic behavior. I shook the thoughts away. Perhaps I was imagining things.

To my surprise, Crown Prince Bennett offered me his arm. "Shall we go together?"

It seemed like he was in a friendlier mood today. I accepted his arm gingerly and we made it to the dining room in silence. His gait was stiffer than usual. No doubt he was suffering from a sore backside from riding yesterday, as Misty had predicted.

Served him right.

"Your Highness, Lady Narcissa," Lord Frederick greeted us from the table. Two women beside him stood and curtsied—one older and the other younger. They introduced themselves as Lady Huntington and Miss Isabelle Huntington, respectively.

"It is an honor to share our home with you, Your Highness," Lady Huntington said as Crown Prince Bennett took his seat at the head of the table. I sat in the empty spot to his right, across from Lord Frederick and next to his daughter.

"Papa always keeps the grounds so lovely," Miss Isabelle said, leaning forward. I caught a whiff of strong lilac perfume. "Perhaps Mama and I can give you a tour, Your Highness." She gave him a deeply dimpled smile.

"His Highness is busy, Isabelle," Lord Frederick said, buttering a piece of toast. "You're going into town today, isn't that right, Your Highness?"

The crown prince nodded.

"There now, Izzy. Perhaps you can show him and Lady Narcissa around another time."

Isabelle pouted. I swore I saw her shoot me a glare from my periphery.

What is there to eat? Misty emerged beneath my chair, looking up expectantly.

I scanned the spread on the table. Fresh bread and butter, tea, several bowls of fruit, and pitchers of cream.

No fish, I thought to her. *How do you feel about cantaloupe?* Misty always liked the fruit. She claimed its texture was similar to raw flesh.

Cantaloupe? In winter?

I blinked. *That is unusual. Do you want some or not?*

I suppose it will do.

I took a piece of fruit and put it on a separate dish for her. Misty jumped up eagerly.

"Eek! What is that *thing*?" Isabelle screeched, jerking up from her chair.

Misty hissed, pupils dilating. I quickly stroked the back of her head to soothe her.

"A cat, Miss Huntington," I said with a grimace. Her scream practically tore through my ear.

Lord Frederick looked simultaneously appalled and embarrassed. "Really, Isabelle!"

"Frederick, I thought I told you Izzy is allergic to animals," Lady Huntington said. "How could you allow one in here?"

"Don't be ridiculous. She has nothing of the sort."

Lady Huntington ignored her husband and turned to me. "Excuse my daughter's manners, Lady Narcissa, but Isabelle has…delicate health. I'm afraid your pet cannot dine with us. Serena!"

The maid rushed in, face flushed. "Yes, Lady Huntington?"

Lady Huntington narrowed her eyes. "I thought I informed you about Isabelle's allergy."

"Y-yes milady."

"Then take Lady Narcissa's cat to the stables at once," the lady said, "unless you wish for your young miss to fall ill."

I stood from my seat. "Misty cannot stay in the stables. She is a house cat."

Lady Huntington looked at me through heavy lashes. She forked a cube of cantaloupe. "Will she not be able to hold her own? Is she not magic?"

"My cat is not a witch, Lady Huntington," I said slowly. "I am."

Her lip curled ever so slightly. "Forgive me. I'm rather ignorant to witch matters," she said. "Nevertheless, your cat cannot dine with us. Serena, take it to Lady Narcissa's chambers."

Serena curtsied, and without looking at me, took Misty from my chair.

I reached for her. "But she's hungry!"

Serena evaded me under Lady Huntington's glare.

"Not to worry. It will be fed oats along with the other animals," the lady said.

I clenched my jaw in frustration, surprised to find moisture in my eyes. She wouldn't have dared speak to me in such a manner half a year ago. But now, without Mother…

I dug my nails into my palm. No. I didn't need Mother's prestige to protect me anymore.

"Surely some exception can be made—" Lord Frederick began.

I shook my head. "Apologies," I said with as much grace as I could muster. I was all too aware of Crown Prince Bennett's silent presence, a reminder that I was expected to behave a certain way. I had disappointed him, no doubt. Misty's meows disappeared into the other room. "I didn't mean to disrupt."

Isabelle returned to her seat with a huff. In the next minute, she was back to jabbering and I had composed myself enough to join the small talk. I ate the cantaloupe I had prepared for Misty. It was sweet and juicy, as if the fruit were really in season.

But even surrounded by chatter and a pleasant breakfast, I felt Misty's absence more than anything. I would have to apologize to her later.

13

We set off to town right after breakfast, much to Isabelle's chagrin. Crown Prince Bennett wanted to observe Coriva disguised as civilians, so we borrowed the servants' carriage. This, I realized, was why he suggested the tour in the first place. It certainly wasn't to spend more time with me, judging from his studious silence during the carriage ride.

The roads were busy, though not overly crowded. Several stray cats darted into an alleyway, avoiding a group of rambunctious children playing ball on the street. Misty would've hated the noise, but I still felt awful leaving her in Serena and Lady Huntington's clutches.

Something must have shown on my face.

"You seem preoccupied, Lady Narcissa," Ulysses said, glancing up at me over his spectacles. "Is everything alright?"

"I'm fine. It's just my cat—" I cut myself off when the crown prince looked up. I knew I would sound ridiculous and spoiled if I continued. Misty was just a pet to him—and squabbling over a pet was not becoming of a future princess. I shook my head. "It's nothing."

Crown Prince Bennett opened his mouth. I braced myself for whatever was coming, but the carriage rolled to a stop before he could speak.

"There's the shop in question, Your Highness," Ulysses said, pushing his spectacles up his hooked nose. He flipped through the pile of reports in his lap. "William's Plants and Produce. It opened two months ago."

"Two months only?" Crown Prince Bennett murmured, dropping his gaze from me. "Curious."

The shop had been upsetting adjacent store owners, Ulysses told me earlier, and many had written complaints to the king. It was a mystery what the shop owner had been doing to cause such a reaction.

We clambered out the carriage. The storefront had glass walls and a yellow ochre door. Even from outside, the place was bursting with greenery.

"Are you familiar with plants, Lady Narcissa?" the crown prince asked.

I grew mildly irritated, though more at him than at his question. I wished he would just berate me for my behavior at breakfast and have it over with. "Not every herbwitch has a partiality to plants, Your Highness," I said. The words came out stiffer than I intended.

"Apologies. I..." He cleared his throat, his gaze fixating on something down the street.

Before I could identify what it was, a floating pot of soil obstructed my view, wobbling precariously in the air. I blinked rapidly at the odd sight.

A few other civilians gaped. Others barely batted an eye.

A witch humming a lilting tune sat a few feet away. The pot drifted into his hands, which were engulfed in yellow, dirt-encrusted gloves. The sunspots on his forehead sparkled gold as he looked up.

"Ah, did I startle you, miss?" His nose scrunched as he smiled. He looked about Father's age, but with a slimmer build and silvery hair.

"Are you William?" I asked, approaching him.

"That I am. And you are?"

"Cissa," I said, using my pet name.

William turned. "And you, good sir?"

The crown prince looked past him, seemingly distracted. "Bennett."

"Like the crown prince?"

He gave a start, as if just realizing he had given himself away.

The witch chuckled. "That is a poor disguise, Highness. Maybe slouch a little next time. Even without your crown, you look like you're wearing one." He gave me another look. "And you must be Lady Narcissa."

Crown Prince Bennett sighed. "We may as well discuss this openly, then. Shall we take this inside?"

William's shop was crowded with plants of all shapes and sizes. Some of them were sprouting fruit, others flowers. Some sat in elegant little pots on shelves of gold filigree, others on the floor, their leaves spilling onto the walnut paneling. A hexagonal dome in the ceiling let in a shaft of natural light. Crates of fruits and vegetables lined the opposite wall. The place was equal parts a plant store and a produce store. Charming, albeit unusual.

We sat behind the counter with William, where two sets of benches were placed. Ulysses looked hesitant.

"Your Highness, is it wise to reveal our identities so openly?" the steward whispered. "News could spread and perhaps the rioters—"

CANTALOUPE

"Not to worry, sir," William said. Ulysses had been whispering rather loudly. "There are no rioters here. But if they come, I've got a nasty little jinx at the door." He chuckled good-naturedly.

Ulysses' face turned green.

"Hopefully it won't come to that," Crown Prince Bennett said. He leaned forward, resting his elbows on his knees. "William, over the past month we've received complaints from local store owners about your shop."

William's brows shot up. "Whatever for? I'm merely serving my customers."

"Are you selling them magic plants, perchance?"

The witch widened his eyes. "Not at all. Some witches don't wish to sell magical wares, you see. Myself included. My plants and produce are perfectly non-magical."

Crown Prince Bennett sat back. "Why would they be displeased unless you have something they don't?"

"By all means, enlighten me, Your Highness. I've spent most of my life among witches. I cannot fathom what I'm doing to anger the others."

The crown prince glanced around the crowd of greenery, though he could not possibly glean anything from the observation. He was no skilled botanist. Neither was I, but I didn't need to be. This morning with Misty was enough.

"Are you selling produce that is out of season?" I asked. "Cantaloupe, perhaps?"

"Indeed!" William said. "Cantaloupe has been popular lately."

I pursed my lips. I had heard that Witch Village was an underground expanse enchanted to look like the outside. Seasons were harsh at times and inconvenient at others. Perhaps the witches didn't bother simulating unfavorable weather and grew what they wanted.

"Are there seasons in Witch Village?" I asked.

"Hardly. None of us wanted to deal with snow or sweltering heat," William said, confirming my theory.

Ulysses seemed to catch on. After clearing his throat, he found his voice and proceeded to remind William of in-season and out-of-season produce.

"Are you saying I cannot sell my cantaloupe?" the witch said, brow furrowing. "I'm afraid that is all the customers want from me lately."

"They want novelty. You offer them things no other shop can because of your magic," Crown Prince Bennett said. "Cantaloupe would be fine in a witch market, but not when you're competing directly with human businesses. That is why they are angry with you."

William leaned back, looking lost. "But if I offer exactly what the others are offering, why would anyone want to come to me?"

"Remember the riots," the crown prince said grimly. "Reducing the variety of your stock is a small price to pay."

"B-but Your Highness! My life is here now, in this shop. I don't have anything left down in Witch Village."

"All the more reason to retreat from the spotlight. Once I return to Delibera I will work with my father on solutions. Perhaps it would be safer for witch businesses to stay in the witch markets."

At this, William frowned. The expression didn't suit his jovial features.

Sacrifices had to be made for the wellness of the kingdom, that I knew. But it was abundantly clear that the crown prince was making a mistake. Forcing witches to stay in witch markets would only isolate them further from human civilians, not to mention limit their pool of consumers.

I turned to William. "That doesn't have to be the case."

Crown Prince Bennett looked at me. Whether his gaze held curiosity or anger, I was too afraid to meet it. I knew adamantly agreeing with him would have won his favor, but leaving William upset with our interference didn't line up with the purpose of the tour. It was my duty to fix this.

"Do you know what the other shops are selling?" I asked.

"Basic fruits and vegetables and whatnot," William said with a grumble. He had removed his gloves.

I racked my brain for fruits that were in season. "Do you have lemons?"

William screwed up his nose. "Lemons? Who's buying lemons?"

"The Food and Produce Census say lemons are quite popular in Alevine," Ulysses piped up from within his pile of reports.

No one paid him any mind.

"Pears!" I said, recalling the cheddar pear soup I had several times at Greenwood Abbey. "Do you have pears?"

William nodded, seeming to have a more favorable opinion of this fruit. "I have several saplings in the back."

"Do the others have pears?"

"I'm sure they do, Lady Narcissa."

"But none will be as large and sweet and dependable as witch-grown fruit, will they?" I asked.

William raised his brows. "I suppose not."

"Do what the others are doing, but better," I said firmly. That was one of Mother's sayings. It felt odd passing it on to William, but it was fitting. "Tell me, are people only coming to you for cantaloupe?"

"The customers like how I decorate the shop," he said proudly. "They say it's charming and curious."

I couldn't help but smile at his enthusiasm. "Your presence is novelty enough, then. In the meantime, make friends with the other shop owners. Give them a peace offering of some sort."

"A peace offering?" William leaned forward.

I nodded. "Perhaps a helpful tip about gardening. Something to show that you are on friendly terms with them despite being their biggest competitor. Once you stop selling your cantaloupe you will be on even footing with the rest. But you'll still have an advantage with your unique presentation."

Make them think you are equals before flying far and beyond them.

I held back a grimace. Yet another one of Mother's mantras.

The spark had returned to the witch's eyes. He pulled his dirty gloves back on. "This has been enlightening indeed. Thank you, Lady Narcissa!" William made a move to shake my hand, but seemed to think better of it. "I will certainly take your advice to heart."

On our way out, William insisted on giving us a crate of his leftover cantaloupe. A gift, he said, for helping him.

Ulysses trudged along the stone path behind Crown Prince Bennett, weighed down by his papers and the crate of melons. The steward craned his neck to look at me. "Well, handled, milady. I daresay your compromise was clever indeed—"

The crown prince halted, nearly causing Ulysses to crash into his back. "Wait here."

Ulysses righted himself. "Er, what is it, Highness?"

"I will be back in a moment." Without further explanation, he continued down the street, melting into the crowd.

I looked down at my skirts, frowning. I hoped he didn't recognize my advice as the petty games Mother used to play in court.

"Wait! Your—Oh dear," Ulysses said. We stood beneath a large painted sign that read *Pies by Pippin*, the shop right next to William's. A peek into the windows showed a variety of desserts, and of course, pies of all shapes and sizes. The tantalizing aroma of baked goods lingered in the frigid air.

I was half-tempted to walk inside, but my attention drew back to the steward, who was bouncing on his feet like a marionette puppet.

"Is something wrong, Ulysses?" I asked after a few minutes of his fidgeting.

His lips pulled downward. "Of course. I am in charge of keeping my eyes on the heir to the throne and heaven knows where he went. I do wish he would have taken a guard."

The crown prince didn't strike me as the type to dart off for foolish fancies. Whatever compelled him away must've been important, but it felt impertinent to ask where he went. I had the feeling the steward didn't know either.

"Is His Highness not allowed to be alone?" I asked instead.

"He hardly ever is, milady." Ulysses exhaled, ruffling his papers.

At that moment, Crown Prince Bennett appeared up the street. Except this time, there was an orange tabby cat slung over his shoulder like a sack. I blinked twice. Surely the light was playing tricks on me.

"Your Highness!" Ulysses exclaimed as he approached. The steward froze when the feline stared at him with pale green eyes. "This cat is...?"

"Mine."

"Yours? B-but—"

Crown Prince Bennett patted the cat's head. There was a wet spot on his lavender cravat, as if it had been thoroughly chewed on. "I left him here to be groomed. His name is..." He glanced up. "Pippin. Or do you not remember, Ulysses?"

"P-pippin?" Ulysses squeaked, flipping frantically through his papers with one hand and balancing the crate with another. "Er—"

"Shall I tell Father you are no longer in prime condition to do your job?"

"No! No, not at all. Of course I remember...Pippin," the steward said.

The crown prince removed the cat from his shoulders and offered it to me. "Lady Narcissa, if you don't mind?"

I took the creature, staring incredulously as Crown Prince Bennett turned on his heel and headed back to the carriage.

The cat meowed in a voice far deeper than Misty's, squirming in my arm's length hold.

What's your name? I thought to him. *And where did you come from?*

Didn't you just hear? It's Pippin, the tabby cat replied. *As for where I come from? Don't be daft. My mother's womb, of course!*

When we returned, Crown Prince Bennett claimed to have unfinished paperwork and disappeared to his room.

Ulysses went to the kitchens to drop off the melons, leaving me with Serena to show me back. She gave me and Pippin a sidelong glance, a tortured expression on her face. She gave no additional comment about Miss Isabelle's aversion to animals, however, and left promptly after I entered the common room I shared with the crown prince.

I set Pippin down. He began exploring eagerly.

"This is your home for now," I said, putting my hands on my hips. "I sincerely hope you are house trained."

Of course, of course, Pippin said, peering underneath the couch in the center of the room. He jumped back abruptly. *Say! Who are you?*

Misty slunk out from beneath, groggy from her nap. But when she caught sight of Pippin, she hissed and bolted behind my legs.

You actually got a ginger tabby to replace me! she yowled.

I knelt to stroke her head. "I did nothing of the sort! This is Pippin. He's...the crown prince's cat."

Pippin's tail stood upright as he strode toward Misty. *Has anyone told you what a stunning creature you are?*

Misty bristled. I spread my skirts to keep her back. She didn't have the best history with the males of her species. I was secretly glad of it. I'd rather her stay with me than go off with some tomcat.

Before Misty could throw a fit, the crown prince's door opened with a loud creak.

Giselle walked out. Her eyes widened. "Narcissa! I didn't know you would be in here." She shut the door quickly, pulling her braid over her shoulder.

"I live here. Why are you here?" I asked.

"Er, right. I was just...taking His Highness's measurements."

"Was he not doing paperwork?"

"Of course, but I had to interrupt him. Lady Huntington is hosting a ball next week."

That sounds like fun, Pippin said, the tip of his tail curling. *Will there be music? And fish?*

"Aw!" Giselle cooed when she noticed the new feline. "This must be Pippin," she said, kneeling down to pet him.

"You know him?" I said incredulously.

"Of course. He's His Highness's cat."

I looked blankly at the top of Giselle's head. How did I miss that the crown prince had a cat?

Giselle sighed loudly. "Well, I have a load of sewing to do," she said as she jumped up. "See you later."

"You don't need to take my measurements?" I asked when she was halfway through the door.

"Unless you've grown two feet taller in the past day, no.

Besides, I already have something special in the works for you." With a wink, the witch skipped out into the hall, whistling an off-key tune.

THE NEXT MORNING, I made sure Misty was properly fed before going down to breakfast. Pippin was nowhere to be seen. He most likely wandered off to explore the abbey further. I only hoped he wouldn't bump into Isabelle, lest she damaged my ears with another one of her screams.

"It will be a wonderful ball, Papa, I will make sure of it," Isabelle said from beside me. Her cheeks were flushed pink with excitement. She had been going on without pause about the upcoming ball the moment breakfast began. I wondered when she managed to down her two pieces of toast.

"I'm sure you will, my dear," Lord Frederick said for the third time.

"Mama taught me everything about event planning, isn't that right, Mama?"

Lady Huntington smiled. "And you have been the perfect pupil, my darling girl."

I raised my teacup over my lips in case I made a face. Mother would dote on me in the same manner in public, though I never realized how sickening it was to watch.

Lady Huntington turned to Crown Prince Bennett. "It certainly won't be as grand as the balls you are used to, Your Highness, but gatherings at our abbey are delightful nonetheless."

"Certainly. I look forward to it," the crown prince said. He bent down and lifted Pippin from underneath the table.

Isabelle let out a strangled squeal.

Lady Huntington set down her tea with a clatter. "Lady Narcissa, I believe I made it clear that—"

"This is my cat, Lady Huntington," Crown Prince Bennett interrupted, letting Pippin onto the table. "I reunited with him yesterday and find myself rather attached again. I presume it will be acceptable to have him dine with us."

Lady Huntington sputtered. "Y-your Highness!"

"Of...of course," Isabelle said with a high-pitched giggle. "How lovely it is that you dote on your pet, Your Highness."

Lord Frederick cocked his head, eyes flicking from Pippin to Crown Prince Bennett to me. "Isabelle, do you not have an allergy—?"

"It's a seasonal thing!" Isabelle exclaimed as Pippin strode over to lick a dollop of whipped cream off her plate. "A...seasonal thing," she squeaked.

Crown Prince Bennett held out a piece of toast to Pippin, who approached but merely stared at it. "He's lonely." He gave me a sidelong glance. It was the first time he looked at me since the carriage yesterday. "Lady Narcissa, will your cat join us?"

I blinked. "Misty already ate, Your Highness."

He nodded. "Next time, then."

Lady Huntington pressed her lips together so tightly they disappeared.

She forced a smile nonetheless. "Frederick says you are free today, Your Highness. Perhaps you'd like a tour of Huntington Abbey after breakfast?"

"A grand idea," Crown Prince Bennett said. "The cats can stretch their legs." He removed the napkin from his lap and stood, leaving Pippin. "Let us start in ten minutes."

I stared, first at the crown prince's retreating figure, then the faces of the remaining parties. Isabelle and Lady Huntington were both beet red, watching Pippin meander on top of the table with bulging eyes. Lord Frederick gave me a knowing smile, as if we were sharing a secret joke. I wasn't sure what the joke was.

The tabby cat leaped from the table to my lap. His stomach gurgled. *I'm starting to think that cream wasn't a good idea.*

14

It was not. Rarely should a cat consume anything derived from milk. Still, a dollop of cream and a mildly upset stomach did not deter Pippin from joining us on the grand tour. Misty, after hearing that he would be present, declined to go.

Pippin pranced around the courtyard as Lady Huntington droned on about the bear fountain. Crown Prince Bennett stood in rapt attention, though my focus was not so unwavering.

"This fountain was carved fifty years ago by a distant relative who was a well-known artist in his time. Completely by hand, not with magic like some...newer artists are doing these recent months."

Pippin hissed playfully at the marble bear. Lady Huntington coughed.

"I don't know if you have heard of him, Your Highness, but his name was Hugo Valiant Huntington the Third, and he was known for his life-like sculptures of bears, especially black bears…"

I frowned at Crown Prince Bennett's broad back. He never mentioned having a cat before yesterday and I had never seen Pippin during all my time at the palace.

Pippin.

The cat paid no attention, pawing at the weeds underneath the lip of the fountain.

Pippin! I thought harder.

He rolled onto his back. *Yes, yes. I hear you. What is it?*

Are you really the crown prince's cat?

Of course I am! He looked affronted. *Why do you ask?*

He tried to feed you bread.

So? Pippin said. *He spoils me with variety.*

I narrowed my eyes. *How long has he had you?*

Pippin made a little noise that sounded like a huff. *Long enough. I don't believe that's any of your business.*

What do you know about him?

He's the crown prince. He's big and warm and gives the best kisses. Don't you already know that?

The crown prince kissing anything, much less a cat, was a difficult image to conjure. I held back a sigh. Pippin was clearly a loyal pet. I'd have to find another way to weasel out what His Highness was hiding.

"Lady Narcissa?"

I jerked my attention back to Lady Huntington and Isabelle, who were both staring at me haughtily. "Pardon?"

"Mama was asking if you were familiar with Pierre Mullgren," Isabelle said. She seemed convinced I didn't. Little did she know, Mother drilled me endlessly on volumes of "ladylike" knowledge, art included.

"I believe Mr. Mullgren was the first to experiment with

bold pigments in his paintings after they were made available in Olderea," I recited. I felt the crown prince's eyes turn to me. "Instead of the rustic color palette typical of Olderean portraits, he used vibrant teals and oranges, inspiring an artistic movement that lasted for decades."

"Very impressive, Lady Narcissa," Lady Huntington said, raising her thinly penciled brows. "I hope you're just as knowledgeable in matters of the kingdom."

I dipped my head. "When I am committed, milady, I do my best in *all* disciplines."

She gave me a calculating look, but gave a sudden gasp. "Heavens! The grass has just been watered and trimmed!"

Pippin was squatting beneath the fountain, in the middle of something unspeakable.

Crown Prince Bennett blinked rapidly. "Much apologies, Lady Huntington. I'm sure he didn't mean to...deface your lawn."

Lady Huntington took a step back, holding a handkerchief to her nose. "Lady Narcissa, if you could please magic this away, it would be much appreciated."

Insolent woman! Banishing Misty was bad enough, but this? "Lady Huntington, I cannot make excrement disappear from lawns," I said before I could stop myself.

"Lady Narcissa! A respectable lady of your age ought to mind her manners when speaking to her hostess," she said sharply.

"My manners only reflect my hostess's."

Lady Huntington gaped. I almost thought I shocked her until she gave a little laugh. "Do accept my apologies, Lady Narcissa. With your mother and father's influence, you certainly haven't learned propriety. Forgive me for not being more compassionate toward your...situation."

I clenched my jaw, my face burning with anger and humiliation. How dare she bring up Mother? And how dare she mention Father as if he were anything but good and kind?

Crown Prince Bennett stepped in front of me before I could retort. "I believe there were some interesting vases in the foyer, Lady Huntington," he interjected. "I would like to see them up close." His tone was stony despite his words.

He must be angry with me. Crown princesses didn't have tempers. And they certainly wouldn't be scolded by their hostesses. I closed my eyes briefly, glad that I could only see the back of his coat and not the disappointment in his eyes. Why couldn't I pass one day without blundering something?

Lady Huntington gave a nervous giggle. "Of course, I'm happy to oblige," she said. "Isabelle, show Lady Narcissa around the gardens, will you? And if you happen to see the gardener tell him to take care of...that."

"But Mama, I'd much rather join you and His High—"

"Isabelle, please."

"Yes, Mama," Isabelle grumbled.

Crown Prince Bennett turned and motioned to one of the guards at the gate. "In that case, a guard should join you."

"Our grounds are perfectly safe, Your Highness, and Isabelle will be good company—"

"A mere precaution. Lady Narcissa must be protected at all times," the crown prince said. "Now, the vases?"

Lady Huntington pulled on a toothy smile and led His Highness to the foyer. The guard from the gate approached. His blond hair made him instantly recognizable.

I sighed. Just my luck.

Isabelle scowled at Maddox as if he were a crushed bug beneath her boot. "Keep at a distance, will you? Men should not eavesdrop on ladies' talk."

"Yes, miss," Maddox said monotonously.

Isabelle harrumphed, latched onto my arm, and led me to the back gardens. Her grip was unnecessarily tight.

I was no fool. Miss Isabelle Huntington, like half the girls in the kingdom, was infatuated with the crown prince. That infatuation certainly did not extend to me.

First the mother and now the daughter. The only good thing about this battle was that it wouldn't be witnessed by anyone important.

"Father says His Highness plans to be on horseback for the entire tour," Isabelle said as we passed a hemlock tree surrounded by blooms. The pansies were abundant, taking over the scene with bursts of inky purple and gold. She gave me a cool glance. "Why won't he join you in the carriage?"

This was a petty challenge indeed.

Forcing a smile, I picked a yellow pansy and offered it to Isabelle. "This will look lovely in your hair."

Isabelle accepted the flower, squirming as she tucked it behind her ear. I had disarmed her for a moment.

"The crown prince and I are not familiar with each other. Our union is purely out of obligation," I said. Perhaps blatant honesty would conclude the battle.

No such luck. Isabelle crossed her arms. "Marriage should be out of love, not obligation. His Highness should be with someone who makes him happy."

Heavens. She sounded like someone who read a few too many romance novels. I would know.

"What makes you think he's not happy?"

"He never smiles around you," Isabelle said triumphantly.

I wanted to scoff. The crown prince *never* smiled.

"Olderea is and always will be at the forefront of his mind. His Highness needs someone who can solve the unrest and put the kingdom first," I said, pulling on a regal expression. "Are you able to do that, Isabelle?"

She sniffed. "At least he doesn't find *me* so repulsive that he would rather endure a five hour horseback ride in the blistering cold."

I stiffened. The daughter was just as poisonous as the mother.

"Well it's true, isn't it?" Isabelle said, jutting out her chin when I didn't reply. "And I am sure he hasn't even kissed you."

At this phrase, I threw all caution to the wind. "Oh! Are you very familiar with his kissing habits? I'll be much obliged if you would share. I am quite mystified by them myself."

Isabelle flushed red. "H-His Highness hasn't spent a willing minute with you is all I meant! There are plenty of respectable candidates out there. If I were a witch, I'd—"

"Make him fall in love with you and cut me out of the picture?"

Isabelle stamped her foot. "You have no right to be so self-righteous after all you've done." She ripped the pansy from her hair, pale cheeks flushed. "I'm going to find Mama. You can go back to your...wicked potions and magic!"

She stormed off, knocking into Maddox's shoulder as she passed. I exhaled. The battle was hardly won, but it *was* over.

Maddox looked at her incredulously and hiked up to me, knee deep in pansies. "What are you doing standing there?" he demanded. "Did you not hear anything she said?"

I gave my half-brother a dry smile. "Can't handle ladies' talk?"

"Her words were treasonous!"

"I recall you said some of the same things to me," I said flatly.

Maddox sputtered. "Well, it's treasonous now that you're the crown princess."

"Not yet. Besides, she's not wrong," I said as we waded through the flowers. My mood was irrevocably soured now that I had roused the ire of both Huntington women. I took pleasure in smashing as many pansies in my path as possible. So much for behaving like a proper princess. "His Highness *does* find me despicable, as does half the kingdom. So despicable, in fact, that it seems to have addled his brain and caused him to kiss his cat."

"What? Truly?" Maddox said.

I shook off my skirts as the ground leveled, raining petals on the courtyard. I whirled around to face him. "What are you still doing here? Don't you have a gate to protect?"

His face, which had previously worn an expression of befuddled curiosity, twisted back into a scowl. "W-well. In fact, I do!" he said, and stormed off.

I raised my eyebrows. He didn't call me any names. Perhaps joining the Royal Guard was changing him for the better after all.

15

A week passed at Huntington Abbey. Other than a few uneventful trips and parades through town, my days were spent in the company of Lady Huntington and Isabelle, the latter of whom made it a point to ignore me after our last interaction.

It was a shame that hiding in one's room as a guest was frowned upon, for I would've gladly done that instead of spending my evenings in the company of two women who detested me.

Crown Prince Bennett, having the luxury of being the crown prince, was allowed to lock himself in his quarters without being questioned. Ulysses joined him to write up reports. Pippin joined as well, after realizing that the crown prince's bed was far softer than mine. Even Giselle frequented the room, claiming to have a variety of fitting issues she needed to consult him with.

It seemed that everyone was invited to hide out in his

quarters except me. I suspected he was still angry with me for offending Lady Huntington and this was his punishment.

Luckily, as the ball drew closer, Isabelle and Lady Huntington were too preoccupied to pay me much attention. I was allowed to retire immediately after dinner the evening before.

"A family friend is arriving tonight so I'm afraid I cannot entertain you, Lady Narcissa. It is getting late. He will be introduced tomorrow morning," Lady Huntington said.

I couldn't have been more thankful to this mysterious friend, glad to have an hour or two with Misty before bed. But when I returned to my room, I found Maddox squatting beside the door, spreading out a bedroll.

"What are you doing here?" I asked when I approached.

He looked up and scowled. "His Highness says you are to be guarded in the presence of strangers." He shifted his weight to his knees and straightened his purple tunic. Another bedroll leaned against the wall. "Do you mind? I have to make room for Flannery."

I stepped aside as Maddox spread out the other bedroll. "It's only one of the Huntingtons' family friends. Is this necessary?"

"Ask the crown prince," Maddox said. He leaned to the side. "Oi, Flannery! Over here."

Another guard came down the hall, red cheeks puffing. I recognized him as the guard who gave me his pear during the procession. "Burning barnyards! This place is a labyrinth. Why are there so many hallways?" Flannery said, panting. Somehow, he got even redder when he saw me. He bowed abruptly. "My condolences, milady."

I furrowed my brows. "Condolences?"

Flannery choked up. Maddox flailed his arms in my periphery. "Er, excuse me, milady. I'm rather parched. I'll be back in a bit!"

He ran off down the hall, which was decidedly not where the kitchen was. I whirled around and put my hands on my hips. "What is going on?"

Maddox grew as red as Flannery. After a second, he mumbled, "I...might have told the guards about what you said the other day."

"What did I say?"

"That...His Highness found you so despicable that he kissed his cat."

I stared. I had been exaggerating, merely verbalizing my most ridiculous thoughts after my frustration at Isabelle and Pippin.

"And why exactly," I said slowly, "did Flannery give me his condolences?"

Maddox blew out a slow, painful breath. "He thinks the crown prince prefers cats instead...instead of women. And so does the whole guard."

I slapped a hand over my mouth before I cursed, or worse, laughed. I knelt across from him.

"What in the blazing fires were you thinking?" I demanded in a hushed voice. I was so worried Isabelle would spread rumors that I didn't even consider Maddox would.

"How was I supposed to know they'd take it that way?" he said, matching my volume. "Apparently, His Highness has never shown interest in women *or* men in the past. Before I knew it, the entire guard spun their own story around what I said. I don't think I've met a more vulgar group of people. It's impressive, really."

"Has Lord Frederick heard?"

Maddox shook his head vehemently. "He doesn't like gossip. Says we shouldn't be gossiping to begin with."

"Well, he's right!"

"If you knew how deathly boring this job is I doubt you could stop yourself! Besides, it's hardly my fault. The guards are always gossiping. What am I supposed to do, stuff my ears with cotton?"

"Preferably!"

"I already do that at night. Their snores are thunderous."

I exhaled slowly. "Take everything you said back. Tell everyone you lied."

Maddox scoffed. "It's too late. Maybe if the crown prince actually liked you, we wouldn't have this problem."

"How is this my fault? I can't help that he doesn't like me."

"Then make him! You can do anything and everything according to Father," Maddox said.

I didn't miss his bitter undertone. "Wait. Are you *jealous* of me?" I said, incredulous.

"In your dreams!" Maddox jerked his head forward so aggressively that it knocked into mine. "Ow!"

I rubbed the throbbing spot on my forehead. "Blazing fires. Your head *is* as hard as it looks."

"You're one to say!"

Before I could come up with another biting remark, footfalls came from behind me. "Is everything alright?"

I jerked up at the crown prince's quiet voice. Heavens. I prayed he hadn't heard anything.

"Perfectly, Your Highness." I bobbed an unsteady curtsy before braving a look at his face.

Crown Prince Bennett glanced from me to Maddox. "I hope you do not mind the extra security. It's merely a precaution."

"Not at all." I cleared my throat. "I was going to retire. Good night."

I slipped through my door, shooting Maddox a glare before slamming it shut.

Misty bounded over to me. *You're here early*, she said, nudging her head under my hand. I let the events of the past fifteen minutes wash over her.

Misty rolled onto her back and purred. I was sure if she had the ability to laugh, she would be in tears. *My, that is hysterical! Imagine kissing Pippin—of all cats!*

"Seriously? Is *that* what you find funny?"

It was still dark when a knock came at my door.

"There's something for you," came Maddox's groggy voice. I buried my face into my pillows and squinted at the gap between the curtains. Judging from the brightening horizon, it was very early in the morning. I donned a dressing gown and opened the door.

"What?"

Maddox held out a bundle of fabric, barely illuminated by the torch in the hallway. "Your dress or something," he mumbled.

The ball was today. I had forgotten. I made a move to take it, but something scaly and glistening poked out of the fabric.

Maddox yelped. The dress tumbled onto the ground in a heap. "What in the blazing fires is that?"

I squinted as a snake slithered out. It was muddy in color with stripes running down its length.

Where am I? Where is the garden? he hissed.

"A garter snake." I reached down to pick it up. "I'll bring

you back shortly," I told him as he coiled around my hand.

Maddox looked at it in horror. "I-I...how did that thing get in there?"

A groan came from the bedroll on the other side. "What is it, Mad—agh!" Flannery screamed, face going stark white.

I winced at the high-pitched sound. "Take this to the garden, will you?"

"B-but I...snake!"

"He's harmless. I promise." I took Flannery's hand and transferred the garter snake to his palm. "Garden, please."

"Oooh," Flannery whimpered, holding the creature at arm's length as he half-walked and half-ran down the hall.

I knelt and picked up the dress, unfurling it. Instead of a ballgown, it was a plain work dress made of rough cotton. "Did Isabelle send this?" I asked, stifling a yawn.

Maddox frowned. "A servant did. She looked like she was in a hurry or...oh." He nodded. "Isabelle. Should I report her?"

"Report her to whom? Her father?"

He opened and closed his mouth. "She can't get away with this!"

"Of course she can. Besides, we're leaving tomorrow."

Maddox fumed. "I don't understand how you can just... take this!"

"I'm going back to sleep."

I did precisely that. After a moment of blissful slumber, Serena entered.

"Breakfast, milady." She set a tray on the bedside table. "Preparations are going on downstairs. You won't meet Mr. Turner until the ball tonight."

"Who?" I mumbled, squinting as Serena drew open the curtains, letting white winter light into the room.

"Mr. Dominic Turner, the gentleman who arrived yesterday. He's the son of General Killian Turner. You've heard of him, no?"

I jerked up at the familiar name, then groaned.

Just when I thought my stay here couldn't get any worse, my former fiancé reappears after years of separation. I had spent countless balls and soirees from ages fourteen and up avoiding him ever since Mother broke off our engagement. I always hated the boy. He was pompous and irritating from what I remembered—and oddly attached to me despite my coldness toward him.

After informing me that Giselle will pay a visit later, Serena left me to dine in bed. A plate of fish was left out for Misty, who immediately went to the window to eat. I was carefully applying rouge to my lips when Giselle barged in.

"Good morning! Let's get you in your corset, shall we?"

I jumped, smudging the berry red across my chin. "Is it that much work to knock?" I muttered, wiping the color away.

Giselle unslung her bag from her shoulder and removed several yards of royal purple velvet from within. "We have a fitting to do."

"A fitting?" I demanded as she dug through the drawers for my corset. "The ball is tonight."

"I'm aware of that," she said, fishing out the garment. "I told you I sew quickly."

I raised my arms as she pulled the corset over me. She made quick work of the laces. "That doesn't mean you should," I muttered, comforted by the snug support of the boning.

A torrent of velvet cascaded over my head without warning as Giselle tugged the gown down. When I emerged

from the other side, it came into view. The bodice was a harmonious blend of elegantly curved seams and clever darts that hugged my figure. Rows of luminous seed pearls trailed down to a center point at my waist. I blinked, surprised at how different my reflection looked.

"Let's see," Giselle said, stepping back with a scrutinizing gaze. "A little loose under the arms, but otherwise, perfect!"

I shivered. "Isn't it too cold for this?" The dress exposed my shoulders, a daring cut some would wear during the summer months. Although it was a bold style, I didn't feel as exposed as I used to in the gowns Mother picked for me.

"Fashionable ladies never get cold," Giselle said, briskly pulling a pair of matching gloves over my arms. "Now spin for me."

I obliged as Misty watched us disinterestedly over her breakfast.

Giselle clapped. "My, my. I've done it again! So. What do you think?"

I spread the gathered skirt, which flared dramatically at my feet. "I've never worn purple before."

Mother had practically worn red all her life, favoring shades of ruby and crimson. So had I. She said it was the boldest hue there was. Now, I wasn't sure I would agree. The velvety purple was deep and mesmerizing, especially when it caught the light.

Giselle grinned. "It's his favorite color."

I gave her a blank look.

"The person next door," she said impatiently. "You know, your fiancé?"

"Why does that matter?"

Giselle threw her hands in the air and muttered under her breath about "those two idiots."

16

After the fitting and breakfast, I went to the common room to read a romance novel I found in the Huntington's library. It was undoubtedly Isabelle's, about a princess who ran away from her marriage to find true love with a stablehand. I found it rather vapid—no princess in her right mind would abandon her kingdom for a simpering stable boy—but I was hooked nonetheless. I had just gotten to the part where they were discovered by a palace maid when Giselle knocked on my door, informing me that the ball was about to commence.

I left the book begrudgingly. Before long, I was dressed in the finished purple gown and escorted to the entrance of the abbey's ballroom where Ulysses and Crown Prince Bennett waited. Murmurs of conversation and warm candlelight streamed through the archway, a taste of what was to come. My heartbeat quickened.

"Several illustrious families from Coriva are present this evening, some of whom have made their distaste known about the kingdom's recent changes," Ulysses murmured, removing several folded papers from his waistcoat. The ball's guest list. "To them we must pay extra attention. They have as much of a hold on Coriva as Corivians themselves." He read off a list of names. Interestingly enough, my former fiancé was included. "And that is why, Lady Narcissa, you above all must make an impeccable impression tonight."

I dipped my head. "I will certainly try my best."

Impressing high society was second nature to me. But being Mother's daughter, which was once a merit, was now a disadvantage. There was Father, of course. But being born out of wedlock was no merit either.

"Lady Narcissa?" Crown Prince Bennett's voice broke through my increasingly frantic thoughts. I looked down at the crook of his arm, which he had offered to me. It was clad in the same velvet as my dress.

His face, though expressionless as always, was almost reassuring. It reminded me that I still had an identity—the future crown princess. I was not just a friendless girl who talked to animals. Not just a traitor's daughter.

I exhaled and took his arm, and together we entered the sparkling splendor of the ballroom. Isabelle had certainly outdone herself with the decor. Crystals dripped from the ceiling like hail that had frozen in time—an eye-catching display. But the guests' attention was on us. I dropped my gaze to the marble tiles. Fortunately, the crown prince was a steady guide. I didn't have to look up until Lady Huntington and Isabelle approached.

"Welcome, Your Highness! I hope you enjoy yourself tonight," Lady Huntington said, inclining her head. The large ostrich feather in her updo teetered dangerously.

"Certainly," the crown prince said.

"Allow me to introduce our guest from yesterday." Lady Huntington gestured to a gentleman I hadn't noticed before. He looked about Maddox's age, with bronze skin, dark hair, and a shadow of stubble along the hard curve of his jaw. The last time I saw him he was scrawnier. "This is Mr. Dominic Turner, son of General Killian Turner. Your Highness is familiar with the general, I'm sure?"

Crown Prince Bennett dipped his head. "An honor to meet you, Mr. Turner. Your father has done a great deal for Olderea."

"As proud as I am of my father's accomplishments, you have done a great deal more, Your Highness. The honor is all mine." Dominic Turner bowed with a flourish. When he straightened, he fixed his brown-eyed gaze on me. "Lady Narcissa Whittington."

It took everything in me not to flinch at the name. "It's Greenwood now, Mr. Turner."

"Ah, apologies. But by all means, call me Dominic," he

said, flashing a grin. "I always thought Mr. Turner sounded senile."

Isabelle giggled, fluttering a lace fan under her nose. "Don't be silly, Dominic. It's only proper for everyone to address you so."

"How can I ever be proper with you around, Izzy?"

This garnered a blush from Isabelle, who hid behind her fan.

Dominic returned his attention to me and the crown prince. "Forgive me, I do love joking with old friends. Rules of society seem to be lax these days anyhow, with the *new-comers.*"

I frowned when he threw me a wink. If the general shared his son's opinions, he didn't show it. But there was no doubt Dominic Turner disliked witchkind. It seemed that he had grown into a shameless flirt too, which wasn't surprising. He had been rather vain in his youth. But whatever hid beneath his charms was more cause for concern.

The string quartet began playing a light air. Isabelle perked up at the music and looked over at Dominic. Had her feelings changed so quickly in the span of a day? Only this morning she had sent a snake to my room.

"Your Highness, would you mind if I steal Lady Narcissa for the first dance?" Dominic asked. Isabelle deflated.

Crown Prince Bennett lowered his arm. "If she has no objections."

My fingers tightened around his wrist. What was he saying? It was customary for engaged couples to have the first dance with each other.

The crown prince gave me a questioning look. Horse-feathers. He expected me to accept. Ulysses *did* say I was supposed to make a good impression on all the guests above all else.

I released his wrist, albeit reluctantly. His skin was comfortingly warm through my gloves, unlike my clammy fingers. The exchange went mostly unnoticed thanks to the volume of my skirts.

"Not at all." I accepted Dominic's hand.

Lady Huntington said something about refreshments and led a pouting Isabelle away. The crown prince stood alone for a moment before he was bombarded with guests. I was forced to give my full attention to Dominic, who had led me to the dance floor and taken the liberty of holding me closer than needed.

"It has been too long, Narcissa," Dominic murmured. He was a rather inflexible dancer, jerking me through the steps. "You have grown more beautiful than I could have imagined."

I narrowed my eyes at his familiarity. "*Lady* Narcissa, Mr. Turner. I do not believe we are friends."

He grinned. "No. We were something more at one point. Do you remember the strolls we used to take around my father's estate?" he asked lightly. "You always preferred that spot near the hedges, though I didn't have your sensibility to see any beauty in it."

I doubt he remembered the flourishing daffodils lining the path when he tried to steal a kiss from me behind those hedges. Nor the stinging slap I had given him afterward, it seemed.

"That is in the past," I said stiffly.

"So it is." He gave me an assessing stare. "I must admit, Lady Narcissa, the events of the last Season intrigue me greatly. I would have never expected you to be one of *them*."

A witch, he meant. I looked past his shoulder so I wouldn't have to meet his prying gaze. "I do not want to speak about that, Mr. Turner. It brings back painful memories."

Brutal honesty did not seem to work on him as it did on Isabelle.

"Of course. But you are not like those others. You're refined. Elegant," Dominic said. The last word sounded like a caress.

Revolting.

"I suppose that is why King Maximus chose you instead of any old witch girl," he continued, giving me a sweeping look that was far too bold for my comfort.

My silence did not deter him.

"Take for example, that seamstress. Pretty, but rude."

I flicked my eyes to him. "How do you know Giselle?"

Dominic shrugged and smiled. The combination would have disarmed anyone else. "Bumped into her this morning. She gave me a tongue-lashing, that one. I'm sure you would have treated me better."

I ignored his wink. "What are you saying, Mr. Turner?"

He raised his brows at my curt tone, perhaps realizing that I would not melt into a puddle at his feet like Isabelle. He leaned forward so his breath tickled my ear. "That you aren't a witch. Not at all."

I laughed.

Dominic drew away. "You laugh because I'm right. They say you have a way with animals, but you do not."

"How could you possibly know that?" I asked, curious at how he could make that ridiculous claim with such confidence.

"You screamed this morning. At the snake." A self-satisfied smirk spread over his face as I processed the information.

The scream was Flannery's, but it was certainly high enough to have been mistaken for mine. Isabelle hadn't sent the snake. Dominic had. But why?

"You mean to say you drew your conclusion at an unidentified scream?" I said coldly.

He merely dipped his head.

I narrowed my eyes. His stupidity and boldness combined was appalling. "You overstep your boundaries, sir. Are you not afraid by confessing to me, I will tell the crown prince? And thereby King Maximus?"

Dominic chuckled. "Surely they don't expect the whole kingdom to believe they want the future queen to be a witch," he said, spitting out the last word. "This tour is but a show, is it not, Lady Narcissa? To silence those who have a right to complain?"

"Your words are starting to sound treasonous," I said as he let me go for a spin.

He reeled me back in with more force than necessary. "You are but a pawn in their game, Narcissa," Dominic said softly. His expression was hungry. "It's not too late to leave all this. Don't you see how the crown prince treats you? He didn't even want you for the first dance. Perhaps he doesn't want you at all. You're untrustworthy after what happened last summer—no one will have you except me. I can take you away and make it seem like an accident."

I tightened my grip on his hand. His knuckles cracked under the pressure. "Is that a threat, Mr. Turner?" I had the satisfaction of seeing him wince.

"No. Merely an offer," Dominic said with a pained smile.

The song ended. On the last step, I dug my heel hard into the toe of his boot. He yelped.

"Apologies," I said, brandishing a low curtsy. My velvet skirts flared out onto the marble. "Perhaps I'm not as *refined* and *elegant* as you think."

I swept off and adjusted my gloves, shuddering. Dominic was as insolent as ever. The way he looked at me made my skin crawl. I thought back to this morning with newfound unease. Had he been there in the hallway, hiding and waiting for a reaction?

I didn't have time to dwell on it further as several guests approached me with greetings. I pasted on a smile and engaged in the pleasantries, though I wanted nothing more than to retreat to my room after being leered at and jostled around the dance floor. The night passed making mindless conversation with different families. Some looked wary, but most others seemed charmed enough.

The grandfather clock chimed ten when Ulysses found me sipping a glass of champagne near the refreshments table.

"Heavens, Lady Narcissa! Where have you been all this time?"

I squinted up at the steward. A sheen of sweat peppered his brow despite the cold. "Talking with the guests. Did you not want me to make a good impression?"

"I meant with His Highness, not alone!" Ulysses polished his spectacles on his waistcoat and put them on, perhaps so he could glare at me better. "Have you at least danced with him?"

I shook my head. "Couldn't find him," I mumbled, looking down at my champagne. Was it my second or third?

Ulysses slumped onto the seat next to me. "Horsefeathers," he said, taking a glass of champagne for himself. "I'm worried His Highness doesn't like you very much."

Giselle, Isabelle, Dominic, and now Ulysses. I gave a dry laugh. "Is it that obvious?"

Ulysses shifted and pulled yet another piece of paper from his waistcoat. This time it was a newspaper clipping. I recognized the column: *Sister Scarlett's Scandals*. It was the biggest gossip column in the post, started by a former nun.

I took the clipping from Ulysses, who downed his champagne in one swig.

Olderea's Future Queen: A Traitor?

Shock rolled over the kingdom on the twenty-seventh of December when His Majesty King Maximus Median announced the engagement of Crown Prince Bennett and Lady Narcissa Greenwood (formerly known as Lady Narcissa Whittington). The couple is now touring the kingdom in celebration, their first public appearance at Delibera's Witch Market. As of now, the procession is residing in Coriva at Lord Frederick's Huntington Abbey.

Though the crown prince and his betrothed make an elegant pair, it becomes increasingly clear that this union is not one of love, but of politics. The increase of riots due to magic-related issues has left Olderea confused and on edge. The crown prince's marriage may be a means to distract the people from the glaring issues at hand, though a poor one at that. It only raises another question: Why Lady Narcissa?

The events of the last Season are no secret. Duchess Wilhelmina Whittington was imprisoned after being unmasked as a traitor, but her daughter was allowed to roam free despite taking equal part in her treasonous acts. Is it possible Crown Prince Bennett had tender feelings for Lady Narcissa and prevented her from suffering the same fate?

However, one of our anonymous sources (a young lady who claims to be close to the traitor's daughter) says otherwise.

"His Highness refused to ride in the same carriage with her," our source says. "He was on horseback from the palace all the way to Huntington Abbey—a five-hour ride in the blistering cold!"

It is fortunate that Crown Prince Bennett possesses a muscular physique, for no ordinary pair of thighs could handle such strain. But what could drive His Highness to endure such icy hardship, if not a burning hatred for his new fiancée?

The words began to blur together. I closed my eyes briefly, having no wish to read further about Crown Prince Bennett's muscular thighs or all the reasons he hated me.

"I didn't know you read Sister Scarlett, Ulysses," I teased, my words slurring.

He frowned. "It's my job to read everything, milady," he said, taking the clipping back. "I have the utmost faith in you. That faith has only strengthened when I saw how you handled the produce shop. You are meant to lead."

I looked away. I had used Mother's methods. Now Ulysses was giving me Mother's praise.

"The only thing left is to stop rumors like these," he said, shaking the clipping before tucking it back into his waistcoat. "His Majesty will not be pleased if they end up on his desk."

"Are they really rumors, Ulysses? Or are they the truth?"

Rumors were that the crown prince preferred cats. Sister Scarlett was not wrong. I finished the rest of the champagne in my glass, relishing the bite as it ran down my throat. I reached for another, but Ulysses blocked me.

"Rumors," he said firmly. "Milady, you must try harder. We set off for Vandil tomorrow. It will be a fresh start."

I hadn't even won the crown prince's trust. Now I was supposed to win his heart? Not only that, I would have to convince the entire kingdom of the feat. I squinted at my empty glass. The surface felt like ice.

"There are only two things a woman needs to ensnare a man, Ulysses," I said, recalling something Mother once told me. "Beauty and wealth. Therefore, I have done all I can. Why don't you tell His Highness to try harder?"

I got up before he could reply. Lady Huntington was by the exit, saying goodbyes to the departing guests. I slipped past her into the hall and turned the corner, crashing into something solid.

Warm hands steadied me.

Crown Prince Bennett held my shoulders, frowning. No doubt I was flushed from the champagne.

"Lady Narcissa, are you alright?"

I giggled at the irony. Why did he bother asking? He left me to dance with the slimiest man in the room and didn't come looking for me the entire night.

The crown prince repeated his question.

"Perfectly well, *Your Highness,*" I said. I pushed his hands off my shoulders, surprised at the cold in their absence.

He stared at me. It felt like an eternity. An errant thought crossed my mind. In the romance book I was reading, the stablehand had fallen in love with the princess by staring at her. Was that all it took? A good, long stare?

"You have, um…" Crown Prince Bennett gestured vaguely to his chin.

I wiped a hand over mine. Berry red rouge stained my fingertips.

Lovely. As if this night couldn't get any worse.

"I want to go to sleep," I declared.

He regarded me for a moment before stepping back. "Of course. We are setting off early tomorrow."

"You might want to…" I paused and hiccuped. "Stretch your thighs. Good night."

Crown Prince Bennett let me pass without a word.

Serena helped me to bed when I returned to my room. I locked the door when she left in case Dominic decided to test me again.

With my room secure, I let sleep take me.

17

"So? How was it?" Giselle asked as we rattled along the dirt road. The last spire of Huntington Abbey had disappeared behind the forest an hour ago. We set off early—the sun was just now making its appearance, streaming watery beams into the carriage.

I pressed my fingers to my temple, trying to fight down my nausea and headache. But no matter how hard my head pounded, it was nothing compared to the joy I felt knowing I'd never have to see Isabelle or Lady Huntington again. "How was what?"

"Dancing the night away with the crown prince, of course," she said, flashing me a smile.

"We didn't dance."

Giselle made an exasperated noise. "Great. It's not like I made you two matching outfits for a reason."

Thick fir trees rolled past the window. "There's more to this tour than making appearances," I said, petting Pippin's ears. He had insisted on riding in here, much to Misty's chagrin. But currently she was asleep and couldn't throw a hissy fit about his presence.

Giselle grunted. "Well, most of it is. It's unlikely you're going to personally visit every witch-owned shop in the kingdom like before. How did that go, by the way?"

I gave her a sidelong glance. "The crown prince didn't tell you?"

"Not the gritty details," she said. "Besides, from what Ulysses said, you handled it pretty well."

Giselle, I figured, was not one to let go of a subject once she brought it up. I filled her in on our conversation with William, though reluctantly.

"My, my. If you weren't going to be crown princess you certainly have a future as a business owner," she said, pulling an embroidery hoop from her bag. "It was a good thing William was one of the nice ones, otherwise he wouldn't have taken well to the crown prince's suggestion."

"What do you mean?" I asked. From what I knew, witches were known to be a passive people.

Giselle chuckled mirthlessly when I told her so. "It's true. I don't think we could've lived underground with each other for so many years if we weren't. But there are bad apples in every batch, if you know what I mean."

"Are there wicked witches? Like in the storybooks?" I asked, recalling the tales I heard from other children. Father read me no such things as a child. Mother never read to me at all.

Being the only magic-wielder I knew, I never considered myself wicked. That was no longer the case in later years.

"Some certainly have the potential to be. Perhaps that's just as bad." Her face darkened as if recalling some unpleasant memory.

I decided to pry. After all, there was a long journey ahead of us. "Did you know someone like that?"

"Once," she said, bending over her embroidery. "Nasty child, that one. Used to play pranks on us witch children all the time by taking away our magic. She would only return it when my sisters and I chased her down."

I blinked rapidly. "Take away your magic? How?"

Giselle shrugged. "She was a charmwitch who specialized in gathering substances. For example, she could take trace particles of gold from the ground and compile them into solid bars. Impressive, if she bothered to use it for good."

"I didn't know magic is a substance."

Giselle unraveled a length of gold embroidery floss. "Charmwitches consider everything substances. They can be taken, manipulated, and returned—but never created or destroyed. This includes the intangible, like music or pain. Even hatred is a substance."

I played absentmindedly with Pippin's gingery fur, wondering what hatred looked like.

"Well, the point is she was a menace. Her mother was an herbwitch who sold potions that removed witch magic for good. Nasty business, but there was a demand," Giselle said with a sigh. "I'm guessing she learned a few tricks from her. It was a shock to wake up without your magic. I wouldn't recommend the feeling. Anyhow, the older folks always made her return it and apologize. But between you and me, I bet she didn't care a whit."

"What happened to her?" I asked. "And her mother?"

"Eventually, having them around just got to be too much. They were driven out by the rest of us. The two packed up and left the kingdom. Didn't know how they managed, but I'm glad I never have to see her face again," she said, tying off a thread. "By the way, when's lunch?"

A couple hours passed with mindless chatter, mostly from Giselle. Despite the distraction, she managed to finish a row of elaborate embroidery along a hem that was at least two yards long. At noon, we stopped at a forest clearing to refresh the horses and stretch our legs.

Misty awoke from her nap when Giselle took her leave. *Oh. He's still here*, she said, green eyes narrowing when she saw Pippin on my lap.

Pippin rolled onto his back. *Of course. Wherever you are, I'll be there*, he said. He gave Misty a look I figured was supposed to be flirtatious.

How annoying, Misty hissed. She leaped onto the forest floor. *I'm going for a walk. Don't you dare follow me.*

Pippin rolled over again, fully intending on following her, but I held him still. *Come on, Narcissa. How am I supposed to ignore that blatant invitation?* he said, nudging my hand.

His round cheeks and pink nose made him ridiculously adorable, but I couldn't have Misty mad at me.

"Give her some space, Pippin. After all, absence makes the heart grow fonder," I said, smiling. "Come with me. I'll find you something to eat."

This seemed to perk him up as he eagerly scrambled into my arms. Lord Frederick helped me down the carriage, his whiskered cheeks flushed from the cold.

"The men are preparing lunch, Lady Narcissa. You may stretch your legs along the river in the meantime, if you wish." Lord Frederick handed me a plain wool cloak. "Here. For warmth."

I thanked him. We were in a sparse forest of pine trees, surrounded by frosty greens and dreary skies. A gentle slope led down to a narrow stream, where a few guards were watering their horses. The rest were setting out stools and building a small fire.

Pippin was disgruntled that food would have to wait, but was nevertheless content to remain in my arms. I made a few rounds around the clearing before venturing downhill. The river ran clear and free, rippling over the smooth stones at its perimeter.

Pippin meowed in delight. *Looks refreshing! Let's swim.*

"You're a strange one," I said. Most cats would've taken one look at the water and bolted. I knelt and dipped a hand in, wincing at the icy bite. "Perhaps another time."

Pippin nosed the stones. *But–*

I scooped him up and flicked a playful finger over his cheek. "Silly goose. It's too cold for–"

I stood, startled to find myself face to face with the crown prince. My smile faded. Water droplets clung to his lashes in a rather arresting way, as if he had just splashed his face.

"Your Highness." I curtsied as best I could with Pippin.

"Lady Narcissa." Crown Prince Bennett wiped his face with the back of his hand.

I cursed my luck. I was hoping I'd be able to avoid him. Our interaction the other night was fuzzy. I didn't remember what I said—only that I was too drunk for it to be appropriate.

The frost on the ground glimmered in the weak sunlight. A beat of silence passed.

"Do you like him?" the crown prince finally asked, gesturing to Pippin.

I paused, shifting the tabby in my arms. "Oh...yes. He's a very sweet cat."

The crown prince nodded.

I cleared my throat. "How was the—?"

"May I hold him?" Crown Prince Bennett reached out to take Pippin. I frowned at his interruption. Mayhaps he was unwilling to engage in conversation as I was. What *had* I said to him last night?

Someone's eager to see you, I thought to Pippin as I handed him over.

Of course, he said, purring. *I'm his cat.*

Crown Prince Bennett slung Pippin over his shoulder and wiped his palms on his thighs, looking everywhere but at me.

Blazing fires. I had told him to stretch his thighs.

Odd that he didn't look forbidding and disapproving, as I thought he would.

Luckily, we were spared from continuing our discourse. Maddox trudged over to me with a hunk of toasted bread and cheese wrapped in parchment.

"Lunch," he grumbled. There were bags under his eyes, presumably from taking watch all night. He straightened and bowed when he saw Crown Prince Bennett. "Your Highness."

Thoroughly embarrassed and having no wish to speak another word, I whirled around and hurried behind Maddox as he returned up the slope to a ring of guards around the fire. I knew it wouldn't be appropriate for me to join them, so I circled aimlessly about the clearing before picking a dry spot a few paces away from the group.

I took my seat, leaning against the trunk of a wide tree and wrapping the cloak around myself. My arms felt empty without Pippin or Misty.

Chittering sounded from above. A young squirrel scurried down from a branch, tilting her head at the warm bread in my hands.

"Would you like a piece?" I whispered.

She nodded. I tore off a bit of crust and offered it to her. The squirrel grabbed it with tiny paws, chittered her thanks, and went off. I watched her go with some disappointment.

As I turned back to my meal, I caught Crown Prince Bennett's eye. He still had Pippin, but he didn't seem to be paying him half as much attention as he was me.

I ducked my head and bit into my bread, mortified to be seen without company. Had he seen my aimless wandering too? I tuned into the guards' conversation, hoping to distract myself from his presence.

"...you all see that? I didn't believe it at first, but now it's undeniable," a guard with a gravelly voice said. "He couldn't wait to get his hands on that cat!"

"Someone ought to keep an eye on His Highness. I'm afraid the lad is severely disturbed. Poor Lady Narcissa."

"Did you see her leave? She was practically running!"

"She couldn't have known being the crown prince's fiancée would entail such indignity."

The gravelly guard chuckled. "If Lady Narcissa were my fiancée, I'd—"

A dull thud sounded and he groaned. "No need for violence, boy. At least let me joke a bit."

"No more of your jokes, Thompson," came Maddox's hard voice.

"Oh. I forget you two are siblings," Thompson said, sounding disappointed. He lowered his words to a whisper. "Say, do you think the crown prince kissed her yet?"

Someone snorted. "Not our Prince of Propriety."

"He'll have to during the wedding ceremony."

"But it won't be more than two seconds, that's for sure," Thompson said, howling with laughter until there was another dull thud. "Ow!"

My face was burning by the time I finished my lunch and returned to the carriage. If that was what they thought of their future king, things were dire indeed.

Sister Scarlett's Scandals had a readership prone to gossip and exaggeration, but if the members of the Royal Guard went about spreading such rumors, there was no saying what effect it would have on the tour.

Maybe Ulysses was right. I had to try harder. If not to win the crown prince's heart, then to convince everyone else that I had.

After all, deceit was my strong suit. I played the duchess's spoiled daughter all my life. This would be no different.

18

It took another two days to arrive at Vandil. King Maximus's sister, Lady Marianna Median, had agreed to let us stay at her estate at the outskirts of the city. It was nowhere near as large as Huntington Abbey, but it had space enough for the guards and cargo. The building was homey, built with dark wood and creamy stones, overlooking miles of flax fields—a fraction of which Lady Marianna owned.

Vandil was known as the capital of Olderea's textiles. Most of the land was reserved for farming—flax for linen, lavender for dye, and sheep for wool. Some corners were saved for breeding silkworms for silk, or producing luxurious velvets.

This was the place where the textile riots had happened, as most foreign merchants only wanted fabrics from a certain witch-owned store in the city. Ulysses said the shop sourced raw materials from Witch Village rather than from

Vandil, despite being on Vandil land. It was no wonder the human civilians were angry.

"We must exercise caution, more so than in Delibera and Coriva," Lord Frederick had told us the day before. He ordered four guards to follow me and the crown prince closely when we approached the city, two of whom turned out to be Maddox and Flannery. After what happened with the snake, they were decidedly not the most competent guards. But it was comforting to have familiar faces nonetheless.

Lady Marianna met us in the courtyard when we arrived. She was a short woman with a curvy figure and thick, dark brown hair. Her jovial features lit up when she caught sight of us, though it was late and blisteringly cold.

"Bennett! It's been years since I've seen you, dear," Lady Marianna said, trapping the crown prince in a tight embrace. "And look at you! Handsome as ever."

"Aunt Marianna." The crown prince smiled as she pulled back. Even in the dark, it transformed his face, making him look several years younger.

I stared. I had never seen him quite so happy before.

"And you must be Narcissa," Lady Marianna said, hugging me as well. Her embrace was warm and firm and soft. I hadn't been held like that since I was a child. "You two are going to make this old woman very happy. I haven't had guests in ages!"

"Is Ash not here?" the crown prince asked.

I recalled that Elowyn said he was in Vandil for business.

"He is. But if he's not writing letters, he's at the city library," she said with a sigh, though there was a smile on her lips. "He'll show up, eventually. Come. Let me show you to your rooms!"

Lady Marianna didn't have a taste for the extravagant as evidenced by the simple yet elegant interior of her manor, a stark contrast to Huntington Abbey. My suite consisted of a bedchamber with a plush bed, seafoam green furniture, and an adjacent washroom. Gentle winds brought in the scent of the flax fields through the balcony. It overlooked the back of the manor where the city decorated the horizon.

The crown prince was situated at the opposite end of the hall. Pippin decided to take lodging with him, much to Misty's satisfaction. She claimed she was in a better mood now that we were no longer on the road, though I suspected it was because Lady Marianna had a soft spot for cats and showered both her and Pippin with treats and playthings.

The evening passed pleasantly, and the next morning, Lady Marianna herself knocked on my door.

"Bennett's busy, so I thought you could join me on some errands in the city," she said cheerily. She was already bundled up to the neck, basket in hand.

I looked over my shoulder at Misty, who was slumbering peacefully on the bed. She wouldn't like it if I left without notice.

"You can bring your kitty if you'd like," Lady Marianna said. "Or rather, if she'd like, since you can talk to her. They do tend to prefer sleep over anything else."

I woke Misty and asked her if she wanted to go

She meowed. *Not a chance. It's far too early.*

"How lovely that you can understand animals," Lady Marianna said, eyes shining when I informed her of Misty's answer. "I suspect if I could, the kitten I had as a youth wouldn't have run away."

We set out, the sun barely peeking out through thick white clouds. Lady Marianna chatted pleasantly about the land and scenery as we rode down the road on her horse chaise, which was led by Cozbi after the groom proclaimed her a mighty strong horse. She looked much happier in her old role of pulling carts.

"See the lake over there?" Lady Marianna asked, pointing at the body of water to our left. A few reeds stuck out of the surface, swaying in the wind. "The farmers use it to irrigate the fields. It's large enough that it extends into the city canals. Ah! You and Bennett must have a ride on one of the canoes before the water freezes over. It's truly a beautiful experience."

She gave me a sidelong glance, leaning back in her seat after a minute of silence. "It's Bennett's birthday next week. Did you know that?"

I fiddled with my gloves. "I was not aware, no."

Was she testing me? Seeing if I was a suitable niece-in-law? I hardly knew anything about the crown prince, besides his favorite color. And that was only because Giselle told me.

To my relief, she chuckled warmly and patted my hand. "Not to worry, dear. Very few people know because he prefers it that way. He doesn't like the fuss of it—parades and celebrations and all. I suspect that's why he's been so stiff this entire time."

Lady Marianna continued on about the crown prince's youth and the scenarios he had gotten into as a rambunctious toddler. By the time we arrived at the center of the city, I knew that he had once soiled himself during an important meeting with a foreign ambassador and that he had a deathly fear of candles.

I couldn't help but laugh. "Candles?"

She smiled. "Fire, to be exact. He always insists on having the flames contained in a lamp."

We left the horse chaise and I followed Lady Marianna as she picked out vegetables and a few yards of striped linen.

"I make it a point to buy from human sources," she whispered, tucking the fabric in her bag with a sheepish grin. "Keeps the peace, somewhat."

I found it strange that she went about running errands a housekeeper would normally run, especially since she was the king's sister. But as the day went on, I found there was a certain charm to visiting a mundane fabric shop or a farmer's market where no one knew who we were. Mother would've never stood for it, but I found the smiling faces and polite greetings of civilians more welcoming than a ballroom of nobles stifling in their own perfume.

At last, we reached a gray building with tall pillars framing the doorway.

"The city library," Lady Marianna said, squinting as we hiked up the steps. "I have a few recipe books I want to find. If anything strikes your fancy, let me know and we can check them out together."

I thanked her, but I preferred to keep my fascination for romance novels a secret. When we entered the building, she went off to the recipe books and I wandered about myself.

Civilians lounged at the desks and armchairs, some perusing the books. The shelves were nowhere near as vast as the ones in the palace, but it offered a variety of options nonetheless. I was content with looking around the romance aisle and waiting for Lady Marianna until I ran into a familiar figure.

"Narcissa?" Prince Ash blinked, balancing a stack of books that teetered dangerously in his arms.

I gave a brief nod. "Prince Ash."

I stood by awkwardly as he set the heavy stack on a nearby table and began sorting through them. The last I saw of him was at the masquerade ball last summer, when all hell broke loose. And before that, he was unconscious in my mother's chambers along with Amarante. I braced myself for a tirade of questions, but the second prince merely flashed me a polite smile and gestured to the bench next to him.

"Fancy seeing you here. I'm assuming you're with Aunt Marianna?" he said as if we were old friends.

"Yes. She's getting recipe books." I perched myself on the edge of the bench. It seemed his dislike of me had vanished since last summer. Or he hid it well.

Prince Ash gave me a sidelong glance. He looked different since I last saw him—his hair longer and his skin tanner. I wondered how long it had been since he left the palace. "I have to admit, I never doubted that you'd end up marrying Bennett. I just didn't think it would be good for the kingdom."

I stared at him.

He gave an uncomfortable laugh. "That was a joke."

The mess of books formed into neat stacks as Prince Ash arranged them. "I hope my brother hasn't been treating you too badly," he said, coughing at a particularly dusty volume.

"His Highness has been nothing but respectful."

He raised a brow. "Maybe a little too respectful, if you're still calling him that."

I bit my cheek. Perhaps I needed to refer to the crown prince by his first name when speaking to others.

"You know," Prince Ash began, his voice hesitant, "Bennett is a good crown prince, but he's terrible with people. That's why he begged me to attend the Season on his behalf."

Mother had been furious when she found out, claiming that it had been a waste of a Season for me. *Her* plans were sadly undeterred.

"I reckon this tour business isn't his strong suit either," Prince Ash continued, shaking his head. "The poor soul was forced into it, wasn't he?"

"Not at all. His Highness was the one who suggested it," I said.

A look of surprise passed Prince Ash's face, before understanding dawned. "Ah. To speak with civilians and figure out how to reform the witch laws, correct?"

I nodded.

"Makes sense. Father would have never allowed it," the second prince said with a snort. "Anyhow, do Bennett a favor. If anything goes badly, take over. He always freezes up in front of an audience."

"I will." I looked down at my hands, which were pale from the cold. I flexed my fingers to warm them.

It was difficult to imagine Crown Prince Bennett freezing up. He seemed to have a silent confidence about him, a certainty to his words and actions.

Then again, he was afraid of candles. Perhaps I didn't know him at all.

"Is there...anything else I should know?" I asked. Even if I didn't consider Prince Ash my confidant, he was a better source than anyone else.

He tapped his chin. "It's Bennett's birthday next week. You should give him a gift."

I furrowed my brows. "Is there going to be a public celebration?"

Prince Ash laughed. "No, he hates that stuff."

"Then why should I get him a gift?" I asked.

He laughed again, but stopped when he saw my expression. "Oh. You're serious."

I waited for an answer.

The second prince gave a dramatic sigh. "I should've known," he said. "You're not actually trying to woo him, are you?"

"I tried," I said flatly. "It's impossible."

Prince Ash shrugged. "Can't blame you. Bennett's never been interested in anything except dusty old books on Olderean history." He paused and narrowed his eyes. "What did you try, exactly?"

I pinched my lips, having no wish to recount my attempts at seducing his brother. If it could even be called that. The most I tried was smiling at him, and before that, flirting according to Mother's instruction. Blazing fires, the man wouldn't even come to my eighth birthday party. Even with my dedication, every attempt was met with discouragement. I saw little point in trying again.

After all, my capacity for humiliation was not infinite.

The second prince shook his head. "Never mind. Listen. My brother doesn't trust easily. I reckon he doesn't fall in love easily. But at least try to befriend him. It'll do the tour some good."

"How do I do that?" I said.

"The birthday gift, of course." Prince Ash gave me a strange look. "There's nothing that extends the hand of friendship more than a gift. Everyone knows that."

It made sense. After all, I had given William the same advice. But all gifts came with strings, didn't they? The only reason I was doing this was to win the crown prince's favor and thereby sway the public's opinion about me.

"What should I give him?" I asked.

Prince Ash hummed. "Well. Bennett likes clothes."

"Clothes?"

He nodded, rubbing the back of his neck. "I'm not sure if he wants people to know. A crown prince has to make a certain impression. Clothes help him do that, and he enjoys it. But on the flip side, you know how the press is. Next thing you know they'll be saying he's a dandy unfit to rule."

Mother always told me to take pride in my appearance—a rare lesson that wasn't nefarious at its core. It was one of the things I was able to find joy in, no matter how frivolous it may seem. For it to be encouraged among ladies and laughed at amongst men was absurd.

Besides, Crown Prince Bennett's impeccable dress was certainly a part of his allure.

I winced. What business did I have thinking about his allure when the man wouldn't even hold a conversation with me?

"Ash, there you are!" Lady Marianna appeared around the corner with her basket full of recipe books. She beamed. "Perfect. We can all go home together."

SQUEEZING THREE PEOPLE into her horse chaise, Lady Marianna eventually realized, was an impossible feat. Prince Ash opted to stay a little longer at the library.

"Don't mind me," he said cheerfully. "I still have to finish my letter to Amarante."

We left him to compose his love poem—for that was what it was—though the glimpses I caught needed desperate work.

I spent the ride back half listening to Lady Marianna talk about beet stew and half pondering about what gift I should give to the crown prince. It was well into the morning when we returned. Lady Marianna split off to unload her purchases, and I took Cozbi from the groom, hoping to have a quiet time tending to her in the stables.

But I was surprised to see Lady Marianna there, her basket still full. She was standing near the stalls in a hushed discussion with none other than Crown Prince Bennett. I stopped in my tracks. Cozbi's nose bumped into the back of my head.

What is it? she nickered.

"My boot laces are untied. A moment please," I murmured. They were not, but I bent down anyhow, hoping the two of them would leave. I wasn't in the mood to face the crown prince–not when I was thinking about how best to woo him. If we exchanged a word I was sure to give up the idea entirely.

"I don't see why you can't ask her for help," Lady Marianna said, putting her hands on her hips. The bottles in her basket clinked. "She's a sweet girl as far as I can tell."

I shuffled behind a bale of hay. It was bad of me to eavesdrop, but there didn't seem to be another choice if I wanted to avoid the meeting.

"She has her own schedule. I mustn't disrupt it." The crown prince's voice sounded fainter. A peek above the hay told me that he had entered his gelding's stall.

"You're afraid to talk to her," Lady Marianna accused.

"I am not."

"You're going to have to sooner or later. She's the only one who can understand animals around here."

Crown Prince Bennett withdrew from the stall, taking care to brush off his boots before replying, "Lady Narcissa is not to be used for her magic on anyone's whim. The stable-hands will figure it out."

I blinked, wholly forgetting to pretend to tie my boot laces. The memory of his anger at Huntington Abbey resurfaced. His eyes had flared when Lady Huntington demanded me to clean up her lawn. Had it been on my behalf? My heart inexplicably skipped a beat.

"Since you seem to have a newfound aversion to carriages, Bennett, I recommend you have your gelding fixed immediately," Lady Marianna said.

He stilled. "I do not have an aversion to carriages."

She made an exasperated noise. "Oh for heaven's sake, my boy. You *do* know that producing an heir is impossible if you can't bear to be a foot away from your future wife?"

"I beg your pardon!" The crown prince looked positively scandalized.

Cozbi nickered, nibbling at my hair. I stood quickly, wincing when a few strands tore from my scalp. "Cozbi, really!" I hissed.

Our ruckus drew their attention. My stomach clenched when Lady Marianna's gaze met mine.

"Narcissa! There you are. Bennett has a favor to ask of you."

His eyes widened. "Aunt Marianna—"

She waved her hand, silencing him. I had never seen the crown prince look more mortified—or disheveled. He had abandoned his tailored coat, the sleeves of his shirt rolled to his elbows. Pieces of hay clung to his breeches and hair.

"Your Highness," I said, bobbing a curtsy.

He nodded, but said nothing.

Lady Marianna gave him a look I couldn't decipher. "Bennett's gelding is misbehaving. Perhaps you can ask him why?" She took Cozbi's reins from me and winked. "I'll take care of this one."

Before I could object, she was off with the mare, leaving me, the crown prince, and his gelding alone. I realized it was the first time we had been alone since the king's study, though now there was less probability of interruption. Lady Marianna was not likely to come back and the stables were empty of stablehands, no doubt ordered to leave the crown prince to tend his horse in privacy.

The horse in question stuck his great white head out of the stall with a snort.

Seeing that Crown Prince Bennett had not yet spoken, I turned to the horse. "Er…is there anything bothering you?" I wasn't used to conversing with animals out loud in the presence of other people, but I figured anything was better than silence.

I don't like my stall, the gelding said.

"He does not like his stall," I said to the crown prince.

"I see. I will have him moved, then." He reached for the gelding, but the horse stepped back.

The other ones aren't any better.

A speckled pony poked her head out from the stall next to him. *It's true. There's mice everywhere. We've been dealing with them for a week now.*

"Mice?" I stepped into the gelding's stall, pretending not to notice Crown Prince Bennett jump when my shoulder brushed his chest. I crouched, surveying the space. It was neatly swept, a fresh pile of hay in the corner.

"I don't hear any mice," I said, looking up at the gelding. Usually I'd be able to sense animals if they were near enough. I couldn't decipher any rodents amidst the stalls.

Well they're there. They nip at my hooves at night and eat my apples, he said indignantly. He gestured to a bucket with his nose. An apple sat at the bottom, the skin thoroughly nibbled.

Crown Prince Bennett crouched beside me, running a hand over the far wall. The gaps between the boards were unusually large, mostly from disrepair. I noticed, too, that his fingers were long and elegantly boned. "Perhaps the mice come from the fields. The stablehands will have to repair the walls."

I sat on my heels. "I suppose that explains it."

"Indeed. Thank you, Lady Narcissa."

I cleared my throat. Though the stall was by no means small, it was not meant for a horse and two people, all fully grown. The crown prince's proximity was unnerving, and so was my realization that his lips were full and pleasingly shaped. As was the curve of his jaw.

"What is his name?" I asked, scrambling to my feet.

Crown Prince Bennett followed suit, though slower. "My horse? He doesn't have one."

"Oh." My mind blanked, hardly knowing what else to say.

Yes, the crown prince was handsome. I had acknowledged it before, but somehow the fact never bothered me until now. And I couldn't seem to stop *noticing* things about him.

I curtsied instead, the action awkward in the cramped space. "I must go. All the best with your gelding, Your Highness."

He nodded and I headed out of the stables as gracefully as I could.

The moment I was out of his sight, I broke into a trot, scouring the building for Giselle.

The seamstress sat in the common area of her chambers, her work sprawled out in front of her. She was mending a pair of dark brown breeches.

"Close the door. Don't let the cold air in," she mumbled over the pins between her lips.

"I need a gift for...Bennett," I said, leaning back into the door. It clicked shut.

Giselle raised her brows. "Oh. *Bennett* now, is it?"

My throat clenched, punishing me for speaking his name when I didn't have permission. I schooled my features into composure. "It's his birthday next week. Did you know?"

"Now I do," the witch said. She removed the pins from her mouth and gave me her full attention. "What kind of gift?"

I sighed and explained to her the crown prince's penchant for clothing.

"Huh," she said, refocusing on her work. "You'd never know from the way he treats his breeches. This is the third pair he's worn out this month. Must be all the riding."

I shrunk against the door frame. "If you could make something, I can give it to him and—"

She laughed. "My dear, dear girl, that is what he's paying me for. It won't mean anything if I make him something."

"Who else is going to do it then?"

Giselle's expression grew mischievous. "You are."

"I don't know how to sew," I protested, but she was busy rummaging through her bag.

"Don't you society girls embroider all the time?" Giselle asked, voice muffled.

"That is not the same as garment making."

"Oh, pooh. As long as you know how to handle a needle, you'll be fine."

I swallowed, looking askance. The last time I handled a needle, it wasn't for sewing or embroidery.

Giselle emerged with a bundle of beige wool. "What do you think about breeches?"

I took a step back. "Absolutely not."

She made a face, tossing the fabric aside. "Fine. A shirt, then."

I protested again, but Giselle pulled out a mass of ivory linen and spread it over the floor. She whipped out a charcoal pencil and a spool of measuring tape.

"So. The body of the shirt should be roughly twice as wide as his shoulders. As you probably noticed, His Highness's shoulders are rather broad." Giselle gave me a sly smile. "We may require extra yardage."

I thought it proper not to comment. After thirty minutes of instructions and cutting, the seamstress let me return to my room.

"Show me when you're done," she called out. "I'll have to make sure it's wearable."

I heaved a sigh.

Why did I let Giselle convince me to do this?

19

A few days later, I still had not touched the shirt. Perhaps it was the sewing needle that reminded me of a different time. The linen sat on my bedside table collecting dust—and that was where I was content to leave it.

"Lady Narcissa. Lady Narcissa!"

I was on my way to the library. Ulysses trotted up behind me, lugging his usual pile of papers.

"Are you off to lunch, Ulysses?"

"Not yet." He paused to catch his breath. "And you, milady?"

"I'm trying to find Misty."

"Apologies for the interruption, but I have urgent news about tomorrow's schedule." Ulysses adjusted his spectacles. "His Highness is delivering a speech at city hall tomorrow morning. You're expected to make an appearance."

I blinked rapidly. "Tomorrow? Why didn't you tell me sooner?"

"Alas, it wasn't scheduled," he said with a sigh. "The lord mayor—Lord Irving, his name is—contacted me this morning. He says the people want to see the crown prince."

"Does the lord mayor make it a habit to obey their whims?" I asked. "He can't possibly expect us to deliver a speech on such short notice."

"Crowds in Vandil are known to be rowdy. The first inklings of the riots originated here. He's attempting to calm them in the meantime."

I bit my cheek, wondering how the people of Vandil would react to my presence. "Should I be prepared for anything else?"

Ulysses waved his hand. "Nothing to worry about, milady. There will be guards aplenty. And His Highness will do most of the talking. I've prepared a script for him beforehand for the press, but it can easily be modified into a speech." He cleared his throat. "Tomorrow will be a good opportunity to make your relationship appear more…convincing."

"I see. Is that all?"

Ulysses lowered his spectacles. "I'm hoping, Lady Narcissa, that you understand how important this opportunity is. It's still early in the tour. Better now than later to paint the picture we want."

"I told you I've done all I can," I said stiffly. "Whether His Highness deigns to put in the same effort remains to be seen."

I turned and strode away before he could reply. If only the steward knew how impossible winning over the crown prince was, he wouldn't be so pushy.

Lady Marianna's library was smaller than the city's, but much cozier with plenty of daylight and soft seats. Misty only had to visit once to fall in love with the cushiony pillows and tall, narrow shelves.

"Misty!" I called out.

Over here.

I turned, raising my brows. A pair of green eyes gleamed between two shelves pushed against each other.

"There you are." I peered into the sliver of space. "Good heavens, Misty. What did I tell you about wedging into miniscule crevices?"

Can't a cat enjoy her tight spaces in peace? The annoyance in her voice was evident, though I couldn't imagine what could have irked her. Misty's morning was practically feline bliss, rising late in a feather bed and dining on the finest fish Lady Marianna's kitchen had to offer.

I reached for her, but my arm barely fit through the gap. I withdrew with a sigh, rubbing my wrist. "Alright. What's bothering you?"

It's that Pippin. He's following me everywhere, she said. *Why did you have to bring him with us?*

"That's hardly up to me. He's not *my* cat," I said. I couldn't help but smile. Wooing Misty was about as difficult as wooing the crown prince.

She made a disgruntled noise, turning on her back.

"It's lunchtime. Lady Marianna wants to know if you want salmon or tuna," I said after a beat.

Salmon. Always salmon, she said, seemingly in a better mood. She shifted. Then wriggled. But as much as she tried, she didn't move any closer. The shelves rattled.

I crossed my arms. "You're stuck, aren't you?"

Misty meowed in indignation. *Stuck? I am not!* She flailed, her limbs contorting beyond recognition.

"Misty…" I sighed. Her feline flexibility allowed her to cram herself into impossibly tight spaces, but somehow she never could get herself out. I spent hours of my childhood moving couches and bed frames to release her.

Alright, she said. *I'm stuck. Some help, darling?*

I sized up the massive pair of shelves. They were narrow in width but towering in height, filled to the brim with thick volumes. I doubted my meager strength would suffice, but I rolled up my sleeves nonetheless.

"Promise me you won't do this again," I said, gripping the leftmost shelf.

Fine, Misty said. We both knew she was lying.

I pushed hard, arms straining. The shelf did not budge. I blew a breath and tried again.

Come on, darling. Don't tell me you can't move it, Misty said warily.

"Just one moment." I wedged my shoulder into the gap and shoved hard. Besides the pain now blooming at my shoulder, nothing changed. I was half-tempted to try a running start until I caught sight of a figure standing at the opposite row of shelves.

Crown Prince Bennett cleared his throat.

"Your Highness." I dipped into a quick curtsy, ignoring my throbbing shoulder. Blazing fires. How long had he been standing there? And why did I keep running into him? Lady Marianna's manor must be smaller than I had thought.

"Lady Narcissa." His voice betrayed nothing. But the questioning look in his eyes was hard to miss when he approached.

I stepped aside so he could see Misty. "My cat is stuck."

"Is she hurt?" The crown prince knelt on the tiled floor.

"Not at all."

"Maybe some bait will help?" He drew out a half-eaten biscuit from his pocket.

Misty meowed. *Could this get any more humiliating?*

"Some space would suffice," I managed.

Crown Prince Bennett withdrew his hand, raining crumbs on the floor and over his breeches. He stood again. Did he think I was asking *him* to move the shelves? My face warmed. I wasn't nearly bold enough to ask the future king of Olderea to do manual labor on my behalf.

"I'll go ask Lady Marianna for help." I whirled to the exit, but when I looked over my shoulder, he had already removed his coat.

"It's no problem," Crown Prince Bennett said shortly, rolling up his sleeves. He had done the same that morning at the stables. I stopped myself before I could begin to admire his toned forearms, the breadth of his chest, or how handsome he looked when his hair fell over his forehead, so unlike his usual polish. The pieces curling at the nape of his neck were especially endearing, I decided.

You like him, Misty accused.

I tore my eyes away as he got to work.

I am grateful for his help and you should be too, I thought to her irritably. My face burned. It was moments like these I wished Misty *couldn't* read my thoughts.

Moving shelves is certainly an admirable trait in a mate, Misty said. *I wonder if he moves couches as well.*

I looked heavenward, refusing to indulge her. The shelf squeaked. Crown Prince Bennett had managed to shift it an inch over, but it was enough. Misty meandered out, licking her paw.

Where's the salmon? she said.

"Misty says thanks," I said, shooting her a glare.

The crown prince looked down. "Of course. Consider this a return of your favor." He pulled on his coat and gave me a quick bow. "Good afternoon, Lady Narcissa."

He straightened his lapels and left.

Misty brushed against my leg. *So, about his muscular b—*

"The salmon is in the kitchen," I said with a scowl.

20

Lord Irving, a bony man with an abundance of black hair, greeted us at the steps of Vandil's city hall the next morning.

"This way, Your Highness, Lady Narcissa," the lord mayor said, leading us up the stairs behind a row of large pillars. At the top of the granite steps was a platform. On top was a single podium where Crown Prince Bennett was to give his speech.

Below, the Royal Guard positioned themselves at their stations with help from the city guard, armor clinking amidst the murmuring of a growing crowd.

Lord Irving wiped his brow as the civilians gathered along the street. "My deepest apologies for the short notice," he said, eyes darting from us to the rabble. "I wasn't sure if you were going to make a public appearance, Your Highness, but I'm afraid news of your arrival traveled faster than I expected and the people—"

Crown Prince Bennett held up a hand. "We must do what we can to keep the kingdom at peace." There were dark circles under his eyes, as if he had stayed up late last night.

The lord mayor nodded profusely. "Would you like some tea?"

For the next fifteen minutes he kept offering to bring tea, which Ulysses declined with increasing firmness. I fidgeted in my seat as the steward fussed and Crown Prince Bennett stared intently at his script, feeling rather useless. Ulysses said all I had to do was stand there and look pleasant.

It wasn't long before the street flooded with people craning their necks to catch a glimpse of us. The guards held them in, though they were nothing but a flimsy chain compared to the sea of civilians.

I stole a glance at Crown Prince Bennett. There was a crease between his brow as he studied the script. I was surprised he hadn't burned a hole into the paper yet.

"You'll do fine," I said.

This seemed to startle him. Crown Prince Bennett glanced at me before lowering his gaze again. "Thank you," he said softly. The low timbre of his voice sounded almost gentle.

To my alarm, I blushed. I pressed a hand to my cheek. Was I feverish?

Before I could think too much on it, Lord Irving headed toward the podium, gesturing us to follow. Ulysses raised his eyebrows at me meaningfully, jutting a chin to the crown prince.

As the crowd's murmuring grew, I grabbed Crown Prince Bennett's hand, interlocking his fingers with my own. The action was difficult with the bulk of our gloves, but I hardly knew what else to do. It seemed that I had to take our image into consideration after all. He certainly didn't.

"Welcome, citizens of Vandil!" Lord Irving said, projecting his voice over the rabble.

The crown prince eased his hand out of my hold. He looked uncomfortable. I was half-tempted to try again, but the crowd didn't seem to be paying Lord Irving half as much attention as they were us.

"...this wonderful city. And now, it is my honor to welcome His Highness, Crown Prince Bennett Median, and his fiancée, Lady Narcissa Greenwood!"

The crowd cheered, but among the applause were several curses. I followed the crown prince to the podium, trailing a step behind as he greeted the quieting rabble.

The guard to my right gave me an encouraging grin. Red hair poked out from his helmet. I returned Flannery's smile half-heartedly as I watched Crown Prince Bennett's back. His posture was stiffer than usual as he began reading his script.

"It is the highest honor to tour Olderea this winter in celebration of my engagement with Lady Narcissa. As your future rulers, it is vital that we observe our kingdom at a personal level and connect with the land and the people who upkeep it—people such as yourselves. By the end of the tour, we hope our union will inspire those of all backgrounds, magical or non magical, to live in harmony and bring our kingdom to prosperity."

The crowd began murmuring again. A woman shouted, "What a load of rubbish!"

The crown prince ignored her and continued his speech. His voice, though commanding in a room, was far too quiet for outdoors.

A young man in the crowd jeered. "We can't hear you, Your Highness!"

This made him pause. I wrung my fingers and looked back at Ulysses, who shifted nervously on his feet. This group was certainly not as calm as the one in Delibera. Very few were smiling. The faces of the ones closest to us were tense and displeased.

Giselle had not joined us, claiming to be under the weather. I wished we had her peacekeeping magic at hand. Some individuals looked like they could use some restraining.

Ulysses's pretty speech would not satisfy them.

Crown Prince Bennett stopped speaking as the crowd's murmurs grew into chatter. He was freezing up. Prince Ash told me to take over if that happened. I certainly couldn't stand and look pleasant in these conditions.

Pulling off my gloves, I stepped forward and slammed my hands on the podium. The sound was blunt, but effective. The noise quieted.

"Ladies and gentlemen, may I have your attention?" I said, enunciating each syllable.

Mother had a way of speaking to the public that almost ridiculed them—slowly and clearly as if to a child. Yet her demeanor was so pleasant that one couldn't help but listen.

Public speaking was a skill essential to a crown princess. That was why Mother taught me all she knew.

Shoulders back. Chin up. Breathe from your stomach. Project. Take up space.

Hopefully, it would be enough to tame such a crowd.

Their eyes followed me as I walked across the platform. "We understand the last six months have been...uncomfortable for all of you. So much so that some situations have escalated into violence. The purpose of this tour is not only celebratory. We hope to address the issues the people of Olderea are facing with the end of the Non-Magic Age."

Crown Prince Bennett met my eye before speaking. This time, he matched my volume. "Therefore, we will listen. In two days, I will meet with those who make an appointment with Lord Irving here at city hall. You may report your concerns. I will do my best to solve them when we return to Delibera."

Ulysses scurried forward. "Er. Your Highness this is most unprecedented—"

But the crowd drowned out his voice. The people at the front still didn't look happy, but the tense lines around their mouths had eased. I exhaled slowly.

"Only you, Your Highness? Will Lady Narcissa be there?" someone shouted. A few murmured in agreement.

"She's a witch, is she not? She can answer our questions."

Crown Prince Bennett tucked his hands behind his back. "Lady Narcissa will be present if you wish."

"Are you actually going to marry her? Or is it just for show?" an elderly woman with round spectacles demanded.

The crowd grew rowdy again, this time accusing our engagement of being disingenuous. Someone threw a head of cabbage at us, though it only made it halfway up the stairs.

"You wouldn't even hold her hand!" someone shouted.

I looked over at Ulysses, eyes wide. The steward looked at a loss. Neither of us could deny what the crowd was saying.

"You royals hate magic as much as we do! Why keep up the charade?"

Crown Prince Bennett thinned his lips. "Lady Narcissa and I indeed will be married."

"Prove it, then. Kiss the witch!" the elderly woman shouted.

When Ulysses had warned us of the rowdy crowd, I expected cursing and profanities. But certainly not this amount of impropriety.

"Unless you find her too repulsive!"

"You wouldn't even ride in the same carriage as her!"

I blinked, taken aback as a gaggle of young people hooted in agreement.

At that moment it became clear to me how much had changed. I was no longer a noblewoman's daughter. Not even the crown princess. I was nothing but a witch.

A repulsive witch.

The crowd's chatter soon turned into a chant. "Kiss the witch! Kiss the witch! Kiss the witch!"

I fought for composure. First it was Lady Huntington and Isabelle's disrespect. Now it was the entire city of Vandil. Was Mother right? Was I friendless and weak and pathetic without her? Was I *nothing* without her? The back of my eyes burned.

I should have never left the walls of Greenwood Abbey.

Ulysses looked bewildered. Lord Irving had taken shelter behind a pillar. The guards held their station, ready to take action if things escalated.

For once, Crown Prince Bennett's emotions were written plainly on his features. He was terrified. He couldn't deny what the crowd accused him of. The realization was harder to swallow than I thought. Perhaps we were both unequipped to go through with this tour.

I squeezed my gloves and stepped back. But the crown prince touched my shoulder. I blinked back my tears.

"If I may…?" he mouthed.

I stared. Surely he wasn't considering it.

He repeated the inquiry.

Heavens. I had underestimated him. He became engaged to someone he believed was a traitor. Why wouldn't he kiss her too, as long as it pleased his people?

And why wouldn't I go along with it? There was no

future for me in Greenwood Abbey. I had dedicated myself to be the perfect crown princess. A crown princess must be unfazed. A crown princess must not be jeered at.

A crown princess I *shall* be.

Taking a breath, I nodded.

Crown Prince Bennett leaned in. I braced myself as the crowd roared.

Hesitant lips grazed the corner of mine. I waited for a firmer press, but he merely stood frozen, a full two feet away. He was either the most unenthusiastic kisser I had ever come across, or he had never done this before.

It was most likely the latter, if the guards' gossip had any ring of truth. I was dangerously close to laughing at the absurdity of the situation. Heavens. The people of Vandil would humiliate him into the next millennia.

There was no time for wallowing in self-pity. I had a performance to give, and it must not disappoint.

I yanked the crown prince into me, holding his face in hopes it would shield the spectators from his inexperience. My gloves dropped to the floor.

The crowd crescendoed.

Crown Prince Bennett's cheeks burned hot against my palms. Though he still didn't move his lips, they were soft and smooth and pliable beneath mine. His skin carried a heady scent of cedar and spices, masculine and warm. My knees weakened. I began to count, hoping it would steady me.

One.

Two.

Three.

It was a shame—or perhaps a blessing—that he didn't know how to kiss properly.

Four.

I was sure I would dissolve into pudding if he did anything more than stand there.

Five.

Six.

His breath hitched.

I released him.

Cheers and hoots exploded from the audience. I opened my eyes in time to see Crown Prince Bennett gape at me. His mouth was smudged with berry red rouge.

"Apologies," I whispered. I quickly wiped it away with my fingers, lest the people found something else to make fun of him for.

"I..." He exhaled, staring at me with wide eyes.

I stared right back.

"Er, that was a lovely speech, Your Highness," Lord Irving said.

The crown prince stumbled back like a child caught doing something he shouldn't have. I touched my lips, wishing they would stop tingling, or better yet, disappear all together.

Because a quiet, curious part of me wanted to kiss him even without the chanting crowd.

Crown Prince Bennett bent to retrieve my gloves from the floor. "Yours," he mumbled.

I took them. "Thank you."

He gave a jerky nod before turning on his heel. "Lord Irving, be sure to take the appointments and bring them to me. Ulysses, let us go."

Ulysses was uncharacteristically silent during the carriage ride back. Crown Prince Bennett stiffened whenever our knees brushed and wouldn't meet my eye when I inquired about the following days. They both split off upon arriving at Lady Marianna's manor.

I was left standing in the parlor. My boldness had since fled, leaving nothing but a nagging sense of shame as a servant took my coat and gloves. Misty meandered toward me from the hall.

How did it go? she meowed, brushing against my leg.

I bent down to sink my fingers into her fur. It was softer since Lady Marianna had her groomed. After telling her everything, I fanned my hot cheeks and slumped onto the floor. "I think I need to apologize."

Apologize? How do you know he didn't enjoy it? Misty said cheekily.

"Well. It wasn't *that* kind of kiss. It was just for show." I grew flustered when I replayed the moment. I doubted the crown prince would have felt the difference between an earnest kiss and a kiss for show, seeing as he had nothing to compare it to. Heavens, *I* didn't even know the difference.

I wanted to kiss him. Very much so. He, on the other hand, had no choice. Not with the goading crowd. Had I been too zealous? Did I take advantage of him?

"He wouldn't even look at me," I finally choked out.

Misty crawled onto my lap as I stroked her back. *How about I ask Pippin to observe him and report back?*

"Since when did you start talking to Pippin?" Only yesterday she was throwing a tantrum because of the tabby cat.

Misty flicked her tail. *None of your concern. Do you want to hear from him or not?*

I shook my head. It didn't seem right to spy with my magic again. It would be better to confront him straight on.

I found myself before Crown Prince Bennett's door. Forcing my erratic heartbeat to calm, I raised my hand to knock, but promptly stopped at the sound of voices within.

"His Majesty would never allow such a thing," came Ulysses's voice. The steward sounded agitated.

"Allow what? Listening to our people?" Crown Prince Bennett asked. The door was slightly ajar. I caught a glimpse of him rising from his chair, his back to me.

Ulysses exhaled. "No. He would never allow such disorganization. Listening to the people involves written reports and schedules—"

"You know how Father is with reports. He only reads what he deems important," the crown prince said. "Why else did you think the problem with Vandil's textile trade came as a surprise?"

"You've changed. You're bending too much to the people's will. What is this supposed to be? Some desperate attempt to defy your father?"

"No, Ulysses. You know me too well to say that."

Ulysses quieted. After a beat, he said, "This isn't because of Lady Narcissa, is it?"

I stilled at the sound of my name.

Crown Prince Bennett sat back down. "What do you mean?"

"You're influenced by her," Ulysses said, his tone accusing. "If she hadn't interrupted your speech, none of this would have happened."

"She saw things more clearly than we did," Crown Prince Bennett said, turning away.

"She is a good speaker. You should learn that from her, but everything else—"

"Don't you think the future queen should have a say in kingdom matters? Olderea has two rulers for a reason, Ulysses. That is something you and my father do not seem to understand." His voice rose and quieted. "And you're wrong about her influence. It's not what you think."

"Perhaps, Your Highness, I would be more convinced if you hadn't just been thoroughly kissed," the steward said flatly. "I was young once. I'm aware of the effect these things have on people."

My cheeks flamed. I wouldn't be able to look Ulysses in the eye for at least a week.

Crown Prince Bennett seemed similarly ruffled, but I didn't linger to hear his response. I was too humiliated, knowing that my actions may have gotten him in trouble with King Maximus.

THE NEXT COUPLE of days were as busy as could be. I rarely saw the crown prince, much less had time to apologize. I poured myself into sewing his shirt instead, a project I had forgotten about until Giselle barged in several nights to remind me. I quickly fell into a rhythm of stitching. Uneven, lopsided stitching, but stitching nonetheless. The needle grew familiar between my fingers, and though wielding it was painful in more ways than one, I found the pain more bearable than the embarrassment that arose whenever I recalled our kiss.

When Lord Irving sent us the list of appointments he

had collected, the sheer volume sent Ulysses into a frenzy.

"Fitting these all into a day is impossible," Ulysses said, throwing his hands in the air. "This was *not* part of the schedule!"

After hearing his complaints, Lady Marianna and Prince Ash volunteered to take part in the hearings. This quelled the steward considerably.

The next day at city hall, we listened to the citizens' qualms.

"I detest waking up in the morning and seeing things float about like they've been possessed!" a laundry woman exclaimed.

"The witches always startle my sheep. I don't know what they are doing to them," a shepherd said.

"My store cannot compete with the ones at the witch market," an elder who owned an antique store complained. "Did you know their porcelain figurines are enchanted to talk? Unbelievable!"

A blacksmith shook his wild-maned head. "They're making swords and axes and saws that make no noise. Can you imagine a silent saw? The woodworkers are snatching those up right, left, and center!"

One woman asked me if witches such as myself drank the blood of children, to which I replied no. After several strings of profanity thrown my way, she was escorted out by Maddox and Flannery. There didn't seem to be any witches in the midst, merely humans who wanted to ask me how magic worked. Some even asked how to get rid of it.

"No one needs my horses anymore," a horse-breeder said, scowling heavily at me from across the table. "It's because your kind enchants carts to carry themselves whenever someone asks. Next thing you know, the fields will be plowing themselves. How is anyone supposed to make a living with all this magic around?"

I noted that Cozbi got put out of work for the very same reason. The horse was living a more pampered life because of it, but I didn't feel it wise to mention that to the breeder.

By the end of the day, the four of us rattled back to the estate, tired to the bone.

"Many in Vandil still have a strong prejudice against witchkind," Lady Marianna said, shaking her head.

Prince Ash heaved a sigh, looking out the small window of the carriage. "I've been here for a month observing the situation. The main issue is the Vandil witch market outperforming other shops, despite being so new. People flock to see all the oddities. And with prices being so low for magical items...well let's say the average family can have self-cleaning dishes."

I furrowed my brow. "Why are the prices so low?" One would assume a self-driving cart or a talking porcelain figurine would cost a fortune.

"Witches aren't used to being paid fair wages for their products and services. I suppose they're low because they don't know where to start," Prince Ash said.

"How is the textile trade with foreign merchants?" Crown Prince Bennett asked from beside me.

Prince Ash made a face. "Not good. They're still asking for witch-made fabrics, but I've managed to convince them to revisit their original sources. It seems to be working for now."

"Is the demand for finer fabrics, or utilitarian ones?" the crown prince said. His shoulder brushed mine as the carriage rolled over a bump.

"Both. They think anything witch-made is better, though I'm not sure if that is the case."

The crown prince nodded, gazing out at the flax fields rolling past us. "Perhaps if we limit the witches to making their specialty fabrics, the merchants will be more inclined to go to human sources for more practical materials."

I shifted in my seat. "Will that not take away from the witch businesses?"

Crown Prince Bennett met my eye for a split second before looking away. It was dark, but I swore his ears grew red. His voice, however, was as soft and level as ever. "Finer fabrics will naturally be more expensive. Witches can increase their prices. If their fabrics are as good as everyone claims—good enough to riot over—the merchants should have no issue paying a higher amount."

I nodded, hoping my cheeks didn't look as warm as they felt. "Fabrics aside, I believe we should limit anything too life-changing for the average civilian. Self-driving carts, for example. People seem the angriest over such items."

"Good thinking, Narcissa, Bennett. I will send a letter to Father right away," Prince Ash said. "I'll keep our solutions vague. You know how he gets when we do all the work for him."

The brothers exchanged a knowing glance.

Before I could read too much into it, Prince Ash yawned loudly. "But first, a bath. I believe someone spat on my leg today."

I was ready to fall unconscious when we returned, but when I arranged myself and Misty on the bed and reached over to blow out the candle, my hands brushed over the pile of linen bunched next to it. I stared until Misty pawed my arm.

Don't tell me you're going to stay up all night working on that thing again, she meowed.

"I did not stay up all night."

She stretched herself out on the pillows. *Of course. Just until three in the morning.*

"I'm almost done," I said. "I only need to attach the sleeves and sew the sides and gather the body and…blazing fires."

I was nowhere near done. The icy air bit my ankles as I slipped out of the sheets and dug out my sewing supplies. It didn't matter that my limbs were begging for rest.

If I couldn't apologize verbally, at least the crown prince would have a new shirt as a consolation gift.

Misty mewed in annoyance and stuck her head under the covers. *Torture yourself if you want.* I'm *going to dream of pleasant things and* not *impale myself multiple times for a garment.*

21

I was determined to spend all of next day finishing the shirt, as I had only managed to press the collar and stitch up the sides during the night. But my plans were ruined when Lady Marianna knocked on my door in the afternoon.

"Narcissa? Join me in the kitchen, will you?" she said mysteriously before disappearing.

I was disgruntled at being interrupted, but annoyance at Lady Marianna wasn't sustainable. The delectable aroma of baked goods and the toasty temperature instantly improved my mood as I entered the kitchen.

"Gently, dear. Don't dent my cookware," Lady Marianna said to Prince Ash, who was putting away pots with unnecessary clanging. She smiled when she saw me. "Just in time. Come, come."

She led me to the counter in the center where a selection of desserts, golden brown and glazed, were spread out

in neat rows. "I thought you could help me choose what Bennett would like for his birthday."

I bit my cheek. "I'm afraid I'm not familiar with his tastes."

Prince Ash joined us at the counter. "Redheads," he said in a singsong voice.

I blinked. "I beg your pardon?"

He laughed. "Don't tell me you never noticed Bennett staring at you when we were younger."

I scoffed. If he liked me, Mother's plan would have come to fruition years ago. "You told me he wasn't interested in anything but old books," I said.

Prince Ash shrugged. "Mostly. But I'd say he thought you pretty for a year or so. Your personality, on the other hand—"

"Don't finish that sentence."

"Ash! Stop teasing her," Lady Marianna scolded. "We were talking about desserts."

Prince Ash popped a puff pastry into his mouth, wiping the crumbs on his waistcoat. "You should try the raspberry tarts. Amarante gave me the recipe. They're heavenly."

The three of us spent the next thirty minutes tasting the desserts. Mother would have never allowed me to eat so many sweets at once, and for good reason. Though I felt nauseated by the end of it, I rather enjoyed the warm atmosphere and Lady Marianna and Prince Ash's banter.

At last, we narrowed it down to three dishes—honey-glazed puff pastries, sugar-dusted raspberry tarts, and pumpkin pie baked to golden-brown perfection.

"It's your call, Narcissa," Lady Marianna said.

I chose the last without hesitation, though for purely selfish reasons. I hadn't tasted a pumpkin pie since the tour began. If Crown Prince Bennett were as impassive as Lady Marianna said, he would have no issue with it.

Prince Ash reached for his tenth puff pastry. "Perfect. We'll surprise Bennett with it tomorrow night."

"His birthday is tomorrow?" I said, alarmed.

Lady Marianna nodded, clearing off the counter with a smile. "He's turning twenty-one. Doesn't time fly?"

Younger than Maddox. Somehow I always assumed the crown prince was older from the way he carried himself.

I excused myself shortly after and returned to my room, charged with energy from the sweets. I had to finish the shirt today.

Misty wasn't present, though a glance out the window showed her perusing the yard with Pippin. I didn't have time to dwell on their newfound friendship before pouring myself into sewing.

It was midnight when I knocked on Giselle's door. The

witch was miraculously awake, surrounded by piles of fabric and half-drafted patterns. There were dark circles under her eyes, which I was sure matched mine.

She took the shirt and inspected it. In the dim light, it looked like a misshapen bedsheet.

"You didn't finish any of the seams," she said accusingly, picking off a loose thread.

I nursed my throbbing fingers. "Does it matter? He can still wear it."

Giselle sighed and pulled out her own needle and thread. "Give me a minute."

Quite literally a minute later, Giselle had the seams neatly felled. She folded the shirt, tied it off with a velvet ribbon, and gave it back to me. "I'm sure Benny boy will be thrilled," she said, rubbing her eyes. "Off to bed with you now."

Despite being blissfully done with the shirt, sleep did not overtake me immediately. I spent a good two hours staring at the ribboned bundle in the dark, wondering how I could possibly give it to him, if at all. Would Giselle know if I didn't? The only reason I bothered with this was because of the overbearing seamstress.

THE NEXT MORNING was a strange one. Breakfast was quieter than usual, the silverware making more noise than the people. Crown Prince Bennett excused himself halfway through, claiming to have unfinished paperwork.

"He's always like this on his birthday," Prince Ash whispered to me after the crown prince left the table. "He avoids us like we're about to spring a surprise party on him."

"We won't," Lady Marianna said, smiling at my questioning look. "Let him busy himself all he wants. Tonight he's getting a home-cooked meal and pumpkin pie. And a gift from you, I heard."

The embellishment on my plate suddenly became very interesting. Horsefeathers. I had no choice but to give it to him now that everyone knew.

"It's nothing special, Lady Marianna," I said stiffly, arranging my eggs to the center of the plate.

Her eyes glimmered with mirth. "Please, dear, call me aunt. You are going to be my niece-in-law."

Ulysses came down soon after to inform me of today's events. We were going to the Vandil witch market to inspect the popular fabric shop the textile merchants favored.

"Dress warmly, milady. I have a feeling it may rain," he said.

We set off for the city with a few guards. Besides speaking with Ulysses about the schedule, Crown Prince Bennett spent the trip stone-faced and silent. I had never seen someone look so dismal on their birthday—with the exception of myself.

Mother rarely put effort into making the day feel special unless it was for show. The crown prince, on the other hand, had family members willing to throw genuine festivities. What was keeping him from celebrating?

THE WITCH MARKET was bustling with people despite the early morning cold. In contrast to the rigid stone structures of the rest of the city, the market had the rounded architecture of the past, with curved storefronts and thatched roofs.

Grocery stores, quaint bakeries, and the notorious shops that robbed many of business lined the cobblestone streets, overlooking the canal. The water lapped against the ruddy bricks of the bridge, clear and sparkling in the overcast sky.

The three of us entered a fabric shop, our guards lingering back at the entrance. I was assaulted by a torrent of bright colors and unique textures, each arranged in neat bolts. One of them was a lilac that shifted to pale green, very much like the fabric of Elowyn's dress.

A middle-aged witch greeted us, fair brows raising in recognition. "Your Highness, Lady Narcissa. It's an honor to have you here."

Crown Prince Bennett began asking questions about the logistics of the store's operation. The witch, who introduced herself as Pamela, spent the next hour showing us around the store and to the back, where several witches sat hard at work. Some looms were weaving by themselves. I asked what kind of magic was involved with their duochrome silks.

"The concept is quite simple. There doesn't have to be magic involved at all," Pamela said with a laugh. "We use two different colors for the warp and weft yarns. It produces a shifting effect."

"Are there any fabrics that do involve magic?" I asked, curious.

Pamela gave me a smile. "Certainly. Our satins and chiffons require the most delicate handiwork. Impossible to do by hand, so we use magic," she said, gesturing to a self-weaving loom. The moving threads were practically invisible, but the fabric looked like water, shimmering delicately in the light.

We perused the workroom for another hour. At some point, it felt that the crown prince was repeating unnecessary questions, and it became clear we were overstaying our welcome. Ulysses eventually convinced us to leave.

Crown Prince Bennett, however, had no intention of returning to the manor any time soon. The three of us spent the entire day inspecting the market, taking our lunch at one of the bakeries, and riding along the canal.

Lady Marianna was right. It was lovely. Or, it would have been if Ulysses didn't lose his lunch into the water.

We drifted along for some time, our guards following close, until the sky darkened with clouds and a light drizzle began to fall.

"Really, Highness. I must insist we return," Ulysses said, motioning for the boatman to let us back onto land.

"Do you think, Ulysses, that the kingdom can tour itself?" Crown Prince Bennett said irritably as we climbed up onto the street. The steward tossed the boatman a coin and ducked underneath a lamppost. It did little to keep the rain off him.

Miraculously, the roofs of the shops were dry. The precipitation was repelled by an invisible sheen of magic. I wished it extended a little further so I could take cover.

"No, but drifting in circles hardly counts as touring the kingdom, Your Highness," he said. "Just because it's your birth—"

Crown Prince Bennett gave him an icy look that rivaled the raindrops drenching my hair.

"We are all exhausted, Your Highness. And the guards can't very well do their jobs properly when they're frozen stiff," Ulysses said, straightening. He wiped his spectacles on his coat, but it only wet the lenses more.

I was sure my ears were going to fall off from the cold. Thankfully my wool spencer kept the rain off my shoulders. I couldn't say the same for my skirts. Still, I feigned indifference as the crown prince regarded us.

"Fine. Let us return." He turned on his heel, his greatcoat billowing behind him.

It was difficult not to sigh in relief when we returned to the warmth of the manor. Lady Marianna ushered us in, tutting at our drenched state.

"You three ought to dry off at the fireplace," she said. "Oh, and dinner is ready!"

The crown prince shrugged off his sopping coat and gave it to a passing servant. "I have reports to start."

Lady Marianna stopped him with a stern look. "Nonsense. You just came back. At least sit down and have something to eat."

"I'm sorry Aunt Marianna." He left before she could say anything else. Hurt flashed across her features.

I looked incredulously at his retreating figure. What did he have against birthdays that made him blow off his aunt and a decent meal?

After drying off, Ulysses and I joined Lady Marianna, Prince Ash, and Giselle in the dining room where a variety of dishes were laid out with more care than usual. In the middle of it all was a pumpkin pie, finished off with a dollop of cream in the center.

The ambiance of the meal felt rather bleak, and though the food was delicious, it didn't entirely distract from Lady Marianna's frown and Prince Ash's uncharacteristic silence.

"Narcissa. Do me a favor, dear?"

I looked up from the remnants of my pie. Lady Marianna met my gaze across the table. I was surprised to see a glint of determination, and if I wasn't mistaken, mischief, in her eyes.

"Yes?" I said hesitantly.

"Bring Bennett some food, will you? And a nice big slice of pumpkin pie. He should be about done with those reports."

I hardly had time to stand before Lady Marianna grabbed a plate of food and some utensils, arranging them neatly on a silver tray. She thrust it into my hands.

Giselle jumped up. "Wait one second!" The seamstress ran up the stairs and came back with a familiar bundle tied off with a purple velvet ribbon. She placed it beside the plate, giving me a wink.

"I—"

"If anyone can get Bennett out of his birthday blues, it's you," Prince Ash said before I could protest.

"But why?" I said, bewildered.

"Because you're going to be his wife and one simply cannot be angry at one's wife. That would be most unwise," Lady Marianna said, pinching my cheeks and rearranging my hair. "There. Pretty as a pansy. Albeit a little damp. Hurry now, before the food goes cold!"

I was ushered up the stairs despite my aching feet and my objections. Crown Prince Bennett's suite was at the end of the empty hallway, his door firmly shut.

I huffed. I much preferred finishing my pie instead of subjecting myself to his cantankerous mood, but I knocked thrice nonetheless, the sound feebly quiet.

The door opened. Crown Prince Bennett glanced at the food, then at me. His waistcoat was rumpled, shirt open at the throat. He was still damp from the rain.

"Your aunt wanted me to bring you dinner," I said after a beat.

"I'm not hungry."

I was half-tempted to shove the tray in his hands and leave, but one look down the hall showed me Giselle and Lady Marianna making encouraging gestures. I exhaled, shoving my shoulder against the door before the crown prince could close it.

"Yes, you are," I said. "You hardly ate anything today."

He blinked. "Lady Narcissa, I believe I am more acquainted with the state of my stomach than you are."

I pressed my lips together. Why was he being so difficult? "At least let me come in and sit. My feet are sore. And I'm freezing."

This seemed to get through to him. He stepped aside to let me pass, and I set the tray down on the nearest table. The woodsy scent of cedar and spices enveloped me as I surveyed his room. A wide window seat took over the opposite wall. His bed was neatly made and the rest of the furniture was arranged in a way that lined up perfectly with the floor tiles.

The space was spotless. The only exception was the mess of papers strewn across his desk. A fire burned happily in the fireplace, warm and inviting. I didn't miss the sturdy grate secured over it.

The crown prince shut the door. He regarded me with an unreadable expression.

"Are you going to sit?" he asked.

I grabbed the armchair before his desk and took a seat, scrambling for my next words. I felt like a pigeon on a bench. And the crown prince was the cat staring at me.

It seemed my knowledge of language had vanished without a trace. I blamed it on the lungfuls of masculine fragrance I was inhaling, though why it was affecting me so much was beyond me.

"Try some of the pie," I managed to say, nudging the plate over to him.

Crown Prince Bennett took it wordlessly, though he didn't make a move to eat.

I was reminded of the time Lady Vanessa had visited me, pumpkin pie in hand, to tell me about her arranged marriage to Father. Had I been as frustratingly unresponsive as the crown prince?

I cleared my throat. It felt odd that one of us was sitting and the other wasn't. "Should we move to the window, Your Highness?"

"Bennett," he said abruptly, breaking away from the door and taking a seat at the window. He wet his lips. "Your Highness is too ceremonious at this point."

I took the tray and joined him, shifting slightly on the cushions. "As you wish. Bennett," I said, trying the name.

My throat still felt tight even now that I had permission, though perhaps this time it was because of his gaze. Prince

Ash was wrong about him staring at me as children. I would have felt it a mile away.

I gripped the tray tighter. The shirt was dangerously close to soaking up the gravy on the plate beside it. All I had to do was give it to him and leave. My palms felt clammy as I reached for the bundle.

"Here," I said, holding it out.

Bennett took it and turned it over, fingers trailing across the linen. "What is it?"

It was difficult meeting his eyes. I settled on the spot between his groomed eyebrows instead.

"A gift," I said. Scowling at his questioning look, I turned to the window panes. They fogged up at my breath. "People give gifts on birthdays, don't they?"

The velvet ribbon unfurled. Bennett held up the lop-sided garment I had painstakingly stitched together in the past week.

"It's not my best work," I mumbled, rattling the tray as I prepared to leave. "I'm assuming you have reports to finish?"

He made a move to stand with me but leaned back at the last second. "No. No, not at all," he said, carefully tucking the shirt over his arm. "You may sit for longer. If you like."

The door was tempting. But for some idiotic reason, I returned to the window. "Only if you tell me why you hate birthdays so much," I said.

He paused. "I do not."

I narrowed my eyes. "You were as sulky as a child today, Your Highness."

"Bennett," he corrected. "I was not sulky."

I stared at him long enough until he broke his gaze. "Very well, so I was," he said. He swallowed. I tried not to be too distracted by his open collar. "I've lost my taste for birthdays when the Earl of Alevine celebrated his eighty-fifth."

"The one where he fell into his fountain, drunk?"

I recalled the event vividly, despite being seven at the time. I had been shocked by the elderly earl's behavior as he sang bawdy tavern tunes and guzzled down two bottles of whiskey. His lordship passed away the week after. I suppose he wanted to make a lasting impression.

Bennett gave me a sidelong glance. "You were there?"

"The whole five hours."

His lips quirked, but he smoothed the grin away with his fingers.

I wished he hadn't.

"You know, my birthday celebration wouldn't have been as distasteful," I said.

"Yours?"

Of course, he didn't remember how he had refused to go to my eighth birthday party. Or how rude his rejection was.

I was about to brush it off, but realization dawned on his face. "I—" He stopped. "I should have been more polite. Apologies."

The injured child in me spoke before I could stop her. "I didn't have a birthday because of you."

Bennett tilted his head. "What do you mean?"

My mouth went dry. What was I supposed to say? That Mother desperately wanted us to be friends in hopes of us becoming something more? That she punished me for my failure? That she had given up for a moment and betrothed me to the general's son when I was still a child? He would be disgusted. Heavens, *I* was disgusted.

"Nothing. I'm bothering you. I should go." I stood again. My skin felt clammy, a chill biting my collarbones. My dress had yet to dry completely.

"No. Stay...if you please."

Our gazes collided. My knees weakened on their own accord and lowered me back beside him, closer this time. The ends of my hair brushed Bennett's arm. His was in boyish disarray, dark locks falling over his forehead. I looked askance, suddenly shy.

"My father didn't want me wasting my time," he said quietly. "He said celebrations were frivolous. He didn't like them much himself. I assumed that was part of being a ruler."

Frivolous. At least *now* I knew what it meant.

"Celebrating your own birthday isn't against the rules," I said.

"The mentality is a little difficult to get rid of," Bennett said with a short laugh.

I stilled, feeling his breath ruffle my hair. I twisted a strand hard between my fingers to center myself. "Lady Marianna only wanted to give you a nice dinner."

He shrugged. "My aunt has been overbearing in her celebration tactics in the past. I've learned to avoid her," he said. "But you're right. I should apologize."

How odd that the crown prince of Olderea wasn't comfortable celebrating his own birthday because of the king.

Bennett's gaze fell to my left hand, which rested between us. "You're not wearing your ring."

I had forgotten it in my dress pocket last month. It was surely back at Greenwood Abbey. He was wearing his, a plain gold band on his ring finger. I never noticed it before. If we were a love match, I would have given him a ring too. But our union was one of necessity. What would he think of me, leaving behind the very thing that symbolized our duty to the kingdom?

"It...didn't fit," I lied, cursing myself for my forgetfulness.

Bennett touched my hand, his fingertips rough and stained with ink. He ran a thumb over my ring finger. It was a light touch, but it sent a jolt through me. "Odd. I thought it would."

I held my breath as his hand rose to brush a coppery strand of hair away from my face. He twisted it between his fingers and stared, as if admiring the color. It was awfully forward of him.

"Um…" I couldn't manage a coherent word.

Bennett's eyes flicked to mine, closer than ever. They were hazel, not brown like I thought. How did I miss that?

"Apologies," he said, his voice barely a whisper. "I find myself in a strange mood."

My stomach turned as it did the night of the Winter Solstice Ball, but this was a different sort of feeling. One I wasn't sure I wanted to identify.

The window seat was shrinking. Or was he leaning closer?

"Your Highness!"

The door burst open. Bennett and I sprung away from each other as Lord Frederick came in, eyes wide and hair disheveled. He bowed quickly.

"Forgive me for the interruption, but there's news from the palace. The former duchess has attempted a prison break. The Royal Guard managed to stop her, but…I think there's something you should see."

22

Lord Frederick held out a folded paper, which Bennett took. My blood froze at the sight of my name in Mother's spidery script.

My darling Narcissa,

It seems that I have underestimated you, daughter. Whether it was through your own cunning or through fateful circumstances, you are exactly where you need to be. That is all that I care for. My heart is singing with joy as I write, for we will be reunited soon. You mustn't let this opportunity go to waste. Get close to the crown prince. Make him trust you. Better yet, make him love you—heaven knows you're beautiful enough to do it.

I tire of this cell. My health is deteriorating, and for that reason I cannot wait until you are queen to leave the dungeons. I will plan my own escape soon. When you receive this, know that I am somewhere in Delibera, awaiting your return.

All my love,
Your dearest mother

The parchment crumpled in the crown prince's hand. He stood. The air suddenly felt colder.

"Bennett, I—"

"Where is Wilhelmina now, Lord Frederick?" he said, voice hard.

"Back in her cell, with extra security. It seems that her previous guard was allowing her various resources." Lord Frederick turned to me, his usually kind face serious. "Lady Narcissa, if you have been communicating with your mother—"

I clenched my fists. "I haven't."

"Your father says you've been visiting her monthly," he said. "Why? What were you speaking to her about? What did she say to you?"

"I…nothing. I promise." My vision clouded. I blinked back my frustration. What could I say? That I was visiting her to make sure she was still there? That she wasn't hatching another treasonous plot? It was the truth, but it sounded fraudulent. Like I was protecting myself.

Lord Frederick sighed as I went silent. "I'm not accusing you of anything, milady. It's only procedure. If you could tell me everything you know—"

He cut himself off when I began to cry. I clamped a hand over my mouth, mortified that I couldn't control myself in front of him. In front of Bennett.

Bennett turned away abruptly. "It's getting late," he said quietly. "We will deal with this matter in the morning."

The shirt that he had carefully draped over his arm now lay in a pile on the window seat, forgotten.

I stood and fled, having no wish to manipulate them with my tears.

Giselle tried to stop me in the middle of the hall, but I pushed past her and locked myself in my room, heart threatening to burst out of my chest. But my heart was nothing compared to the anger bubbling in my stomach like a fiery cauldron ready to explode.

Even hundreds of miles away, Mother managed to destroy all I obtained without her. Lord Frederick's generous kindness. The fragile trust I had only just built with the crown prince. My *future*.

Misty bounded over to me from the bed, tail twitching in concern as I sobbed. *What's wrong?* she meowed.

I hugged her close and buried my face into her fur. "I

was fooling myself when I thought I could be anything more than a traitor's daughter, wasn't I?"

Misty put a paw on my chest. *Stop being dramatic. Tell me what happened.*

I pushed my jumble of emotions over to her and let the memories of the last ten minutes flash by. Misty hissed. *So! That no good mother of yours is back at it again.*

"I knew you didn't like her," I said with a mirthless laugh.

What are you going to do now? Misty asked.

I exhaled, sagging against the door. My damp skirts tangled around my legs. "I don't know."

She nudged her head against my arm. *How about we run away? Find somewhere else to live—somewhere nobody knows us. Pippin must come too. We'll need someone to carry the cargo.*

"No. That's as good as pleading guilty. They'll scour the entire kingdom to arrest me."

Misty settled on my lap. *We're in a rut, then.* She let me pet her for a bit. *A good night's sleep might do you good.*

I didn't object, though the last thing I wanted was hours of silence to brew in my own thoughts.

The crown prince's warm hazel eyes would be the first thing I'd think about.

I AWOKE TO Misty's meows. The room was still dark. It couldn't have been more than an hour since I fell asleep.

There's something happening in the city, she said, green eyes glowing.

I slipped out of the bed, shivering in my thin chemise, and went out to the balcony. Vandil was usually silhouetted in the distance, but this time a glowing ember flickered at the far edge, illuminating the minuscule buildings.

"Is that...fire?"

Misty joined me outside. It was still raining, though the droplets were finer and sharpened by bites of icy wind.

If we can see it from this distance, think of how bad it is in person.

I rubbed the sleep from my eyes. "The witch market is at the edge of the city."

Well, that's—

I didn't hear the rest of her words as I raced back inside, wrestling myself into a gown and pelisse. I didn't bother with my corset.

Where do you think you're going? Misty demanded, leaping onto the mattress.

I stuffed my feet into stockings and the half-laced boots under my bed. "To the city."

She paced, bristling. *What are you planning to do? Single-handedly put out the fire?*

"Something like that," I muttered, straightening after tightening the laces. I rushed blindly toward the door, but Misty jumped in front of me.

Are you insane? What am I supposed to do if you don't come back? We're supposed to be together. Forever. Doesn't that mean anything to you?

I knelt, pressing my palms into the icy tiles. The cold made my elbows tremble. Mother would go into hysterics if she could see me now.

A lady, go off into the city in the middle of the night, and without her underpinnings no less! Your reputation will be ruined! Don't you care about anything I've built for you?

You've ruined everything already, Mother, I said to her savagely. *I have nothing left to ruin.*

Stop that! Misty yowled, sensing my conversation with my non-present mother. *You're delirious!*

If I was delirious, so be it. I needed to do something reckless. Something heroic. Something like what I had done at last Season's Masquerade Ball.

"Misty," I said quietly, "I have to go. I'm tired of having no control over how everyone views me."

Oh, yes. And running headfirst into an inferno will fix that how?

"I don't have time to argue. Are you coming or not?"

Misty gave an exasperated meow. *The things I do for you.*

MINUTES LATER I burst into the stables with Misty tucked under my arm. The odor of hay and manure wafted over us as I trotted past the stalls.

"Cozbi?" I called out.

A nicker came from my right. *Over here,* Cozbi said, sticking her head out. She blinked at me sleepily. *What is it?*

"We need to get to the city. There's a fire," I said.

Fire? She drew back, stamping her hooves. *No, thank you.*

I pressed a hand over my forehead, trying not to appear too frantic as I concocted a plan. "You're one of the fastest horses I know. You can get us there quickly before the fire spreads. Think of all the pears you'll get once you come back as a hero," I said.

Her nostrils flared. *Hero?*

I nodded. "You'll be a hero. And so will the other horses who come, if they choose to," I said, raising my voice. "You all will be rewarded."

The crown prince's gelding stuck his head out from his stall. *Why should we go?*

She did help us with the mice problem, a chestnut-brown horse said.

Another horse whinnied. *Will there be sugar cubes?*

"Sugar cubes for all," I promised, opening Cozbi's stall. I frowned at the gelding. "But you should stay." Endangering Bennett's horse would only make him hate me more.

Only fitting. He is *a coward,* Cozbi thought to me.

I reached for the saddle hanging above her when the door creaked open.

"Narcissa? What are you doing?" Maddox said, rubbing his eyes. Hay clung to his tunic and hair.

I hurriedly explained as I saddled Cozbi.

"Is there another riot? Did someone set the fire on purpose?" Maddox asked, alarmed.

"I don't know. But there is a chance," I said, putting Misty into the saddlebag. "I'm going to help."

"Wait here. I'll tell Lord Frederick and the crown prince." He turned to leave, but I grabbed his arm.

"You can't!"

Maddox scrunched his brows. "Why not?"

I swallowed. I was being selfish, wanting to solve this alone. Lives depended on my desperate need to prove myself. But what else was I supposed to do? Sit in my room and wait for Lord Frederick and Bennett to publicly condemn me in the morning?

I was half-tempted to bribe Maddox with heroism and Father's approval.

"There's no time to get them. I have a plan," I managed to say. It was a half-baked plan at best, one that I had scrounged together during my flight to the stables. "Do you trust me?"

He dragged a hand over his face. "I really don't have a reason to."

"Maddox—"

"And yet," he said, looking heavenward, "I do."

Once Maddox readied himself, we galloped past the flax fields with a fleet of horses behind us. There were about twelve, not counting Cozbi and Maddox's horse, all equipped with buckets, saddles, and lengths of rope we had begged from a bewildered stableboy who performed his duties with impressive haste.

The city came into view. The cobblestone streets were sleepily silent with the exception of the pattering rain. No one was yet aware of the chaos on the other side.

As we got closer, the night air grew thick with smoke, the surrounding buildings set aglow by the raging inferno ahead. Witches ran to and fro, crying in dismay as crackling flames devoured the thatched roofs of their shops and homes.

They had enchanted their roofs to stay dry. It seemed someone decided to take advantage of that.

Maddox's eyes widened. Cozbi grew skittish beneath me, as did Misty, who ducked her head into the saddlebag.

"Quick. To the canal," I said, stamping down my own panic. "We won't be any use burnt to a crisp."

Making sure the horses were in a single file, I led us through the buildings until we came to the canal. Several witches were already there, magicking buckets into the dark water. It seemed that one individual could only enchant two or three at a time. The buckets only moved as fast as they ran.

I dismounted. Pulling out a length of rope from the saddlebag, I tied it to a bucket and threw it over the edge. It crashed into the water below. My arms strained as I hauled the full bucket back up, palms stinging.

Maddox did the same, strands of hair falling from his drenched ponytail. "At this rate we won't do any good," he said with a grunt, lowering the bucket onto the ground.

The rope unfurled from the handle. "We should go back and get help."

I rested my hand against a lamppost. My feet and back ached. The adrenaline from before had masked how sore my body was from the past hours of touring. This was an idiotic idea. I tilted my head back in frustration.

Three lamps shone brightly at the top of the post.

"Wait."

Stepping back, I tossed the rope over a curved arm of the lamppost, tying one end to the bucket and the other around my hand, fashioning a crude pulley system. The rope was just long enough. I lifted the bucket with a tug, this time with much more ease.

Several more lamps lined the railing of the bridge.

"Gather as many witches as you can," I told Maddox with newfound energy. "I've improved my plan."

I had fashioned the same pulley system on five posts when Maddox reappeared with ten witches behind him, all covered in soot. I recognized one of them as Pamela from the fabric shop.

"Lady Narcissa, what are you doing here?" she cried, looking over her shoulder at the billowing smoke snaking down the streets. "Have you brought men to help?"

I shook my head, ignoring the twinge of guilt at her words, and squared my shoulders. "I brought horses."

I proceeded to explain my plan. Some witches would stay to man the pulley systems while those who could ride would levitate buckets toward the fire on horseback, taking the animals as far as they can go.

"That'll speed things up tremendously," one of them said, panting.

"It'll be ideal if we have more than five pulley stations," I said, looking at the bare lampposts further down. "If you could tell the others to join us—as many as possible—the sooner the fire will be tamed. We can do this together."

Pamela blew a breath. "Us witches have never seen the value of leadership. Now it saves us in our time of need." She gave me a grim smile. "Now. Where is the rope?"

As Pamela and the others set up more stations, I led the horses down the bridge. They stamped their hooves nervously as the odor of smoke and ash grew stronger.

"Heroism and sugar cubes await." I looked at Cozbi. "And pears."

The horses whinnied in a resounding cheer. I let the witches take their reins, one after the other, as they galloped down the street. I trusted the animals to protect themselves and their riders.

I turned and began filling buckets as more disheveled witches streamed toward the canal, picking a role to play in the system. The cacophony of splashing water, hooves clattering against stone, and panicked shouts seemed to last for hours until the crackling fire ceased and the streets were no longer illuminated by its eerie red glow.

The rain had helped tremendously in our efforts once everyone removed the enchantments from their roofs.

Maddox put a hand on my shoulder. "I think it's over," he said, coughing into his tunic. I let go of the bucket I was about to lower.

"Is it?" My voice was feebly hoarse from the smoke I had inhaled. "Are there any casualties?"

He ran his fingers through his hair. "I don't know. We should go check."

I nodded and took the horse nearest to me, a sturdy brown mare. We trotted down the street toward the fire site. I patted her mane, sensing her exhaustion. "You did well."

The center of the witch market, which had been full of

color and life this very morning, was now dark and dilapidated. Charred piles took the place of buildings. The structures that managed to survive were burnt beyond recognition. Witches huddled in small groups. Some wandered around the rubble, looking for lost belongings.

I dismounted, letting the horse go back to take a well-deserved break and a drink of water. The air was dense and sooty as Maddox and I approached.

Pamela came over to us, a handkerchief over her nose.

"Is everyone—" I went into a coughing fit as I choked on a mouthful of smoke.

"Everyone is fine, milady," Pamela said. She pulled out a spare handkerchief, which I gratefully accepted. "Our shops, on the other hand..." She heaved a sigh as she regarded our bleak surroundings. "We are fortunate to have magic. Otherwise, reconstruction would take a great deal longer."

"Do you know how the fire started?" Maddox said. His voice was muffled by his tunic which he had lifted over his nose. "A rioter, perhaps?"

Pamela shrugged. "You'll have to ask the others. I woke up in the midst of it." Her gaze softened when she looked at me. "We owe you many thanks, Lady Narcissa."

I expected to feel pride at her words—some sort of accomplishment—but I couldn't muster anything of the sort. My palms were raw and throbbing from the rough rope. "I wish you the best in reconstruction," I said. "The crown prince will be notified. I'm sure he can aid you and find the culprit, if there is one."

She nodded. "Thank you again, milady. The two of you will make great rulers."

My stomach twisted at her parting words. Perhaps I would no longer be engaged to the crown prince by the time the witches had repaired their market. I turned to Maddox, who was looking at me strangely.

My limbs suddenly felt leaden. The past sleepless nights had not helped, either. If only I had listened to Misty and—

"Misty!" I grabbed Maddox's arm. "Have you seen Cozbi?"

"Who?"

"The speckled mare with a dark mane. She had a saddlebag. My cat—" I was taken over by another coughing fit.

Maddox furrowed his brow as I righted myself. "I'm sure she's back at the canal with the other horses. I don't see any of them here," he said. "But are you—?"

I dashed down the way we came, chest constricting. How could I have forgotten Misty? What if she had been caught in the fire? Had I been so desperate to prove my worth that I abandoned my only friend?

The buildings blurred together. I wasn't sure if it was due to my speed or the throbbing in my head. The lampposts grew nearer. Cozbi was drinking from a bucket of water with the other horses. I caught a glimpse of Misty sticking out of her saddlebag, alive and well.

Rough hands grabbed me from behind before I could let out a sob of relief, jostling me into the side of a building. I stumbled, having no energy to resist.

"Don't move, princess, or I might cut you," a gravelly voice said in my ear.

I fell limp against my attacker when I felt the cold bite of a blade against my neck.

"Who are you?"

She laughed, a throaty, unpleasant sound. "An unsatisfied customer."

I didn't dare to turn and look at the speaker. "Don't play games with me. What do you want?"

"Simple. Tell the crown prince and the king to banish those witches. Or we might have to banish them ourselves."

So there were others, assuming she was the one who set the fire. But no sign of other assailants appeared in the dark corners of the street.

"They won't be scared away by pesky little fires," I said, mustering as much venom as I could.

"They would've been if *you* didn't show up. They're an unorganized lot, spoilt by the conveniences of their own magic," the rioter spat. I flinched as she pressed the dagger harder into my neck. "Get rid of them. Exterminate them like the vermin they are or my hand might slip."

I steeled myself, too exhausted to bother coming up with a plan. Perhaps my future was doomed to the dungeons even if I managed to escape. My death might even make me a martyr of some sort—a heroine. Mayhaps the best crown princess Olderea ever had, one willing to sacrifice herself for the kingdom. I smiled humorlessly at the thought. Even my own death had selfish reasons.

"No."

My assailant stilled. "What?"

"No," I said louder. "There's nothing you can do to make the royals bend to your will, not even take me hostage."

She forced a laugh. It sounded nervous. The hand at my throat was rough and calloused. Underneath the odor of smoke was the scent of earth and flax.

"The witches are not sourcing from your fields, are they?" I said.

I took her silence as confirmation. She was one of the flax farmers.

"His Highness is planning to limit witch weavers to their specialty fabrics and convince them to source from Vandil farmers. The textile merchants will have to go back to human-made linen and you will get additional business from the witches, if you wish it," I said, closing my eyes briefly as my head pounded. "You don't have to do this."

"Don't think you can lie your way out of this." Her voice was hesitant now, but her grip on me tightened.

Pounding boots sounded from the way I came. Members of the Royal Guard appeared, some on horseback, but most on foot. I had taken their horses. Lord Frederick and the crown prince led them, their faces grave.

Why was Bennett here? He was terrified of fire.

My assailant tried to pull me back into an alleyway, but we had already been spotted.

"Stop right there!" Lord Frederick shouted.

The dagger bit into my skin. I flinched as blood trickled down my throat. "Stay back!" the farmer shouted, fully panicked. "Stay back or I'll kill her!"

"Don't do anything stupid," I muttered.

Bennett dismounted from an unfamiliar stallion, face tight. "Release Lady Narcissa at once."

The farmer's legs were shaking like a newborn fawn, no doubt unused to the role of assassin.

"Do as they say," I said quietly. "They won't hurt you."

She dropped me and fled. The blade nicked the back of my neck and clattered to the ground beside my knees, stained red. A slip of paper fell beside it. Almost on instinct, I stuffed it into my pocket.

Shouts came from the guards as they pursued the farmer. I only hoped she hid somewhere sensible.

Someone hauled me up by my upper arms. The scent of cedar and spices identified him well enough, but I didn't have the strength to stand myself. I fell against his chest.

"You're bleeding," Bennett said, attempting to hold me upright. His face swam in my vision, speckled with growing black spots. His brows were knit, hazel eyes dark despite the glow from the gas lamps.

Heavens, he was beautiful. I could stare at him forever.

Bennett's hand cupped the back of my head. "Narcissa? Say something. *Please.*" I detected a note of panic, but I couldn't be sure from the blood rushing to my ears.

"Make sure...make sure the horses get their sugar cubes," I managed to say before darkness overtook me.

23

"Straighten up, Narcissa. You are slouching," Mother said, circling me. The click of her heels echoed in the cavernous room.

We were in an empty ballroom. The space was lit by a soft pink glow. I looked down. A dress of scarlet satin drowned my body, glittering with rubies.

"The ball is tonight," Mother continued. "You must dazzle. Stupefy. Entrance."

She lifted my chin with her fan, staring at me with her hard, steely eyes. "Very good," she murmured as I stood, frozen in perfect posture. My ribs were constricted as if Mother had tight-laced my corset. She only did that for the important balls, where our appearance mattered most. "You will rip the hearts out of every nobleman in the room."

"But Mother," I said, my voice barely a whisper, "I don't want to."

"What you want does not matter," she barked. Her face softened when my eyes blurred with tears. "You are a vision, my dear. You will rise to greatness as I did at your age." She stroked my cheek, pinching the flesh between her fingers. "Even more so, if I can help it."

Mother released her hold, but kept her hands outstretched. I watched in horror as they became drenched in blood, splattering onto the marble tiles. The hem of my gown deepened into crimson.

"No." I stumbled back. "I don't want this."

"You do not have a choice, Narcissa. We are bound by blood," Mother said.

I ran as her words reverberated around the ballroom. The tiles slipped beneath my feet and disintegrated. I fell into my chambers at the palace, the walls and windows distorted. Amarante knelt before me as I carved my initials into the back of her hand, blood red.

I felt frozen in my own body, sickened as it performed such cruelty upon another.

"Cruelty is a weapon, dear girl," Mother crooned into my ear. "Use it and no one will dare hurt you."

"Stop!" I sobbed. "Stop it!"

Suddenly, I was left with nothing but darkness. Ice seized my limbs. I whirled around, grasping at nothing.

"M-Misty?" I called out, desperate for warmth.

I stumbled forward. A familiar alleyway materialized before me, crowded with wagons of decaying produce. The palace dumping grounds. A tiny kitten cowered between two heads of brown cabbage.

"Misty!" I reached out, but she hissed and darted away. My heart constricted. This wasn't right. She was supposed to leap into my arms, then together we would go to the kitchens to sneak a piece of salmon.

We swore to be together forever.

But I was alone, surrounded by mildewy brick walls. I collapsed onto the rotting vegetables and wept.

Stop being dramatic. I'm here, a voice echoed.

The alleyway disappeared. Pillowy warmth enveloped the top of my head and whiskers tickled my cheek.

Sleep well, darling.

Then, it was blissfully quiet. No visions of Mother plagued me. Sounds of murmuring voices and rustling emerged occasionally from the lulling darkness. Someone brushed my hair back. A damp towel stroked my cheek, followed by a lingering brush of soft lips on my forehead. Cedar and spices hung in the air. The scent was familiar, though I couldn't put my finger on why.

A door slammed faintly, followed by a woman's voice.

I can't believe you let her run off like that. What were you thinking?

I didn't know she was going to put herself in danger, another voice responded. It was soft and deep and comforting. I wanted nothing more than to sink into it.

Of course, no one knew that! But you let her believe you thought the worst of her when that letter came.

But I never thought—

Has anyone told you, Your Highness, that you have a brick for a face?

Giselle, please. The man sounded pained. I tried to reach out and comfort him, but my limbs did not respond.

You need to be more upfront about your feelings. What if something horrendous happens again?

The towel and the scent of cedar disappeared, and so did the voices.

After an unknown period of time, I drifted back into consciousness. My eyelids were heavy as I took in the seafoam green wallpaper. I was back in my room at Lady Marianna's manor. Misty slumbered peacefully near the window.

A loud snore came from the doorway. Maddox slouched against the wall, a string of drool pooling from his open mouth. I made a face.

My rustling bedsheets awoke him. "You're awake!" Maddox wiped his chin and came to my bedside. "Don't move. The physician said you might reopen your wound."

I touched the bandages on my neck. "It's only a scratch, isn't it?" I croaked. My mouth felt like sandpaper.

"A little deeper than that," Maddox said, grabbing a bottle of tonic and strips of linen from the bedside table. "Turn around. I have to redress it."

I turned and moved my hair aside with some hesitance. My witch traits marred the spot behind my neck. Only Tizzy had seen it so far, and her reaction hadn't been the best.

Maddox said nothing, however, and uncapped the tonic. I winced at the sting as he wiped my wound clean.

"How long have I been asleep?" I asked after downing the glass of water he offered me.

"Two days. The physician says you were overexerted," Maddox said. He blew a breath. "Narcissa, you almost got yourself killed."

"You would've liked that a month ago," I said, discomfited at the concern in his voice.

"No. I wouldn't have." Silence pervaded as he took out fresh bandages and dressed my wound. "I…didn't mean a lot of the things I said," he muttered.

I began to turn my head, but thought better of it when my wound pulled. "Not even when you called me a cold-blooded snake demoness?"

Maddox cleared his throat. "You heard that?"

"That and more."

"Oh," he said. "Well, no. I was just angry."

The sky was white beyond the rain-speckled window, the time of day indiscernible. I looked down.

"Why were you angry?" I said. "You have a loving mother and you're Father's legitimate heir. My presence didn't change any of that."

Bottles rattled as Maddox put the supplies away. "I suppose. But I have to work for Father's approval," he muttered. "He loves you unconditionally."

The bedframe creaked as I shifted to face him. Maddox glared at his hands, which was crisscrossed with several new scars. From sword training, no doubt. "I didn't know you felt that way," I said awkwardly. After a beat, I added, "For all it's worth, I apologize."

He rubbed his face. "Don't. I was a hateful idiot."

I smoothed the wrinkles from my pillow, hoping to bring levity to the conversation. "So, you don't abhor witches with all your being?"

Maddox smiled mirthlessly. "I didn't trust them entirely. I suppose that was amplified by your presence, but no, I don't. Not to the point of setting fires."

I thought back to the flax farmer who had held me at knifepoint. "Where are my clothes from the other night?"

He jutted his chin to the pile of sooty fabric beside the medical supplies. "Looks like they didn't have time to launder them."

Despite Maddox's protestations, I eased out of bed and dug through the pockets. My hand met the slip of paper. I unfolded it eagerly.

"'Come see star soprano Celeste Carr at the Grand Alevine Opera in *Ode to the Moon.* February twenty-eighth, midnight'," Maddox read from the flier in my hands. He raised his brows at the illustration of a dark-haired woman sitting on a crescent moon.

I put it down in disappointment. "This came from the woman who held me hostage. I thought it would tell us more about the rioters, but…" I sighed.

"Don't worry about that. Lord Frederick is investigating the rioters," Maddox said.

I began to ask if Lord Frederick had decided what to do with me, but stopped. Maddox didn't seem to know about the incident with Mother's escape.

"I'm hungry," I said instead. "Get me something to eat."

He frowned. "That's not how this works. I'm the older one. *I* get to boss *you* around."

"But I'm bedridden." I coughed twice to emphasize my point.

Maddox rolled his eyes.

News that I was awake spread immediately after his departure. Lady Marianna came first, bearing a tray laden with food. After fussing over me for some time, she let me tend to my meal, though I had barely gotten through the soup before Ulysses rushed in. There was no sign of the crown prince behind him.

"Thank goodness, milady," the steward said, wringing his hands. "Those in the witch market were asking after you. They'll be glad to hear you're awake. I'll have someone relay the news."

"Never mind me. How are they?"

"Not to worry. King Maximus has already agreed to give them extra funds for reconstruction. Half the guards are down there helping with immediate relief. His Highness has also gone to help."

I nodded. I hadn't even considered what the aftermath of the fire would be like. At that moment, I only cared about proving myself. What would have happened if I didn't succeed? I squeezed my eyes shut. "I'm sorry I ran off."

Ulysses shook his head. "I'm not sure if what you did was extremely stupid or extremely clever. Look." He took out a newspaper clipping, a recent column from *Sister Scarlett's Scandals*.

The Herbwitch Princess: Seductress, Martyr, Hero.

January twentieth, at Vandil's city hall, Lady Narcissa locked Crown Prince Bennett into a passionate embrace before a crowd of astonished spectators. After this shocking display, the two were spotted touring the city's witch market, thoroughly enjoying each other's company. Our to-be princess has managed to win the crown prince's affection in a mere moment armed with nothing but her womanly allure—but that is not all she has done to surprise us.

A devastating fire tore through Vandil's witch market that same night. Rather than enlisting the aid of the Royal Guard, Lady Narcissa flew down to put out the fire herself, accompanied by no one but a team of horses and one particularly handsome guard. Whether he, too, was captivated by her is up for question. But after single-handedly dousing the fire, Lady Narcissa was captured by a rebel rioter who threatened her very life. An anonymous passerby claimed she did not struggle.

"She was standing very still," our source said, "as if she was going to accept whatever came her way. Even death."

Lady Narcissa was close to becoming the first Olderean

martyr, and though her sacrifice would have been a great honor, Crown Prince Bennett would not have allowed the heroic woman who had enraptured his heart to be taken from him.

"The way he held her after the whole ordeal was nothing I'd ever seen," our source added, shaking his helmeted head in wonderment. "It was like she was the most precious thing in the world to him."

I threw the clipping down in disgust. "Ulysses, I do not understand why you insist on showing me the worst column in the paper. And someone ought to tell the guards not to lie in press interviews, or engage in them at all."

The steward gave me a look. "Gossip columns have a tendency to exaggerate," he said briskly, taking the clipping back.

I stirred the remnants of my soup, watching the herbs spiral in the clear amber broth. "It doesn't matter anymore, does it? King Maximus will retract the engagement in a week at most."

"Whatever for?" Ulysses said.

"My mother attempted an escape and wrote to me. Lord Frederick thinks I'm scheming with her. And so does Benn—" I paused. "His Highness."

Ulysses lowered his spectacles. "Are you sure?"

"I...no," I said. "But why wouldn't they?"

"Ask them," he said calmly. "Perhaps you will find you're wrong."

He left before I could argue. The soft blankets weighed heavily upon my legs. Why wouldn't they think the worst of me? The citizens of Vandil did. Lady Huntington and Isabelle did. Lord Frederick and Bennett were only being merciful, letting me heal from my injuries before taking me to the dungeons. That was why I was still here.

Misty woke when I finished my meal, meowing in

delight when she saw me awake. She jumped into my lap, rattling the tray. I hugged her to my chest, her presence chasing away all negative thoughts.

You're an idiot. I told you not to go, she said amidst purring.

I kissed her head. "I'm sorry I left you," I whispered.

Misty nuzzled my chin. *We are back together. That is all that matters.*

We chatted a bit after and I finally asked her about her friendship with Pippin, which she willfully refused to elaborate on. It wasn't long before we were interrupted by yet another visitor.

Lord Frederick came in, his steps hesitant. "Are you feeling better, milady?" he asked.

"Better than before," I said. I felt relatively energized from the meal, though everything still ached.

A beat passed before Lord Frederick met my gaze. "What you did was admirable. Those at the witch market say they owe you their lives."

I turned away. He couldn't possibly expect me to accept his compliments. "We both know I only went down for selfish reasons," I said, steeling myself. "What better way to prove I'm not a villain than to barrel straight into a fire like a self-sacrificing hero?"

It sounded worse out loud.

The stool beside my bed creaked as Lord Frederick sat. "Whether it was selfish or selfless does not change the good you have done," he said. "Intentions can evolve indefinitely. Results are concrete, unchangeable."

I gave a dry laugh. "In that case why does it matter if I win the crown prince's heart for nefarious reasons or by chance? Ulysses will be happy and I'll have done my duty either way."

"Because, Lady Narcissa, intention is the soul of an

action. It doesn't always determine whether the result is good or bad, but it establishes character."

"And what if your character is already established for you, Lord Frederick?" I asked, recalling the way he acted after Mother's letter. "If what you say is true, no one can truly understand another's character if they don't reveal their intentions."

Lord Frederick gave me an appraising look. "You're right, milady. Only one can truly understand oneself. But some have lived their whole lives following somebody else's legacy. Whether they choose to continue or break free is entirely up to them."

I was starting to find the conversation rather convoluted.

"Well, Lord Frederick. Am I going to remain engaged to the crown prince or has His Majesty sentenced me to the dungeons?" I said falling back onto my pillows.

He broke into a smile, a twinkle appearing in his eyes. "Seeing that I haven't dragged you off in chains yet, it is the former."

"Why?"

"Why?" He raised his brows. "I meant what I said, milady. I wasn't accusing you of anything that night. And neither was His Highness."

After a beat of silence, Lord Frederick put a weighty hand on my shoulder. "I know what kind of person the former duchess is, Lady Narcissa. You are not to blame," he said firmly. "Not for any of it."

I watched him leave, touched by his kindness. But the warm feelings dispersed quickly. Even if Lord Frederick was convinced of my innocence, I doubted the crown prince was. I struggled to remember how Bennett had reacted that night, but the memories were blurred. I had been too wrapped up in hurt and anger and fear. Fear that Mother would be true to her word and come for me.

The rest of the day was dedicated to more visitors. Giselle, after insisting on switching out my plain pillows for embroidered ones, chatted incessantly about a new riding gown she was sewing. Maddox came back with Flannery, who burst into tears and babbled about how incompetent he was as a guard. After Maddox dragged him away, Prince Ash attempted to read me a book of poetry he had written. I feigned exhaustion to get him to stop.

But as the sky darkened and my eyelids grew heavy, I found myself fighting sleep.

Mayhaps you're waiting for a certain someone? Misty said slyly, making herself comfortable beside me. The flickering candlelight made her dark fur gleam.

"I'm sure the entire manor has visited me at this point," I said.

But the strange, gaping emptiness I felt said otherwise. Was he still down in the witch market?

Misty looked at me knowingly. *He did visit, you know. He was a very tender caretaker during the two days you were unconscious.*

I blew out the candle with more force than necessary, throwing my blanket over my head. "I'd rather be unconscious for twenty days than hear you speak nonsense."

Days at Vandil eventually drew to an end. The guards who had split off to help the witch market returned once workers from Delibera came to replace them. Still, there was no sign of the crown prince.

Pippin, unlike his owner, decided to accompany me during the last day.

It's awful stuffy in here, Pippin said, strolling in through the door.

I folded a chemise and put it in my suitcase. Lady Marianna would be horrified to see me packing my own things, but mundane tasks seemed to calm me more than laying around in bed.

"You're more than welcome to wait outside with Misty," I said, straightening the sheets. The guards were already reassembling the procession for the journey to Alevine, carrying provisions and leading the horses out in the courtyard. Misty had followed, wanting fresh air after so many days of bedrest.

Pippin jumped on top of the bedside table and surveyed the room. *That does sound tempting. But I thought I'd pay you a visit after not seeing you for so long.*

"I'm perfectly fine, as you can see," I said, holding out my arms. I had regained my energy the day before and the cut on my neck had scabbed over nicely. "Now run along. I'm sure Misty will enjoy your company."

Pippin nosed the opera flier that lay discarded beneath him. *Smells like lemons*, he commented, yawning. He padded onto the mattress. *I'll be honest—I am in desperate need of attention. Bennett has been awfully glum lately. He won't even look at me.*

Little did Pippin know we shared the same problem.

I supposed Bennett was busy drafting reports about the situation and helping at the witch market. But others had already taken over the job. He was back to distrusting me, like the past months didn't even happen.

Well, Pippin said crossly, *are you going to pet me?*

I indulged him with a thorough belly rub. Soon after, Lady Marianna came with servants to escort me outside.

"It was lovely having you, dear. Although I wish events could have turned out differently near the end," she said, giving me a rueful smile.

I thanked her earnestly and bid her goodbye, realizing that I would miss her motherly affections. Her attentions hadn't been unlike Lady Vanessa's, if I had bothered to accept the latter.

The courtyard was dark and slick with rain, though some spots were already evaporating in the sunlight. Vandil and Coriva had rather mild weather, but once we reached Alevine, it was sure to grow colder. A few horses nickered as I passed, thanking me for the extra sugar cubes they had received in exchange for their heroism.

When I opened the carriage door, I was surprised to see Maddox, Giselle, Misty, and Pippin crammed inside.

"Has anyone told you how vile you smell?" Giselle asked, scowling as Maddox rearranged his sword.

"Has anyone told you how naggy you are, woman? First you insult my clothing, which by the way, I have no control over, and now—"

"Narcissa! There you are." Giselle held out a hand to help me up.

I seated myself gingerly between Pippin and Misty, who sprung apart at my appearance. "What are you all doing in here?"

"Lord Frederick says the journey to Alevine will take two weeks of traveling," Maddox said. "It'll be better if you had a guard near at all times. Not to mention, Alevine is even more anti-witch than Vandil."

"Is it?" I asked, gathering both cats to my sides.

He nodded. "That's what Ulysses said. It's the furthest from Delibera, so most people there don't care for royalty. You'll have to be extra careful once we arrive."

I raised my brows. "Look who's taking their job seriously." It seemed only yesterday he was complaining about losing his freedom.

Maddox's ears reddened as he struggled to come up with a retort.

Giselle smacked his arm with the glove she was embroidering. "Don't hurt yourself," she said breezily. I wondered when they had a chance to become so familiar. "Anyway, we're here to keep you company. It'll be great fun."

Maddox scoffed. "Assuming you stop nag—Ow!"

24

The crisp winter air and bumpy roads were a welcome change after so many days of bedrest. Maddox and Giselle's bickering did not annoy me as I thought it would, but instead served as entertainment as the hours passed. The full carriage provided an appreciated warmth. Despite traveling toward colder regions, I was not shivering as I had before.

Lord Frederick informed us we would be passing thick expanses of forest for several days, and as a result, would have no choice but to camp outside. "We'll be vulnerable, but we will have plenty of guards on watch," he said. "Nothing will happen if we can help it."

The first few nights of making camp in the forest was as peaceful as could be, my slumber lulled by the soft chatter of forest animals. Despite my initial uneasiness, I let myself relax, which wasn't hard to do with my carriage companions.

On the morning of the second week of traveling, I was surprised by another companion. His presence was not relaxing in the least.

"You're feeling better, I hope?"

Bennett sat with his legs tucked beneath the carriage seat. Pippin was nestled in his lap, as was Misty. I blinked rapidly at the odd sight. I hadn't seen him since…

I pressed my lips together, pushing away the twinge of hurt. "Yes."

He stroked Pippin's back. The tabby was clearly enjoying the attention from his loud purrs. "I hope you don't mind me joining you."

"It's your carriage, Your Highness," I said stiffly, gripping the door.

"Bennett."

My jaw clenched when he met my eye. He avoided me for over a week. Why was he pretending like nothing had happened? Like I still deserved to call him by his name?

Giselle approached before I could demand an explanation. Her eyebrows rose. "Your Highness! Are you in the carriage today?"

He nodded.

The seamstress blew a breath. "Finally!" She sounded exasperated. "Do you want some privacy?"

"That won't be necessary," Bennett said, petting Pippin a little faster.

I recognized the anxious motion all too well.

Maddox opted not to join us, whispering to me with some embarrassment that the crown prince made him nervous. That made both of us, only I didn't have the luxury of leaving.

Giselle took her seat across from Bennett, making a big show of spreading out her belongings so there was no room for me. I shot her a glare as I begrudgingly sat beside him.

Misty hopped onto my lap. *Didn't you want to see your fiancé?* she said, rolling onto her back.

My upper arm brushed against Bennett's as the carriage rattled forward. Then our knees knocked together. Then our elbows. I held back an irritated sigh.

He wanted to see you. He cares, Misty continued, turning over again when I didn't indulge her in a belly rub.

He doesn't and he shouldn't, I thought to her. My nightmare of Mother resurfaced. She had been so real, so solid in the dream. Like she was going to come take me away any moment. Reliving Amarante's servitude was equally gut-churning.

Misty hissed, nudging my thoughts away. *He does.*

I crossed my arms. *You don't know that.*

I do. She blinked slowly. *He said so.*

My hand went to her on instinct, running over her soft fur. *You can't read his thoughts—*

They weren't thoughts. He talked to us.

I stole a glance at Bennett from the corner of my eye. He was looking out the carriage window, his strong profile silhouetted against the white sky. Besides the tabby cat sprawled on his lap, he was the picture of dignified royalty. Him? Talking to cats out loud? I almost snorted.

I appreciate you trying to make me feel better, I thought to Misty, *but nothing has changed. He doesn't trust me and he certainly does not care about me.*

Misty narrowed her eyes. Without warning, she clawed my hand.

I gasped.

The scratch was hard enough to hurt, but light enough not to draw blood. Before I could reprimand her, Bennett turned.

"Are you alright?" he asked. His voice sounded oddly breathless.

My mind blanked, unable to process the pure concern in his hazel eyes as he searched my face.

"I-I'm fine," I managed to say. "Misty was just being... feisty."

Bennett frowned at the red scratch, his expression morphing into one I couldn't quite place. To my utter embarrassment, he raised my hand to his lips and blew on it softly. "Are you sure? Do you need it bandaged?"

My skin tingled at his breath. I yanked my hand away, increasingly aware of Giselle's raised eyebrows and Misty's smug presence. I mumbled my assurance and we fell silent again.

What did I tell you? she meowed.

You are a very bad cat, I thought irritably.

She stretched herself across my lap. *Only for you, darling.*

The rest of the day passed in a similarly uncomfortable manner. Giselle kept winking, either at me or at Bennett. Perhaps it was at both of us. I dozed off in the afternoon and awoke to find my lip rouge smeared across Bennett's shoulder in a garish red streak. Some had transferred to his collar, though I hardly knew how.

I apologized profusely, only to realize that my face was in a similar state when he tried to wipe my cheek with his handkerchief.

When we finally stopped to settle for the evening, Bennett went off to speak to Lord Frederick, whose eyebrows shot up at my rouge on the crown prince's neck. I ducked beneath the window, barely able to contain a moan of mortification.

I didn't know how much more I could take of Bennett's overfamiliar manner. He would have chewed my lunch for me in the afternoon if I allowed it.

"Why is he treating me like…like some sort of invalid?" I asked Giselle.

She looked up from her sewing, raising a brow. "Because," she said, tying off a thread, "you *were* one the last time he saw you. He's used to tending to you now, I reckon."

"He—I…" I struggled for words. The possibility of the crown prince choosing to play nursemaid at my bedside when there was so much reconstruction work to oversee was slim to none. Especially when my injuries were due to my own foolishness.

Giselle held my gaze. "He cares about you, Narcissa," she said simply.

I scoffed, knowing it was fruitless to argue with her.

When night fell and the camp settled, Maddox came with a bundle of bedding in his arms. "If you don't mind," he said, voice muffled by a pillow, "I need to lay out your cot."

I eased down, taking Misty and Pippin with me as Maddox spread the blankets on the seats of the carriage. Lord Frederick claimed the carriage would be more secure than a tent and urged me to stay inside as we got closer to Alevine.

Maddox straightened after patting down the pillow. His spine cracked and he pounded his lower back, wincing. "If you need anything I'll be two feet away."

I put a hand on his shoulder. "Get some rest tonight," I said, giving him a half-smile. "I'd hate to be ordered around if you become bedridden"

He snorted. "I might just to spite you."

My eyes caught Bennett's over Maddox's shoulder. He was looking at us strangely. I hauled myself into the carriage after bidding my brother good night. Misty and Pippin had already settled themselves on the opposite seats.

"Sweet dreams," I said to Misty, giving her a peck on the forehead. Pippin stared at me expectantly. I sighed and gave him the same treatment.

I AWOKE TO a torrent of grainy particles raining down on my face. I sputtered, jerking up.

What is that? Misty jumped onto my chest. She narrowed her eyes as a shadow of a serrated blade bobbed in and out of the ceiling. Three sides of a rectangle had already formed. But despite hacking through wood, the blade made no noise.

I sat up. It was a silent saw. *Magic.* A rioter could very

well be in possession of a witch-made item if it suited their purpose. Whether it was to kill me or kidnap me, I didn't want to find out.

I squeezed myself to a corner, holding the cats close. Fear froze my limbs. I had been in the company of dangerous people before, but I was never their target. The change was paralyzing.

There were four guards in all protecting my carriage. Maddox, Flannery, and the two others, judging from their thunderous snoring, were all asleep. We were placed at the perimeter of the camp, strategically hidden by the underbrush.

But whoever was on top of the carriage had taken advantage of that. They had me in direct target without passing the rest of the guards.

What are you sitting there for? Run! Pippin demanded as the fourth side of the rectangle took form above.

Just as the ceiling came crashing down, I wrenched the door open. But the movement was impeded by something—or rather someone.

"Ow!" Flannery's voice came from the other side.

A figure hovered over the gaping hole in the ceiling, engulfing the carriage in his shadow. I made out dark hair and a stubbled jaw. A large hand swung down to grab me. I dodged, my head knocking into the satchel dangling from his shoulder. It landed with a thump on the carriage floor.

"Intruder!" a guard shouted.

The carriage jerked as the assailant launched himself off. Tree branches rustled as the camp awoke, torches lighting the forest in an eerie orange glow.

Flannery opened the door, eyes wide. He removed a pair of cotton plugs from his ears. "Milady! Are you alright? Why didn't you scream?"

From the way my throat was clenched, screaming was the last thing it wanted to do.

A draft swept in through the top of the carriage. I swung my legs outside and held Misty to my chest. "Did you catch the intruder?" I asked, voice trembling.

Flannery shook his head, letting the cotton fall to the dirt. "We're going now. Stay here, milady. The others will guard you."

Guards from the camp abandoned their cots, scouring the premises for the intruder as Lord Frederick shouted instructions.

Pippin stumbled into my lap, tripping over the satchel. *What an unpleasant way to be woken up*, he said crossly as I gathered him into my arms beside Misty.

I forced my racing heart to calm, though to no avail. Because I was certain that the shadowy attacker was Dominic Turner.

I shivered. Something was horribly wrong with the man. Once I got my hands on him I'd box his ears for having the audacity to invade my privacy time and time again. Did he think he was entitled to my whereabouts because we were once engaged?

I recalled what he had said to me during the ball at Huntington Abbey.

It's not too late to leave all this. I can take you away and make it seem like an accident.

Could he possibly be in cahoots with the rioters? Whatever treasonous secrets he was hiding, I fully intended on weeding them out and throwing him in the dungeons.

I grabbed his fallen satchel and searched its contents. It was nearly empty, save for a flask and a bruised lemon. Stuffed in the corner, however, was a piece of paper. I took it out.

What is that? Pippin asked.

"Another one of those opera fliers," I muttered, turning it over in my hand. But it was the same as the one the farmer had dropped, with no strange markings or anything out of the ordinary.

Do you think that might be where the rioters are meeting? Misty meowed.

"There's only one way to be sure." I furrowed my brow, but before I could think about it further, noise started back up in the camp. Maddox came with Flannery, panting.

"No sign of anyone near the premises," he said between breaths.

Lord Frederick appeared behind him, face grave as he sheathed his sword. "Lady Narcissa, are you alright?"

I nodded. "Yes, but there's something—"

"Narcissa!" Bennett pushed Maddox aside and took my shoulders, wearing little else but a shirt and breeches. "Are you hurt?"

"I-I'm fine."

He pulled me snugly to him, smothering my face into his chest. "Good," he whispered.

Just as abruptly, he let me go. I hardly had time to process the intimacy before Bennett turned to Maddox. "You are supposed to protect her," he said, his voice steely. "Yet a potential assassin managed to *saw a hole* into the carriage and you didn't hear?"

"Your Highness, I—"

He looked down at the cotton plugs Flannery had left on the ground. "Tell me one reason you should stay if you cannot perform your duties properly."

Maddox ducked his head. "I am sorry, Your Highness."

Bennett turned to Lord Frederick. "Have him removed from the Royal Guard. Have them both removed."

Flannery squeaked. "But Your Highness!"

Bennett silenced him with a stony stare. I grabbed his wrist before he could leave. "The saw had a silencing charm on it," I said. "Maddox wasn't on watch when it happened and Flannery is not the only guard in charge of my safety."

Bennett turned away. "Nevertheless, they should have been alert and prepared. The fact that they weren't demonstrates their incompetence."

Maddox seemed to shrink in on himself. Being scolded by Father was one thing, but being reprimanded by the future king of Olderea in front of his commander and colleagues was something else entirely. Poor Flannery had tears running down his cheeks, which were red from trying to keep them in.

I set my jaw. "The entire camp should have been alert and prepared. Are you going to demote them all?"

"If it comes to it."

"You are being unreasonable."

His jaw clenched. "I am *never* unreasonable."

My grip on his wrist tightened, his skin burning hot against my fingers. "Then you're a fool."

Bennett whirled around, his eyes ablaze with unfamiliar fire. "Very well, Lady Narcissa," he said. "If you wish to be in the company of inept guards, that is your choice."

He wrenched himself out of my grasp and marched away.

It never occurred to me that I would be begging on Maddox's behalf, but I found myself doing exactly that the next morning. Lord Frederick barely got a bite of breakfast before I began pleading his case.

"You're going to have to speak to His Highness, milady," Lord Frederick whispered after my fifth attempt. I rode a few paces behind Bennett, whose stiff posture and blank expression betrayed nothing. "He has the final say on these matters."

"Perhaps," I whispered back, "you can decide first and then convince him."

He raised a wiry eyebrow. "Milady, I am not so bold as to bend the crown prince to my will. That job is reserved for those who can call him a fool and suffer no consequences."

My face heated.

Lord Frederick shook his head and increased his pace to match Bennett's. It seemed he was fed up with me. I looked over my shoulder at Maddox and Flannery, trudging beside the ruined carriage. They were both especially grim this morning, and it wasn't only because of the dreary weather.

Where would they go if they were demoted on the spot? They would be left to fend for themselves. The forest path was wet with frost. I counted it as a blessing that it wasn't snowing heavily, thanks to Olderea's mild weather. Maddox and Flannery wouldn't stand a chance against a blizzard.

Misty stuck her head out of the saddlebag. *Have you convinced him yet?*

I shook my head, glaring at Bennett's back. Insufferable man. I couldn't imagine what made him overreact to the point of cutting my brother out of the Royal Guard.

Lord Frederick turned around. "Alevine is just ahead!" he shouted.

The forest had melted away into paved road. About half a mile ahead was the city gate, towering and gray.

Ulysses rode up next to me, eyes shining. "Ah, I simply cannot wait to sleep in a proper bed," he said. The events of last night didn't seem to faze him—perhaps because he managed to sleep through everything.

"How close is Lady Ruan's manor?" I was already tired of riding.

Lady Vivia Ruan was to be our hostess during our stay. She was thrown into wealth in recent years after acquiring some property or other, so I was told.

"Oh, we won't be staying at a manor, Lady Narcissa. She owns and runs the Grand Alevine Opera," the steward said, straightening his necktie.

"Oh," I said, raising my brows. That must be the property. "She lives in the opera house?"

"But of course! It's not *just* an opera house. I heard the living quarters above the theater are phenomenal," Ulysses said.

I studied Cozbi's mane, which had gotten windblown with travels, and thought back to the fliers. Somehow we were staying at the very place I had suspicions about.

You're not going to tell anybody about that? Misty asked.

Not yet. I petted her ears. I figured Lord Frederick was already tired of hearing me speak.

I needed solid evidence first.

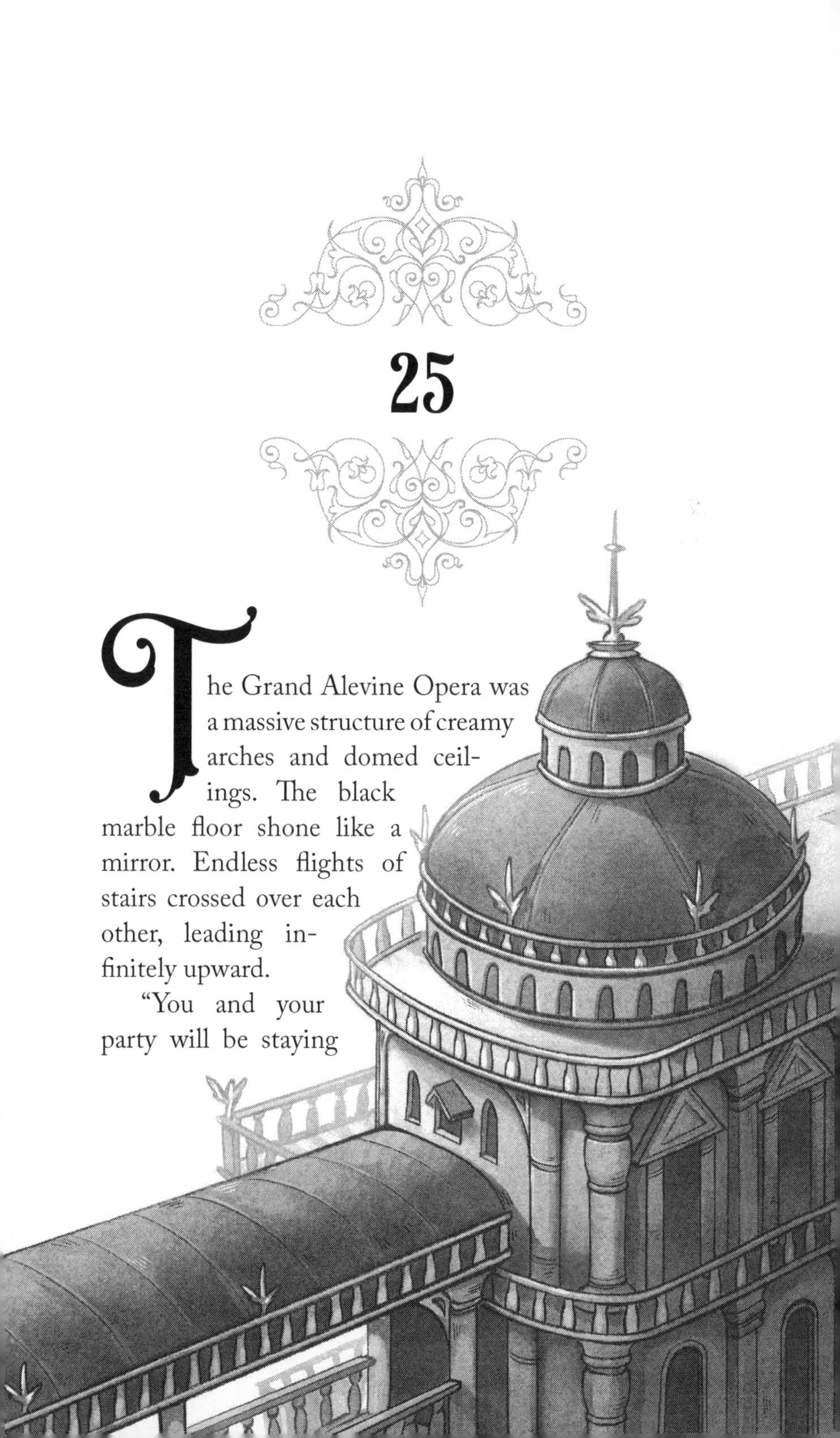

25

The Grand Alevine Opera was a massive structure of creamy arches and domed ceilings. The black marble floor shone like a mirror. Endless flights of stairs crossed over each other, leading infinitely upward.

"You and your party will be staying

on the third level, Your Highness," our hostess said as we hiked up the steps. Lady Ruan was a middle-aged woman with glossy black hair streaked with gray. She had all the formality and elegance of a noblewoman, but it didn't take away from her open amiability. Her brown eyes sparkled with pride when the stairwell opened up to a lavish living area. "Your Highness, Lady Narcissa, here is your suite." She showed us to a luxurious chamber of white and gold.

Bennett frowned. "Are we to share a room?"

Lady Ruan faltered. "Ah, apologies, Your Highness." She offered us a sheepish smile. "If you prefer separate chambers I will have someone prepare another. For now, why don't you both sit down? I'll bring tea."

"Thank you, Lady Ruan," I said.

She departed, as did Lord Frederick and the others. I touched Bennett's arm before he could leave.

He looked at my hand. I detected a hint of surprise before it fizzled out. "What is it?" he asked curtly.

"I need to speak to you."

He took a step back. "I have duties to see to. Perhaps another time."

I flattened my lips and took his wrist, pulling him inside before he could object. There was no sense in letting this drag on.

I seated myself on a plump armchair near the door. The room was flooded with skylight, but I didn't linger on the lavish interior. Bennett rubbed his wrist.

"You are not cutting Maddox and Flannery from the Royal Guard."

"Narcissa, they are not fit for their positions," Bennett said, his voice deceptively calm.

I crossed my arms, peevish. "Do you *ever* raise your voice?"

This seemed to irritate him. He stepped forward, fixing me with his hazel eyes. "Do you always concern yourself with the positions of guards?"

I stood. "What does it matter to you?"

"I am your betrothed. And for you to have gone off with one of them in the middle of the night at Vandil—" Bennett stopped abruptly, his color heightened.

I scrunched my brow, wondering what that had to do with anything. "My brother was helping me that night. He doesn't deserve to be punished for that."

Bennett blinked. "Who?"

"Maddox Greenwood."

"Greenwood?" He looked taken aback. "So he's…not a favorite of yours?"

"Pardon?" I sputtered. My face burned at his insinuation. "You thought I would be *unfaithful* to you?"

My offense seemed to surprise him. Bennett shook his head vehemently. "I—no that's not what I meant," he said. He exhaled. "It's just the two of you seemed close. I…I made assumptions."

I sat back down, reigning in my feelings. His poor opinion of my character was nothing new, after all. But to think I would have favorites among the guards!

"Forget it," I said with as much composure as I could. "We don't have time for this."

Bennett's voice grew quiet. "Time for what, Narcissa? Protecting you?"

Romance. Tender feelings. Ridiculous lovers' spats. He admitted to being jealous of *Maddox* of all people. Wherever this conversation was leading, I didn't want to go.

"I do not need to be protected," I said hotly.

"You are the future princess."

"I've been in danger before. I can handle myself."

He frowned. "Crown princesses do not *handle themselves*. Part of my duty is to care for you and—"

"*Care* for me?" I laughed. What gave him the right to avoid me for weeks, then tend to my scratches and argue for my protection in the next breath? "Is this a performance for the public, like at Vandil? What about after the fire? Where were you then?"

The question hung in the air.

I blushed at the silence that followed. What a fool I was. What right did I have to want his care, especially when I injured myself due to my own selfishness? When I knew he would never choose me over the witches of Vandil?

Bennett finally spoke. "I thought you didn't want to see me because it was my fault you got hurt."

I stilled. "What?"

"Dragging you through the rain for an entire day was irresponsible," Bennett continued. "You were exhausted and feverish. Then Lord Frederick came and I let you run off. I put you in danger when I should have protected you." His eyes strayed to the scar on my neck. "Your mother's letter…I shouldn't have let you read it."

He framed that night as if everything was his fault. But it was *mine*. Wasn't it?

"T-The letter was addressed to me. Of course I had to read it," I said, hardly knowing what else to say.

"You don't have to associate with that woman anymore, Narcissa," he said.

I parted my lips, taken off guard. What was he saying? That he wanted to protect me from Mother?

My heart soared on its own accord, but I reeled it back. Perhaps when I was a child I deserved to be protected, but I had long since passed the age of making my own choices. The things Mother made me do, I did them willingly. I did them because I craved her approval. Now I had to face the consequences.

Bennett ventured closer. "Did she ever hurt you?"

I gripped the armrests. Speaking to him about Mother was the last thing I wanted, especially after what she had done to the queen. It was the ugliest part of our past, the root of everything bad between us.

And he wouldn't understand. How could I explain the raps on my wrist, the cold stares, or the sharp words any more than the affectionate embraces and pretty gifts? The days Mother was happy with me I cherished for too long. The days she was not, I could not forget even if I tried.

"She loved me," I said instead, as if those words encompassed all. In a way, they did. I tucked my hands under my elbows. "In her own way. But…not anymore."

Or perhaps she still did. Her elation through the letter was evident. It wasn't difficult to imagine her back beside me, praising my progress and kissing my hair.

"Narcissa."

"I told you I am fine." I sounded like a stubborn child, but I didn't care. I shouldn't have dragged him inside to talk. I was more confused than I had been before. And he still seemed intent on firing my guards. "Don't you have duties to see to?"

Bennett grabbed my hands, his expression earnest and confused at once. It was the look he had given me all of yesterday.

I sucked in a breath. "What are you—"

My annoyance snuffed out, along with all thoughts of Mother and guards, when he jerked forward and pressed a soft kiss to my forehead. The gesture was achingly tender. I tipped my head back in surprise.

I recognized the feeling. He had done the same when I

was unconscious. While he was…heavens. He *had* tended to me.

It was fortunate I was sitting, otherwise I would have melted into a puddle beneath his warm eyes. They widened, as if he had surprised himself. My gaze fell to his lips.

Bennett pulled away abruptly, stumbling over a ridge in the carpet. "Apologies. I—excuse me."

I flushed as he gave an uncharacteristically awkward bow. He fled to the door, but before he could make his escape, Ulysses appeared.

"Your Highness! Am I interrupting?" the steward asked.

"I was about to mail my reports," Bennett said quickly.

"I see." Ulysses cleared his throat and glanced between us. "A letter came from His Majesty, and…well. Read for yourself."

Ulysses held out a cream envelope. Bennett took it and scanned the contents. The embarrassment on his face gave way to something more serious. A beat later, he stuffed the letter into his coat pocket.

"So Father disapproves of the hearings in Vandil," Bennett stated. "All the more reason to mail my reports."

Ulysses sputtered. "Wait. Your Highness. There's something else you should know—"

The steward barely took a breath before Bennett left. Ulysses looked from me to the hallway until finally scrambling after the crown prince, coat flying.

My forehead was still damp and tingling by the time Lady Ruan came with tea. "Where is Crown Prince Bennett?" she asked, looking around the suite.

I wiped his kiss away with the back of my hand. A sinking feeling settled in my stomach. I didn't dare identify it. "He left for errands."

"Ah, what a shame. I was about to propose a tour," Lady Ruan said. "I suppose we can postpone it until he returns. Celeste was looking forward to meeting you."

"Celeste? As in Celeste Carr?" I said.

She brightened. "So you've heard of her! She would be thrilled to know."

I scrambled at the chance to distract myself. Rising soprano Celeste Carr. This could be my chance to see if she was connected to the rebels.

"Wait!" I said as Lady Ruan was about to leave. "Perhaps you could still give me the tour? I'm sure Bennett wouldn't mind."

Lady Ruan paused. "Well, alright. I suppose I can show you the auditorium and backstage," she said, smiling. "I'll be back to get you in ten minutes. Bring some friends along, if you wish."

Once Lady Ruan left, I scoured the floor for Giselle. She was the only one I could think of who would want to go with me.

I eventually found the seamstress kneeling in an outdoor hallway with stone arches overlooking the city. Another figure sat beside her.

"Maddox?" I turned my collar up as I approached the pair.

Maddox looked up glumly, his eyes bloodshot. Pippin was curled up in his arms. The tabby enjoyed attention from everyone, it seemed. "So? Did His Highness decide to remove me after all?" His voice was a croak as if he had been crying the entire night.

Giselle stood and handed Misty to me. "He's been like this all day," she whispered. "You better have good news."

I shifted Misty onto my shoulder and told them that

Bennett hadn't made a decision. "He left before I could convince him," I lied. I hoped the cold was enough to excuse my flushed cheeks.

Maddox groaned and hugged Pippin to his chest, burying his face into his fur.

Giselle sighed. "You should have kissed him. That would've changed his mind."

I knelt before Maddox. "Everything will be fine. And if you do get removed from the Royal Guard, I will tell Father it was for unfair reasons."

"It won't matter to him," Maddox said, his voice muffled by Pippin's fur. "I'll still be a failure. He's coming here, did you know? With King Maximus."

"The king is coming?" I asked, surprised.

Giselle squatted beside me. "King Maximus is paying a surprise visit to see how we're doing, since this is the last stop of the tour. The whole procession knows but..." She paused. "Rats. I don't think I was supposed to tell you that."

"I'm going to get a scolding and then he's going to disown me," Maddox said. A sob tore out of his throat.

I bit my cheek, not entirely sure how to proceed. He had never been in such a state before and I had little experience in comforting people. "Do you two want to join me for a tour of the opera house?"

Giselle heartily agreed and dragged Maddox to his feet, though he looked like he wanted nothing more than to crawl into a hole. After some cajoling, I managed to get him to wipe his face and hand Pippin over to Giselle.

We met Lady Ruan at the stairs. She seemed surprised at my choice of company, including the two cats, but proceeded with the tour graciously.

"You have already seen these grand steps, of course," Lady Ruan said as we descended the endless flights of stairs, "but the real star of the show is the auditorium."

She was right. The auditorium had rows upon rows of velvet seats and a high, domed ceiling from which a magnificent crystal chandelier hung. The stage was framed by yards of royal purple velvet, drawn open to expose a painted background of a starry night. Stagehands hauled a heavy wooden board in the shape of a crescent moon across the stage. Behind them, a swath of painted clouds were suspended on cables.

Giselle gave a low whistle. Even Maddox forgot to look miserable.

"A peek at tomorrow's show," Lady Ruan said with a wink. "It is Celeste's opening night after a month break. We expect to have a full auditorium for the rest of the week. And bless her heart, she decided to give the witches of Alevine free entry for one of her performances."

I shifted Misty's weight to my other arm. It was an odd thing, after hearing so many human businesses complain about witches. Why would the Grand Alevine Opera allow them to see a show free of charge?

"Will you not lose money?" I asked.

"Celeste is willing to cover the costs herself," Lady Ruan said. "She's quite sympathetic to witchkind. And with all the unrest..." She trailed off and shook her head. "Forgive me, Lady Narcissa. I did not mean to bring up these matters."

"No need to apologize. We are here to address them."

Giselle looked around with interest. "Are we invited to the show?"

Lady Ruan returned to her previous cheer. "But of course! You'll be our honored guests."

"Think of all the evening gowns," the seamstress said dreamily. She set Pippin on the floor. "Excuse me, this has been nice, but I have some projects in mind I would like to get a start on."

Giselle flounced away to the hall. "Oh, hello Your Highness!"

Moments later Bennett appeared, nose and cheeks flushed from the cold. Ulysses followed behind him, panting.

"Your Highness!" Lady Ruan said, "I was just showing Lady Narcissa around. We're going backstage to see Celeste, our newest singer. Would you like to join us?"

"Of course. Carry on." Bennett gave a brief nod to Maddox, then turned his eyes to me. I couldn't discern the look in them. All I could think about was his kiss.

I dug my nails into my palms as we followed Lady Ruan down the carpeted aisle. As we ascended a short flight of stairs, I tapped Ulysses's shoulder.

"Yes, milady?" The steward wiped his nose with his handkerchief.

I gripped the railing. "Apologies. Where did you go with Bennett just now?" I whispered.

Ulysses sneezed, then gave me a watery-eyed look. "The post office and...bah. You'll find out soon enough," he said with a sigh. He blew his nose again and trotted to catch up with the others.

Backstage was almost as impressive as the front, though in a rustic, chaotic sort of way. Masses of rope and cord hung from high wooden beams just below the ceiling. Lady Ruan led us through a narrow passageway into a separate hall.

"I hope she's still here," she said, turning to a painted red door. She knocked twice. "Celeste? Are you in there, dear?"

"Yes, come in," a husky voice said.

We entered. A young woman sat swathed in pale blue satin before a cluttered vanity, her glossy dark hair hanging loose down her back. Her eyes widened.

"Your Highness, Lady Narcissa," Celeste said, executing a graceful curtsy. She turned to Lady Ruan. "My, if I had known you'd come with distinguished guests I would have tidied up." Her smile moved the beauty mark on her cheekbone. I was impressed by how much she resembled her likeness on the flier.

"It's no trouble," I said.

"What lovely kitties you have!" she exclaimed, reaching out. Misty hissed at her gloved hand. Pippin hid behind Bennett's legs.

"I'm sorry. They're nervous around strangers." I looked at Pippin oddly. I expected Misty to be prickly, but not Pippin.

"Don't be." Celeste recovered with a smile and gestured to the sitting area across the room. It was furnished elegantly, though much was drowned beneath a collection of frilly pillows. "Come, everyone, sit! It is such a pleasure to welcome the future rulers of Olderea. I'm sure touring the kingdom has been quite delightful."

I studied her as we all took a seat. The singer was delicately beautiful, save for the fake beauty mark that stood out in contrast to her skin. Nothing looked suspicious in her room, but I couldn't be sure with how cluttered it was.

"Thank you, Miss Carr. I can think of no better place than the Grand Alevine Opera to conclude our tour," Bennett said, placing his hand over mine.

I jumped. I barely registered that he had taken a seat next to me. "Neither can I," I managed to say, covering my surprise with a smile. "It is the gem of the city, as far as I can tell."

This was another act for appearances, surely. Though why he chose *now* to make an effort was beyond me. I shifted Misty onto my lap as an excuse to remove my hand from his.

Lady Ruan laughed. "Oh, I'm honored, though the real gem here is Celeste."

The singer pushed the older woman playfully. "You flatter me, Lady Ruan," she said, tossing her silken hair behind her shoulders. "I would love for you to come and see my performance tomorrow night, Lady Narcissa, Your Highness. I'll be starring in *Ode to the Moon*. Have you heard of it?"

I stroked Misty's back. "I'm afraid I haven't."

Celeste reclined dramatically in her seat, looking every bit like the actress she was. "It's a recent composition. I find the story so romantic. A lunar goddess falls in love with a mortal king, only to be shunned as a nefarious succubus by his people. Her grief is so great it takes her life, but her spirit returns to the moon."

Bennett nodded slowly. "That sounds...pleasant. We'll be there."

Lady Ruan clapped her hands. "Perfect! I'll reserve your seats tonight. I've only seen the rehearsals, but it is absolutely phenomenal. Celeste has the most wonderful voice," she said. "Guests have been swarming the opera house since she arrived."

After chatting a little longer about opera, we left Celeste to rest. The singer seemed kind enough, and according to Lady Ruan, had a philanthropic view toward witches.

Soon after, Lady Ruan ended the tour, claiming that there was nothing interesting left to see besides storage rooms and stagehands' quarters.

"It's getting late, but if you wish for an in-depth tour, I'll be glad to give one in the near future," Lady Ruan said. She bid us a good evening and informed us that supper will be brought to our rooms.

Bennett didn't split off with the others once we hiked up the stairs. The darkening hallway was empty, save for Misty and Pippin. It was with growing dread that I realized no one had arranged a separate room for us. He seemed to catch on.

"Stay," he said abruptly when I opened my mouth. "I'll find someone to prepare another room."

I nodded. Bennett stuffed a hand into his coat pocket and shifted on his feet.

I cleared my throat. "Is something—?"

"I've always been awful at this."

"What?"

Bennett removed his hand from his pocket. His mouth opened, but no sound came out. Then, "May I take Pippin?"

I gave an awkward laugh. "Of course. He's your cat."

Bennett knelt and gathered the tabby cat into his arms. He didn't sling Pippin over his shoulder like he used to. He bowed quickly. "Good night."

Misty mewed when he left. *He's acting strangely, don't you think?*

I passed a hand over my face. "When is he not?"

26

A dainty gold chain lay in its velvet box, sparkling with rose-cut emeralds and miniature pearl drops. Matching earrings rested in the center. I marveled at the intricacy of the set, but it was nothing compared to the note that came with it.

For you. —Bennett

I never knew three words could addle me so much.

"Incredible. Men usually have horrendous taste in jewelry," Giselle said after the maid who delivered it scampered off. "And it matches the dress I made for you for tonight! This is perfect!"

Misty sniffed the jewels. *Completely inedible. How disappointing.*

Giselle helped me into the gown she had made for the viewing of *Ode to the Moon*—an exquisite emerald number with a slight train. The fabric was rich and mesmerizing, hugging my waist and exposing a daring expanse of skin. I hadn't worn anything quite so ravishing in ages, but I felt comfortable, as I did in all of Giselle's creations.

The seamstress sat me down before the vanity and fastened the necklace around my neck.

I put the earrings on hesitantly, touching the cool gems at my throat. "Isn't this a little much?"

High society always made it a point to adorn themselves extravagantly for opera nights. I've donned my fair share of outrageous pieces, but somehow dripping in the crown prince's jewels felt even more outrageous.

First he kissed me. Now he was sending lavish gifts. Those actions spoke more than mere concern for my person. I was almost afraid to acknowledge what was happening.

Giselle took my shoulders. "Don't be silly. You look perfect except..." She squinted at our reflection and snorted at the smudge of rouge on my chin.

I rubbed it away, embarrassed. The color seemed to end up everywhere no matter how careful I was.

"Not to worry, I have a solution," Giselle said, taking the powder puff from my vanity. She lightly tapped it over my mouth. "There. That ought to keep it in place."

I ran my finger over my bottom lip. "Really?"

She waggled her brows. "Maybe Bennett can help you find out."

"Giselle!" I stood up. A fierce blush burned my cheeks.

She pushed me back down. "Hold on. Just one more thing." She took two pearl combs from the drawers and began to twist my hair up.

I covered the back of my neck on instinct. "Wait, I—"

"Don't be shy now. You have a lovely neck."

I surveyed the scar that marred my throat. The wound had closed, but the scab had yet to fade. The gold of my witch traits speckled the back of my neck. I had never shown it to anyone willingly. The combination was surely a garish sight.

"I'm going to take this out once you leave," I said bluntly.

"Ah, then I won't leave. I'll escort you to the auditorium myself. Feel free to disassemble your coiffure when it's dark, but not before your fiancé sees you."

My ears heated. "Has anyone told you how domineering you are?"

Giselle tugged on a curl. "Yes. Your brother."

As if he had been summoned, Maddox burst through the door. "I'm still employed!" he crowed, practically skipping inside. "And my wages have *doubled*."

I stood, ignoring Giselle's protestations. "What?"

"Thank you, Cissa." Maddox pulled me into a bone-crushing hug and danced out the room. "You're the best sister ever!"

THE AUDITORIUM WAS abuzz with chatter when I arrived. Lady Ruan arranged for us to be on the third level, directly across the stage and equally as visible to the audience. It was no surprise that the entrance to our box was crowded with guests.

Ulysses stood in the midst of them, politely denying entry. "The crown prince would like some privacy, gentlemen. Er, madam, please put down that spyglass."

Giselle managed to slip me and Misty past the thickening crowd.

"There's the witch princess," someone whispered.

"What is that on her neck?"

We ducked through the curtains.

Giselle gave a low whistle, glancing back at the rabble. "Not a subtle group, are they?" She made a face when she saw me clutching Misty to my chest like my life depended on it. "Narcissa! Don't try to shield my work of art with a cat."

Misty hissed. *I* am *the work of art.* She jumped to the floor.

I covered the back of my neck. "This can't be wise," I said, peering at the opera-goers between the curtains. They looked as upset as the Vandil crowd did. If Alevine was as anti-witch as Ulysses claimed, the blatant exposure of my witch traits would only rile them.

"They'll have to accept they have an herbwitch princess sooner or later," Giselle said firmly.

"What if they don't?"

Giselle's expression softened. "They will," she said, squeezing my hand. "Now, I'm going to see if there's a smithy somewhere. I've lost my smoothing iron and all my skirts are horribly wrinkled."

"You're not staying?" I asked, slightly panicked. Without Giselle, I'd be the only witch present.

She merely gave a coy wave and disappeared behind the curtains. I sighed and picked Misty back up.

"Narcissa. You're here."

I whirled around.

Bennett stood stiffly beside the seats, his gaze sweeping over me. I tucked a stray curl behind my ear, unsure of what to make of his expression.

"You didn't discharge my guards," I said after a beat.

"You were right. I was being a fool."

"I didn't mean to insult you, I was just—"

"It's fine." Bennett cleared his throat. "You...you look good."

Misty squirmed out of my arms again. *I think I hear some mice in that corner.* She darted to the far end of the box.

"You as well," I choked out, taking a seat. It wasn't a lie. He looked devastatingly handsome in his suit of black and white. Giselle had sewn slivers of emerald silk along his cuffs and lapels.

Bennett rubbed a hand over his face—though it did little to conceal his reddening cheeks. He sat down beside me.

"Thank you. For the jewelry," I said. Silence seemed worse than awkward conversation.

"Do you like it?" He turned to me eagerly.

I was startled by the light in his eyes. And the way my breath caught in response. I nodded.

"Perfect. Green suits you."

I dipped my head—my poor attempt at concealing *my* reddening cheeks.

Bennett cleared his throat. "I originally wanted to go to the aviary but Ulysses convinced me otherwise."

"The aviary? Whatever for?"

"Er...you like animals, yes? I thought a bird would—never mind. T-the necklace...you look lovely," Bennett finished lamely.

I blushed.

Thankfully for both of us, the lights dimmed and the murmuring quieted. The show was starting. Misty meandered back to my feet. Perhaps it was best that Bennett's gift wasn't edible for my cat.

Is he done whispering sweet nothings?

I shot her a glare. *He was not whispering sweet nothings.*

She made herself comfortable on the plush carpet. *Sure.*

He was only being friendly, I thought to her fiercely.

Bennett took my hand and slipped something cool onto my finger. It was an emerald ring, glittering in the dim light, the impressive stone surrounded by luminous seed pearls.

"Good. It fits," Bennett whispered. His breath tickled my ear.

I swallowed. "You didn't have to."

I made a move to pull away, but Bennett closed his fingers around mine. He seemed emboldened by the darkness. "I wanted to send it with the others, but I thought it best to give it to you myself," he said softly.

My appreciation for the dimmed lights increased tenfold. I was sure my face was the same shade as my hair.

Oh yes. Very *friendly*, Misty said wryly.

"You...didn't run off to get this yesterday, did you?" I asked, turning to him.

That was a mistake. Bennett was much closer than I anticipated. He merely smiled—*smiled*. "It was a worthy errand."

The orchestra began playing a lilting overture. "I'm afraid Ulysses did not think so."

"Let's not talk about Ulysses," he murmured.

The curtains lifted slowly from the stage. I gently tugged my hand out of his. "The show is starting."

But Bennett's eyes were still on me. I took a pair of opera glasses from the stand beside us and shoved it in his hands, babbling something about having a better view.

I grabbed Misty from the ground despite her protests and tucked her over my shoulder, shielding my face with her fur. Anything to get his eyes off me. I didn't think I could take another smile without doing something very unwise. Like kiss him senseless.

Misty pawed at my collarbones. *You're suffocating me.*

Just one more minute, I pleaded.

She mewed in exasperation. *Perhaps he was a little* too *friendly*.

The curtains drew back fully, exposing a bright stage. It displayed the celestial scene we had seen yesterday, but now flooded with intense limelight. On top of the giant painted moon sat Celeste, swathed in a glittering blue robe that trailed to the stage floor. The clouds behind her floated along the suspension wires.

She opened her mouth and sang.

Her voice was high and sweet, yet resonant. She sang about loneliness, longing, curiosity for the world below. The orchestra rose and fell like waves with her song.

The audience was enraptured. It was nothing like traditional opera that at times pierced one's ears. Celeste's voice was softer. Melodious. Entrancing.

The composition played out within the span of two hours, the intermission brief. The moon goddess descended to the earth and fell in love with a human king. He showed her the wonders of his kingdom, but it wasn't long before his scheming concubine spread the rumor of the goddess being a wicked succubus. The citizens drove her away to a desolate desert. It was there she died, abandoned by her love. In the finale, Celeste, dressed in shimmering white, returned to the moon, concluding the story.

Applause roared within the auditorium when she took her final bow. The curtains fell. The room filled with warm candlelight once again.

"Well, that was simply phenomenal!"

I turned to see Ulysses behind us. "When did you come in, Ulysses?"

"Oh, just a few minutes after the opera started." The steward polished his spectacles and gestured to the curtains.

"We ought to slip off before the crowd thickens. Your Highness, Lady Narcissa?"

An unexpected dizziness came over me when I stood. I steadied myself against the railing and rubbed my temple.

Bennett took my arm. "Are you alright?"

Misty meowed in concern. I shook my head. "A passing headache. It's nothing."

He pressed a hand against my forehead and cheeks, his palm large and warm. "We shouldn't have left Vandil so soon."

Embarrassed, I pulled away. "I'm fine."

Ulysses cleared his throat. "Perhaps Lady Narcissa will benefit from early rest. Shall we go?"

Bennett didn't look convinced, but followed us out nonetheless. Several guests were already outside, but one look from the steward prevented anyone from approaching. Unfortunately, it didn't stop them from speaking.

"Did you see her?" a middle-aged woman whispered behind a feathered fan.

Her companion nodded. "She has bewitched the crown prince, that is certain. He barely looked at the stage twice!"

"What sort of witchcraft do you suppose she was using?"

Bennett frowned at the two women. They scrambled into curtsies.

"Your Highness!" The woman with the fan gave a nervous giggle. "Did you enjoy the show?"

Bennett merely took my hand and brushed past them, his strides longer than usual. I had to trot to keep up. Ulysses opened his mouth and rushed after us in the open hallway.

"Your Highness! That was Dame Fiona Powell of—"

"I don't care who she was, Ulysses. They all should know not to blatantly disrespect royalty," the crown prince said as we hiked up the steps.

Ulysses's shoes squeaked against the marble. "Of course, Your Highness, but it is of utmost importance to keep good relations with families of power, especially here in Alevine!"

The steward was right. The point of the tour was to uphold the image of the royal family. Bennett had his fair share of gossip surrounding him as evidenced by Sister Scarlett's column, but never had he behaved so brashly. What had gotten into him?

"We should apologize." I stopped, nearly bumping into Misty.

Bennett paused a few steps above me, his hand still holding mine. "You need to rest."

"But Ulysses is right."

He turned and sighed, closing his eyes briefly. "I will handle it." His gaze dipped to my scar. "Take care of yourself."

He kissed my fingertips with painful gentleness, then let go. Ulysses looked between us with an unreadable expression before sighing.

"Rest up, Lady Narcissa. Tomorrow will be a big day."

27

"Father is here!"

I had just finished my toilette when Maddox burst into my room, face flushed from the cold. Misty yowled and dove under the mattress.

"What? So soon?" I fished her out, attempting to calm her.

That was what Ulysses meant when he mentioned a big day. I had forgotten about the king's impromptu visit. Did he ever tell Bennett?

Maddox bent over my vanity mirror, smoothing stray hairs back into his ponytail and straightening his uniform. His sword knocked against a stool, toppling it to the floor. "How do I look?" he asked, splaying his arms out. The bottles on the table rattled.

"Fine," I said flatly, righting the stool. "What has you so nervous?"

"Didn't I just tell you? Father is here."

I let a disgruntled Misty onto the windowsill and put

my hands on my hips. "You'll be fine. You're still a guard. And I said I'll speak for you if he's unsatisfied."

Maddox nodded, but his posture was still stiff. "Let's go then. I'm here to escort you outside to meet Fa—I mean His Majesty."

"Oh." Of course. Maddox wasn't the only one who had reason to be nervous. I had to face King Maximus, who hopefully would be happy with how the tour had progressed. If not, I doubt Maddox could talk him out of his dissatisfaction.

I went over to the window to stroke Misty's head. "Stay here for now. I'll be back soon."

I followed Maddox outside the opera house, where Lady Ruan was already present, along with Bennett, Ulysses, and Lord Frederick. King Maximus rode forth on his steed, a small procession behind him. Father was beside him in full uniform. A pang of homesickness hit me, taking me by surprise. Since when had I considered Greenwood Abbey home?

Maddox stopped behind me as I took my place beside Bennett. He wore a gray coat, a contrast to his usual rich colors.

"How are you feeling, Narcissa?" he asked softly.

"Fine, thank you." I blushed at the memory of our interaction the other night, though a gust of icy wind cooled my cheeks instantly. The procession approached. "Did you know King Maximus was coming?"

Bennett shook his head. "I should have. He rarely lets me handle things myself," he muttered. He furrowed his brow when I shivered at another gust of wind. "You're cold."

"I'm not," I lied. I should have layered on an extra petticoat.

Something warm and heavy weighed down my shoulders. I looked up to see Bennett without his greatcoat, but there was no time to protest. King Maximus dismounted and strode toward us. Father followed him, the picture of a loyal guard.

"Bennett, Narcissa. Good to see you two alive and well," His Majesty said.

I curtsied. Father's beard had grown longer since I saw him last.

"Father." Bennett dipped his head. "How was your trip?"

"No one attempted an assassination if that's what you mean," King Maximus said. He surveyed us beneath his heavy brow. "We have much to talk about. Maverick, you would like to reunite with your children, no doubt. We'll meet inside."

Ulysses and Bennett followed him up the steps.

Father's formal demeanor seemed to melt in the king's absence. He broke into a smile and pulled me into a hug that swept me off my feet. I let out a startled laugh.

"I've missed you, Cissa!" He put me down to clap Maddox on the shoulder. "And you as well, Maddox."

My brother's eyes shone, but he couldn't seem to muster any words.

"Maddox has been a great guard," I said quickly.

Father raised his brows. "Has he?"

Maddox remained wide-eyed and silent.

I coughed. "Bennett doubled his wages."

Father's brows rose even higher as he took in the coat around my shoulders. "Bennett?"

"Um…" I found myself tongue-tied. Luckily, I was saved from speaking when someone else approached, her blond hair barely concealed by a petal pink cloak.

"Mother!" Maddox's voice returned. He ran forward to embrace her, laughing in delight. "What are you doing here?"

Lady Vanessa held his face between her hands. "I couldn't resist coming to see you," she said. She turned to me. "Narcissa! Are you well? I read about what happened at Vandil!"

Father grunted at the mention of the fire. I figured he was holding back on a scolding.

I fidgeted. "I-It turned out all right in the end," I managed. "And you, Lady Vanessa?"

"Perfectly well, dear." She smiled softly. A few months ago I would have looked away. But now, her presence felt welcome. Comforting, even.

The four of us managed to have a pleasant conversation without either Father or Maddox exploding. Eventually, the cold was too much to bear and Father didn't dare to make His Majesty wait any longer. We joined King Maximus and Bennett inside the opera house before the grand steps.

"I haven't step foot here since I was a boy," King Maximus said, his voice echoing in the hall.

Lady Ruan smiled. "I'm sure much has changed, Your Majesty. Would you be interested in a tour?"

King Maximus nodded slowly. "I suppose there's time. We can discuss kingdom matters tonight."

A meow came from the left. Pippin strode out from beneath the stairs, his ginger fur disheveled, dragging a rat half his size along the marble floor.

Lady Ruan pressed a hand over her mouth.

"Are there strays roaming the opera house now?" His Majesty asked, looking down at the tabby in disgust. Bennett took a step back as Pippin laid the carcass at his feet.

Pippin! This is hardly the time, I thought to him.

What? Is a cat not allowed to bring his master food anymore? Pippin said, peering up innocently.

He's the crown prince. He has plenty of food. I said, covering my nose when I caught a whiff of the rat. *Where did you get that? The sewers?*

Yes, in fact, I did, Pippin meowed. *You should see them. They're enormous.*

"Lady Narcissa, is this your cat?" King Maximus asked.

I realized everyone was watching me having a silent conversation with Pippin. I cleared my throat. "He's the crown prince's."

The king frowned. "Bennett does not have a cat."

Bennett stiffened. "A recent acquisition," he said, so quickly that his words slurred together. "Did Lady Ruan mention another tour?"

Lady Ruan once again showed us the auditorium, the hallways, and the back rooms of the various singers and actors, and the third floor where the living quarters were. Eventually, after King Maximus expressed interest, Lady Ruan led us back down to the auditorium to take a closer look backstage.

"We just had our rigging system redone," Lady Ruan said. "Hopefully it'll be finished by tomorrow." We craned our necks to see a few men above, standing on crisscrossing wooden beams and a myriad of wires.

Bennett lingered behind to stare at them for a little longer as the rest of us followed Lady Ruan further backstage.

"And here are the fliers Celeste signed," Lady Ruan said, pointing to a nook where a small desk sat piled with papers.

The very same fliers I found in Dominic's bag and the farmer's pocket. "Isn't the illustration just lovely? It's a favorite among the audience–we had to print so many!"

A stagehand rushed past us, arms laden with a wooden set piece. A corner knocked into my shoulder. I stumbled back, steadying myself against the desk. A few fliers rained to the floor.

Father furrowed his brow. "Cissa, are you hurt?"

Before I could respond, Bennett rushed to me.

"Narcissa!" he said, grabbing my wrist. "Are you injured? Where does it hurt?"

I blushed. "I'm fine. I promise." It felt like the billionth time he had asked about my well-being.

"No need to raise your voice, Bennett," King Maximus said, raising a brow. "Lady Narcissa has not been impaled."

Bennett released my wrist.

"Apologies, milady." The stagehand who bumped into me bobbed a shallow bow, wringing his hands.

I inclined my head.

Lady Ruan frowned. "Patrick, you really ought to watch where you're going!" She ushered the youth behind the curtains, no doubt to give him a good scolding.

Pippin rolled onto the pile of fliers carpeting the floor. *It smells like a lemon grove*, he said.

One caught my eye. It had a wet spot. I picked it up. The scent of lemons wafted to my nose. I frowned, turning it over. Why would there be lemon juice on the fliers? The mark looked deliberate, a trail of liquid forming into something that resembled a letter. But the rest had dried, indiscernible.

King Maximus rubbed his face. "I'll take my leave. I am tired."

Lady Ruan rushed out from behind the curtain. "Of

course, Your Majesty. I will have a meal sent to your suite as soon as possible."

King Maximus nodded. He motioned for Father to follow as he left.

"Settle down first, my dear," Father said to Lady Vanessa. Turning to me and Maddox, he smiled. "I'll see you two soon."

The group scattered, but I stood, puzzled, as I held the flier. Bennett rested a hand on my arm. I turned to him.

"There...might be something going on here," I said.

Bennett searched my face. "You think so too?"

I blinked in surprise. "Yes."

His expression turned serious. "Come. We can discuss this elsewhere." He looked down at the tabby cat rolling in the fliers. "You too, Pippin."

28

I laid out the opera fliers side by side. The first from the farmer, which was creased and covered in soot. The second from Dominic's satchel, and finally, the third I had taken from backstage. I sunk my fingers into the carpet. We were in the middle of the floor in my chambers, Bennett crouched across from me. He studied them, brows furrowed.

"Both attackers had these on their person," I said. "I had a feeling the opera house is connected to the rioters in some way."

"It's fitting to call them rebels at this point," Bennett said quietly. "Do you remember the Winter Solstice Ball?"

I nodded.

"The rigging system backstage is identical to the one fashioned above the ballroom, down to the color of the wood and the thickness of the wires. It could be a coincidence, but I highly doubt it."

I nodded. Olderea didn't have many opera houses, the

Grand Alevine Opera being the only one in comfortable proximity to Delibera.

I pushed the third flier to Bennett. "There's something else too. Pippin said they smelled of lemons. This had a lemon juice stain on it earlier."

Bennett held the flier to his nose and regarded it for a moment. He did the same for the others, coughing after the sooty one. "I can't smell anything on the other two."

Pippin shoved his head beneath my arm and nosed them. *I still can*, he meowed.

"Pippin can," I said, pulling him onto my lap.

Bennett smiled and scratched the tabby behind the ears. I still hadn't gotten used to the sight of his mouth curved upward. He cleared his throat, wetting his lips when he caught me staring. "So you found the second flier on the assailant in the forest?"

"Yes." I took a breath. "I think...I think he was Dominic Turner."

Bennett straightened. "Are you certain?"

I wrung my fingers and told him what Dominic said to me during the Huntington Abbey ball, and how he tested me with the garter snake. Bennett's brow furrowed.

"That is a severe overstep indeed. I wish you told me sooner," he said, frowning. "What made him so certain you aren't a witch?"

"We were engaged once," I muttered. "He doesn't believe—"

"You were engaged to him?"

"It only lasted a month," I said quickly. "We weren't close."

I hardly knew why I had to explain myself when the arrangement had long dissolved, but the crease between Bennett's brows disappeared.

"If he is rubbing elbows with rebels, I'm afraid this involves more people than I would like," Bennett said, looking out the window.

"General Turner?"

"I sincerely hope not." He sat back on his heels and exhaled as if he had a burden the size of a kingdom on his shoulders. I suppose as the crown prince, he did.

"We should tell King Maximus."

Bennett nodded. "One more thing. Where is Giselle?"

The seamstress came immediately when summoned. She flicked her eyes between us. "What do you need, Your Highness?"

Bennett stood, brushing off his breeches. "A smoothing iron. Do you have one?"

She perked up. "I bought one yesterday! Wait here." Giselle ran off to her room and came back with a hefty hunk of iron, the base shaped like a rounded arrow. She held it away from her, a wad of cloth wrapped around her hand. "Just heated it. What do you need to press?"

Bennett splayed the third flier onto my vanity and took the iron, laying it over the back of the paper. As he moved it slowly across, thick brown stains appeared in the shape of letters and numbers.

12:30 AM. SEWERS. 2L, 4R, 1L

Giselle gaped.

"How?" I managed to say.

"Lemon juice can be used as invisible ink. It won't appear unless heat is applied," Bennett said. He colored under our incredulous gazes. "It's something I learned from a previous case."

He gave the same treatment to the other two fliers.

1:30 AM. ROOF. 3L, 2R

12 AM. SEWERS. 4L, 5R, 2L

"Meeting times and directions," I said. I turned the fliers over, trailing my finger down to the dates of the shows printed on the bottom. "And those are the dates. There's one tomorrow night."

If Celeste was writing these, it meant she was a rioter. Her concern over witches was false, as I had expected.

Giselle pressed a hand over her mouth. "Does that mean what I think it means?"

Bennett looked grim. "Rebellion."

"What?" King Maximus stood and slammed his hands on his desk, face growing cherry red. "Rebels are meeting here? In my presence?"

We went to the king immediately after our discovery. He was understandably upset as we had interrupted his meal, but news of a rebel gathering ended up being more important than roasted chicken and pear soup.

"I don't believe they anticipated your arrival, Father. But it's likely they'll think us ignorant and meet anyway," Bennett said, spreading the fliers before us.

His Majesty seated himself again, exhaling heavily. "What do you suppose we do, Bennett? After all, you did insist on this tour out of a stubborn will to defy me."

Bennett didn't react. "Surrounding the building is out

of the question," he said. "I propose we send two guards to infiltrate their meeting tomorrow night."

King Maximus nodded. "A cautious approach is best. Once we unveil the culprit we can target them accordingly. I must speak to Lord Frederick tomorrow." He sank back into his armchair, looking gray and haggard against the bright red cushions. "Is there anything else I need to know?"

"Yes, Your Majesty," I said. "We've discovered several points of unrest in Coriva and Vandil regarding witch businesses."

"I am aware," King Maximus said. "Though I have yet to hear anything from the crown prince."

Bennett ducked his head. "Apologies, Father. I sent them to the palace before I knew you were coming."

"You didn't know I was coming? You surprise me."

"As you meant to surprise me," Bennett said with a dry smile. "I was preoccupied."

I recalled that Ulysses wanted to tell him something the other day. But Bennett had left so quickly after our talk that the steward couldn't get a word in. I turned the ring on my finger, watching the gem glitter.

"I see." King Maximus sucked in his cheeks. "Then perhaps you can give an oral report instead."

He did. Bennett explained William's produce shop and the complications behind Vandil's textile trade. He proposed his idea of limiting witch weavers to their specialty fabrics so textile merchants would have to return to human weavers for linen and wool.

"A flawed plan, as those who specialize in luxury fabrics are still robbed of business," Bennett said, "but it is better to pass a law now that we can amend later. Perhaps as time passes, it will be possible for witch weavers to collaborate with human weavers."

King Maximus nodded slowly. "It is viable, though the fire in Vandil's Witch Market put a damper on things. A number of people are upset at the extra funds I allowed the witches for reconstruction. They believe I'm favoring them."

I frowned. "But their entire market got burned down. A rioter did it out of spite."

"Logic gets lost in riots," King Maximus said dryly. "The future princess running to put out the fire herself only added to the favoritism narrative."

I shrank into my seat. Everything I did during the fire was for selfish reasons, but I never thought it would harm the royal image.

"Perhaps it did. But Narcissa showed the witches of Vandil the importance of leadership," Bennett said. "They'll be more likely to cooperate with future laws that restrain their business. They are deeply grateful for what she did, Father."

I looked at him in surprise. Bennett responded with the slightest smile, hazel eyes glimmering.

King Maximus grunted.

Bennett walked me back to my room. The hallway was lit with the torches mounted along the walls, bathing the glossy marble floor in a warm glow. Our shadows danced in the flickering firelight.

"Thank you for coming to my defense," I said tugging on my hair ribbon. It loosened in my hands. I twisted it between my fingers like I used to as a child. "But King Maximus is right. I was impulsive."

"No," Bennett said. "You did a noble thing. Father can be...Father."

I frowned at the floor, studying the veins of cobalt and gold in the tiles as we passed. It felt wrong, being praised. Lord Frederick's words came to mind. Intention was the soul of an action. Intention determined character. Mine were far from noble.

Bennett didn't know that. Nobody knew that except me.

I was so lost in thought I didn't realize Bennett had stopped. "Your room is here, is it not?" he called out, voice echoing. I turned, flustered to see him rather far away. I trotted back, smoothing my features.

Something must have shown on my face.

He dipped his head to catch my eye. "Is there something wrong?"

Why was he being so kind to me all of the sudden? I couldn't stand the sincerity in his gaze, not when I knew it wouldn't last.

I steeled myself. "I was not noble."

Bennett laughed. "I am certain dousing a devastating fire is on the list of virtuous acts."

I ignored his smile and faced my door instead, keeping my voice level. "I had an ulterior motive. We both saw my mother's letter before it happened. It was not your fault I ran off and hurt myself. It was mine."

"Narcissa—"

"What did you think of me then?" I finally voiced the question that had been haunting me. "Did you hate me?"

Bennett blinked, caught off guard.

"Did you think I was part of some scheme with her?

That I was back to my old ways?" I twisted my ribbon harder. "I never communicated with her during the tour. Not once. Back in Delibera I only visited to make sure she was still there, but nobody would have believed me."

Bennett took the end of my ribbon, unfurling it from my grasp. I watched as he smoothed the wrinkles out of the emerald silk and wound it into a neat spool around his fingers.

"Narcissa." He said my name so softly, as if it was devoid of harsh syllables. "I never hated you."

"I..."

He tucked my hair ribbon into his waistcoat pocket, right over his heart. I couldn't seem to find the right response.

"You are not to blame. I know you are not like your mother."

Bennett didn't know what I was capable of. He didn't know the things I had done willingly for Mother. He was only infatuated with my recent acts of heroism. I anchored myself with those facts, refusing to be drawn in by his hazel eyes.

"Even if the others don't believe you, I do," he whispered after a moment. "Isn't that enough?"

I stepped back. How could he say those words, as if only the two of us mattered? How could he look at me so tenderly after what I told him?

"No. It isn't," I said stiffly, even as my heart screamed otherwise. "The entire kingdom hates me, and for good reason. Even if you don't—"

Bennett pulled me to him in a sudden embrace. My breath caught.

I was terrified by how much I craved his affection. How was it that when he held me, I couldn't bring myself to worry?

"That's not true," Bennett said. His voice made his chest rumble. "And even if it were, you'll win them over."

I meant to push him away entirely, to extricate myself from his arms, but I only managed a mere two inches. His eyes caught mine. And suddenly it felt like we were closer than ever.

"Kiss me again, Cissa?" Bennett whispered.

My pet name coming from his mouth undid me. I didn't know what I was doing. Or what I was feeling. My hand found his cheek on its own accord. His scent, the curve of his philtrum, his lashes that fluttered closed—everything about him was so magnetic. I tipped forward, pressing a lingering kiss to his jaw. Then to the corner of his mouth. One more kiss wouldn't hurt, would it?

Our lips brushed. Bennett's breath hitched.

You mustn't let this opportunity go to waste. Get close to the crown prince. Make him trust you. Better yet, make him love you.

And suddenly, Mother was there, looking imperiously over me as I did her bidding.

I jerked back.

Bennett opened his eyes, his expression shy. He touched the faint red prints where my rouge had stained his skin. "Apologies. That was inappropriate of me. You didn't have to—"

I forced a laugh, hoping to lighten the mood. "If I recall correctly, you already stole a kiss when I was unconscious."

He blushed. "I promise I didn't mean it that way."

I stepped away and opened the door, slipping inside to put some distance between us. My heart was threatening to burst out of my chest for more reasons than one.

Bennett was playing his part of Mother's plan far too well. He was falling for me.

And most confounding of all, I was falling for him. But how could I truly love him if that was exactly what Mother wanted?

"I'm teasing." I pulled on a smile. Luckily, he was too embarrassed to notice its fraudulence. "Good night, Bennett."

He returned the smile, though his was genuine. "Good night, Cissa."

I watched him leave before I closed the door, dragging a hand over my face and pressing it to my neck. My skin felt feverishly hot.

This was dangerous.

Mother escaped once. She could do it again, ready to resume where we left off. How thrilled she would be at the progress I had made.

My lungs constricted as I recalled Mother's gore-drenched hands in my nightmare.

You don't have a choice, Narcissa. We are bound by blood.

It would be best if I held Bennett at arm's length until I knew it was safe.

I trudged over to Misty's sleeping form and ran my fingers over her head, wishing I could drown my worries in her company. I sighed. There was little sense in waking her when I told her the same concerns less than two months ago. She thought I was too paranoid.

But was I?

29

I woke the next morning to Misty pawing at my face.

"What is it?" I grumbled.

Oh, she speaks! Misty sat on my chest, looking grumpier than usual. *Would you like to explain why you've been ignoring me for the past day and a half?*

I rubbed the sleep from my eyes. My vision focused, though I couldn't see beyond Misty's furry form.

"I have not been ignoring you." I picked her off my chest and sat up.

Don't try to deny it, Misty meowed, licking her paw. *I know you've been busy kissing your betrothed, but I highly doubt he'll be half the companion I am.*

Thoughts of kissing Bennett flooded into my mind despite myself. I pinched my arm, hard. Misty gave an unimpressed meow.

"Now, now," I said, petting Misty in her favorite spots to ease her. "So you've been in this room for too long. Let's go for a walk."

Misty evaded my hand. *I'd prefer feline company today, if you please. Take me to Pippin.*

I was going to agree, but realized that the tabby was with Bennett. Knocking on his door first thing in the morning certainly wasn't keeping him at arm's length. "Maybe later. Pippin is probably still sleeping."

Misty meowed in displeasure, but I pulled her into my arms, burying my face into her fur. "Alright! I haven't been attentive, but I'll make it up to you today. Promise!"

I won't forgive you so easily, she said, but made no move to wriggle out of the hug.

After making sure Misty had something to eat, I broke my own fast in a small sitting room down the hall. Misty joined me shortly after and we descended the myriad of stairs to take a stroll around the opera house. The staff were running about, busy preparing for Celeste's second performance tonight.

So this Celeste woman is a rebel? Misty asked, walking along the banister.

I had recounted everything that had happened to her, from the king's arrival to the hidden messages.

"The messages were on the fliers she signed," I said quietly so my words wouldn't echo. "Whether she was the one who wrote them is unclear."

Misty flicked her tail and stopped to sniff a potted plant. She nibbled on a leaf, then spat it out. *I hope to be there when whoever is behind it gets arrested. I'm in dire need of some excitement.*

Ulysses had yet to come with news about another event scheduled and Bennett was busy with King Maximus, which meant I had the entire day to myself. I had forgotten how carefree it was with just Misty and me. We hadn't been alone for this long since the tour began.

After a morning of exploring the halls and an afternoon of playing with quills and lazing about in every available patch of sunlight, I took Misty outside for one last evening stroll. The air was refreshingly crisp. A gaggle of citizens had already gathered before the steps of the opera house with their tickets, waiting to be admitted.

I made sure to stay out of sight behind the hedges and pillars, as I didn't have any guards. I wasn't sure what the Alevine crowd would do if they saw me.

Misty nudged my leg. I picked her up at our unspoken sign, arranging her comfortably in my arms so my cloak shielded us both from the chill.

"Well, Misty. Can you find it in your heart to forgive me?" I asked.

She purred as I rubbed her belly. *I suppose I can.*

I kissed the top of her head, then stifled a yawn. Despite the opera house just coming alive, I was ready to retire. But the sight of someone familiar stopped me in my tracks.

Dominic Turner. He was hunched behind a hedge only several paces away. I hid myself behind a pillar. My jaw clenched. What was he doing here?

It's him again, Misty meowed, narrowing her eyes into slits. *He positively reeks.*

I stroked her head to calm her. "What does he smell like?"

Rats.

I frowned. "If he's here it's only for one reason."

The rebel meeting.

You want to spy on him, don't you?

Misty looked ready to fall asleep. I bent down, letting her onto the ground. "Go back without me. I left our door ajar," I said. "You can find Pippin, if you'd like."

Are you sure?

I nodded. "I'll be back soon."

Misty didn't need much convincing. She slipped back into the entrance, no doubt eager to cuddle up with a pillow. Or with Pippin.

I poked my head out from behind the pillar. Dominic was still there, conversing with a figure obscured by unruly branches.

"...saying you have personal information on Lady Narcissa and Crown Prince Bennett?" the figure asked. It was a woman, her voice high and nasally.

"I am a friend of theirs, in fact. I met them in Coriva."

"I see. And pray tell me, why do you refuse to reveal your name?"

Dominic tilted his head. "No offense, madam, but I want to make sure you don't run off with an incomplete version of what I have to say and slap my name on it."

The woman tittered. "I assure you I never name my sources, unless they wish it."

"Nevertheless I would like to keep my anonymity," Dominic said. "At least until the day after tomorrow."

"Really. You convince me to travel all this way and yet refuse to tell me what you promised. I'm starting to think you have other intentions," the woman said slyly.

"As lovely as you are, Sister Scarlett, I called you here strictly for business. Trust me. You will be glad you were present for what is to happen in the next three days." Smugness was practically dripping from his voice.

"Very well. You best deliver what you promised," Sister Scarlett said.

Dominic bowed low as she emerged briskly from the bushes. I braved a peek at the infamous gossip columnist. The woman had a curvy frame and brown hair, about forty years of age. Her lips were painted scarlet, the color stark against the dreary gray sky. Fitting.

I whirled around to see the tail of Dominic's coat disappear around the corner of the opera house. My feet followed before I could process everything I had heard. I highly doubted Dominic called Sister Scarlett to Alevine just to give her some petty gossip about me and Bennett. What he said was to happen in the next three days had to be connected to the rioters.

My eyes were trained on Dominic's back. I didn't see the two figures emerge from my right until I stumbled over their feet.

"Ow!" Flannery cried out, hopping back in the grass. He dropped his lamp, the flame sputtering.

"Flannery?" I turned. "Maddox?"

The two were not in uniform, which was a rare sight. Maddox shushed me, eyes wide.

"What are you doing here?" he asked.

I raised my brows. "What are *you* doing here?"

"Didn't you hear? Lord Frederick and His Majesty sent us to infiltrate the rebel meeting," Flannery said, shaking out his foot.

"They chose...you two?"

"Thanks for the unwavering faith," Maddox said flatly. He looked over my shoulder. "Look, as much as we would love to stay and chat, we have to find the entrance to the sewers."

Flannery sighed pitifully. "We've been looking for half an hour."

Dominic had gone further down the side of the building, nowhere to be seen.

I bit my lip. "I know where it is." I told them what I had

witnessed and my suspicions of Dominic being part of the anti-witch rioters. "He could be meeting them right now."

Flannery nodded. "Let's go then. Otherwise we'll be late."

Maddox frowned at me when I followed them down the building. "You are not coming with us." He quickened his pace, leaving us behind.

I trotted to catch up, the grass squelching beneath my boots. "But I—"

"Lord Frederick will have my neck. Not to mention the crown prince. Did you know he was looking for you all day?" Maddox said.

Bennett was looking for me. I ignored the warmth in my chest at the thought of him. All the more reason to go. "I'll stay close, I promise," I said.

"You'll slow us down."

Flannery panted from behind us, slinging his lamp over his shoulder. The flame nearly sputtered out again as it swung wildly. "Maddox is right, milady," he said, between breaths.

Despite their protestations, I kept pace with them until we reached the back end of the building. Beneath a patch of tall grass was a metal disk, slightly ajar.

Maddox moved it aside. A ladder led down to infinite darkness.

"Here it is," he said.

Flannery gulped. I tucked my hands behind my back and bent over the hole. "There are all sorts of animals in the sewers. Rats, possums, perhaps a stray cat or two. Did I mention rats?"

"Rats?" he squeaked.

I nodded. "Feral ones. But I'm sure with some reasoning

they could be kept at bay." I turned on my heel. "I suppose I'll see you two tomorrow. If you survive."

Maddox exhaled as Flannery whimpered.

"Fine. If you get hurt or kidnapped I'll—"

I held up a hand. "After you, brother."

THE AIR GREW impossibly colder when we descended, bringing with it the putrid odor of rot and sewage. I smothered my nose in my cloak as Flannery held the flickering lamp before us. A thin river of water ran through the center of a narrow hall, rippling from a slight draft.

"Two lefts, four rights, then one left," Maddox said, squinting at the slip of paper he had written the instructions on. "Are we supposed to skip past any entrances?"

"If there were entrances to skip, it would have been included." I gave him a nudge. "Let's hurry."

We proceeded down the hallway and turned left, then again. We turned four rights. Miraculously, it was silent save for our boots against the damp bricks. No critters made an appearance, thankfully. Feral animals seldom listened to reason.

At the cusp of the last left, the sound of rumbling voices emerged.

"We're here," Maddox said, rubbing his palms on his trousers. Flannery threw a concerned glance my way.

"Are you sure you want to do this, milady?"

I wasn't. I pulled my hood tight over my head, making sure not a strand of hair poked out. This would be my first time diving into a roomful of vagrants without Mother being in charge of them. But what Dominic did was unforgivable.

The sooner he was discovered the sooner I'd be rid of him. I took a deep breath and promptly regretted it.

"Yes," I wheezed, burying my nose in my cloak again. Sewage air was less than pleasant.

Sandwiched between Flannery and Maddox, I shuffled forward.

"What in the blazing fires..." Maddox whispered.

The final hallway was in stark contrast to the others. The walls were smooth and white, decorated with golden accents not unlike the rooms of the opera house above. Torches lit the interior, but the firelight cut off abruptly at the edges of the hall.

"There's magic all over this," I said under my breath. It didn't make sense. Why would an anti-witch rebellion involve themselves with magic?

Benches sat along the walls, filled with men and women of all ages. Those who didn't have a seat stood, crowding either entrance. There were perhaps thirty or forty of them. Judging from their dress, most were of the working class. Dominic was nowhere to be seen.

A large crate stood in the center, an empty ring of space around it.

I held my breath, wondering who would step up and speak.

"I've never seen you before," a gruff voice said to my left. A grizzled man with scarred, muscular arms frowned at Flannery. Soot blackened his fingertips. A blacksmith. I squeezed my eyes shut. We were doomed.

"Reckon you haven't seen lots before." The suave, uncaring words were almost unrecognizable as Flannery's. But there he was, looking lazily up at the blacksmith as if the stranger wasn't thrice his size.

"Why are you here?" the blacksmith asked, narrowing his eyes.

Flannery shrugged. "Same reason as everyone else. Witches ruining my business. Do you know how well they can cut a quill? It's ridiculous. My pens can't compare."

Imagining Flannery as a pen-maker wasn't difficult. Good thing he didn't claim to be a locksmith or anything of the sort.

The blacksmith grunted, relaxing his stance. "Those blasted royals didn't know what they were doing when they let those witches up here again. Did they think some petty tour was going to fix everything?" He scoffed. "No one gives a damn about the crown prince's marriage. If anything, having a witch queen would make matters worse."

The people around him agreed heartily. I bit my lip. The tour was coming to a close. King Maximus had to enforce new regulations quickly before the rioters did something drastic.

Just then, a figure stepped onto the crate. It wasn't hard to miss the insolent set of his jaw.

Dominic held up his arms to quiet the rabble. A few grumbles sounded from around the hall.

"Who let him up again?" a woman muttered.

"Arrogant peacock."

The general's son cleared his throat, the sound embarrassingly weak in the tunnel. "The mistress is preoccupied tonight," he said, "so I have taken her place. She will return for tomorrow's meeting."

"Why do *you* get to speak for her?" a woman shouted. "A pampered nobleman has no business leading a movement for the people."

Dominic's face pinched, searching for the offender in

the crowd. I lowered my head, hoping my cloak was plain enough to blend in. "Because I have proven myself capable. Do not forget that my father has made the winter solstice attack possible."

I stilled. General Turner had been in charge of the Royal Guard in Father's absence that night. *He* let the assassins in.

The woman scoffed. "That attack achieved nothing. The royals didn't believe the assailants were witches."

Dominic's face grew red. "Place the blame on the fools who concocted the plan," he spat. "My father is a general. As long as he is willing to assist us, we have a fighting chance at bending the royals to our will."

So General Turner wasn't the mastermind of this. Instead, it was this mysterious "mistress". Someone who clearly had access to magic, judging from the nature of the meeting space.

"Are you suggesting overthrowing the crown?" a younger man asked, paling. "We'll be traitors. They'll have our necks!"

His companion smacked his shoulder. I realized with a start that he was Patrick, the stagehand who had bumped into me. "We're already halfway to treason," Patrick said, sneering. "Besides, it's not like the king has a particular aversion to traitors. Look who he married his son off to!"

Another murmur of agreement rose.

"A traitor *and* a witch."

"She must have enchanted them to her will."

Dominic stamped his boot. "Silence!" The crate wobbled dangerously beneath him. "Lady Narcissa is innocent in all this. She is merely misguided. I have strong suspicions she is not a witch at all. This has all been a ruse to distract us, to convince us that the royals are actually taking action."

The blacksmith beside Flannery bellowed a laugh. "Don't tell me you're smitten with the witch princess."

"Narcissa was promised to me once," Dominic said haughtily. "I know her character best, not to mention whether she is a witch or not."

I clenched my fists. Who did he think he was, brazenly claiming to understand me when we hadn't interacted in half a decade? Rage simmered beneath my skin. He was a despicable man, presumptuous and brash and too ignorant to know it.

The same woman from before groaned. "If you're so sure she isn't a witch, then how did she single-handedly douse the fire in Vandil?"

Dominic faltered. "An exaggeration, no doubt," he said. "Besides, the...the fire was started by a rogue farmer who heeded no caution!"

A few snickers sounded.

"You should be grateful. The whole situation made your Lady Narcissa look like a saint," the woman jeered. "And look at that farmer now. She's not coming to these meetings anymore."

The crowd's muttering grew louder until Dominic was completely at a loss. Maddox and Flannery exchanged glances.

It was prime time to go while the group was distracted. Besides, it was clear this was not a usual meeting. The "mistress" was missing.

"And what of the mistress's secret weapon?" someone shouted over the rabble. The three of us paused.

Dominic straightened up. "That is going according to plan. She's taking it for a test run."

"How come we aren't allowed to know?" the blacksmith demanded. "How come only you do?"

The general's son smiled smugly. "Seeing as none of your ideas have worked, the mistress has decided to execute her own plan. You will find out once it is implemented."

"You're lying," the woman spat. "The mistress always informs us of our next steps."

Dominic raised a brow. "Careful, now. Remember that you swore allegiance to the people, not to a witch."

Maddox tugged on my arm. I let him pull me away from the muttering crowd, the three of us slipping back into the darkness of the other tunnels. My mind spun. This mistress was a witch, leading anti-witch rioters?

We retraced our steps and eventually returned to the opera house, weary and dazed.

Flannery let go of a breath. "Well. Seems like we have a lot to report."

30

"You brought Lady Narcissa with you?" King Maximus's voice flooded the confines of his room with barely concealed rage.

"Deepest apologies, Your Majesty," Flannery squeaked. Maddox hung his head, his face growing pale as the king glowered at all three of us.

I shifted uncomfortably, though it was more from Bennett's frown than King Maximus's shouting.

"Your orders were to infiltrate the meeting without drawing attention to yourselves, not take the future crown princess into a pit full of rioters who want her dead!"

"Your Majesty, I was the one who insisted," I said.

King Maximus scowled mightily. "Why? Do you have an incurable impulse to throw yourself into unnecessary danger?"

My cheeks grew hot as I stared at the damask rug. "The important thing is that we escaped unnoticed. Maddox and Flannery have information."

He grunted irritably. "Well, get on with it."

Maddox recounted everything we found, including the magic tunnel, the rioters' opinions, and the mysterious mistress. Flannery chimed in to explain the involvement of Dominic Turner and his father.

"The general," King Maximus said, face darkening. "You were right about him from the start, Bennett."

Bennett dipped his head. "I took the necessary precautions in Coriva when his son appeared," he said quietly. His gaze slid to me. "Though extra guards didn't seem to be enough."

The king exhaled. "I will discuss next steps with Lord Frederick and Captain Greenwood. You two are dismissed."

Maddox and Flannery shuffled out, both looking thoroughly ashamed. I felt a pang of guilt as I trailed behind them.

King Maximus stood from his seat.

"Father, you look pale," Bennett said, brows furrowed.

"I just discovered my general is in cahoots with rebels. I need some air." His Majesty frowned. "Don't leave, Lady Narcissa. Since you insist on involving yourself in these matters, I will return shortly to speak to both you and Bennett."

He walked briskly past me, the door slamming shut.

Silence pervaded the room. I tugged on my sleeve, unable to speak as Bennett rounded the table. "Cissa. You do not have to prove that you're some kind of hero. Not to me. Not even to Father."

I turned my face away. "I didn't go down there for heroism." It wasn't completely a lie. I did it to avoid him.

Bennett pressed his lips together, his expression identical to the king's. "You cannot run off and douse fires and infiltrate enemy grounds like you're immune to danger. Why do you have to do this?"

"It's my duty as crown princess," I said quietly.

"It is *not*."

Something in me cracked. My eyes snapped to his. "Well, it is for me!"

"Cissa."

"If I didn't prove myself a hero, no one in Olderea would trust me. In fact, *you* didn't trust me," I accused. "Before all of this I was a...a spoiled society girl. And a traitor. Everyone *feared* me because I was cruel."

He stared. "I know that. I was there."

Heat rose in my cheeks. I didn't think he was going to agree.

"But you're not those things anymore," Bennett said. "You're different now."

"Bennett, I carved into a girl's hand with a needle and made her my servant. That's not something that just...goes away!"

His expression did not change. "Did you enjoy it?"

"What?"

Bennett tilted his head. He looked almost as he did at our first tête-à-tête. I hardly knew how he could ask those things with such composure.

I took a breath. My hands were shaking. "No. I did not *enjoy* it. But I wasn't so opposed to it as you may think."

"But it sickens you now, doesn't it?" His voice was so level. "Cissa, you are capable of change. You *have* changed. Why isn't that enough for you?"

I clenched my fists. "You only know that because I ran off and doused a fire."

Bennett shook his head.

Frustration clawed at my throat. He wasn't making any sense.

I spent my life appeasing whomever had power over me.

I always knew what Mother wanted—ruthlessness and obedience. King Maximus and Olderea wanted a good crown princess. But Bennett? I never figured out what he expected from me.

"What do you want from me, Bennett? My obedience?" I stepped forward. "A silent figurehead? A good queen to help you rule?" Every word brought me closer. Close enough to see the stubble along his usually smooth skin. "Or do you want something else?"

My proximity seemed to break his calm. Bennett's throat bobbed. His cravat was missing, exposing the inside of his collar. I recognized the lopsided stitches as my own. There was the faintest red stain along his jaw where I had kissed him last night, and the unmistakable emerald green of my hair ribbon poked out from his waistcoat pocket.

I stared, wondering when he started looking like he was mine.

"I want you to be safe. With me," Bennett said, touching my cheek. The touch, though brief, sent a jolt through my skin. "You don't know how scared I was in Vandil. When I thought I was going to lose you."

I searched his eyes. "What are you saying?"

He swallowed, leaning closer and settling a hand on my waist. "Cissa, I think I'm—"

The door opened. Bennett withdrew at the king's entrance, though not quickly enough.

King Maximus frowned mightily. I thought my face would burst into flames.

"Sit down, Narcissa. Bennett," His Majesty said.

We sat. This time, Bennett took his seat next to mine. I tried to compose myself, though my heart was beating wildly from his unspoken words.

"I have spoken with Lord Frederick," the king said. "Other than the word of those two guards, we have no solid evidence that the general is joining the rebels. We will have to surround the next meeting and detain Dominic Turner and the others."

I blinked, his words washing over me like a bucket of icy water. Since when had our focus been on the general? Ambushing the rebel meeting didn't seem wise when there was still so much we didn't know. Who was this witch mistress and what was her secret plan? What was her purpose in supporting a cause that wanted nothing to do with her kind?

I swallowed. "Your Majesty, if I may interject?"

His stormy expression hadn't disappeared, but King Maximus inclined his head. "Go on."

"The person who held me hostage during the fire... she was a flax farmer who no longer had weavers source from her fields. I told her about the new regulations and the other rioters say she's no longer attending the meetings." I recalled the young man who balked at the mention of crime against the throne. "Many of them are too afraid to rebel. The sooner we reform these laws, the sooner the uprising will quell."

King Maximus grunted. "Naturally. I will draft them as soon as General Turner is punished for treason. His son will confess his father's crimes once we arrest him."

Bennett sat forward. "Is that the best course of action? If we surround the next meeting we risk further agitating the rioters. How will it look if we use force on our people?"

"Leaving General Turner to his own devices is a greater risk," King Maximus said. "He commands the troops. Those rioters could already be loyal to him. He could plan an uprising all his own and take the crown for himself if he so wished." He pressed his fingers to his temples. "All this time I thought he was trustworthy."

"But the general has shown no signs of planning a rebellion," Bennett said. "He's counting on the rioters to do it for him. We need to find out what they're planning and thwart them in private. Then pass the laws, as Narcissa suggests."

King Maximus turned to him, face creased with a scowl. "Are you claiming fault in my course of action?"

Bennett sucked in his cheeks. "No, Father. I believe you have muddled your priorities."

"Is stopping a military uprising not a priority to you?" His Majesty demanded.

I suddenly felt uncomfortable. "I believe Bennett makes a good point, Your Majesty."

King Maximus glared at me. "Being the crown princess does not involve inserting yourself into royal decisions."

I flinched.

Bennett frowned. "Maybe it should, Father."

The king's weathered face grew red. "The two of you seem well prepared to run the kingdom yourselves."

"I didn't mean it that way." Bennett said. "I was only—"

"Giving me your opinion," King Maximus finished. "So you always say. Though whether it is wholly yours is questionable."

The look he gave me was hard to miss.

His Majesty pushed his chair back. "You have always been the voice of reason, Bennett, but tonight you do not seem to have your wits about you. Therefore, I will do what I believe is right. I *am* still king."

"Father—"

"Tomorrow night Frederick and his men will surround the meeting and take care of those traitors accordingly,"

King Maximus said, eyes flashing. "You may assist me or you may stand aside, but under no circumstances may you defy me. Is that understood?"

Bennett lowered his head, clenching the fabric of his trousers. "Yes, Father."

I watched the exchange, my gut churning at how familiar it felt.

"Good. You are dismissed."

31

Dear Lady Narcissa,

I hope you are enjoying your stay here at the Grand Alevine Opera. The living quarters are absolutely divine, are they not? I suppose you won't be staying long as the end of the tour draws nearer, but it would mean the world if you could attend my show one last time with His Majesty and the crown prince tonight.

Looking forward to seeing you,
Celeste Carr

I stared at the neat, swirling script, so unlike the coarse lemon juice messages on the back of the fliers. Misty surveyed the letter before walking across it, crumpling the paper.

She wants you to see a show you've already seen? Sounds suspicious, Misty meowed.

It was suspicious. But what was the point of investigating whether Celeste was involved in the meetings? King Maximus already decided on his plan of action. This was no longer my concern.

"Suspicious or not, we're going," I said, standing from my vanity. "You heard Ulysses this morning. The tour is ending in four days."

I hadn't expected it to end so soon. The past few months had gone by in a blur.

"And after that, of course," Ulysses added, "is the wedding. Thank heavens I don't have to plan that."

I balked at the mention of the wedding. Being Bennett's wife was something I never considered. It had always been about my role as the crown princess of Olderea. It was difficult to forget our conversation last night in the king's chambers. Bennett made his feelings for me abundantly clear. He didn't want anything from me. He just wanted...*me*. Yet I couldn't bring myself to believe him.

Don't act so surprised. He was bound to like you, Misty said, hopping onto the carpet. *Besides, is it so bad?*

I turned to the window, leaning against my bed post. "It's not *bad*," I said, struggling to form my thoughts. "I did not expect it, that's all."

Misty sat back, giving me a hard stare. Her whiskers and elegant form made her look wise beyond her years. *Solitude is essential in moderation, but crippling in excess. Even strays like me find solace in company.*

"You're not a stray anymore," I said, joining her on the carpet. I petted her ears fondly. "Besides, we have each other. We always have. Together forever, remember?"

That was what we had promised each other—a lifetime of love and friendship.

Misty pushed her head into my hand. *I know, darling. But don't you think it'll be better with more than two of us against the world?*

I gave her a peculiar look. "What has gotten into you?" Misty always liked it when it was just the two of us. She was upset with me the other day for this very reason. Realization dawned on me. "Is this because of Pippin?"

Misty licked her paws. *Partly. I love you to the moon and back, but having a feline companion is an entirely different experience. He made me realize what I was missing.*

I frowned. "I didn't know you were missing anything."

I'm only being honest.

A pang shot through my chest. Misty had always been with me the moment we found each other at the palace dumping grounds all those years ago. The thought that I had kept her from living how she pleased pained me more than I could describe.

"Do you think you would've been better off if...if you hadn't met me?" I asked.

Misty meowed indignantly. *Don't put words into my mouth. I'm only saying that accepting Pippin's companionship has been for the better. It gets lonely when you're out and about.*

Protestations died on my lips.

Misty was always by herself whenever I had events to attend. But the thought of not having her waiting when I got back was unbearable. She had always been the one to comfort me, to make me laugh, to help me sleep at night.

She was the only one who knew me in and out—the only one who *loved* me.

I hope you're not delusional enough to think that, Misty said, pulling away from my hand. *You're surrounded by love, both potential and existing. You have been for months. Whether you dare to accept it is another matter. I, for one, am going to find Pippin.*

She turned up her tail and stalked toward the door.

"Misty—"

The door, she meowed.

I wordlessly turned the knob and watched her slink down the hall. Whistling and light footsteps came from the other end. Giselle raised her eyebrows at the sight of me.

"Why so gloomy?" she said.

I shook my head. "It's nothing."

It turned out that the seamstress was on her way to fit me for a new dress. Lady Ruan had convinced King Maximus to attend the show tonight, and to my surprise, he had accepted. Giselle was in charge of dressing us all.

"But His Majesty plans to ambush the rebels tonight," I said as she buttoned me into a midnight blue gown, complete with a chiffon shawl.

"Oh? There's no reason he can't attend while Lord Frederick does the dirty work," Giselle said through a mouthful of pins.

I stood still as she adjusted the length of the slight train. "I suppose. I just think..." I sighed and shook my head. "Never mind. It doesn't matter." Whatever mystery was left to solve, it was up to Lord Frederick and the king. Perhaps Father as well. Bennett and I had done our part.

Giselle didn't seem to be listening. She was scrutinizing the fliers that lay at the corner of my vanity, the pins abandoned.

"This woman..." she said, pointing at the likeness of Celeste. "She looks familiar."

"She's the new soprano everyone is raving about," I said. "Do you know her?"

Giselle shook her head, but the crease between her brows didn't disappear even as she finished making adjustments on the dress. I stopped her at the door.

"You should come with us," I said. Misty would likely not join me after our conversation, and I had little desire to be stuck in a box with a father and son upset with each other.

Giselle waved her hand in the air. "Oh, I never liked theatrical productions. Besides, I want to sleep early tonight. Enjoy yourself."

After she left, I found myself meandering about the halls, pacing in front of a certain door. My palms felt clammy. I shut my eyes before mustering up the courage to knock twice.

The door opened.

"Narcissa," Lady Vanessa said, blue eyes widening. She was still in her dressing gown with curl papers in her hair, despite it being nearly noon.

"Is this a bad time?" I asked.

She broke into a smile. "Not at all. Come inside, I'm having tea."

Lady Vanessa's room was less grand than mine, though the tasteful pastel furnishings suited her perfectly. I took a seat at the edge of a chaise longue.

"Can I help you with anything, dear?" Lady Vanessa asked, pouring herself a cup of tea.

I fidgeted, pushing the fringe of the rug with my shoe. "I was wondering if you would like to attend the show tonight? With me."

She set the teapot down, her expression all surprise. I couldn't blame her. I avoided her at every turn in Greenwood Abbey.

"It's alright if you do not have time," I said when she didn't answer.

Lady Vanessa shook her head, a few curls falling from their papers. "No, I do! I have all the time in the world." She beamed, lighting up the room.

"So you will come?"

"Of course! I'm quite fond of the theater," Lady Vanessa said. "I was hoping your father would take me, but alas he's on duty."

I cracked a smile. "He'll be there. Just facing away from the stage."

She laughed. "Yes, precisely." She looked around the spotless room. "Though…I'm afraid I don't have anything appropriate to wear."

"I know just the person to help."

It wasn't long before the night came.

A pair of guards escorted Lady Vanessa and I to the auditorium where King Maximus and Bennett already stood in our box. Father was stationed outside with a couple of other guards, their uniforms matching the deep purple carpeting.

He beamed when he saw us. "My dear, you look divine."

Lady Vanessa was swathed in a luxurious gown of soft periwinkle chiffon. The color livened her complexion.

Giselle had certainly outdone herself in such a short amount of time.

"I'll have to thank Narcissa for inviting me and lending me her dressmaker," Lady Vanessa said with a smile.

Father raised his eyebrows, pleased.

King Maximus welcomed my stepmother when we entered the box. I stood back with Bennett.

"I presume His Majesty didn't change his mind?" I whispered.

"No." Bennett sighed. His lapels was uncharacteristically lopsided, though he didn't seem to notice.

I reached over to straighten them. "Is he always like this?"

Bennett's expression softened. "For all my life." He smiled sadly.

I looked down. How wrong I was when I assumed Bennett didn't understand my relationship with Mother. King Maximus was the same sort of parent. Rigid. Demanding. He expected great things from Bennett yet wouldn't let him go beyond his control. I wondered what nuggets of affection the king would give him to show that he loved him in spite of everything.

"Recently he has been more…paranoid," Bennett said quietly. "He's threatened by the riots and his policies being disliked. Ash and I think his age is making it worse."

I couldn't find the words to comfort him, so I squeezed his hand instead.

"Hopefully nothing too disastrous happens tonight," I said, peering over the crowded auditorium. There was no saying if the rioters would decide to take the chaos here.

"Hopefully." Bennett exhaled and gave me a small smile. "You look beautiful."

I still hadn't gotten used to his compliments. I ducked my chin. "As do you."

He looked as if he wanted to say something more, but King Maximus cleared his throat. I pulled my hand away.

"Bennett, Narcissa. No reason to lurk in the shadows like criminals," he said gruffly.

So he wasn't entirely cured of his sour mood. Bennett turned stone-faced and sat next to his father. The king sighed.

The chatter quieted as the lights dimmed. Once again, the curtains lifted to reveal Celeste in all her glory. She caught my gaze and smiled. I wondered how she could see me in the dark, but I gave her a nod.

Then she started singing. Nothing had changed, yet somehow I found her dulcet voice grating, like sandpaper against skin. I sat, entranced, unable to move as the opera progressed. A dull pain pulsed at the base of my head. It spread up my scalp, tingling and burning its way to my ears and then shooting to my throat. I coughed.

Lady Vanessa's concerned expression floated at my periphery. I blinked, eyes watering.

"I think I need some air," I whispered to her. She nodded and moved aside so I could leave the box.

Father stood on the other side of the curtains, the hallway dazzling compared to the darkness inside.

"Are you ill, Cissa?" he asked, frowning. I must have looked as pale as I felt.

"I just need some air," I said, rubbing my throat. The tingling subsided. I excused myself to the washroom, not wanting to disturb Father while he was on duty.

When I exited, the hallway was sprinkled with audience members. Was it intermission already? I returned to the box, feeling faint. I was surprised to see Celeste there, still in her stage costume, conversing with King Maximus.

"....to say, Your Majesty, that I greatly respect what you have been doing for Olderea," Celeste said in her soft, husky voice. "Your perseverance in helping those poor witches is admirable."

His Majesty responded, looking immensely flattered. Celeste turned to me.

"Lady Narcissa! Thank you for obliging me tonight," she said, smiling. Her stage makeup looked garishly intense up close. "I was sorry to see you leave before the first act was complete. Are you quite alright?"

I managed a nod. The headache had faded into a dull throb, not unlike the one I felt the other night. "I needed some air."

Celeste tilted her head. "Oh dear. I hope it was nothing serious." She rearranged her robe and pulled out a small lavender vial, spritzing something into her mouth. "Keeps my throat comfortable after all the singing," she said with a wink. She tucked the spray bottle back into her robe pocket. "Now, off I go. The ensemble will be cross with me if I'm late."

She swept into a low curtsy and glided off.

King Maximus grunted. "Good to know someone still respects royalty."

Bennett touched my arm when I returned to my seat. I knew the question on his lips before he could vocalize it.

"I'm fine," I whispered.

Intermission ended far too soon. My hands were shaking inexplicably when the curtain drew open once again, flooding the auditorium with colored light. There was something I couldn't put my finger on. Something strange…

Celeste's singing drowned out all thoughts. My eyes were glued to the stage, my limbs stiff in my chair, my head sluggish with dull throbs.

Then, something slashed my eardrums.

I keeled over in pain, clutching my head. My reaction must've been more disruptive than I thought.

"Narcissa!" Lady Vanessa and Bennett said in unison. I slid from my seat. Bennett knelt before me, grabbing my forearms.

"Get back to your seat, Bennett. And quiet down," King Maximus whispered harshly to my left. "Narcissa, what ails you?"

I didn't understand how the king's voice was perfectly audible when my ears felt like they had been cut off. "A-a headache," I said. It came out more like a whimper. Something wet dripped onto Bennett's hands. Tears. My tears.

I wiped them away quickly.

"Something's wrong," Bennett said. Somehow he managed to pull me up. My knees buckled. He wrapped his arm around my waist, holding me against him. I gasped into his chest when another surge of pain hit me.

Whispers started along the surrounding boxes.

"Good heavens. What happened?"

"Lady Narcissa appears ill."

"Look at the crown prince. That is the most I've seen him emote."

Then, the agony stopped. No residual throb remained. My limbs felt strong enough to support me. I teetered back from Bennett's embrace, bewildered.

Bennett cupped my face, wiping my tears away with his fingers. "Cissa. What's wrong? What is it?"

King Maximus stood, exhaling.

"Should we call for the physician?" Lady Vanessa asked, touching my hand. "My dear, you're shivering."

I shook my head. "No. No, I'm fine."

Bennett began to protest, but King Maximus quieted him with a stern stare. He did not look pleased.

"Narcissa. Bennett. To my office," he said, and abruptly exited, disappearing behind the curtains.

"I-I'm sorry," I managed to say to Lady Vanessa.

She furrowed her brows. "Don't worry about me, dear. You must rest if you aren't feeling well."

The king's stormy expression told me I wouldn't be resting any time soon.

32

Bennett helped me into the hall, his arm wrapped firmly around my shoulders though I was steady on my feet. Neither of us spoke as we followed King Maximus upstairs to his office, guards trailing behind us.

"Come inside, Narcissa," His Majesty said, opening the door. He frowned when Bennett followed. "Not you."

"But Father, Narcissa isn't well," Bennett said.

The king barked a laugh. "Do not think I'm ignorant of your plans. I'm not so senile as to let the two of you go off together on this particular night."

Realization dawned on me. He suspected us of thwarting his orders of surrounding the rebel meeting.

I clenched the fabric of my skirts. "Your Majesty—"

King Maximus gestured wordlessly to his desk. I exhaled, easing out of Bennett's hold. He reluctantly let me go.

The king shut the door and sat across from me, crossing his arms. His expression was steely.

I inhaled. "Your Majesty. Bennett would never defy you and neither would I. I had an episode. That is all."

"You are a very good actress," King Maximus said.

"I'm telling the truth! The headache…I-I do not know where it came from but believe me, Your Majesty, I had no intention of stopping your orders."

"I once believed my son unmovable and level-headed," King Maximus said, "but it seems I was mistaken."

I sagged against the back of my seat, suddenly exhausted. "What do you mean, Your Majesty?"

He regarded me for a minute, as if assessing my character. I wasn't sure what he saw.

"Do you know why I chose you as the future crown princess, Narcissa?" King Maximus finally asked.

I blinked. Where was he going with this?

"My mother made sure I was prepared for the role. Half the work was already done." I stared at the smooth wooden floor. "I just happened to be a witch."

The king shook his head. "No. Any witch can learn the ways of royalty. But you. You were the only witch in the kingdom my son could not possibly fall in love with."

I ignored how the thought of Bennett in love with me made my heart leap.

"Your Majesty, that can't—"

"Don't try to convince me otherwise, Narcissa. I've seen how he looks at you. After what happened last summer I didn't think it was possible. Bennett was wary of you, but he was willing to do what I thought was best. Olderea needed a peaceful marriage. A union between two individuals without hatred or passion. I was sure you two would be able to achieve that."

I swallowed, my throat tight. "Why?"

"A marriage with malice will lead the people to suspect that witches are accepted on the surface as hatred boils beneath. A marriage with love will suggest the crown prince is influenced by his feelings instead of what is right for the kingdom. Or worse, that the bride is controlling him with magic."

"People will think what they like regardless of reality," I said, recalling Sister Scarlett's past articles. "The press writes whatever they deem interesting."

King Maximus stood from his seat, turning to the window. "It's not only about what the people believe. It's also about what I believe." He clasped his hands behind his back. "I overestimated Bennett's passivity. He has changed since Delibera. He's loud, erratic. He doesn't think when he acts when it comes to you."

I almost laughed. None of those words described the soft-spoken crown prince who dedicated himself to his kingdom. "I beg to differ."

"He acquired a cat in the middle of the tour for you, Narcissa."

Pippin? I thought back to his abrupt appearance in Coriva. It had been the day Isabelle and Lady Huntington forbade me from bringing Misty to the dining room. The next morning Bennett had brought Pippin. Was that for my sake?

Why had he done that when he still wouldn't speak to me? Wouldn't dance with me at the Huntington Abbey ball? My face heated when I recalled his silence, his awkwardness. Was it because he didn't know how to act around me?

"Not only that," King Maximus said, his wide shoulders stiffening, "Bennett has never defied me before. Not once."

"I wouldn't call a difference of opinion defiance."

"You and your mother had a difference of opinion. Look where she is."

My stomach soured at the mention of Mother.

"That's different," I said quietly. "He still wants the best for Olderea, as you do. I never persuaded him otherwise."

"I want to believe you." King Maximus gazed out at the dreary landscape. "But I think it is best if you do not see him for a while."

"Your Majesty?"

"Bennett is to become king. A king cannot be influenced by his emotions or by anyone. Not even his wife."

I clenched my fists. "But Your Majesty, didn't you let witches back into the kingdom at Queen Cordelia's request?"

"Yes. And look how that turned out." He turned, his lips flattening into a grim line. "Love is a dangerous thing, Narcissa. It addles the mind. Intoxicates the soul until you're no longer in control. Your mother should know that."

"She's a monster."

King Maximus shook his head. "She wasn't, once."

"Are you breaking off the engagement, Your Majesty?"

He sighed heavily. "After all this publicity? No, not at this moment. But Bennett needs distance from you. The wedding will be postponed for another year. You will not see him until then. Still, perhaps once we enforce more policies regarding magic, there will no longer be a need for the union. You know how the press is. They'll forget."

My throat tightened.

Every ounce of effort I exerted to be the perfect crown princess was for naught. Even when I tried I was not enough. Not cruel enough for Mother. Not suitable for King Maximus's vision—so much so that he wanted to rid his son of me. What purpose did I have now?

And Bennett. I would not see him for a year. If things went as the king planned, he would no longer be in love with me by the end of it.

"I see," I whispered hoarsely.

"As for this situation with the rebels, I forbid you from meddling further. Do not think being the future crown princess entitles you to such liberties," the king said, his voice hard.

I dipped my head. "Yes, Your Majesty."

His demeanor softened. "I do not mean to cause you harm. Everything I do is for Olderea. It is time Bennett learned that too." King Maximus met my gaze. "You may take your leave, Narcissa."

Mustering as much composure as I could, I stood and left the room.

Bennett waited on the other side. My heart leaped treacherously at the sight of him. I wanted to ask him a million questions at once. I wanted him to hold me again. But I held myself back.

He stepped forward. "Cissa. What did Father say? Are you alright?"

I wondered if he knew the concern in his voice felt like a dagger to my chest.

"I'm fine." I stared at my hands, which were tightly clasped before me. The emerald ring winked in the torch-light.

The union was not off, but I couldn't keep this ring for the next year knowing that it symbolized something that may not be there by the end of it. I would get another one at the wedding, if there was one. At least the new ring would mean duty. Not whatever distracting thing was between us.

Easing it off, I placed the emerald ring into Bennett's palm. "You were wrong. This doesn't fit."

He looked to the ring and back at me, realization dawning on his face.

"Come inside, Bennett," King Maximus said.

Bennett took another step forward, but I evaded him. "Cissa," he said beseechingly. "Father, whatever it is—"

"Inside, now."

"You can't possibly break this off after everything she has done," he burst out, looking more panicked than I had ever seen him. "Narcissa is more than qualified to be crown princess."

"Inside! Come inside and close the door," King Maximus said, raising his voice. "Or have you forgotten your duty?"

Bennett's breath hitched. A foolish part of me thought he would speak for me. That he would take my hand and stand his ground. That he would yell at his father and beg him to let him feel a little. But he merely stared at me—stared as he had never before.

Then, Bennett shut the door.

Every ounce of my composure shattered. What had I expected? That he was going to chase after me? Defy the king?

It didn't matter that he adopted a cat for my sake or bought me gifts or worried about me. He would do anything the king wanted. He would fall right out of love with me.

Duty came before all else for Bennett. I was a fool for ever hoping otherwise.

Antonio pulled back. Carla wanted him, not the duke. It was too good to be true. "Do you mean it? In earnest?" he asked.

"Yes." Carla threw her arms around his strong shoulders. "I love you, Antonio."

Antonio's spirits soared as the last of the sun dipped below the horizon, plunging the dock into a purple haze. Looking into Carla's dark eyes, he knew that he would do anything for her—even steal her away from the most powerful man in the city. But right now, he wanted to kiss her. To kiss her until they were both breathless.

—from *A Sailor's Seduction: Tales of Romance at Sea* by Erasmus Lenard

3

THE SPRINGTIDE FLOWER

33

I ran to my room, searching for Misty's slumbering form on the pillows. She was nowhere to be found.

Of course not. She was with Pippin.

I started down the hall, but I didn't have to go far before I saw her with the tabby.

"Misty!" My voice cracked.

She leaped into my arms, putting her paws on my shoulders when she saw my tears.

I knelt. My throat was too tight to speak, so I let my jumbled thoughts flow to her. Or tried to. But her usual presence—a comforting ball of warmth at the front of my mind—wasn't there.

"Misty?" She was on my lap, looking at me with those intelligent green eyes. And yet, she wasn't. Panic crawled up my throat. Why couldn't I hear her? "Misty, talk to me. *Please.*"

Her ears turned back, eyes dilating. She meowed again.

Pippin approached, nudging my arm with his head and joining with deeper meows of his own.

For the first time in my life, I didn't understand. A sob tore through my throat. Then another. And then another.

Something in me broke. It felt like my lungs collapsed. Hot tears welled in my eyes and ran down my chin in salty, uncontrollable rivers as I gasped for breath. I had lost *everything*.

I let myself weep like I had never before, clutching Misty to my chest, and eventually Pippin too. My whimpers echoed in the empty hallway. I didn't care if anyone overheard. I was alone, like I've always been.

Now, more so than ever.

That was how Lady Vanessa found me—sobbing in the middle of the hall and holding onto the two cats like my life depended on it.

"Narcissa?" She knelt, taking my clenched hands in her own. They were warm and smooth, her beautiful face creased with concern.

I shook my head vehemently. It was all I could manage before I gave another strangled sob.

"What is it, my darling?"

The endearment only brought fresh tears. Lady Vanessa hesitated before gently prying Pippin out of my arms.

Her soft eyes steeled with determination. "Let's get you to bed."

I was too numb to know how she did it, but in a blink of an eye, I was in my nightgown, my face wiped clean and my hair combed out. Lady Vanessa helped me onto the mattress and drew a thick blanket to my chin. Misty curled herself above my pillow, her whiskers tickling my forehead.

"This one too?" Lady Vanessa asked, lifting Pippin from the floor. When I didn't answer, she shrugged and tucked the tabby cat in next to me.

Pippin purred and licked my chin. A hot tear trailed down my temple, soaking into my pillowcase. My skin stung. I never realized how much crying hurt.

"Oh, my dear girl," Lady Vanessa said, her face softening. She took a seat, dipping the mattress, and stroked my hair in a slow, comforting rhythm. I buried my face into the pillow, chest racking with new sobs.

My hysterics didn't seem to bother her in the least. She continued gently, as if petting a kitten or consoling a child.

Eventually, my breathing evened. My eyelids were swollen and throbbing, glued shut by dried tears. Lady Vanessa had withdrawn her hand. Soft footsteps fell on the rug, punctuated by the sound of a doorknob being turned.

"Maddox? Where have you been?" Lady Vanessa asked in a hushed voice. A slice of warm light cut into the room. "You look awful."

"Fulfilling the king's orders." He sounded exhausted. "We surrounded the rebel meeting."

Lady Vanessa gasped. "Rebels? Here? And you and your father didn't think to tell me?"

"I'm sorry! I didn't think anyone was supposed to know," Maddox said sheepishly.

Lady Vanessa exhaled. "What happened? Is it safe now?"

Maddox's armor clinked. "Most of them got away, but

we contained some. And the general's son. That's the most important thing, His Majesty said."

"The general's…?" Lady Vanessa made a noise at the back of her throat. "Never mind. You're safe—that is all that matters. Did you see the king recently?"

"Yes. He just dismissed us for the night. Why?"

There was a pause. "It's just that your sister..."

"What about Narcissa?" Maddox asked.

Lady Vanessa's skirts swished. I pictured her wringing the fabric. "She hasn't been well since King Maximus asked to see her tonight. He didn't look happy."

"Does he ever?" Maddox's boots squeaked against the marble. "What's wrong with Narcissa?"

"I don't know. She had a splitting headache in the middle of the show and had to leave. I found her in the hall crying. I'm not entirely sure what happened."

"Maybe Giselle knows. I'll go ask her," Maddox said, stifling a yawn.

"Nonsense. Don't disturb a respectable girl in the middle of the night."

He snickered. "Ha! Respectable."

Lady Vanessa smacked him. "Off to bed with you. Your Father and I will deal with this in the morning."

"Er...Father left. With His Majesty and the crown prince."

"Oh?"

"His Majesty wants to settle the situation with the general as soon as possible. He took a few of the rioters, too. It's a time-sensitive matter and Father—"

"I understand," Lady Vanessa said. She took a shaky breath. "Go rest, alright?"

"Alright. Good night, Mother." Maddox kissed her and went off. The door closed softly. I was surprised to hear footsteps on the rug again. The mattress dipped and Lady Vanessa's gentle hand found my hair once more.

"There now, darling," she whispered. "Sleep well."

A LOUD CRASH jolted me from my slumber.

"I know her! I *know* her!" Giselle barged into my room, shaking a paper violently over her head.

I squinted, trying to decipher the blur of ink. She sat hard on the bed, waking Pippin and Misty. The cats yowled in displeasure.

Last night's events rushed over me. The king's decision. The disappearance of my magic. Bennett leaving. Tightness seized my throat again, but I didn't have time to wallow.

Giselle shoved the paper into my hands. It was the opera flier, wrinkled from her handling. "Her," she practically spat, pointing at the likeness of Celeste on the page.

"Celeste? I thought you didn't know her," I croaked.

"Not as Celeste, the famous opera singer. As that good-for-nothing witch child Cecelia who tormented my youth." Giselle ground her teeth. "I knew she looked familiar. If only I had known before. I'll bet my life that she's behind the rebel meetings!"

I vaguely recalled Giselle's anecdote about the witch who had played pranks on her. The witch who...

"She's the one who removed magic?" I asked hoarsely. Misty perked up, scrambling to my side. The absence of her voice in my head throbbed like a fresh wound.

"Exactly," Giselle said.

I drew Misty close, desperately seeking comfort as I relived the splitting headache last night. Not only that, but the mild headache I had when I heard her sing for the first time.

Was that the removal of my magic—or the beginnings of it? Misty claimed I was ignoring her that night. I wasn't—I just didn't hear her. But I understood Pippin perfectly well the day after. Was that why Celeste wanted me to see her show a second time?

Giselle's jaw slackened, as if noticing my state for the first time. "What happened?"

I pulled my blanket around me as I recounted last night's show, how Celeste had begged me to come, how her singing affected me. "I...I can't understand Misty anymore." The words alone brought fresh tears to my eyes, though they burned and ached for respite. Misty pressed herself into my side.

Giselle's face fell.

"Oh, Narcissa." She pulled me into a tight hug and drew away, a deep crease appearing between her brows. "She found a new way of working her magic. I would have never imagined singing. How did she manage that?" Giselle seemed to be talking to herself more than to me.

I stared at my lap, my hand still buried in Misty's fur. At least she was still with me physically. But I would never hear her talk again.

Father was right. The silence hurt. How could he ever bear to remove his magic voluntarily?

Giselle pounded her fist into her palm. "Cecelia, Celeste, whatever her name is, is obviously targeting you. But why? What is her purpose in all this?" She frowned at me. "Narcissa, we have to tell Crown Prince Bennett and King Maximus."

I looked away. "They left last night. His Majesty made it clear he no longer needed my efforts."

"What? What do you mean?" Giselle demanded. "This is important! She's obviously involved with the rebels."

I squeezed my swollen eyes. "His Majesty thinks I am an unwelcome distraction to the crown prince," I said quietly.

I told her his suspicions that Bennett was under my influence and that we planned to go against his orders.

Giselle's face grew redder by the second. "*Unwelcome distraction*? He might as well blame his son for having a working pair of eyes!" She stood and paced the room in a swirl of turquoise skirts. "You're telling me King Maximus thinks capturing the general's boy is more important than passing the laws that could very well end this whole debacle?"

"He detained Dominic last night," I said. "He'll pass the laws soon enough."

"Yes, but what about the press?" Giselle said, tugging at her dark hair. "He might as well have sabotaged himself, using the Royal Guard like that. The only reason the people are rebelling is that *his* policies are lacking."

She was voicing the same thoughts I had before, but somehow I couldn't muster an ounce of concern. What was the point now? King Maximus already discharged me from my duty.

Bennett was wrong. I was not fit to be the crown princess. My devotion was a charade, something I adopted to ease my guilt. I was every bit as selfish as Mother. Now, I was facing my punishment.

The memory of Bennett shutting the door resurfaced. At least *his* devotion to Olderea hadn't wavered. I lifted my chin so the tears wouldn't fall. It was better this way. I never deserved his affection in the first place.

"Are you seriously going to let Celeste go unnoticed?" Giselle demanded.

"If she's really behind this they will find out eventually," I said. My voice sounded hollow.

The seamstress thinned her lips, eyes blazing.

"Forget it. I'm going to find Maddox," she said. "Maybe *he* will listen to sense."

Lady Vanessa came in a moment after, looking more surprised than offended as Giselle marched off without a word.

"I thought you'd be hungry by now," Lady Vanessa said.

The tray in her hands was laden with a steaming bowl of cheddar pear soup and biscuits baked golden brown. A tantalizing pairing, even in my state.

She set it down on the bedside table. I ducked my head, sure I looked a mess.

"Thank you," I said, hugging Misty to me.

Lady Vanessa tapped her fingers. "Are you cold? There are quite a few blankets in my quarters. An excess, really," she said with a laugh. "I could bring a few if you'd like."

I realized the feeling blooming in my chest was shame. Shame and guilt. The combination made me want to curl into a ball.

Why was she so kind to me? I spurned her the moment I stepped foot in Greenwood Abbey. I had intruded on her home. I was a stranger, the illegitimate child she knew nothing about. The daughter of a woman her husband had once loved. A traitor.

That was enough for anyone to scorn me, yet Lady Vanessa was nothing but compassionate. She didn't pry. Didn't demand answers, even when she found me sobbing in the middle of a hallway. She had put me to bed and coddled me like her own child.

The pressure in my chest compelled me to speak. "I-I'm sorry."

Lady Vanessa tilted her head. "For being cold? It's no trouble, dear, I'll just—"

I grabbed her sleeve when she made a move to get up. "I'm sorry," I repeated. I blinked rapidly as another surge of tears pressed against my eyeballs. Blazing fires, when would it stop? "And...thank you. Again."

My stilted words encompassed all I wanted to say but couldn't.

Lady Vannessa melted and drew me into a hug. She smelled of gardenias and biscuits, her embrace soft and motherly. After a moment's hesitation, I wrapped my arms around her.

"There's no need to apologize," Lady Vanessa said. "We're family, are we not?"

Misty slipped out discreetly, settling next to Pippin.

I managed a nod. I knew if I tried to speak, I'd burst into tears.

34

"Cissa! There you are."

Maddox trotted down the opera house steps and rounded the corner to the sparse garden I sat in.

After eating my fill, I had taken Misty and Pippin for a stroll. The two deserved play and exercise after being clutched like rag dolls for the entire night.

It was much later in the afternoon, though it was difficult to tell with the unchanging gray skies. I knelt on the threadbare lawn as Maddox approached. His lack of uniform meant he was off duty, but he looked harried and exhausted nonetheless.

"Yes?" I hated how weak my voice sounded.

He furrowed his brows. I must've been an awful sight. My face was still swollen from crying. "Giselle told me everything," he said.

"Oh." I pursed my lips. I had no wish to hear the same spiel from him.

"Don't look at me like that," Maddox said with a huff. He joined me on the ground, wiping the dirt off his boots. "I'm not going to lecture you."

I picked at the grass as Pippin explored the bushes. Misty never left my side. I was grateful, but her constant presence only accentuated the silence.

"What is it, then?"

"King Maximus and Crown Prince Bennett left for Delibera this morning," he said.

"I know," I said, looking at my hands. "Did His Majesty give orders about where I should go? Or was that not a priority?" I didn't bother masking the bitterness in my voice.

Maddox crossed his arms over his knees. "We're to remain for another week," he said slowly, as if worried I'd explode if he talked any faster. "After that...well I don't know what'll happen."

"He's leaving an entire entourage of guards idle. How considerate."

"Not exactly. Lord Frederick let most of the tour guards return with His Majesty. Flannery's gone."

I twisted my torso to face him. "Then why are you still here? The tour is finally over. You could've taken Lady Vanessa with you."

"You weren't well last night. Mother said so," Maddox said simply.

He had done nothing but complain about being a guard from the beginning. Now he was staying because I wasn't well?

"But...you can go back home. You don't have to be a guard anymore."

Maddox shrugged, poking at the damp debris with a fallen branch. His hands had accumulated more scars since the last I had seen of them, and the purple bags beneath his eyes had never disappeared. "It's funny. I didn't have anything to do at home except ride and practice swordsmanship. Being a guard...it's purposeful. Don't get me wrong. It's bloody exhausting and downright boring at times," he said, "but I have a duty now. It's almost comforting."

Lady Vanessa, Father, me, and now Maddox. What was with this family and duty? It seemed to bring nothing but disappointment.

Maddox dropped the branch. "I don't plan on doing this for long, though," he said, surprising me.

"You don't?"

He snorted. "Are you kidding me? Look at Father. He dedicated his entire life to protecting the royal family. It's admirable, yes, but foolish. And unfair to us." He paused and glared. "Don't tell him I said that."

I held out my hands. "But if you give up your duty as a guard, what else is there?"

"I'll have other duties. To family, to friends, to myself. Blazing fires, sometimes you don't need duty. It's enough to exist and relax. But to be fair," Maddox said, stretching his legs, "I've been relaxing excessively before this."

"Then...what do you plan to do after?"

"I haven't a clue. But I can't go back to being a guard."

"Why not?"

"Because," Maddox said, standing up and offering me a hand, "we're going to commit treason."

I stared. "Excuse me?"

"Come on. We can't let Celeste get away with this," he said. "Have you forgotten? She's inviting witches to come to her show tomorrow night. For free. What she did to you, she's going to do to them."

My head spun as I recalled Celeste's charitable charade. Had this been her plan all along, to gather witches and remove their magic in masses? Had I been some sort of preliminary experiment for her?

"If you won't do it out of duty, at least do it for those witches. Giselle told me what it's like, having magic taken away," Maddox said, hesitating. "Father had a choice, but the others...it'll be against their will. It's not right."

Misty put a paw on my hands and meowed. It was a beseeching meow, that much I could tell despite the severance of our connection. She wanted me to take action.

I stared at her in despair. How I wished I could hear her speak again.

Perhaps...perhaps I could. Giselle said Celeste was always forced to return the magic she stole. Her method of stealing had evolved, but if she could return magic before, surely she'd be able to now.

Olderea's approval was no longer my concern. I had to do this for Misty, if I wished to speak to her again. For the witches who didn't deserve the pain of losing their magic. For Bennett, who didn't have the option to defy the king. If we never saw each other again, at least I'd be able to do this for the kingdom he so dearly loved.

I drew Misty to my chest and took Maddox's hand. "Let's do this."

He grinned, pulling me to my feet. "That's my sister."

Lady Ruan knocked on my door when I returned, her round face lined with distress. It turned out that my episode the other night did not go unnoticed, and neither did King Maximus's order of surrounding the rebel meeting. There was a great commotion, I heard from passersby, though there was no sign of any violent scuffle.

"I didn't know about these meetings, Lady Narcissa, I swear it," Lady Ruan said, her eyes bloodshot. "But when I went to beg audience with His Majesty, I was told he departed with the crown prince this morning. I don't know what to do."

I assured her that she would not receive punishment for her ignorance, but the worry lines between her brows did not disappear.

"A poor visit this has been, hasn't it? I'm afraid I haven't been a very good hostess." Lady Ruan sniffed and shook her head. "Is there some way to make it up to you?"

"There may be one thing," I said, leaning against the doorframe. Maddox and I had come up with a haphazard plan on the way back to my room. Now everything depended on how well I could act.

She perked up. "What is it?"

"My brother has developed an interest in theatrical engineering." The lie came smoothly. "He would like to inspect the suspension wires above the stage tonight."

Lady Ruan widened her eyes. "I'm sure that can be arranged. But tonight we have Celeste's rehearsal for tomor—"

"Perfect! He can see the wires in action, then," I said.

"I'm afraid having outsiders during rehearsal gets distracting, Lady Narcissa. Celeste is only here for rehearsals and shows and she's very strict with her schedule. Perhaps your brother can come another time?"

"He'll be as quiet as a mouse."

Lady Ruan gave me an apologetic look.

Tears welled up in my eyes. They came easily as I channeled the damsels of the romance books I had read. "Being separated from my betrothed has been unspeakably difficult, not to mention the chaos of the other night." I sniffled. "If only my brother could be allowed to engage in his interests. Seeing him happy would greatly improve my mood."

"Oh. You poor thing," Lady Ruan said, tutting as I dabbed the tears dripping down my cheeks. "I'm sure I can make an exception. Where is your brother so I may tell him?"

Maddox leaned over from the other side of the door, making the matronly woman jump. "Here," he said, flashing a smile. "Thank you for your generosity, Lady Ruan. I do hope to work here once I become a theatrical engineer."

She tittered. "Of course. I will send for you when the time comes, dear."

We watched her leave until she disappeared around the corner.

Maddox raised a brow. "Are you alright?"

My face was still dripping. I sniffed and hastily wiped the tears away, dampening my sleeves with salty blotches. Perhaps the lie I told Lady Ruan had some ring of truth.

"I'm fine," I said to my brother. I took a deep breath. "Well, that's the first part of the plan. What now?"

"Now," Maddox said with a sigh, "we find Giselle."

35

We found Giselle stuffing her enchanted bag with the contents of her room. She glared as Maddox and I came through the door.

"What are you doing?" he asked, appalled, as Giselle crammed her box of sewing supplies into her satchel.

"I'm leaving." She ran a hand through her disheveled hair, loose from its usual braid.

Maddox blocked her as she reached for an ornate candlestick that certainly wasn't hers. "What? Why?"

Giselle glared, eyes flashing. "I am fed up with serving royalty," she said. Her acorn pin was missing from her bodice. "Your sister is heartbroken and impossible to reason with and the royals left without me after claiming I was one of the best on the committee. Plus, they're too idiotic to figure out who is behind all of this. And nobody appreciates my outfits!"

The seamstress sidestepped Maddox and grabbed a candlestick, snapping it in half with the sheer force of the action, and stuffed the pieces into her bag. I had never seen her so incensed.

"You can't just pack up and leave," he sputtered. "You have a job!"

She threw her hands up. "I am a *witch*, Maddox, what do you expect? We're used to going where we please, laws and authority be darned! By all means, keep guarding those uptight pricks if you want. I'm leaving and don't think I'll miss you just because you have a handsome face!"

Maddox choked. I stepped forward. "Giselle, we just wanted to—"

"I don't know why *you're* still here!" she said, whirling around to me. "If my betrothed asked someone to test me with love charms I'd have left ages ago!"

"Test me with…?" I parted my lips, remembering that she had offered me love charms the first time I met her. "Bennett asked you to do that?"

"They were never real, you know? Every witch knows love magic can only be bottled in a potion." Giselle snorted. "That idiotic crown prince was already halfway in love with you when I told him you refused them. Then he got that stupid cat for you and I had to play along because he was too spineless to confess. He is *dreadful* at romance." Giselle hauled a bolt of lilac silk from the floor with unnecessary violence. "And now look at him! Crawling back to the palace with his father like the spineless, duty-obsessed ninny he is."

Maddox and I were both rendered speechless. I battled my sudden surge of feelings into submission. There was no use thinking about the past. It didn't matter that Bennett asked Giselle to test me. It didn't matter he was smitten with me for so long.

Horsefeathers. It didn't matter.

A minute passed of Giselle shoveling knick-knacks into her satchel before Maddox regained his voice.

"How are we supposed to deal with Celeste without you?" he demanded, grabbing a porcelain vase of violas before she could get her hands on them.

Giselle's frown deepened. "What do you need me for? I don't want anything to do with that woman and I am leaving before she can get her grubby hands on me again."

"You are the only one familiar with Celeste and her magic," I said. "What she did to me, she's going to do to the others who come to her show tomorrow night. We cannot let that happen."

My words seemed to have the desired effect.

Giselle paused, a corner of an embroidered bedsheet in her hand. "What?"

"The audience will be *witches*, Giselle." I tugged the bedsheet out of her grasp. "You said Celeste could return magic as well as take it. The others don't deserve what you and I went through. And I...I just want to talk to Misty again."

"We need you," Maddox said simply, setting down the vase. "You can show the royals how invaluable you are once you help us stop her."

Giselle's lower lip trembled as she straightened. She looked from me to Maddox.

"Fine," she snapped, dropping her satchel. It landed with a heavy thud. "But only because we're friends. I'm leaving after this."

I exhaled and pulled her into a hug. "For the record," I said, "I appreciate your outfits."

THE NEXT HOUR was dedicated to getting rid of Lord Frederick. He had insisted on guarding me himself now that much of the Royal Guard had departed for Delibera, but after half an hour of having him trail behind us in the halls, I told him that Maddox alone was quite enough.

"Besides," I said, "the rebels are taken care of. They'll have no reason to come to the opera house again."

"And you mustn't forget your back, sir," Maddox piped up from behind him. "If you injure yourself you'll become a liability if there is danger."

Lord Frederick begrudgingly left for his room.

"About time," Maddox grumbled as we descended the staircases. "So how exactly are we going to stop Celeste from taking everyone's magic? And how do we get Narcissa's back?"

"You're lucky you've got me," Giselle said. She had been scribbling notes while we were wandering about trying to lose Lord Frederick. "Celeste's mother was an herbwitch who specialized in magic removal. Celeste is a charmwitch. Her natural talent is gathering substances, including magic, but I suspect she's using sickleweed potion in conjunction with her charms and enchantments."

I furrowed my brow, recalling something Father said. "The potion that removes witch magic?"

"Precisely," Giselle said. "In the past Celeste kept the magic she had taken within herself. She was the sort of witch child who didn't need an enchanted object to contain her magic—annoyingly talented. But I doubt she'd be able to handle an auditorium full of magic without one, or without sickleweed potion. Every witch has their limits." She sighed. "All conjecture of course. We'll need to scour every nook and cranny to find out what she's up to."

That was why the three of us were heading to Celeste's backstage room. The singer was only in the theatre when there was rehearsal or a show. It was too early for rehearsal, so her room should be deserted.

Sneaking in was the riskiest part of our plan, but after talking in circles for half an hour, I concluded that theft and eavesdropping was our only solution.

That was yet another one of Mother's lessons. Always be willing to resort to unsavory methods. This time, I couldn't bring myself to care about what she would think of me using it.

We started the last flight of stairs.

"Maddox, I need you to keep watch when we search her room," I said.

Maddox quickened his pace, boots squeaking on the marble. "Why does it have to be you two? I can do it. You're the crown princess, for heaven's sake. And what if Celeste recognizes Giselle?"

"I need you as a guard," I said. "And Giselle knows charmwitch magic. She'll know what to look for."

Maddox didn't look convinced. "What if you don't find anything? And what if Celeste barges in when you're in there? Don't tell me you're going to engage in an epic battle of magic like you did last summer. Because you don't have any."

"Thank you for the reminder," I said flatly. The thought of summoning that many animals again made my bones ache. How I managed that was still a mystery, but exploring untapped parts of my magic hadn't appealed to me in ages.

Giselle blew a breath at Maddox's paranoid ramblings. "It'll be a quick search," she said. "And I highly doubt we'll need your guarding either."

I swallowed as the steps ended. My fingers were frozen and shaking, but I steeled myself and marched to the auditorium with Giselle and Maddox.

All that mattered now was Misty. Our last conversation had been a disagreement. Now I knew there were things worse than her choosing Pippin over me. Losing the ability to talk to her was one of them. I had to set things right.

The auditorium was dimly lit, the space infinitely larger without the hustle-bustle of an audience. The velvet curtains were drawn. I would have assumed the space was empty if it weren't for the occasional racket from the stagehands. Giselle, Maddox, and I slipped up the backstage steps.

Luckily, there were only a few people running errands. Several were repairing the giant painted moon from the beginning of the show. No one looked up at our entrance. I surveyed the space for any possible obstacle.

"There," Maddox whispered, tilting his head to offstage left.

A dark-haired stagehand loitered before the short hallway we needed to pass. It led to the performers' rooms. I sucked in a breath when I recognized him. Patrick. He had been at the rebel meetings. It seemed he had managed to escape arrest.

"You two go on. I'll take care of him," Maddox said.

I nodded and watched him saunter over to Patrick, leading him away from the hall. Giselle and I crept into the hallway.

"Rehearsal in ten minutes!" someone hollered from the stage.

I cursed. We must have lost track of time upstairs.

"Change of plans. You should hide," I said to Giselle in a low voice. "If Celeste is here, she can't recognize you."

Giselle looked like she was about to protest, but sighed. "I would love to pummel her upside the head," she grumbled, "but you're right. Remember, look for sickleweed potion."

I gritted my teeth, wishing I had been more prepared or more educated in witchcraft.

"What does it look like?" I asked. "Or smell like?"

Giselle pressed her mouth into a grim line. "It smells like the thing you desire most at the moment. Could be food or drink. Even atmosphere and ambiance. I suppose it makes it easier to get down, but it's nasty magic nonetheless."

The thing I desired most. What did defeating Celeste smell like?

Giselle wished me luck when we approached Celeste's red door. "I'll be here," she said, disappearing behind a dusty tapestry on the opposite side. She poked her head out after a second, flashing a slip of patterned paper between her fingers. "If anything goes wrong, I've got you."

I didn't get to ask what the papers were before she disappeared again. Mustering up courage, I approached Celeste's door and pressed my ear against the wood.

Silence.

But that didn't mean she wasn't inside. I took a deep breath and knocked. Talking to her hadn't been a part of my plan, but I was sure I'd be able to manage if it came to it.

No response came, to my relief. The doorknob turned smoothly in my hand. I stepped inside.

Celeste's room was a chaotic mess of pastel cushions and elegant furniture. A single lamp illuminated the space. Nothing changed since I had seen it last. Security didn't seem to be a priority for her. Perhaps no one frequented the performers' chambers save for Lady Ruan.

I started with the vanity. The tabletop was crowded with bottles of various shapes and sizes.

My eyes drew to a large, diamond-shaped container made of a multicolored crystal on the top shelf. Empty. I uncapped an oblong vial next to it instead and sniffed. Rosewater. A yellow orb encrusted with citrine crystals smelled of hair tonic. The clear cube beside it was a strong lilac perfume.

The back of my throat was burning by the time I went through a third of the containers. I coughed into my arm, eyes watering as I reached for a small lavender spray bottle. There was a row of them in the back, all identical. I inhaled. My fingers tingled with warmth when I recognized the scent.

Cedar and spices.

I peeked into the vial, as if the clear liquid would tell me something. There was barely enough to cover the bottom. I closed my eyes and gave it another whiff, inhaling deeper this time. Ghostly arms twined around my waist, holding me against a strong chest.

I opened my eyes. The sensation faded. What was Celeste doing with Bennett's fragrance? I stilled as I watched the lamplight flicker off the lavender bottle. The narrow body. The amethyst studded cap. Celeste had brought it with her the night I lost my magic. It wasn't fragrance.

It was her throat spray.

I capped it and stuffed it into my pocket, although a part of me longed to keep smelling it. Had Celeste somehow reformulated her mother's sickleweed potion into something that expelled outward instead of taking her own magic? My mind raced. I wasn't familiar with all the possibilities of witch magic, but it only made sense. I was halfway out of the room when I realized what it meant.

The thing I desired most at the moment was Bennett.

My heart jumped treacherously at the thought of him. I turned back into the room.

"Don't be ridiculous," I muttered to myself. This wasn't some romance novel where the female lead does little else but yearn endlessly for her lost love. Perhaps cedar was popular among throat spray formulators.

There had to be something else hiding in the rest of Celeste's lotions and sprays. I would know what the scent of defeating Celeste smelled like once it presented itself.

I was about to uncap an aquamarine bottle when footsteps came from down the hall. I cursed, hastily putting it back. From the sliver of space between the door and doorframe, I spotted Celeste in deep conversation with someone.

The hallway was shadowy enough. Without a moment's hesitation, I slipped outside and ducked beneath Giselle's tapestry before Celeste could turn.

Giselle gave me a wide-eyed stare, which I returned. There was no chance of moving now. Hopefully, Celeste wouldn't notice how lumpy the tapestry was.

The footsteps drew closer.

"You've made a very dangerous decision coming back here," the singer said. She had dropped her sugary sweet act, opting for a lower, menacing tone.

"I'm dedicated to this cause as much as you are."

I stiffened at the sound of Dominic's voice. What was he doing here? He should be on his way to Delibera.

"Touching," Celeste said airily. "Aren't you afraid of the guards seeing you?"

"They have no reason to seek me out when they think I'm detained," Dominic said.

"What do you want? Rehearsal is starting soon."

"Nothing from you. I have unfinished business."

"Not with Lady Narcissa, I hope." Celeste scoffed after a moment of silence. "She is a witch, Dominic. I don't understand why you can't get that into your thick head."

"She *was* a witch. Now she's perfectly normal," came his reply.

I trembled. Giselle squeezed my hand.

"Thanks to me."

The door opened, then shut. I strained to hear, but their voices were muffled by the thick tapestry, and now a wall. This was too good of an opportunity to pass up. I stepped out.

"Narcissa, what are you doing?" Giselle hissed.

"Eavesdropping," I mouthed back. "Stay."

She frowned and made a series of hand motions and faces I barely understood before ducking back into her hiding place.

I pressed my ear to the door, my muscles tense.

"...have made some minor adjustments to the enchantment. The way she reacted was far too violent. We can't have all the witches in the audience keel over in pain tomorrow night, now can we?"

The clinking of glass ensued. Celeste was rifling through her vanity. The spray bottle I had taken weighed heavily in my pocket despite being nearly empty. Would she notice its absence?

"And you're sure no one will suspect you?" Dominic demanded.

"I've perfected this enchantment. It'll be nearly undetectable to even the most skilled of witches," Celeste said smugly. "Besides, even if someone does find out, there's nothing they can do about it. With sickleweed potion alone, a witch's magic disperses, never to be seen again. But with my reformulation and enchantment, I alone will be able to contain it. And I never intend to give it back."

"Then what? Are you going to take all that magic for yourself?"

The clinking stopped as Celeste laughed. "Of course not. That's impossible."

"I don't understand," Dominic said. "Why are you doing this unless you want power?"

Light footsteps sounded. "Such a handsome face," Celeste crooned. "Too bad you don't have any brains to go with it."

Dominic made a strangled noise. "Answer the question. The rioters are loyal to you, despite knowing what you are. You spent months building their trust, yet you have no qualms with the royals and no desire for power. What is your purpose, Celeste? You've shared everything with me except this."

I held my breath. *Celeste* was the mysterious witch mistress.

"Is it not enough to know I have no intention of harming your plans?"

"No."

Celeste scoffed. "Very well. It's a personal matter," she said. "I want all those lowlifes in Witch Village to pay. They treated my mother's magic as a curse and mine as a menace. I want to drive them out of Olderea like they drove me out of the village, to take their magic and hold it in my hands. I have no intention of giving it back, of course. Witches are nothing without their magic. This is for justice, Dominic. For me. For my mother. Are you satisfied?"

"What are you going to do after you strip the witches of their magic? You're not going to stay, are you?" The disgust in his voice was evident, though I doubted it was a reaction to her unscrupulous actions.

She scoffed. "Are you so prejudiced as to exterminate every witch from the kingdom? Even me?"

"Our partnership is temporary," Dominic said stiffly. "If you are convicted, my father will give you safe passage out of Olderea. That is all. I owe you nothing."

"Of course not." I thought I detected a hint of disappointment in her voice. The clinking of bottles resumed. "Go then, to your unfinished business."

Footsteps grew close. I turned to hide, but the door swung open.

36

Dominic's shadow materialized on the floor as I whirled around to face him. His eyes widened.

My legs were begging me to flee, but I stood my ground. There was no sense in running. I had questions and he had answers.

He shut the door.

"Narcissa," Dominic whispered. He didn't want Celeste to know I was here. Was it because he still had the delusion that I was innocent in all this?

I jerked my head down the hall and began walking. From the corner of my eye, I spotted Giselle following several feet behind us. I prayed Celeste would not come out and see her.

We halted at the end of the narrow passage that opened up backstage. I glanced past Dominic's shoulders. Giselle had disappeared.

There was no time to wonder. "You should be on your way to Delibera. How are you still here?" I demanded.

Dominic stepped closer. "There was a decoy—"

"A magic one. How do the rioters have access to magic? Are they using services they claim to detest? Or is it because of Celeste?"

"Narcissa, listen to me." He reached for my arm.

"You do not have permission to touch me," I said icily.

This seemed to intimidate him, though he did not step back. "I can take you away. The royals left you here. They have no need for you anymore, so they abandoned you as I predicted." The fervent look in his eyes made my skin crawl. "Come with me and you'll be safe from all this."

"You and your father are committing treason. It is you who should come with me."

Dominic took another step forward. "You were promised to me first. Why are you still fighting this? Why are you still doing the crown prince's dirty work when you don't believe in his cause?"

"What makes you think I don't believe in rights for witches?" I retorted. "I *am* a witch."

"Not anymore." A small smile tugged at his lips. "I know you, Narcissa. You're loyal to whoever cares for you. It was your mother first, then the royals, and now it will be me. Marry me. I'll give you the life you deserve. I won't make you risk yourself for anyone's sake. You can be whoever you want, live however you like. You can be happy."

Bile rose to my throat. His delusion made him dangerous. "My magic was all I had and I've lost it because of your cause," I hissed. "You are the last person in the kingdom who can make me happy."

A flash of annoyance passed Dominic's face. "Then who can? Crown Prince Bennett?"

My fingers tightened around the narrow spray bottle in my pocket. "Stop this, Dominic. Surrender now."

He grabbed my wrist in an iron grip. "You're coming with me."

Just as I was about to slap him across the face, a piece of patterned paper fluttered onto his forehead out of nowhere, embellished with an intricate design. Dominic's fingers went slack.

"I *knew* you needed backup," Giselle said, crossing her arms as she came up behind me.

I swallowed, rubbing my wrist. "What did you do to him?"

"My, ah, *peacekeeping* magic," she murmured. "Hypnosis, some call it."

Dominic hadn't moved an inch, and neither had the slip of paper. I waved a hand over his eyes. "How does it work?" I asked. "Can you...control him?"

Giselle pursed her lips. "We ought to get out of here." She turned to Dominic. "Follow me."

She stepped forward. He followed in perfect synchronization. I stared, amazed, as I trailed along. Judging from how she boasted about her sewing, I was surprised she hadn't talked about her hypnotic abilities sooner.

We managed to slip unnoticed outside into the hallway. Maddox leaned against a pillar before the stairs. His hand went to his dagger at the sight of Dominic.

"What is he doing here?" Maddox demanded.

"It's fine. I've got him under control," Giselle said. I didn't miss that she was avoiding his gaze.

Maddox blinked rapidly. "Under control?"

"Magic," I said shortly. I turned to them both, removing Celeste's throat spray from my pocket. "Also, I found this."

I told them about how she had used it during the night I lost my magic. She had reformulated sickleweed potion as a throat spray that expelled outward instead of taking her own magic.

Giselle nodded. "There's a reversal charm she likely used to achieve that." Then, she raised a brow. "Are you sure that's the potion? What does it smell like?"

My throat went dry as I recalled Bennett's spiced scent and ghostly embrace. I thrust the bottle to Maddox instead. "It's supposed to smell like what you desire most at the moment."

Maddox gingerly uncapped the bottle and sniffed. His eyes widened. "It smells like the fields at home," he said, amazed. He inhaled deeply. "Grass and fallen rain on an overcast day. And a hint of fresh hay."

He gave it to Giselle. She hovered over the rim. "Smells like pie."

I nodded. "That's it, then. Now we need to figure out how Celeste is keeping the magic she has taken. And how to get it back."

Maddox frowned at Dominic, who was once again still as a statue. I regarded the latter. I still wanted to punch him for his impudence. But he would need his jaw intact to answer our questions.

"Giselle?" I said.

The seamstress exhaled heavily. "Alright. Let's take this upstairs."

THE HYPNOTIZED DOMINIC didn't stumble on a single step on the way up, though his limbs appeared entirely limp. Maddox gave him wary glances. Giselle marched several feet ahead. She didn't want to speak or look at us, though I hardly knew why.

We filed into my room after making sure Lord Frederick wasn't lingering outside. Maddox stood against the door anyway as a precaution. The cats bounded over to me from the window.

"Hello Misty. Pippin," I said softly, stroking their ears. Misty narrowed her eyes at Dominic, hissing. "It's alright. Giselle is using her magic on him."

The seamstress shifted uncomfortably, gaze darting from Maddox to the floor to me. "Do I have to do this?"

Maddox tilted his head. "Is making him speak not part of your magic?"

Giselle pressed her lips into a thin line. "It is. I can also make him dance like a monkey and walk on his hands. I can make him jump from that balcony," she said, pointing to the far end of the room, "or I can make him stab himself."

I stared, taken aback. "You'd never do that."

"I could."

"But you'd never," Maddox said.

She clenched her jaw as she sat on an ottoman, polishing the amethyst bottle with her sleeve. Dominic followed suit but fell bottom-first onto the ground.

"You don't get it," Giselle said. "My magic will always have the potential to be wicked."

I shook my head, wondering at how carefree, confident Giselle could ever think that about herself. "I've been there," I said, smiling humorlessly as I recalled all the dirty work I had done for Mother, "and all I could do was talk to animals."

"If that's the case, then all witches have the potential to be wicked. Humans do too." Maddox scrunched his nose at Dominic, who sat on the floor with his legs splayed like a child. The paper on his forehead added to the effect.

"You could never be wicked if you don't wish to," I said slowly, running my fingers through Misty's fur. "Forcing someone to speak against their will may not be objectively good, but you're doing this for the benefit of other witches. Intention is...the soul of an action."

Giselle stared at her hands thoughtfully, though she still didn't look convinced. "I suppose I never thought of it that way."

I gave a short laugh, half at her cluelessness and half at mine. All these months I had agonized over being under Mother's influence, believing everything I did came from a place of wickedness. But that had stopped last summer, the moment I decided to thwart her plans.

That was what Misty was telling me all this time.

I straightened my shoulders. "Shall you ask the questions or shall I?"

Giselle sighed. She swiveled to Dominic. "Tell us everything you know about Celeste's role in the rebellion."

Dominic's jaw fell open. I half-expected him to start warbling like a lark, but his voice was unchanged. "She joined the rebellion because of her spite for other witches. She spent months weaseling her way into the cause and making a name for herself as a singer. I didn't know how she did it. But after doing favors for several rioters, she eventually gained their acceptance."

Maddox leaned forward. "What kind of favors?"

"She would incite conflict between humans and witches. Convince traders that witch-made items are superior while on the other side complain about traders favoring magic. It fueled the existing tension, which gave rioters all the more reason to rebel," Dominic said, staring blankly into the wall. "She also would give us various magical comforts no one dared to get themselves."

That explained the luxurious meeting places and Dominic's magic double. I held Misty closer to me. "And what about her removing witch magic?"

"That was not part of our plan until the tour began. You and the crown prince were dousing the flames she was fanning. After the failure of the winter solstice attack and the fire at Vandil's Witch Market, Celeste decided to take more drastic measures. The other rioters don't know about her plan of taking witches' magic, though I suspect they'll approve. It'll rid the problem from its source."

Giselle gripped her seat. "This is ridiculous. Witches will notice their magic being taken away. Charms like that leave a trace, and it'll all lead to her."

"She said she perfected the enchantment. It'll be undetectable," Dominic said.

Giselle rolled her eyes. "Her ego is a big as ever," she muttered. "But that doesn't explain how she expects to get away with this."

A bit of drool ran down Dominic's chin, which his limp arms didn't deign to wipe. "Celeste established herself as a popular human singer sympathetic to witchkind. King Maximus does not trust witches as much as the princes do. He will have no reason to believe the witches over her, especially when he is trying to appease human civilians."

The plan was full of flaws, especially since the royals had a witch committee who answered directly to them like trusted advisors. Though from the way King Maximus was behaving lately, Celeste had a good chance of getting away with her schemes.

"How do your plans intersect with this?" I couldn't help but ask, especially when I knew they involved me.

"Once Celeste uses that potion on the audience tomorrow night, I'm going to take you away on one of my father's ships after I report our elopement to Sister Scarlett. Your union to the crown prince will be broken and the royals will be humiliated across the columns."

I clenched my jaw. So that was why Dominic had called Sister Scarlett to Alevine. It wasn't for the rebellion, but for his own vanity. If he knew me as well as he claimed, he would've known I would have never agreed to it.

Giselle made a noise of disgust. "Forget that. How is Celeste using the sickleweed potion?" she demanded.

"Her throat spray," Dominic said, pointing a floppy finger at the spray bottle in her hand. "When she sings it disperses... or whatever. I don't know. Some voodoo and whatnot."

It was a confirmation of our suspicions, though certainly not an eloquent one. The seamstress rolled her eyes. "How is she containing witch magic?"

"And is there a way to return it?" I asked. Misty buried her face into the crook of my arm. I cradled her head.

"She has this giant...crystal container," Dominic said, coughing up a few drops of spittle. "She never opens it. I assume it'll release whatever it's holding once opened."

"So she *is* using an enchanted object," Giselle said.

Maddox curled his lip at Dominic's drool-soaked collar.

Giselle uncrossed her arms, studying the amethyst spray bottle. "Enchanted objects are made to contain very strong magic and are notoriously difficult to break," she murmured. "Then again, I *am* an accomplished charmwitch."

"*Is* there a charm that can break them?" I asked, hopeful.

"There's something similar. One to reduce the capacity of magic an enchanted object can hold. I'll have to rework it tonight," Giselle said, sitting up. "If she's using an object, there's a good chance her enchantment won't work without it. Enchantments are a mesh of interwoven parts. If something isn't right, the whole thing will collapse."

The confidence in her voice reassured me. Giselle knew what she was doing. Her gaze softened. "Don't worry, Narcissa. You'll be back to normal soon."

I hoped as I had never dared to before. Misty meowed, eyes wide and shining. Pippin stuck his head under my other arm. I drew both of them close. "Then we're all ready for tomorrow night?"

"More than ever, now that we have all this information," Maddox said, unsheathing his dagger. He examined the edge. "I should probably sharpen this."

"Be sure you do," I said. We had discussed our plans earlier. Everything counted on how well Maddox's dagger performed.

"And I'll work on my charm. But first..." Giselle said, rummaging through her satchel. She pulled out a coil of rope and a wad of fabric, offering them to me. "Would you like to do the honors?"

I took them. "Gladly."

Dominic was bound and gagged in a matter of minutes. I had learned how to restrain a prisoner properly from watching Mother's lackeys with little relish. However, I thoroughly enjoyed trussing up the general's son like a turkey.

Maddox dragged him to my wardrobe and stuffed him inside after I removed the gowns I was fond of. The thought of them making contact with him was enough to make me gag.

"He won't need this anymore," Giselle said, plucking the embellished paper from Dominic's forehead.

"Hmmphf!" Dominic wriggled in his bonds, but to no avail. Awakening in a wardrobe with three people blocking the entrance wasn't a pleasant experience, I was sure, but I had little sympathy for the man who tried to elope with me against my will.

"Here's what's going to happen," Maddox said to him, pointing with his dagger. I could see now that it was quite dull. "You're going to stay here for the next twenty-four hours and not make a peep. If you do, there will be consequences."

Dominic struggled, rattling the wardrobe. Giselle leaned forward and waved the patterned paper under his nose. He froze.

"That's right," Giselle said with a smirk. "I'll work my voodoo and whatnot on you if you're difficult."

"Hmmphf?" Dominic gave me a pleading look, but I remained stone-faced. He crumpled against the wall of the wardrobe.

Maddox slammed the doors shut. "Well. It's about time I take a look at those suspension wires."

37

Giselle barged in the next morning, a wad of royal purple fabric tucked under her arm. I winced as the door slammed.

"You managed to rework a charm *and* make us matching clothing?" I whispered, surveying her ensemble made out of the same fabric. She wore flowy trousers and a pin-tucked blouse decorated with braided gold trim.

Lady Vanessa breathed softly across the room, still miraculously asleep after the racket. I had spent the night in her room instead of mine, claiming loneliness. In reality, it was because of a certain rioter in my wardrobe, but I decided to spare her the details.

"Of course! I finished the charm in the first two hours. Had to destroy my old enchanted object to test it, but oh well. Never can be too sentimental." Giselle sighed woefully, but brightened as she laid out the pieces on the floor next to my cot, a voluminous blouse and a skirt similarly trimmed. "I had the whole rest of the night and, well, everyone knows matching outfits are absolutely essential when committing mutiny."

I ran a finger over the deep purple silk. "The color is…"

Bennett's favorite, I was going to say. But my throat seized, refusing to speak his name.

"It'll help us blend into the auditorium," Giselle said. "Besides, we all look divine in purple."

"I'm assuming we're not making a public appearance?" I said, raising my brow.

"Maddox and I won't. But you are," Giselle said.

"That wasn't part of the plan."

The seamstress shook her head. Her usual braid was replaced with a slick ponytail. "The witches of Alevine deserve to see their crown princess right before she saves them, don't you think?"

I shuffled back into my cot, comforted by Misty and Pippin's slumbering forms. "I wasn't invited. Celeste will suspect something is off. I'm supposed to be with Dominic now, remember?" I said, shuddering. I hoped his night in the wardrobe was a miserable one.

Giselle grabbed my shoulders. "Exactly. That'll show her that nothing she's doing will stop you. That you're stronger than she thinks you are. Those rioters will think twice before attempting another scheme again."

I set my jaw and nodded. Appearances were everything. The tour was over and done, but I was not.

"Shouldn't you have made something a little more... grand?" I asked, looking at the ensemble. It was lovely, but not exquisite like her usual dresses.

"The audience tonight will be witches," Giselle said. "Most aren't too impressed with luxury. What are you waiting for? Try it on."

It fit perfectly, as always, though the blouse and skirt

made me feel freer than I did in my usual evening wear. Giselle left to catch some sleep, stumbling over Maddox's foot on the way out.

"Watch it!" they said in unison. Giselle blushed, dumped a pile of purple on his lap, and disappeared down the hall.

I decided not to comment on their strange exchange as I stuck my head out the threshold. "You didn't have to stand guard all night, you know."

Maddox rubbed his eyes. "Lord Frederick trusted me to do the job." He stretched his back and blinked. "I should check if Dominic is still alive."

I gladly let him do that, having no wish to see the general's son ever again if I could help it. I'd have to have the remaining dresses in my wardrobe burned.

"What are you two talking about?"

I ducked back into the room. Lady Vanessa sat up in the bed, yawning into her hand.

"Nothing," I said quickly. "Good morning, Lady Vanessa."

"Good morning." She smiled sleepily, pulling her braid out from her chemise. It was mussed, like Misty's fur would be after rolling around in the grass. "It's nice that the two of you are getting along."

I busied myself with rearranging my cot. Misty was still asleep, curled against Pippin. "Right," I said, tucking the edges of my blanket around them. "I suppose we got used to each other in the past few months."

Lady Vanessa stood, straightening her sheets. "It's more than that, surely. Maddox never gets along with anyone unless he respects them in some way."

I shrugged. "Or maybe he likes the idea of having a sister to order around."

"Maybe." She laughed. "Your father will be very pleased with both of you once we return." Her smile dimmed at the mention of Father. He had abandoned her without so much as a word a few days ago. Though it wasn't his fault, it still must have hurt.

"You'll see him soon." I sat back on my heels, cheeks warming. Lady Vanessa's kindness was something I'd never forget. If only I wasn't so uncomfortable repaying it.

"I know. I always do," Lady Vanessa said softly. Her lips quirked up again. "You look lovely in purple."

Misty rolled over onto her back, paws in the air as Lady Vanessa disappeared into the washroom. I rubbed her ears, smiling at how comfortable she looked. Pippin yawned and licked Misty's head fondly.

"You two really like each other, don't you?" I murmured, hugging my knees to my chest.

Pippin meowed in affirmation. I blew out a breath, displacing a few curls. "I'm sorry I overreacted," I whispered, scratching Misty under the chin. "I was just scared. Maybe a little lonely...but not anymore."

Misty mewed.

"You were right all along. I bet you love that." I tweaked her nose and looked at Pippin. "And you have a lot to explain to me after tonight. You looked extremely well-groomed for a cat Bennett picked up off the street."

I couldn't help but laugh at the expression on his little face. Somehow even if I didn't understand them, my heart felt much lighter than it did yesterday.

THE STEPS OF the Grand Alevine Opera were flooded with witches, bundled up to the chin with gray wool coats and colorful knit scarves. A bracing wind howled through the glistening streets. It had rained in the afternoon but the clouds had since cleared, exposing an indigo sky speckled with stars.

I smoothed my skirt, straightening as I approached the golden entrance of the auditorium where witches were filing in. Giselle had slipped off earlier and Lady Ruan had taken Maddox backstage upon my request. The poor woman looked anxious, as if Maddox was going to single-handedly ruin the show.

Well, he was. But hopefully, she would find it in her heart to forgive us once the truth revealed itself.

"Is that Lady Narcissa?" an elderly witch whispered. He had a snowy white beard adorned with a variety of beads.

"I think so, grandpa," said his young companion. The boy couldn't have been more than ten, drowning in a maroon scarf. He stared, wide-eyed. "She looks just like the pictures."

I gave the pair a nod when they approached. "Good evening," I said, my voice barely audible over the footsteps on the marble floor.

"Lady Narcissa?" the elderly man asked. His eyes lit up when I nodded. "What a pleasure. I'm Ferdinand. This is my grandson, Giovanni. Go on Gio. Say hello."

The boy murmured a shy hello.

Ferdinand wedged himself and his grandson to the side, letting the witches behind him pass. "I heard you were here in Alevine but I didn't expect to meet in person," he said jovially. "You've made quite the impression this past year, haven't you?"

I smiled, wringing my hands behind my back. "A good one, I hope."

"Absolutely!" Giovanni exclaimed. The word echoed in

the hall. He ducked his nose into his scarf. "You're a hero."

I laughed in surprise. "A hero?"

"The boy's serious," Ferdinand said, raising a bushy white brow. "Not only did you douse the fire in Vandil, but you also helped a great deal of magical business owners figure out what they were doing wrong. Old William told us everything."

The fire and William's produce shop seemed so long ago, yet I remembered my crippling guilt like it was yesterday. Dousing the fire had been an impulsive decision, but William's shop? I hated that I used the schemes Mother taught me, but now it seemed silly. Mother gained nothing from it and William, everything.

"I only did what I could," I said, cheeks warm at the grandson's awe-stricken stare.

Ferdinand grinned a toothless grin. "It takes courage to go against someone like your mother. You'll make a great queen one day."

I bid them goodbye as they followed the rest in, my face hot. The witches behind them seemed to have noticed my presence. Soon, a smaller line formed with those who wanted to greet me. None of them asked why I was blushing like a schoolgirl, which I was grateful for. The usher seemed scandalized as I exchanged cordial hellos and handshakes with the witches streaming in.

"Good evening, Lady Narcissa."

"Lovely to meet you, Lady Narcissa."

"What a stunning skirt you're wearing! Is it witch-made by any chance?"

"Never in a million years did I think a witch would be in the place you're in. How wonderfully inspiring."

A few witches grew teary-eyed and expressed their gratitude for everything I had done during the tour. I found myself in a few awkward embraces, and by the time the line had dwindled, my ears were hot and my heart throbbing from the sheer amount of praise I had received.

Everyone was so friendly. Friendlier than any group of strangers had ever been to me.

My resolve hardened. Celeste wouldn't touch a single one of them if I could help it.

"Lady Narcissa! Enchanted to meet you in person."

I started at the nasally voice that cut through the noise. A woman in a burnt orange coat and a sleek updo stood before me, pen and notebook in hand. The bright rouge on her lips made her easily identifiable.

"Sister Scarlett," I said, inclining my head.

She tittered. "Oh! I thought I would have to introduce myself. Well, since we're both acquainted," she said, tilting her chin conspiringly, "would you mind doing a short interview?"

I held back a sigh. It didn't seem like I had a choice, from the way the woman was standing. She was so close I'd have to use magic to escape. "Of course," I said, keeping my face neutral.

"Wonderful!" Sister Scarlett scrutinized my ensemble and scribbled something down. I could only imagine what she was writing.

Lady Narcissa Greenwood was spotted at the Grand Alevine Opera dressed plainly in a blouse and skirt, greeting witch civilians as if she were one of them. What could possibly be the purpose of this plebeian display?

"So. I've heard from my sources that you are acquainted with a certain Dominic?" she said, raising a perfectly groomed brow.

"Dominic?" I said slowly, looking off to the ceiling. "Never knew one."

"Oh." She flipped back a few pages and scratched something out, a disappointed frown on her lips.

Good. Whatever lies Dominic had fed her about me would never see the light of day.

"Well, never mind that. Let's talk about what happened two nights ago," Sister Scarlett said brightly, refocusing her attention on me. "The king had the rioters surrounded. It must've been a frightening experience."

"I wasn't there." Perhaps if I kept my answers short she'd leave faster. The last of the witches had filed into the auditorium. Any minute now the show would start. I wanted to make sure Celeste failed.

"His Majesty and the crown prince left you here shortly after," Sister Scarlett continued. "Why is that?"

I forced myself to meet her shrewd eyes, though her words brought a pang from the memory of their sudden departure. "They had prisoners to take care of in Delibera. It would be unseemly for me to join them."

"Of course." She wrote a few words before looking up again. "And how do you feel now that you are separated from the crown prince?"

Another pang. I pushed it down. "Fine. We both have duties outside of being in each other's company." My words sounded more bitter than I intended.

I cringed inwardly as a flow of sentences appeared in Sister Scarlett's notebook.

"How would you describe your relationship with His Highness?" Her fervent expression made it clear this was the main reason she was here. "I'm sure all of Olderea is wondering how you and Crown Prince Bennett went from strangers at the beginning of the tour to the close—ah, individuals—you are now."

The auditorium lights had yet to dim, but the audience had all been escorted to their boxes. "Our relationship?" I murmured distractedly. "It's fine."

Sister Scarlett furrowed her brow at the vague answer. My legs grew restless as the ushers began to snuff out the candlelight.

"Could you elaborate on that?" she said.

I repressed a sigh. Short answers weren't working.

"We're head over heels in love with each other and we plan on having five children once we're married. King Maximus is already scouring the kingdom for nannies. It'll be a grand occasion," I said, barely able to keep the irritation out of my voice. "Is that all? I would like to attend the show."

"Yes! Yes, of course," Sister Scarlett said, scribbling profusely. "That is perfect."

She blathered something else about children and how darling they were, but I slipped into the auditorium, glancing up at the box I had occupied during the past two shows. It was full. I scoured the dim room for an empty seat. A shock of white hair caught my eye in the center front.

"Oh, hello Lady Narcissa," Ferdinand said in surprise as I squeezed into his box. Giovanni gaped at me as I sat in the empty seat beside him.

I felt sorry for the intrusion, but the two weren't going to have a pleasant night either way. "I hope you don't mind me joining you," I said, smiling as if barging into other people's boxes was a normal occurrence.

Luckily, the old witch didn't seem to be versed in the rules of society. "Of course not! We'll be honored."

I thanked him and leaned back, trying to look relaxed. My nerves were practically humming. Had Maddox made it to the wires? Was Giselle prepared to cast her spell?

Unfortunately, I was stuck in my seat. Was this what being royalty was like—making all the decisions but never carrying them out personally? It was maddening. Perhaps this was how Bennett felt before the tour.

I gnawed my lower lip as Ferdinand chattered about his experience with theatrical productions. I did my best to appear engaged. At last, the curtains began to lift. A sliver of bright light and an ethereal background appeared, then the bottom of the hovering moon, then a train of a glittering robe, then Celeste herself, hovering over it all.

Oohs and ahs filled the auditorium. The orchestra began playing the soulful tune to her opening song. Celeste parted her lips.

Now, Maddox, I thought fiercely.

A loud twang sounded before the soprano could sing a note. The moon she hung from dropped, swinging violently to the side. The audience gasped.

"Is that part of the show?" Ferdinand asked, baffled.

My satisfaction with Maddox's timely efforts didn't last. Celeste clung onto the swinging moon with surprising strength and grace, reaching an arm out to the audience. She began to sing.

I cursed when the first note hit the air. Giovanni squeaked, but seconds later he froze, eyes glued to the stage.

"Ferdinand, cover your ears," I said desperately, but the elderly witch was in a similar state. So was the rest of the auditorium.

I should have known it wouldn't be that simple. Breaking the suspension cord wasn't enough to delay the show, much less buy Giselle time to destroy Celeste's enchanted object.

Lurching from my seat, I rushed out of the box, making sure to duck so the singer wouldn't notice my presence. Past the backstage stairs and protesting stagehands, I burst into the back hall where Celeste's room was. The red door was ajar.

"Where in the blazing fires did she put it?" Giselle muttered to herself as I barreled in. She whirled around. "Narcissa? What are you doing here?"

Maddox was with her, frantically flipping through drawers.

"Celeste is singing," I said between breaths. I stared at them both standing in a mess of bottles and embroidered pillows. "Have you found the object?"

Maddox shook his head. "No luck yet."

Giselle held out a knotted charm. "This is supposed to track enchanted objects, but it's not sensing anything." She waved her hand around the variety of vials and bottle around her. "Do you have any idea what this container looks like?"

I cursed again. We should have asked Dominic when we had the chance, but somehow it slipped our minds. Those witches in the auditorium would suffer for our negligence.

I squeezed my eyes shut. "Wait," I said, hiking up my skirts to Celeste's vanity. I recalled the large iridescent container on the top shelf. Sure enough, it was there. I pointed it out. "Is it that?"

Maddox climbed onto the tabletop and retrieved it, knocking over a few vials. He inspected the glossy surface and pulled on the diamond stopper. It did not budge.

For a second, the center flashed gold. Maddox yelped, nearly dropping it.

"Ha! I knew it," Giselle said, taking the container from him. "She concealed it from tracking charms."

"Hurry and destroy it." I didn't mean to sound so snappy, but my anxiety made my voice harsh. The echo of Celeste's singing drifted over from the auditorium. I slammed the door shut.

"In a moment," Giselle said, tucking the glass under her arm. "We're going to have to take this outside. Enchanted objects contain a great deal of magic, especially one of this size. Destroying it could be explosive."

I gritted my teeth. "If we walk out we're going to hear Celeste singing. You can't afford to lose your magic."

Maddox furrowed his brows. "One second." He unsheathed his dagger and hacked into a velvet cushion. I was going to ask him why he was gutting a pillow until he picked out a pinch of stuffing and took Giselle's chin, turning her to face him.

"Really, this is hardly the time to kiss me," she said.

"I was not going to kiss you!" Maddox jerked his hand away, cheeks turning bright red. He shoved the fluff into her hand. "The guards stuff their ears with cotton when they don't want to hear each other's snoring. Pack it in as densely as you can."

Giselle took the fluff nonchalantly and put it into her ears. "Kissing me would've worked just as well. Then I wouldn't be able to hear anything but my own gagging."

Maddox scoffed, muttering something about despicable women. I found their exchange rather amusing, but the smile on my lips died when the three of us exited the room and Celeste's song rang through the halls loud and clear. Giselle pressed her hands to her ears. We increased our pace.

Patrick the stagehand stood with his arms crossed as we emerged backstage, mouth parting. I motioned Maddox and Giselle to go on. They slipped off. The stagehand paid them no mind. No doubt he thought I was the threat.

"You may have escaped King Maximus's guards but you won't escape mine," I said before he could speak, giving him my best condescending glare. I hoped I looked intimidating. Like a proper princess.

He paled, but didn't move. "The mistress will get rid of you. She'll get rid of you all."

I raised a brow. "Will she?"

I began to leave, but Patrick grabbed my wrist with a large, bony hand. He couldn't have been older than fifteen. There was a mad panic in his eyes.

"Not so fast, witch," he spat. "King Maximus and the crown prince left you here. You're no longer under their protection, are you?"

My jaw clenched, but I forced a smile. "Perhaps not. But I can order the sewer rats to eat you alive if you don't get your hands off of me."

Patrick's eyes widened. He didn't know Celeste had taken my magic away, then. He stepped back, letting me go. Somehow, his fear did not ease the knot in my stomach.

He was just a boy who thought his livelihood was being threatened, like all the other rioters. They were desperate because their ruler had failed them.

I took a breath, smoothing my expression. "I hope you will have more faith in the crown, Patrick," I said quietly, "once we set everything right."

He merely stared, his brows furrowed. I pushed past him and hoped with all my heart that I hadn't made a false promise.

Outside the opera house, Giselle stood at the bottom of the steps with Maddox. She set the iridescent bottle onto the sparse grass. The night was still and the stars illuminated just enough. I ran down to join them, a chilled breeze raking through my clothing.

"You might want to stand back," Giselle shouted.

Maddox and I obliged, tucking ourselves behind a tall white pillar. Giselle whipped out a slip of paper, not unlike the one she had put on Dominic. She took a deep breath and made a complicated motion with her hands, too fast to decipher.

The bottle shuddered, teetering on the bumpy ground, then shattered into a million shimmering pieces. A mound of iridescent sand pooled at Giselle's feet.

"Huh," she said, regarding it. "I thought it would be more dramatic."

A whoosh of something blew past me, tickling my cheeks and tousling my hair. It was not wind, neither cold nor hot. I knew it from the moment it touched me that it was magic. Pure magic.

WE FOUND LORD Frederick dozing off in a dim parlor on the third floor. His gray eyes widened when I explained everything to him, from Dominic's stunt double to Celeste's plan. His face softened when I told him of King Maximus's decision to separate me from Bennett.

"What do you need me to do, milady?" Lord Frederick said. I was immensely grateful for him in that moment.

"Help us escort Celeste back to Delibera," I said.

He nodded. "Anything else? As His Majesty's former advisor I believe I can convince him to change his mind about—"

I shook my head. I knew what he was going to say, but I couldn't bring myself to hope.

We waited until the end of Celeste's show to return to the auditorium. It seemed the singer hadn't noticed any change until the moment she saw us backstage. Maddox and another guard seized her upon arrival.

"What are you doing?" Celeste spat, still dressed in her sparkling robes.

"You can't steal magic and expect no one to notice, *Cecelia*." Giselle crossed her arms, arching a brow when the singer's face twisted from surprise to malice.

"Giselle?" she screeched. "You b—"

Maddox yanked her arms back and tied them with a length of rope.

Celeste glared. "You don't have any proof! You can't incriminate me without solid evidence."

"Oh we have evidence, alright," Giselle said, dangling Celeste's throat spray in front of her face. She looked like she was enjoying herself immensely. "*And* we have someone who will attest to your crimes."

The singer narrowed her eyes, just noticing my presence. "Dominic," she said with a hiss. She turned to Giselle. "I'm surprised they haven't arrested you too. My magic isn't half as bad as yours."

Giselle's expression grew dark. Before she could retort, Lord Frederick approached Lady Ruan who had rushed in from the back hallway, mouth gaping at the sight of her star soprano bound up. He explained everything to her. The poor woman looked heartbroken as Maddox and the other guards led Celeste away.

"None of this is your fault," I assured Lady Ruan as I passed.

She merely blew her nose into her handkerchief.

The witches filed out of the opera house. If anyone noticed their magic almost being taken away, they were impressed enough with the show to brush it off as their imagination.

Witches were a passive people, after all.

38

Misty was two months old when she first spoke. She was in her makeshift bed beneath mine, blinking with sleepy eyes when I awoke her. I wanted to show her the new toy I had made—a handful of gray-blue pigeon feathers tied to one of my hair ribbons.

"Look Misty," I said, dangling the contraption over my feet. "I brought you something to play with."

My stockings were torn and dirty from scouring the garden for the nicest feathers, but luckily Mother was out. She would punish me if she saw them.

Your mother does not sound very nice, my kitten mewed.

I started, scrambling to the floor. "You're speaking! *And* you can hear my thoughts," I beamed as Misty meandered to my lap. "I thought it would take another week at least."

Animals were very much like people. They said nothing decipherable until a certain age, but they were much faster learners.

Misty pawed at the feathers. *Like I said, your mother doesn't sound very nice.*

I pouted. I needed to convince Mother to let me keep Misty as a proper house cat. That would only work if Misty was exceptionally well-behaved. And if she liked Mother.

"Of course she's nice," I said, stringing the feathers across the floor. Misty pounced. "She just wants me to be the best. That's all."

Misty gnawed on the feathers and spit them out. I couldn't help but giggle at how silly she looked. I couldn't imagine why the crown prince thought dusty old books were more interesting than kittens.

That doesn't sound fun, Misty meowed, rolling onto her back.

I rubbed her soft underbelly, moving the feathers aside. The movement only made her jump back onto her feet and fly at them at full speed.

I watched her wrestle with the toy for a minute until she tore it apart. The pigeon feathers were in shreds, the scarlet ribbon frayed. I frowned and tucked the mangled toy behind my back.

"Not everything is about fun," I said in my best disciplinary voice I had adopted from Mother.

Misty tilted her head. *It isn't?*

"No, it is not. We will have to behave occasionally too," I said. I peered under my bed frame, wrinkling my nose at the smell wafting from Misty's burrow. "Let's start with house training."

I TURNED THE knob to my room in the opera house, now cleared of everything besides Misty and Pippin who were both fast asleep on the mattress. Weak daylight streamed in through the balcony.

It had rained again last night, droplets drenching the streets and pitter pattering against the window in a comforting hum as I slept. We planned to leave at noon, as everyone had retired late.

I didn't have a chance to try my magic again. The third floor of the opera was considerably vacant pest-wise, and the cats were already asleep by the time I went upstairs. They looked too precious to wake, as they did now.

Misty was curled against Pippin, both of them shaped like two furry crescent moons. I ran my fingers over Misty's side, surprised at the weight she had put on the last time I had studied her.

She shifted. *Morning already?*

A giant smile split my face. "You're speaking!"

Misty sat up and I gathered her into my arms, squeezing her to my chest. I knew she hated tight hugs, but she didn't move away.

To be fair, I have always spoken. You just didn't understand me, Misty meowed, squirming away after a full minute. *Everything worked out, then?*

"Yes." I wiped away the moisture in my eyes. "Yes, it did. I love you."

I love you too, darling, Misty said. She nuzzled my cheek, whiskers tickling my nose.

"We're going home today," I said, tilting my head up to keep the tears in. They were happy tears, but my eyes still ached.

Pippin stirred from the noise, yawning and stretching his paws. *Home?* he meowed.

"Back to Delibera," I said. "You're going to live in the palace, Pippin."

The tabby cat blinked. *Am I?* He stood, his fur ruffled and his brow lowered. *Would I even be welcome?*

"Of course. You're Bennett's cat." I reached over for him, but he evaded me. I raised my brows. He never refused a good petting. "What's wrong?"

Bennett abandoned me, Pippin meowed. *I'm his cat but he abandoned me. Vulgar way to treat a stray, don't you think?*

"Oh, Pippin," I said, sitting on the mattress. "He didn't have a choice. His father—"

Of course he had a choice, he said, turning up his nose. *He made a choice to adopt me regardless of his father. He could have taken me with him this week, or he could have stayed. He just didn't want to.*

I didn't think explaining royal obligation to a stray would be productive, so I changed the subject, telling the cats that their breakfast was ready in the courtyard.

Lady Ruan saw us off, waving from the steps of the opera house. I suspected she was glad to be rid of us after we destroyed her suspension wires and arrested her star soprano.

Celeste and Dominic were in a separate carriage, being watched by Maddox. I hoped they would be well-behaved prisoners for the length of the trip.

Misty put a paw on my hand as the carriage rolled off, rattling down the dreary cobblestone streets. *Pippin is right, you know*, she meowed, blinking up from my lap.

She felt heavier. I shifted in my seat to redistribute her weight. Pippin had fallen back asleep against my thigh, oblivious to our conversation.

"Misty..."

Bennett always had a choice. He chose to love you in spite of the king.

"I don't know if love is a choice, Misty." I turned to the window, my breath fogging up the glass. "And he's the crown prince. It has always been more than just me and him."

Bennett had forgotten his title when he was with me. But the people of Olderea came first. He had a duty to them and to their king. I thought back to Ferdinand and Gio and all the others who greeted me at the opera house.

If Bennett left me for their sakes, I found that easier to swallow.

I sighed. Why did it matter now? He was going to spend the next year without me. By the end of it he would have reverted back to his old self, silent and unmoving. Pretending like nothing had happened. Would I do the same?

Don't tell me we're going to spend the next year miserable and locked in your room again. Misty nudged my hand.

"We won't," I assured her. "We can take more walks."

You're not listening to me. You need to be with him.

I looked at her, surprised at the urgency of her tone. "Misty, I'll have you and Maddox and Lady Vanessa and Father. We will be fine."

No. You'll be miserable. And he will be miserable.

"But King Maximus said—"

The king has issues.

I laughed. "My mother has that effect on people."

Mother always fancied the king—that I knew even as a child. Whether she genuinely loved him or only cared about his title was unclear to me, but from the way King Maximus controlled Bennett regarding matters of the heart, I figured it was the former. Whatever Mother did, she never skimped on effort. Her love must have been a strong one. So strong it made the king not want the same for his son.

I want you to be happy, Misty meowed. I pet her ears

fondly. Father said the same thing earlier this winter. I wasn't sure if I had fulfilled his wishes.

"I am happy," I said to Misty softly. "I have you."

She tilted her head. *I'm having kittens*, she mewed.

My eyes widened. "What?"

Misty nodded, rolling onto her back to show me. I touched her belly, which had certainly expanded in the past few weeks. That explained the extra weight. "Pippin, you rascal," I whispered to the sleeping tabby cat.

By the time I have my litter I expect you to have everything sorted out with the king. Pippin wants to be with Bennett. I can't have us separated.

I hugged her close, feeling tears prick my eyes again. My kitten was having kittens.

Misty squirmed upright, narrowing her green eyes. *Promise me. If you won't do it for yourself, at least do it for me.*

My throat grew tight. Would King Maximus listen to sense? Would Bennett attempt to persuade him? I squeezed my eyes shut. Did Bennett even want to see me again?

Don't talk nonsense, Misty thought to me. *Of course he does.*

Hearing her voice in my head again was so comforting I didn't care if I believed her words or not.

"Alright," I said. "I promise."

THE NEXT FEW weeks passed by in a blur. Celeste and Dominic were thankfully well-behaved prisoners, despite the occasional cursing and insults that erupted from their carriage. We passed through Vandil and stayed at Lady Mariana's again. The witch market reparations were coming along nicely and the inhabitants welcomed me with open arms.

I was showered with gifts from fine, shimmering fabrics to glossy-leafed plants to magical charms and knick-knacks. An elderly witch woman stuffed a packet of herbs into my hands.

"For plenty of children between you and the crown prince." She walked off with a wink, the beaded ornaments on her belt jangling. I kept my composure until I was back in the carriage, where I shoved it into the trunk of gifts, hoping it would magically get lost.

That evening Giselle showed me a copy of the morning post. Sister Scarlett's article was plastered on the front page.

Madly In Love: An Exclusive Interview with Lady Narcissa Greenwood

On a rainy Friday evening, Lady Narcissa Greenwood was spotted before the Grand Alevine Opera, personally welcoming witch guests as they streamed into the auditorium. Though I was not invited to that night's show, I jumped at the opportunity to interview the future princess herself.

When asked about the previous night's rebel arrest, Lady Narcissa claimed ignorance of the incident and declined to comment further on the political side of things. She did, however, eagerly turn the discussion to her relationship with Crown Prince Bennett.

"We are head over heels in love with each other," Lady Narcissa had said, lovely eyes shining, "and we plan on having five children once we're married."

She laments being separated from her fiancé on such short notice, admitting that it has been especially difficult. Her mood seemed to improve when she discussed King Maximus's efforts in scouring Olderea for the best nannies.

I can only suspect that Lady Narcissa is already with child after so many months alone with Crown Prince Bennett. Why else would the king be looking for caretakers before the wedding? Could it be that she is already Princess Narcissa?

I balled the paper up and threw it at Giselle who was guffawing uncontrollably. "Stop it!" My face heated as she dodged and continued cackling. "I said what I had to to get rid of the woman."

Maddox made a series of unpleasant kissing noises. "Whatever you say, *Princess Narcissa.*"

I endured another three days of relentless teasing from both of them.

On our last night on the road, we spotted the gates of Delibera in the distance, silhouetted by the dimming sky. Lord Frederick ordered the men to set up camp in the forest clearing. The prisoners were being tied to trees as I took a turn around the grounds to stretch my legs.

"You know they will never accept us, Narcissa," Celeste called out.

I paused. Lord Frederick advised me not to speak to the prisoners. I was diligent in avoiding Dominic, but not so much Celeste. The singer was now dressed in a plain brown ensemble instead of her glittering stage costume. Her hair had lost its luster, hanging in loose tangles down her back. She looked at me with a grave expression.

"I don't know what you are talking about," I said stiffly, ready to walk off. Celeste scoffed.

"The humans. They will never accept witches no matter how many laws you change. No matter who pledges their allegiance to you." She gave an icy glare to Dominic across the camp. He was dozing off against his tree. She returned her dark gaze to me. "You thought your prince loved you. But where was the fool when you lost your magic?"

I clenched my jaw. "You will speak of His Highness with respect."

Celeste laughed and shook her head. "Don't you get it, Narcissa? Humans don't see us as people. They see us as our magic—something to be used and feared. Once our magic is gone we are nothing. The sooner you realize that the better."

I turned abruptly and walked off to the center of camp, where a happy fire was blazing. Giselle and Maddox sat on a log eating stew, bickering about something. I pressed my lips together, throwing a glance back at Celeste. She was wrong about Bennett. He never feared my magic, nor did he ever want to use it.

If Bennett ever loved me, it was for me.

The next day, we entered Delibera. The familiarity of the city felt foreign after months of new sights and new roads.

Lord Frederick peered in through the carriage window when we stopped for a break. Half the guard split off to escort Dominic and Celeste to the palace, but Lord Frederick stayed with me. "Where to, milady? The palace or…?"

Our trip had given me plenty of time to think. The entirety of the company had heard about King Maximus's one-year-postponement decree at this point. Not to mention, my last impression of the palace had been tainted by Mother's presence, my mind too plagued with thoughts of her.

I never wanted to see her again. The realization should have come to me sooner. I needed to dispel her—if not from my memory—from my life. She had done enough damage.

I set my jaw, gazing at the turquoise tiled rooftops of the city.

"Greenwood Abbey, please."

39

1 month later

It can't end like that!" Giselle said, throwing *The Sailor's Seduction* onto the sofa. The heavy volume landed with a thunk.

Maddox sighed and fell back onto my rug. "We never find out if Carla and Antonio get away from the duke."

I took a sip of tea. "I told you two not to read it."

The three of us fell into companionable silence.

The past month had been painfully uneventful. Though I received a flood of invitations and calling cards for various teas and gatherings, I declined them all. They came from the very people who spurned me months before, including Mother's former friends. I decided I was quite done with them.

Other than taking strolls and visiting our local witch-owned shops, Maddox and I fell back into our previous routine of doing absolutely nothing, though this time we did so in each other's company. Giselle visited frequently after quitting her position on the witch committee.

"It's too much pressure," she said breezily when we asked her why. "Besides, I've always wanted to open my own dress emporium."

Soon after, Giselle secured an empty shop at the corner of Delibera's witch market. When she wasn't there, she spent her time reading *The Sailor's Seduction* over Maddox's shoulder as the three of us lounged in my room. Misty and Pippin joined occasionally, the former looking more pregnant by the day.

Father didn't seem to mind Maddox and me wasting our time. After learning that we single-handedly took down Celeste, he said we deserved a break. I only hoped it would be long enough for Maddox to find something else to do. Lady Vanessa and I were getting used to the lack of shouting matches in the abbey.

"You don't need any help at your dress shop, do you?" Maddox asked, propping himself up on his elbows.

Giselle waved her hand. "No, no. I don't plan on opening until Narcissa gets married."

I nearly choked on my tea. "Why?"

"Once the people see the wedding gown I made for you, I'll have plenty of customers."

"You're not working for the royals anymore, Giselle." I set down my teacup and studied the lace on the curtains across the room. "Besides, the wedding is not guaranteed to happen."

The thought used to hurt more, but I've had plenty of time to come to terms with it.

It didn't matter how unfair it was. It didn't matter how my stomach fluttered at the scent of cedar. King Maximus was a stubborn man, and I didn't want to hope if there was none.

Giselle made a noise. "The king has been locked up in

his library for the entire month. I sincerely hope he's rethinking his decisions."

"Honestly. The engagement was his idea and now he won't even let you see the crown prince." Maddox sat up. "Plus, after everything I did, the least I deserve is an honorary medal," he grumbled under his breath.

Giselle threw me a sidelong glance. "You know, if you ever need an invisibility tonic to sneak into Bennett's—"

"For the third time, Giselle, no." I folded my hands in my lap, wishing the conversation would turn elsewhere. I had long given up on seeing Bennett again before the year was up despite Misty's increasingly impatient reminders about our agreement. And I certainly wasn't going to attempt one of Giselle's many unscrupulous plans.

She pouted. "But it would be so romantic."

"Sneaking into someone's room uninvited is the furthest thing from romantic," Maddox interjected.

Giselle threw a tasseled cushion at him. "What do *you* know about romance?"

"More than you, evidently," Maddox said, rubbing his head.

The two began bickering. They were too preoccupied with each other to notice that I had risen from the sofa. But before I could make a stealthy escape to the gardens, a knock came from the door.

Father poked his head in. "Cissa, you have a visitor," he said. "It's the king."

I WRUNG MY sleeves as I followed Father down the hall. Daylight streamed in from our newly modified windows, now as large and grand as the ones in Huntington Abbey. But the cheerful lighting wasn't nearly enough to quell my anxieties.

"What does His Majesty want?" I asked.

"He didn't say." Father furrowed his gray brows. When we stopped before the parlor door, he took my shoulders. "Cissa, I want you to know how proud I am of you."

"Oh," I said, startled at the sudden praise. "Thank you, Father."

"No, truly. You were brave back in Alevine. Braver than I was. I hope Maximus can see that," he said. He closed his eyes and sighed heavily. "And that his son will be happier with you."

I was close to letting out a sigh of my own.

"Crown Prince Bennett inquired after you."

The words sent a jolt through me. I tried not to let it show.

Though Father had spent the past month around King Maximus and thereby his son, I never dared to inquire after Bennett. I knew doing so would be asking him to be disloyal.

"Father, you don't have to tell—"

"His Highness was worried sick. Wanted to know if you were all right after the episode you had that night," he said. "I told him about your magic being taken and that you were doing fine now. I would've told him more if I could."

I ached to ask after Bennett too, but Father couldn't be passing messages between us—it would be inconsiderate to put him in that position.

Father patted me on the back and turned the knob. "Go on, now. I think you will find His Majesty in a merciful mood, albeit prickly. But if he does not grant your wishes,

I'll have the abbey surrounded until he does." His expression was disturbingly serious when he left me to enter the parlor.

King Maximus didn't look up at my entrance, but his face pinched at the sound of the door closing.

"Narcissa," he said gruffly. He sat on a plump armchair with rose pink upholstery, examining the trim on the cushions Lady Vanessa had sewed on recently. "It's been a while."

I curtsied. "Did you need anything, Your Majesty?"

He sighed, setting down the cushion. "Your father and Lord Frederick have been singing your high praises for the past month. And that Giselle, when she stormed in my office to quit the witch committee. I suppose my son would have done the same if he bothered talking to me."

I parted my lips, but King Maximus held up a hand.

"I know you did not send them," he said. "I am merely here to tell you that Celeste has been tried and imprisoned. General Turner and Dominic as well. The riots have died down ever since I enforced the newest policies on witch-made items, as you predicted."

"That is good to hear," I said. I had seen the papers reporting that last week. I was glad my promise to Patrick last month hadn't been false. Hopefully the stagehand was seeing the effects of the new laws.

King Maximus regarded the window. "As for Bennett, he is how he has always been. Quiet. I never realized how quiet."

"He's not helping you draft laws?" I asked, unable to contain my curiosity.

"Helping is a generous word. He is acting more like a mute scribe than a crown prince," the king said with a snort.

"Isn't that what you wanted from him?"

King Maximus sucked in his cheeks. I was afraid I had overstepped my boundaries, but he slumped forward, looking older and more exhausted than I had ever seen him.

"I acknowledge my faults, Narcissa, but being king involves more challenges than you dare to imagine."

I scuffed the carpet with my shoe. "If I may be so bold, Your Majesty?"

"By all means."

"You're paranoid." Those were the same words Misty had told me so many months ago. "Your sons are not a threat to your throne."

I recalled how Bennett and Prince Ash talked about working with the king, who evidently was used to having the final say on everything. Perhaps that was why Bennett learned to be soft-spoken—because he thought his voice didn't matter.

"And neither was my former general, it turned out," King Maximus said stiffly.

"It's not your age," I said quickly. He looked rather pathetic in the too-small armchair. "I only believe that Olderea will benefit from multiple rulers instead of one."

"Bennett would tell me the same thing. If he would speak," the king mumbled.

I cautiously sat in the seat across from him, unsure of the purpose of this conversation.

King Maximus sighed. "A banquet will take place next week to celebrate the completion of the tour. You are invited, obviously."

I stared. "Your Majesty?"

"You will see him then. I tire of his sulking and you seem to be the only solution."

"The engagement—"

"Is still on. I have already told the press about the one-year delay so you cannot get married until then," King Maximus said, standing from his seat.

I blinked rapidly. He truly loved his son if he was willing to make amends with me. Perhaps he wasn't entirely like Mother after all.

King Maximus gave me a steely stare when he turned to go. "But mark my words, Narcissa. If my son becomes a lovesick buffoon in your presence again, I won't be so forgiving."

I returned to my room, numb. Maddox and Giselle stood at my entrance.

"What did he want?" Giselle asked.

I let go of the breath I was holding. "I can see Bennett again."

40

The day of the banquet came before I knew it. Giselle whipped up a dress for me, a floaty evening gown the color of frosted leaves, pale enough to be mistaken for white. I dressed with greater care than usual that night.

When I arrived at the palace banquet hall, a maidservant escorted me to a curtained alcove before the entrance, where I was told to wait. It was there I sat.

"I do not see why this is necessary," I said, shifting on my feet.

"Apologies, milady." The maid wrung her hands, peeking out at the banquet hall. "Just a minute more."

"You said that for the past fifteen." I tugged at the emeralds dangling from my necklace—the gift Bennett had given me at Alevine.

The maid blushed. "Apologies," she repeated.

"What are we waiting for, exactly? Every other guest has already been announced."

"For the royal steward to come with Crown Prince Bennett," she said.

"Is he not already here?" I asked in surprise. My glances past the curtains have been futile, then.

"His Highness is running late," she said. "King Maximus wanted you to be announced together but…" Her words trailed off and she ducked her head.

Had Bennett heard of my attendance? Was that why he avoided coming? There was no reason to believe that was the case, but a month's separation had blurred the memory of him, of his mannerisms and whether his affections had been as ardent as I thought. Did he only need a month to forget about me?

Murmurs came from the banquet hall. The guests were waiting for me and their crown prince, no doubt.

My hands grew clammy. The alcove seemed to grow smaller. "As His Highness has not shown his face, perhaps I may be allowed a stroll?"

The maid poked her head out when I exited the alcove. "Milady! You mustn't! The guests will expect you soon."

I turned, tucking my shawl tighter around me. "As it is, I cannot be announced without the crown prince," I said, forcing a smile. "Five minutes. I will return shortly."

I didn't stay to hear the rest of her pleas.

The exterior of the banquet hall was lined with gladiolus flowers, opening up to a manicured lawn and a man-made pond where the debutantes had spent a morning during last summer's Season. The surface of the water was undisturbed. The swans had since migrated for the winter. It was likely they would return soon.

I walked along the perimeter of the building, taking care to duck out of sight when I passed the windows. The glittering chandeliers within threw golden panes of light onto the dew-drenched grass. The hem of my gown was soaked from it. Giselle would have fainted.

My steps slowed when I wandered past the exterior of the banquet hall. Rounded shrubberies marked the entrance to the royal family's private gardens. I played there frequently in my youth.

The garden hadn't changed much. Every bush was trimmed to perfection, the grass a lush carpet beneath my slippers. The wisteria tree in the center had the first blooms of spring, drooping elegantly over the large fountain where I used to sit, counting the flowers I picked while waiting for Mother.

I had brought Misty the week after I found her, but she didn't like the water and scrambled up the tree in protest. My lips twitched at the memory.

I began to turn back, but my feet fell into a patch of light beaming from the window to my left. It spanned floor to ceiling, as many of the palace windows did, but I started at the sight within.

A desk was pushed up against the glass. Seated behind it was the crown prince, hunched over a mess of papers, his hand raked in his hair. His shirt was rumpled and his waistcoat halfway buttoned, a stark contrast to his usual impeccable dress.

An emerald green ribbon was tied around his wrist. From it glittered the ring he had given me all those weeks ago. The one I had returned.

"Oh, Bennett," I said under my breath. My words were scarcely loud enough for my own ears. I slipped back into the shadows, content for now to watch and imprint the image of him into my mind.

Bennett crossed something out and threw down his quill with evident frustration. He pressed the heels of his palms to his eyes.

I thought I saw my name scribbled on the paper, but a faint knock came from within before I could take a closer look. Ulysses entered.

"There you are, Your Highness! I've been combing the grounds for you," the steward said between breaths. "You're late for the banquet."

"I'm not going."

I jumped at how close his voice sounded despite the glass.

"Not going?" Ulysses sputtered. "B-but the king has invited—"

"I do not care who my father has invited, I am not going," Bennett said curtly. "I believe he will be pleased to know I'm spending my time in a less frivolous manner."

He turned back to his papers and began scribbling furiously, though from my point of view, there were only loops escaping his quill. I couldn't help but smile.

Ulysses furrowed his brow, disapproving. "Your Highness."

Bennett gripped the quill tighter. "Please, Ulysses. Spare me this one night."

The steward slumped his shoulders. "You cannot pass your entire life in this manner."

Bennett deigned him no reply and continued scribbling nonsense. At last, Ulysses turned and shut the door, but not before giving the crown prince's back a pinched scowl. I almost laughed out loud, but the sight of Bennett's face put off all amusement. He looked positively miserable, and though Ulysses had left, did not stop his scrawling.

My heart twinged. I stepped forward and tapped the glass with a finger.

Bennett's brow furrowed. "Ulysses, for heaven's sake I told you—" His breath caught when he looked up, our gazes colliding.

After a beat of silence, I gave a hesitant smile.

"Narcissa?" My name finally tore out of his throat.

I pressed a hand against the icy glass, warming at the sight of his hazel eyes. "Bennett," I said softly.

To my alarm, he climbed onto his desk, scattering his papers. I was beginning to question his sanity until some hidden mechanism clicked and the window swung open like a door. He jumped to the grass.

I hardly had time to comment before Bennett pulled me into his arms in a tight embrace. I collided into him, my face buried into his neck. His scent lingered there. Cedar and spices. I hugged him back, wondering how I managed the last month without him.

"Cissa! I-I never dreamed I would see you again so soon," Bennett said when he pulled away. His eyes were wet. "I meant to write to you but—heavens you must've thought I…"

Bennett's voice broke off, and he fell into a rapt silence. His stare seemed to finish what his words couldn't.

I was afraid I would cry if he didn't stop. "H-have you been well?" I managed.

The question seemed to bring him out of his spell. Bennett ran a hand through his hair, tendrils falling over his forehead. He seemed suddenly aware of his appearance.

"I'm well," he said, fastening the undone buttons of his waistcoat. Liar. "And you? How are you here? Does Father know?"

"Of course. He invited me," I said. "I was waiting for you at the banquet."

Bennett paused at the last button. "Father invited you?"

"He came to visit last week to make amends, in fact." I took a step closer, concerned when he made no reply. "Are you alright?"

"Father went to you to make amends," Bennett repeated.

"You didn't know?"

"We are not on speaking terms," Bennett said stiffly.

"That makes reforming laws difficult, no?"

He didn't smile. "I'll never forget the day I had to leave you. You were unwell and I…I didn't even get to say goodbye."

"His Majesty just wanted the best for the kingdom," I said, lowering my gaze, "but he also wants you to be happy."

Bennett made a noise that sounded very much like a scoff.

I held back a smile. "He made amends on your behalf. That's more than I could say for my mother. Everything she did was for her own sake." My voice grew quiet. "Perhaps she even had a daughter for her own sake."

Mother never loved me wholly and unselfishly, that I knew now. My feelings were never a concern to her. The thought hurt more than it should have, but I recalled Father's love and Lady Vanessa's gentle support. I found my voice again.

"His Majesty's actions were hurtful, yes, but his intentions were not misguided."

Bennett furrowed his brow. "He—"

"You can't deny you were changed in my presence," I said. "You *did* risk offending several noble personages on my account."

"Because I was madly in love with you."

That made me blush. His words mirrored the title of Sister Scarlett's article on us last month. I hoped he didn't think I was serious about having five children.

"You do not have the luxury of being mad."

After a moment's pause, Bennett reached for my hands. For once, my fingers were warmer than his. "Abandoning you was the first real sacrifice I made as crown prince. Forget the birthday parties, the celebrations. Those I could live without. But you…I left when you were suffering."

"Bennett—"

"I know you lost your magic. I should have defied Father and stayed. I should have been more like you."

I furrowed my brows. "Like me?"

"At the masquerade ball last summer," he said, looking up with red-rimmed eyes. "You stood up to your mother."

I pulled away, hugging my elbows. "That was different."

I tried not to remember that night. The impractical weight of my dress as I hiked up the stairs to the balcony, my heart at my throat, hoping I would make it before Mother did any more damage. The way she had looked at me, her face twisted with rage and betrayal. How hot and disheveled and shaky I felt when I finally said what I had been thinking for ten years.

What you are doing is wrong, Mother.

It was terrifying. But freeing all the same.

"That was the night I fell in love with you. When I saw you up there," Bennett said, startling me out of my thoughts.

There was admiration in his eyes, strong and unfettered. I never thought he could ever look at me that way.

I shook my head in disbelief. "But you didn't trust me, even after that. Why did you ask Giselle to test me with love charms?" I asked.

Bennett's eyes softened. "Because you're beautiful. You were especially so that night. I was afraid I was…infatuated. I didn't trust myself."

"My hair was covered in feathers," I mumbled.

Bennett smiled, but grew serious as he looked down at his hands. "You were so brave. I wish I had that same courage for my father. At least that one time. You needed me. What did you think when I didn't come back for you? Did you blame me?"

All protagonists in great romances sacrificed for their lovers—their wealth, their position, even their duty. But I never expected that from Bennett, nor would I ever. I knew he would never do anything half so foolish as renounce his title. Olderea needed him. And I hated that he was guilty because of it.

"Don't be ridiculous. Of course not," I said.

Bennett's voice cracked. "Truly?"

"This kingdom is lucky to have a crown prince as devoted as you," I said firmly. "Besides, His Majesty is willing to change. My invitation is proof."

Mother, on the other hand, would never change.

"Do you really think so?" Bennett whispered.

"The king has had enough rebellion in the past few months, don't you think?"

He exhaled. He raised my hand to his lips and pressed a lingering kiss on my knuckles. "You are the best crown princess I could ever ask for."

I warmed at his touch. "Perhaps your father can be persuaded into letting me help reform laws, then?"

"You'll be perfect," Bennett said, his voice earnest. "You *are* perfect."

He angled his face closer. I grew flustered, though I hardly knew why.

Perhaps being away from him made him all the more magnetic. Or because he was breathtakingly handsome in the dim lamplight of the gardens, the night sky surrounding him like a crown of stars.

"So you'll forgive your father, then?" I asked, my words stilted.

Bennett paused. "Yes. I suppose I will. He should have told me he invited you," he said. His gaze lingered on my features, as if committing each one to memory. "I usually don't like surprises."

I bit my lip. The movement drew his eye. "Then shall we go to the banquet? Everyone's waiting."

"I confess I don't want to go." Bennett leaned in again.

"Misty and Pippin are having kittens," I blurted out.

"Oh." He raised his eyebrows. "I'm sorry. I didn't expect that to happen when I—"

"When you picked him up off the street," I finished. "Did you think you could get away with that without my knowledge? Even with Giselle playing along?"

He laughed sheepishly. "I suppose not."

"Pippin has been in a sour mood the entire month. He misses you."

"Perhaps not as much as I miss you." Bennett bumped his forehead against mine and gently squeezed my waist. I was suddenly very aware of him. "May I kiss you now? Please?"

I nodded, not trusting my voice. I grew slightly unsteady when he guided me to the window, closer to the light until my back touched his desk.

Bennett smiled when I asked him what he was doing. "So I can see you better," he whispered.

Then he kissed me.

His kiss was gentle, though not wholly without passion. I simply melted into him, noting with some delight that he had figured to move his lips since Vandil.

Bennett pulled away after ten blissful seconds. "Did you know what I was going to say to you in Alevine? Before my father interrupted us?"

I shook my head, still reeling from his kiss.

"I think I'm in love with you," Bennett said softly. He touched my cheek. "And I am. Thoroughly."

"Oh." The word was little more than an exhale.

My torso was already tipping forward for another kiss, but we were interrupted by the sound of rustling bushes.

"Your Highness!" Ulysses emerged into the clearing, and promptly slapped a hand over his eyes when he caught sight of us. "I see you have, er...*found* Lady Narcissa."

"Indeed." Bennett stepped back and cleared his throat. I was so muddle-headed that I was hardly ashamed of being caught. "Apologies, Ulysses. I should have listened earlier."

"Certainly," Ulysses said. He still didn't unshield his eyes. "To the banquet, then?"

Bennett squeezed my hand and laughed. "To the banquet."

41

Hurry!"

"Why didn't you tell me sooner?" Bennett blew a strand of hair off his forehead, his crown tucked securely under his arm as I pulled him down the hallway. We dodged a group of maids dusting vases and paintings.

"I didn't know Misty was going to give birth this morning," I said. We turned a corner and exited the south wing of the palace. My carriage was waiting for us on the cobblestone.

Misty herself hadn't even known. It came as a surprise to all of us after breakfast when I found her in the blanket-lined crate I had prepared for her, the first signs of a kitten emerging. Pippin was pacing nervously before her and yowled at me to get Bennett.

This was, after all, a family matter.

I tapped my foot impatiently as the coachman set out, the carriage moving much too slowly for my taste. It had taken half an hour to get to the palace. Greenwood Abbey was confoundingly far away, and the traffic in the streets was no help either.

Bennett grinned at me from across the seat. "I've never seen you like this."

"Like what?"

"Excited. Your face is glowing."

I pressed a hand to my hot cheek, pretending his comment didn't make my stomach flutter.

It had been over two weeks since our reunion. I saw him daily, even as he was busy drafting laws with the king.

King Maximus was in a considerably better mood now that he and Bennett were on speaking terms. Though His Majesty was still hesitant to include me in royal affairs, it was only a matter of time. His face still pinched whenever he saw me, though I suspected it was out of habit now instead of disapproval.

"This is taking awfully long," I muttered, peering out the window.

We were practically inching down the streets of Delibera, a hackney-coach before us and a horse-drawn cart behind.

"We're in no rush, are we? Cat labor can last twelve or more hours," Bennett said.

"How do you know that?"

He shrugged a shoulder. "I did some research. Drafting laws gets boring at times."

I laughed.

Bennett leaned forward and took my hands. I was still getting used to the feeling. "By the way, I brought you a gift."

He slipped something cold on my finger. I stared at the new ring when he drew away. The band was embellished with floral motifs, wrapping around the diamond in the center like minuscule vines.

"You do have a tendency to lose all the rings I give you," he said when I started to protest.

"You could have returned the last one," I said, recalling the emerald surrounded by seed pearls. "I liked that one."

Bennett wet his lips. I noticed he only did that when he was nervous. "Cissa, I wanted to ask—"

The carriage jerked to a stop. A look out the window showed an enormously long train of carts blocking the road. I groaned.

Misty and Pippin were going to kill me.

Bennett reached for his crown. He had set it beside him when he entered the carriage. Now, he smoothed back his hair and put it on.

"What are you doing?"

He merely smiled and opened the carriage door. "Excuse me? May we pass?" His voice rang clearly out in the streets.

Gasps erupted from the passersby. Murmurs of "Your Highness" rose from the crowd. Bennett barely shut the door before the carriage began rolling again, this time faster.

I threw my arms around his neck and kissed his cheek. "Thank you!" I paused, studying him for a moment. "You've been practicing."

The only time King Maximus encouraged my presence was when I was coaching Bennett on public speaking. Ulysses claimed I had a penchant for it and Bennett had asked to learn.

"I have." His gaze lingered on my mouth. "Is that all the reward I get?"

I tapped my chin and sat back. "Perhaps another ring first?"

Bennett's expression was serious. "Certainly. Do you prefer sapphires or opals?"

He was a shameless flirt when he wanted to be.

Ten minutes later we arrived in the courtyard of Greenwood Abbey. I dragged Bennett to the parlor where I had set up the crate for Misty's birth, nearly running into Lady Vanessa, Tizzy, and an unfamiliar witch at the threshold.

"Misty was having a hard time," Tizzy said, wringing her apron, "so Lady Vanessa and I thought we'd hire some help."

The witch introduced herself as a midwife for animals. "I never understood why birth must be so difficult," she said, waving her hand toward the blanket-lined crate. "You will find your kitty in perfect condition."

I gasped when I saw the litter of kittens curled against Misty, already feeding.

I thanked the three profusely and hugged Lady Vanessa. Somehow in the panic of the moment, I never thought to give Misty magical assistance.

Lady Vannessa laughed, patting my hair. "There now. Go on. She's waiting for you."

Bennett followed close behind as I knelt before the crate. "I'm sorry I missed it," I said to Misty, reaching in to stroke her head.

Misty nuzzled my hand. *Don't be. It wasn't the most pleasant thing.*

Pippin hovered over the kittens, staring with wide eyes. *Look! Those are mine*, he meowed. He nudged Bennett's arm, purring deeply.

There were seven kittens in all. Three were identical to Misty and three were gray tabbies. The last was ginger, like Pippin. I marveled at how tiny they were.

Bennett stroked Pippin's ears. "They're precious."

Would you like to name them? Misty meowed.

"Really? You want that?" I asked.

Of course.

I turned to Bennett, who was waiting patiently for my translation. I had gotten into the habit of telling him everything the cats were saying.

"We can name them!" I said, barely able to contain my excitement.

He broke into a smile. "An honor."

I rested my chin on the edge of the crate. I had been stewing over names for the past two weeks, but I didn't want to assume Misty and Pippin would let me name their children. It was, as Bennett said, an honor.

"Stormi, Dima, and Rani," I said, pointing to the three gray kittens in the center. I turned to Bennett. "What about the others?"

"Iris, Lumi, Sol," he said without hesitation to the three black cats. He laughed at my raised brows. "Like I said, drafting laws gets boring."

Misty purred, pleased with the names. She nuzzled the ginger kitten. *And this little darling?*

"May I do the honors?" Bennett said.

Pippin preened. *Only fitting. She* is *the best-looking one.*

"Daffodil," Bennett said with a soft smile in my direction. "The springtide flower."

Perfect, Misty said. She rested her head against the blankets, blinking slowly. *Now. I'm in dire need of rest.*

We left her to sleep and the kittens to nurse. Pippin insisted on staying. *I am a father now, after all,* he meowed, puffing up his chest.

Bennett took my hand and led me into the gardens. We walked to my old spot before the stone fountain. "Do you have a moment, Cissa?"

I took a seat on the bench. He didn't let go of my hand.

"Don't you need to go back?" I asked.

"Father can wait a little longer," he said. He plucked a daffodil from the base of the fountain, twirling it between his fingers. The flowers were everywhere now, dotting the area with spots of sunny yellow. "I wanted to ask you something."

"What is it?"

Bennett knelt before me.

"You're going to ruin your breeches," I said. The grass had already stained the beige fabric, but he didn't seem concerned.

"Narcissa Greenwood, will you do me the honor of being my wife?"

I laughed. "What are you doing? You already proposed."

"As a prince out of duty. I'm asking now as a man in love." His expression was earnest. At some point, he had removed his crown. It sat beside him, obscured by long blades of foliage. "I want to be yours, as Bennett. If you will have me."

I stared, reminded of our moments alone during the tour. When he helped me move a bookshelf for Misty. The evening of his birthday. That night when we stood outside my room above the opera house and he had spoken as if only the two of us mattered.

"I don't have much without my title…but I can give you companionship," Bennett said shyly. "And love that will last a lifetime."

Together forever. That's what he wanted. No one else had ever offered that except Misty. My heart sang.

"A lifetime?" I whispered. But the wounded child in me was not convinced. "What if…what if you change your mind?"

"I won't," Bennett said simply. "Because you're you."

"That's hardly a convincing reason."

"Because you're fearless and capable and clever. Because you're kind, Cissa, despite what you may think of yourself."

"You don't have to—"

"Because you're gentle. Understanding. *Divinely* beautiful." He traced the curve of my jaw and smiled mischievously at my startled expression. He was getting rather good at compliments. "You're everything I could ever dream of, Cissa. I hope I can be the same for you."

I felt like crying and laughing and dancing and curling into a ball at the same time. A horrendous sight, no doubt, so I contained myself to staring at him instead. Because at this moment, he wasn't the crown prince. He was just Bennett. *My* Bennett.

"You are," I whispered, touching his cheek. He was breathtaking. I never thought so more than at this moment. "And you must know I love you just as well without your crown. Perhaps even more."

Bennett paused, his hazel eyes hesitant. "Really?"

After spouting such a speech, he sounded awfully unsure of himself.

"Silly goose." I leaned forward, bumping his forehead with mine. "You ought to give your brother some poetry lessons. That was quite a declaration," I teased.

His face melted into a smile.

"Well, then." Bennett tucked the daffodil behind my ear. "Are you going to say yes?"

Indescribable warmth flooded my chest. I kissed him.

"Yes," I said. "A million times yes."

ACKNOWLEDGMENTS

I've heard that second books are absolute beasts. Spoiler alert: they are. But like the former, there are people I need to thank who helped me along my journey of making this book a reality!

Jenni, for the past year I've been on bookstagram, you've been a constant pillar of support. Your love for this story was probably the only thing that stopped me from rage quitting in its early stages. Many thanks, my friend.

Cassandra, you're the best beta reader anyone could ask for. Your balance of encouragement and critique is immaculate, and I know I can always count on you for catching plot holes typos, and my "good enough" moments that I would've let slip otherwise.

Susy, I love your chaotic enthusiasm and the fact that you think all the dumb jokes I include in my books are funny. Allis and Kiah, thank you guys for your encouragement. Your support means so much as fellow artists. Kathleen, thank you for being the sweetest and most supportive human being ever.

Thank you to SVSLearn and their podcast for keeping me company while I was chugging along on illustrations. If anyone needs a top tier online illustration school, I highly recommend them!

Shoutout to Enchanted Ink Publishing for the phenomenal formatting yet again.

And thanks to you, dear reader, for making this whole author thing a reality.

Ireen Chau

is a long-time artist, writer, and above all, a lover of stories. She is located in the Bay Area where she works remotely as a concept artist. When not reading, writing, or drawing, Ireen can be found listening to illustration podcasts and watching YouTube commentary videos. Visit her Instagram @theherbwitchsapprentice for more art and news about future projects!

@theherbwitchsapprentice